THE DEBT
War on Two Fronts

ಬಿಾ

BRENDA WILLS OTIS

Nightengale Press

THE DEBT

©2023 Brenda Wills Otis
Cover Art by Valerie Connelly

Library of Congress Cataloging-in-Publication Data
Otis, Brenda Wills,
THE DEBT/ Brenda Wills Otis
ISBN 13: 978-1-945257-37-7
Genre: Historical Fiction, Romance

Published in the United States of America
©2023 Nightengale Press

June 2023
10 9 8 7 6 5 4 3 2

REVIEWS

This charming story takes us to a world and period known by very few readers---the deep South in the '40's. Even fewer people know anything about the middle class black community during this period. Readers will experience this world through the eyes of a young "colored" woman--a teacher who falls in love with a musician who's drafted into the segregated Army during wartime. The book provides a great opportunity to think about the complexity of relationships, race, class, and love.

—Freeman A. Hrabowski, III, President Emeritus,
UMBC: An Honors University in Maryland

The Debt, is a beautifully written story of love, hope, strength and resilience amidst the dangers and anxieties of life in a small Georgia town. In it, she masterfully brings to life the richness of African American culture, history and wisdom of the 1940s American South, against the backdrop of World War II in Europe and the growing storm of racism here at home. Her salt-of-the-earth characters are filled with the indomitable spirit of the ancestors who, through the ages have triumphed even in the worst of times.

—Nell Braxton Gibson, Author,
"Too Proud to Bend: Journey of a Civil Rights Foot Soldier"

"The Debt is a very beautiful, engrossing, and inspirational love story. Within the context of this captivating love story, Brenda Otis has highlighted many of the social and cultural aspects of Black life in 1940s Georgia and the United States. Additionally, she has effectively illustrated the negative and horrific impacts of institutional racism on the daily lives of Blacks during that period and currently."

—Maxie C. Jackson, Jr., Ph.D.
Retired Academic Administrator, Michigan State University

The Debt, Brenda Wills Otis saturates your senses with her uncanny gift for detail. She paints a beautiful descriptive picture of the richness, the trials and the beauty of a Southern black family that easily and eerily could be my own. Brenda navigates us on a journey "down home" where she meticulously evokes memories of treasured experiences with loved ones near and dear. The Debt is a gift to cherish as Brenda artfully paints a picture and masterfully frames each interaction.

—Patricia Knight Gary, Professor Emeritus
Northern Virginia Community College

DEDICATION

To my husband, Amos-Léon Otis ("Roscoe"),

to my adult children, Somá and Noel Brandon,

and to my late, "toddler" daughter, Taj Ieesha,
whose spirit has always kept me going that extra mile.

ಹೋಂಡಿ

THE DEBT
War on Two Fronts

ಹೋಂಡಿ

Chapter 1

Where You Been All My Life?

Nora's crinoline-boosted skirt sways back and forth like a horse's tail. With feather-light foot movements, she floats and kicks in perfect sync with the music of the ballroom jazz orchestra. Nora's style of jitterbugging fits her happy, high-energy personality and brings joy to Jasper and his musician buddies.

"Man, your new lady friend can move," whispers Eugene, Jasper's fellow saxophone player.

What looks like a near-airborne body is Nora being slung over the back of her male dance partner. Others on the dance floor glide aside as if parting the waters for the two show-stoppers. Jasper is Nora's new beau, and keeps inviting her to some of his big-band performances, where he is one of the six, front row saxophone players.

"Man, look at those sharp dressers up there! They're so handsome! I just love those dark gray pin-striped suits!"

"Well, if you say so," her dance partner says, as he spins her three times.

"Oh, my goodness! Look at those red and white polka-dot pocket hankies!"

"You sure can't wear those in church! Hmmmm?" He tilts his head, looks down at her and raises his eyebrows just like he's asking her a silent question.

"And those black wing-tip shoes capped with white spats!"

He smiles like a Cheshire cat, but to end the conversation.

Down the front row, each saxophonist's right foot taps to the beat of the sophisticated, high- energy music. The tall, lean Jasper looks like a good match for his pretty and petite new girlfriend. From his vantage point he keeps an eagle's eye on Nora, who, because she is such a skilled dancer, always has a full dance card. Many of the men who escort other ladies to the ballroom eye Nora as that stand-out swinger.

"Buddy, that's the lady I want to get out on the dance floor with," whispered a chubby attendee who watches the dancers from the back of the club.

Jasper doesn't mind the attention, but some of the temporarily-sidelined ladies—whose beaus are dancing with Nora—are eying her with jealousy.

In between her turns on the dance floor, Nora table hops. She spots friends across the dance hall, tiptoes up behind them in their seats and surprises them with a peck on the cheek and her contagious giggles.

"Hey, how you doing?" She bubbles.

These nights out are such an escape for Nora who is an extroverted person. She lives in a bustling Macon, Georgia household with three of her family members.

The year is late-1943, and Nora has no idea what's in her future with her new romantic interest.

"Where have you been?" asks Aunt Claudine as Nora tiptoes into the house around eleven-thirty one evening.

"I've been over to the Masonic Hall to hear the Ellis Walker Orchestra," Nora offers without hesitation. "Boy are they a good group! Everyone loves to dance to their sound," she says.

"I bet that Jasper man was over there playing wasn't he?" her other aunt, Marilyn, chimes in.

"You all are still treating me like I'm a teenager," Nora reminds them. "I'm grown and working full time, and I do know how to act like a lady!" she says, in her best manners voice.

Then she climbs the stairs to the second level of the old, solid house the family leases. Its red brick exterior is standing up to the ravages of time. And the beautiful flowers the ladies of the house maintain year-round whisper to everyone, *Welcome to our home.*

₭∞⁂

Claudine—the oldest aunt—is the household matriarch and a martinet in dainty, feminine clothing when she isn't in her work uniform. She loves her black crepe, trumpet-style skirts with her white, Peter Pan collar blouses. Claudine is often bossy. She makes decisions for her sisters whether they like them or not, often telling them how they should spend their modest earnings. She disguises her spending requests or decisions as necessary output for the household.

"We really need a new set of cookware—you know, pots and pans," she says one day around the kitchen table. "How about each one of us give five dollars, and I'll see how far I can stretch that at Sears and Roebuck," Claudine squints—as if doing some mental arithmetic computations. She takes no prisoners and has little patience for short-steppers and easy-going males. She long ago dumped her successful, businessman of a husband—old Hempstead—and has since carved out a steady—if monotonous lifestyle—for herself. Miss Claudine, as many neighborhood kids call her, is a handsome and striking woman in appearance. She is about five feet, nine inches tall.

"Miss Claudine, why you always walking so fast up the sidewalk?" asks Buster Brown, a precocious, always curious neighborhood kid.

"I have so much to do in my house and at the hospital. Why do you want to know anyway?" she asks as she furrows her brow. "And why aren't you over in Hanson Park playing with the neighborhood children on this nice afternoon?"

"My stomach hurtin' me and my mama say you are a good

nurse and all, and I thought I could go in your house with you so I can get some medicine," answers Buster Brown in a timid voice. He is always curious about the fast-paced comings and goings of the four adults with hardly ever seeing a man around.

"Buster, didn't your mama give you some cod liver oil this morning?" Claudine inquires as she tilts her head down with her nurse's cap staying in place.

"No, ma'am, I think we all out of it at home," Buster shoots back.

"Come on inside and let me give you a spoonful. I don't want you acting like it's so nasty and stalling and wasting my time, you hear me?" Claudine asks with a strong voice of resignation.

Eight-year-old Buster Brown has struck pay dirt. He has a chance to see what is in this house with all those good looking ladies rushing in and out different times of the day. He will be able to tell the other children what he saw inside. They all see the pretty flowers out front and the well-kept lawn, but none of the children knows what it looks like behind the front door.

"You got pretty hair and skin Miss Claudine," offers Buster as he stands by the kitchen counter waiting on his teaspoon full of that nasty stuff and observing, up-close for the first time, Claudine's wavy black hair and her smooth, cappuchino-complexioned face.

"Just come on over here so you can be finished and get back out to play," barks Claudine as if she is dealing with a recalcitrant patient.

Buster isn't satisfied with going into the house from the kitchen door around the side. He needs to see more than one room, so his mind kicks into gear.

"Miss Claudine, I need to go to the bathroom too, please ma'am." He sounds like a toddler at this point, as he wiggles like he needs to go.

"Are you sure you can't make it to your house without wetting yourself?" Impatience rises in her voice. "Oh, come on, but don't you drip on my clean bathroom floor, you hear me?" snaps Claudine.

80C3

Claudine, in her spare time, enjoys sewing clothes for herself. She is an excellent seamstress. And another favorite pastime is cooking. She enjoys making specialty foods such as homemade mayonnaise, fruit cakes from scratch, creamy caramel cake icing, yeast dinner rolls and lick-the-bowl-delicious homemade, hand-cranked ice cream.

Claudine's sister, Marilyn, who is four years her junior is a rather pessimistic and caustic personality.

"Marilyn, Arnold told me to tell you hello. He was on the same shift with me at the hospital two days ago," Claudine says in a fishing expedition tone. Claudine, Marilyn, Nora and Hattie are all at the dinner table—in the kitchen—on one of those rare occasions when their schedules allow this mid-week togetherness.

"Arnold needs to mind his own business and let his wife's body get cool in her grave," Marilyn chimes in disgust. She, too, like Claudine, is a divorcée. The dissolution of her marriage left her bitter and very much wary of appreciating any attention from the opposite sex.

"All these men around here in Fernwood sniffing around and acting like a mutt in heat," groaned Marilyn as she walks from the oven and puts some candied yams on the table. She finds fault in all her friends' suitors or husbands and doesn't try to hold her tongue when assessing their *up-to-no-good* motives. Marilyn is the self-appointed cook in the family who wields knives and spoons at the kitchen counter like she was a short-order cook in another life. This tacit arrangement is born of Marilyn's sketchy employment history. Unlike her sisters, she is never assigned a permanent, staff nursing position at Cloverdale Hospital.

According to Claudine, "Marilyn just can't relax enough around the white, head nurse who did the interviewing. She gave

11

the impression she would not be friendly enough to the patients and inflexible with her potential co-workers."

She is often home on days when she is not working as a rotation nurse. There are clear physical signs of Marilyn's striking beauty in her younger days with her five foot, seven stature, and a light olive complexion with complimentary hazel-green eyes.

Hattie is the quiet, third sister who generally minds her own business and is not prone to question the social choices of the youngest and fourth female in the house, their niece Nora.

"Marilyn you shouldn't be so judgmental of every man's motives. You act like Arnold is committing a sin because he sent greetings to you through Claudine. And you have no good words for Nora and her new beau. You don't even know him yet, and you're making Nora uncomfortable concerning him," Hattie blurts out as she adds collards to her plate.

"Aunt Marilyn always prejudges the opposite sex, so what else is new?" asks Nora.

"All right now, you all take it easy on Marilyn. We all know her sassy, doubting personality, right Marilyn?" Claudine chuckles after her rhetorical question.

Hattie is a widow who never had children during her brief but, by all accounts, satisfying marriage. She, like her two older sisters, is a registered nurse with a four-year college degree. Hattie is pretty in an odd way, and she has the carriage and bearing of an old maid. When taken out of its customary bun, her straight-back hair strikes the top of both buttocks. Her complexion is fairly light with ruddy-red undertones. She inherited a sprinkling of the characteristics of the family's Native American ancestors among other ethnic blends.

Nora is an elementary school teacher who is fast gaining a reputation as an excellent educator. Unlike her older aunts, she is more optimistic, more outgoing and a very eligible-for-suitors social butterfly.

"You're nothing but a pint-size ball of energy," her girlfriend, Geneva, teases her. Nora is only five foot, four inches tall, but she has a passion for gorgeous, high-heeled shoes that add height and a confidence to her erect posture. She, like Marilyn, is of fair skin with large eyes. But unlike Marilyn's green eyes, Nora's light-brown eyes sparkle with the excitement and wonder of a happy spirit.

"You've got those big smiling eyes," Jasper often says to her in a teasing manner.

Nora has a small cluster of very supportive girlfriends who also enjoy living the independent life afforded young people of that era.

"Come on over to the Elks Club tonight, Nora, so you can meet some of the guys in the band and hear two new arrangements we've been rehearsing," Jasper pleads.

Nora now spends fewer weekends going to the handful of clubs where Jasper performs. She usually goes with Geneva and Velma, her two best girlfriends, because Jasper, though he invites her, would always go ahead to set up early with the other musicians.

She now busies herself with church-related activities at the prodding of Claudine and Hattie.

Claudine says, "Many of the church members ask me why they don't see much of you anymore, and I don't really know how I should answer them."

Marilyn is not a church-goer and doesn't care if Nora attends any events, but she is glad Nora is spending less time with Jasper.

Nora enjoys Jasper's company when they get a chance to spend time together during set breaks at the clubs or dance halls.

"I don't know how I can catch my breath between sets if I spend every minute talking to you," he teases Nora one evening in the hallway right off the stage. And on those Sunday afternoons when he calls on her at the big house—what the family's home is called—she giggles and pumps him for more information about his trips to Atlanta, Birmingham and sometimes Mobile, Alabama to play with other orchestras.

"Tell me Jasper, what do the tall buildings in downtown Mobile look like?" Nora asks. "I sure wish my life was geared to just a little bit of traveling," she says with a forlorn look in her eyes.

Jasper is a mild-mannered person who is devoted to his widowed mother. He is not only her son, but he is also her guardian angel because he is her only child. Nora has been in his mother's company just twice in the three months since she and Jasper began courting.

"Where your folks come from, Miss Nora?" Octavia Martin asks through squinting eyes.

In mid-December, this is Nora's second time meeting Jasper's mother.

"Are they from around Macon, or did your kinfolk move down here from the north?" Mrs. Martin continues questioning. "And where did you get that teachin' education that helped you get into the new colored school here in the Fernwood neighborhood?" She keeps at it with relentless questions.

While she has no qualms about Mrs. Martin, Nora knows she is being sized up as to whether or not she is suitable for Jasper. Mrs. Martin is quite protective of her only child, and she wants him not to be hurt in a wayward romance. Jasper has not attended college like Nora, so that poses a concern with his mother, also.

"Mrs. Martin, my people have been in Macon for two generations now," answers Nora with pride. "And I went to school at Tuskeegee Institute in Alabama," Nora continues in an accelerated pace. Nora so appreciates how respectful Jasper is toward Octavia Martin and how tender he is when talking with her. She is not a delicate or needy type of older woman, so that makes Nora appreciate his relationship with his mother even more.

Nora and Jasper soon realize they both love to dress in stylish, well-tailored clothes. Nora asks," Jasper, where do you and the guys in the orchestra find those really good-looking suits you wear?"

"We get them made in Atlanta from a tailoring shop on Auburn Avenue," he answers without hesitation. "Do you like the way they look on stage?" Jasper continues. "I buy my other clothes anywhere I can get a good price, which sometimes means waiting for a sale or putting something in lay-away."

Nora likes Jasper's honesty and down-to-earth manner when they talk. There is no pretense about him.

But nothing of a material nature is more precious to him than his two musical instruments. He owns an alto saxophone and a clarinet. He maintains his horns like the honored possessions they are to him. His decent, but nothing-to-write-home-about used car runs a distant second in reverence.

Jasper still lives at home with his mother. Nora thinks she might be spending time with a closeted Mama's Boy.

Chapter 2

Let's All Get Under the Umbrella

"Miss Marilyn, these are the best salmon croquettes I have ever eaten in my life. Don't tell this to my mother however," chuckles Jasper in a mock-pleading tone. He is sitting at the kitchen table in the Carpenter's household.

As is the case in most households, the kitchen is the grand central station of the home. The butter-soft yellow walls encase a large window over the kitchen sink where a trio of herbs rest in small clay pots. The ruffles of orange and white gingham curtains frame that window and offer Claudine frequent opportunities to mention her sewing skills.

She likes bragging about how she made them in a couple of hours, casually telling women visitors, "Oh, honey, I went from cutting the fabric to the last stitch in no time flat."

The modest white kitchen stove is powered by electricity, but the cooling and storage mechanism for perishable foods is a square, dwarfy-looking big white box on a pedestal. It is known as an ice box. By most standards it is considered a middle-class luxury in the South.

Many months back Claudine had been on her soap box about wanting to purchase the "appliance" saying, "We have got to keep our food from spoiling so fast, spoiling even before Marilyn can get it cooked and on the table. Food is just too expensive to let it ruin like that."

The crude practice to keep food cold was to pack containers in a large aluminum tub and cover them with ice. Claudine calculated how many months everyone would have to chip in a certain amount of money before they could afford it. The "it" was going to be an ice box, where the process is really the same.

The neat, white box with a huge block of ice keeps food fresh. The ice has to be replenished every few days with a new block of ice. Now, many months later, the purchase at Sears and Roebuck is about to turn into a ceremonial event.

"We've got enough money in the big jar to go and buy the ice box on Saturday," Claudine jumps in with her always, self-appointed role as referee. "Who all wants to go?"

Marilyn is the first to speak up, "Why is it necessary for everybody to go? For sure I will, because I want to know how to operate it and store the ice since I'm doing all the cooking."

"You're not the only one who cooks in this house," Hattie chimes in. "I make my breakfast some Saturdays," she adds in a huffy tone.

"That's just it. Anyone who comes into the kitchen only thinks about what they want at that minute. They don't care to ask what they can cook for the next person. I'm the one who cooks for all of you *and* our planned visitors *and* drop-in friends," Marilyn said in a rising voice, her head cocked and her hands on her hips.

"If it wasn't for Aunt Marilyn chasing me out of the way in *her* kitchen and not taking her nice time to teach me how to cook, I could be of some service," Nora chimed in with a hint of sass.

"You got a nerve acting like you're interested in learning to cook. You so busy chasing behind that Jasper man and dancing around most Friday and Saturday nights, you can hardly catch your breath, let alone learn to cook," Marilyn spouted as she turned on her heels to face Nora—who was standing near the six-seat kitchen table.

Claudine steers the shopping trip conversation back with, "Why don't we all go and pick out the box so y'all can stop this squabbling. I'll arrange for Mr. Willie to drive his truck down so he can load the ice box in it and drive it back. I'll ride back with him and y'all can get back on your own," she ended with her familiar tone of finality.

On Saturday morning all four women board the green and white street car at the back of the car on the corner of Magnolia and Crescent, heading downtown for the big event. While not in their Sunday-best clothes, the three sisters and their niece wore comfortable, but attractive clothes, with cotton scarves over their heads that were tied under their chins. But the self-appointed negotiator of the ice box purchase, Claudine, wore a small black fedora-style hat that was placed at a slight, side tilt.

"This shouldn't take very long, should it?" Nora asks in a tone of impatience as they climb the stairs to board the racially-segregated street car.

Strolling into the appliance section of the Sears and Roebuck, with the women following Claudine in a ducks-crossing-the-street type of procession, the four wait on a salesman to approach.

"What can I help you girls with this morning?" the balding, fifty-something salesman asks in a rather forced politeness.

Before Claudine could open her mouth, Nora jumped in with, "Mrs. Carpenter, my aunt, is interested in buying an ice box." She emphasizes the 'Missus.'

Acting as though he hasn't picked up on the young woman's irritation, he says looking directly at Claudine, "Come on over here to this section to see the different sizes and figure out what you can afford to buy."

Claudine gives *the eye* to Nora—meaning to shut her mouth— before she says in a non-confrontational way, "I hope I can afford to buy at all."

"Oh, you will be able to buy on our lay-away plan, with just a small amount of interest every month, and you can take your ice box home with you in less than a year," the salesman says with a spat of smooth, marketing gusto.

"Could you let me and my family talk this out for a few minutes and then we'll be ready to decide?" Claudine says in a worried-laden tone while dropping her head.

"I'll be back in about five minutes," the salesman says, smiling and walking away with a little bounce in his step.

Nora walks up close to the five or six ice boxes on the raised, display platform and looks down the line at the white, nondescript boxes. She then spins around to her aunts and says, "Which one of these can we afford?"

Claudine says, "Just hold your horses, Nora. Marilyn and Hattie come on let's look inside to see what we can decide."

The four women gather in a sports-team-type huddle and talk in low tones, then walk over and peer into each ice box for a second time. Finally, Claudine speaks up, "Which do you think we should buy, Marilyn?."

"I like the second from the right," Marilyn says without hesitation.

"There's only one other one that's in our budget, right?" asks Nora.

"Yes, you're right," Hattie says.

"Well, let's buy the one I like since I do most of the cooking," Marilyn says, in a matter-of-fact tone.

"Okay, Marilyn, we'll get your choice," Claudine says with pride and satisfaction. "But first we got to be delicate when talking to this old salesman. You know he will expect us to ask for the lay-away plan. He's thinking we don't have the money to buy it out right. I won't act too uppity, but I'll politely say we're buying it today and having it picked up right away. Here he comes now," she says in a whisper.

"Well, what have you girls decided?" the salesman asks. "Oh ,by the way, I don't think I told you my name. It's Mr. Jimmy Mack. I've been one of the top appliance salesmen here for over twenty-five years. Now, which one of these you want to put on lay-away? "he asks, looking straight at Claudine.

"Mr. Mack, we have decided to buy the second one from the right," Claudine says, pointing and walking forward to get closer to the ice box with the other women inching closer, too.

"Oh, good," he says. "What an excellent choice. Is your name the one I'm putting on the lay-away paperwork?" old Mack asks while smiling and opening his smiling eyes wide. "And are you prepared to put down the fifteen-dollar deposit today?" he asks both questions in rapid-fire style. "The total price is sixty-five dollars. This will leave you a balance of fifty-dollars with five dollars due each month. You know there are cheaper models over there," he says, pointing to the boxes on the left side. "Maybe you should look again at those," he says with widening eyes, raised eyebrows and a phony smile.

"We are buying the ice box we want, right out, today. And I'm paying for it in cash since there are no credit terms, other than lay-away, for colored people," Claudine says slowly and politely. "A neighbor friend is picking it up in his truck. He's already waiting outside," she continues.

The salesman crunched his brows instantly and looked slowly at all the women for the first time.

"Well, I declare this is a surprise!" he says with an air of snobbery. "I, I, I can count your kind on one hand, those who won't accept lay-away. How you manage to come up with the cash?" he asks in a disbelieving tone.

"We—we're," both Claudine and Nora start speaking at the same time. Nora looks down sheepishly, knowing she is about to be a bit too hot-headed.

"We are all hard-working women who save our money on a regular basis," offers Claudine almost apologetically.

His complexion turning a light hue of pink, the salesman adds, "I bet some of you have had some college training. Am I right?"

The normally reticent Hattie shoots back, "We all have, Mr. Mack!"

"Let me get my sales pad," he says at a low, difficult to hear level. The salesman walks away, shaking his head as if thinking, *what in the hell is happening here in Macon.*

∞)(∟

Jasper finds himself sitting at the kitchen table again in the Carpenter's household. Nora is staring at him with dewy eyes and so happy her family has finally thought him worthy of being accepted into the fold as a frequent visitor. This is after a few months of dating.

"I'm glad you're enjoying the meal," Marilyn mumbles under her breath. She is still skeptical of Jasper, but she is nonetheless happy to have someone rave over her culinary skills. Her family enjoys her food, but she sometimes feels they take her efforts for granted.

"We need to plan for you to come to Atlanta to enjoy some of my orchestra's out-of-town gigs," Jasper whispers in low tones, even though the radio is on in the next room, and Marilyn has walked out of the kitchen. He knows he is not a member of Marilyn's fan club because Nora hinted, over the last several weeks, about her negative attitude concerning their courtship.

As if reading Jasper's mind, Nora says, "She has no grounds to be against you. It just seems she almost resents anyone experiencing a measure of happiness."

Jasper reaches for Nora's hand and gives it a gentle squeeze as he says with lukewarm optimism, "Don't worry, everything will work out in time."

"I need to check to see if I can get a room at the YWCA to

stay overnight in Atlanta so my family won't raise any objections," Nora says. "Then, I'll have to find someone to go with me," she continues. "You would think a twenty-three-year old school teacher wouldn't be treated like a teenager running off to some wild party." She sits without speaking for some seconds shaking her head in disbelief.

∛

Nora became a member of the Carpenter household after her mother and father were killed in a car accident in April 1923 when Nora was three years old. Her mother, Clementine, was the oldest sister of her three aunts. Nora, an only child, was taken in and treated as the child of all of them. Of course, Claudine played the role of official guardian, saying to friends and church members, "I've always treated that child as if I birthed her myself," she proclaims with a dose of bravado.

Hempstead, Claudine's ex-husband, provided for Nora as his own—as if she were his own flesh and blood. Nora missed Hempstead after the divorce. He was a natty dresser and gentle, six-foot-plus giant. But after the divorce, she quickly absorbed herself in the activities of a normal eight-year-old. Claudine was the most clannish of the aunts and demanded family loyalty from everyone under the Carpenter roof. The women were leasing the house because—after Hempstead and his money were gone and Hattie's husband had died—they changed their residence and moved to the house on Magnolia Street. Home ownership was a financial stretch that couldn't be reached at that time.

∛

"You are going to like the bright lights of Atlanta, Miss Nora," Jasper asserts with a broad grin on his face. "Just wait until I show you all the juke joints as well as the big dance halls," he continues as he surreptitiously squeezes her thigh under the kitchen table. Nora gives him a look that is really a false expression of anger, and they both giggle like college-age sweethearts.

"Well, look who's here," says Hattie as she walks into the kitchen. "It's so nice to see you again, Jasper. It's been a week since you dropped by the house," continues Hattie as she peers over the top rim of her thick glasses. "I'll be out of here in a minute. Just want a glass of milk to take out to the parlor while I read the afternoon newspaper," she offers as she reaches into the cabinet over the counter for a clean glass.

"I'll be out of everyone's way very shortly because there's a rehearsal I'm scheduled for in two hours," Jasper announces after swallowing his last chunk of food. "Besides, I need to drop a package off at the post office for my Mom before it closes," he says as he slides the chair back from the table.

"Nora, when do you think I'll get a chance to meet Mrs. Martin?" inquires Hattie. "I need to tell her what a nice young man she has reared.

"Oh, that's so kind of you to say, Miss Hattie," responds Jasper. "I'm going to make sure my mother meets all of Nora's folks real soon," he continues. "That's a promise," Jasper says as he stands to leave.

"Well, Jasper, you're welcome here in our home at any time," Hattie says with a kind smile on her face as she turns and walks out of the kitchen.

"I hope to get to the Masonic Hall on Friday night, Jasper," Nora says in a sing-song tone. "Velma and Geneva want to bring their special friends with them. Do you think you can get two extra tickets?" her tone shifting quickly to the new business at hand.

"That shouldn't be a problem," Jasper says to reassure her. "You left school earlier today than you usually do, didn't you?" Jasper asks, angling his head down to look in Nora's eyes.

"Yes, I wanted to make sure you didn't beat me getting here.

You never know what Aunt Marilyn's mood might be even though she told me to ask you over to eat some of her croquettes today," answers Nora.

As Nora walks Jasper to the door to leave, she starts to peck him on the lips, after checking to see where Hattie and Marilyn are in the house. But she pulls back, thinking the male is suppose to be the aggressor. Nora has an impatient edge to her personality and she doesn't always conform to the strict social norms of the time.

"I'll see you Friday night, my lady," Jasper says, as he performs a semi-bow at the front door.

Nora closes the door behind Jasper and purses her lips in frustration. *He's still too nervous in this house to even come close to my lips for a little kiss.*

∞∞

Late November is the winding down period for Nora's teaching schedule, as Christmas Break begins the third week of December.

Nora adores her second grade students and the affection is returned in kind.

"Miss Nora, do you go to places like Birmingham and Atlanta for a few days while you are away from teaching?" asks Carol Jean, one of the most talkative and smart kids in Nora's class.

"Sweet Carol Jean, I wish Miss Nora could afford to go away for at least one or two days," answers Nora, with a wistfulness to her voice. The question causes her to freeze in her tracks with a small stack of tattered textbooks in the crook of her arm. She stands at the window looking out onto a small and sparsely equipped playground.

"We school teachers don't get paid all year, so we have to save for the days we don't work during summer vacation," Nora says in a trance-like voice. "I'll be lucky to get up to Atlanta and maybe over to Tuskegee this summer," she said with her voice rising to the consciousness of the moment.

"But Miss Nora, my Mama says Atlanta is a real big city," Carol Jean says in a consoling voice.

ℰᘎℭ℞

Life is humming along at a steady pace at the home of the Carpenters' at 1966 Magnolia Street. Nora and Jasper are becoming more serious about their relationship. Jasper is playing more gigs in ballrooms, dance halls and at fancy society balls, white and colored affairs, separately, all around the state, and his income has increased as well. The mundane affairs and the comings and goings of small-town-segregated Macon are nothing to write home about. World War II is in full court press across the Atlantic Ocean, and the colored and white men around town are not spared military draft notices.

On December 14th, one day into Nora's three-week Christmas Break, the bomb falls on Jasper Lee Martin. In the letter arriving at his and his mother's home, Uncle Sam tells him he needs to report for basic training with the United States Army in three weeks! January 4th of 1944 will be the day Jasper's dance card is punched. His training base will be Fort Leavenworth, Kansas.

Octavia Martin is the first to hear the news. "Don't worry about me, Jasper. You know I'm strong and I've got my good health. I'll be fine for the two or three years you go be away," she reassures him.

"Oh no! No, no, no!," is Nora's initial outburst. "You can't leave now!" she shrieks in disbelief. "We're already thinking seriously about our future, "she says in near-breathless exasperation.

"You know there is nothing I can do about this. I'm called to serve my country, and I know this is the right thing to do—maybe just not at this exact time," Jasper blurts out in an attempt at an officious-sounding voice. "We'll figure out a way to make this work for us," he says.

The three weeks leading up to Jasper's departure on January fourth are a blur. Nora is due in her classroom the day before. She has sent her principal, Mr. Sanders, a letter requesting Monday and

Tuesday, January third and fourth, as official days of absence.

"I am going to be a bundle of nerves going back to work after Jasper's leaves," she tells herself. The Christmas tree and holiday decorations are already up. Jasper has recently performed with his orchestra about a dozen times, and Nora attended all his events that have been in Macon.

After Jasper's draft notice, Octavia Martin steps up her attendance with her bible study group, which meets twice a week. She tells all the ladies, "My son needs all the prayers we can find out there."

Even Nora's stern Aunt Marilyn offers to cook dinner for Jasper and his mother on New Year's Day, saying, "It's about time for this family to meet his mother since Nora and Jasper have become so close in recent weeks."

∞∞

"You're sure a sight for sad eyes," Nora says to Jasper as she holds the front door open on Christmas Day.

"I have a little something for you Nora," Jasper says he hands her a small wrapped gift. "It would have been more had I known I would be shipping out so suddenly."

"It hasn't even seemed like Christmas Day. The whole day has been dragging along. It's going to be so lonely in Macon with you gone over the winter. Do you think your mother is looking forward to coming to dinner on New Year's Day?" asks Nora. "And when will you be leaving Kansas to come back here?"

Nora continues with her mind racing from one random question to another.

"Aren't you going to open my gift to you?" Jasper asks.

"Excuse my awful manners. Come on into the parlor to see our Christmas tree. I had no enthusiasm while putting all the extra ornaments on—after you got your draft letter." Nora's voice trails off. She composes herself after a long pause, and bends down to get a small, neatly wrapped gift from under the fragrant and colorful pine tree.

"You open your gift first," says Jasper in a lighted-hearted tone.

"No, I want you to be the first to see my before-the-draft letter-not-good-enough-now gift," says Nora in a dead-pan voice.

"We both are acting childish. Something material is not as important as who is giving it—and in what spirit. Right?" Jasper asks.

"Okay I'll go first," Nora blurts out.

She begins to unwrap the flat box which reveals a satin neck scarf painted with several, wide-eyed deer frolicking in the snow. Nora gasps at its simple beauty and radiant winter colors.

"Oh, this is pretty and excellent for the season. You have such good taste, Mr. Martin." Nora beams as she makes eye contact with Jasper.

Jasper finds an antique-finished, brass, belt buckle with a crudely-etched car design on its face.

"This is unique and so practical. I won't see any of my buddies with a belt buckle like this." He beams as he moves it around in the palm of his hand. "Thank you Nora. This looks like an original hand-made piece."

Nora and Jasper are seconds into a warm embrace and tender kiss in front of the tree when they hear nearby footsteps and Aunt Hattie's warning.

"Just coming to say hello to Mr. Jasper."

୫୬୯୫

Jasper is scheduled to ship out to basic training in less than a week. While he and Nora are talking about their future, she says, "It's going to be so lonely here with you gone over the winter."

In her non-stop chatter she continues, "Do you think your mother is looking forward to coming to dinner at my home this Saturday night? Exactly when are you leaving Kansas to come back here?" Nora continues, her mind racing from one random question to the next.

"Slow down a minute," Jasper urges. "I might be shipped out from Kansas straight to Europe," he continues. "I won't know until I'm well into basic training which lasts for six weeks," he says.

&∞&

Marilyn and Claudine are both slinging pots and pans all day Saturday preparing for Jasper and his mother's arrival to dinner at six o'clock. Nora is a bit anxious, not knowing if her family will warm up to Octavia Martin. She knows they can be insular and clannish when new people come into the family's close-knit orbit. Jasper has just recently been allowed into the *fold*. They, especially Marilyn, are barely tolerating Octavia's new intrusion. Nora also realizes tonight's invitation is extended with a dual motive: being nice and nosy. Jasper is leaving, so her family is being nice to him *and* her. The real deal about his mother is playing into her family's curiosity.

&∞&

"Oh, welcome to our home, Mrs. Martin," Nora says as she opens the door wide for Jasper and his mother to enter. "Hi, Mr. Music Man," Nora says in a cute and teasing tone. "I like that better than Private or whatever the Army will name you," she continues in a nervous giggle.

"Let me take your things, Mrs. Martin," Nora says.

She pivots to put the items in the closet by the front door. When Nora turns back there are Hattie, Marilyn and Claudine all walking into the parlor.

"Good evening, and welcome to 1966 Magnolia Street," Hattie says in a school teacher tone, even though she changed her mind in college about being a teacher.

"I feel as though I know you already because your son speaks of you often," says Claudine.

"Hello," says Marilyn. "I know you haven't seen much of your son lately because he's been spending most of his non-music-playing hours over here. We all may end up missing him in the next four weeks," she says and then chuckles at herself—by herself.

Establishing eye contact with Claudine first, Hattie second,

28

then Marilyn, Octavia says in a sincere tone, "It's 'sho mighty nice of you to have me here tonight with Jasper. Jasper tells me how nice y'all been to him and how much he enjoy the nice house here, and oh, he can't stop braggin' about Miss Marilyn's cookin'. I can't wait to taste the food."

Nora quickly chimes in, "My Aunt Claudine has been cooking right alongside Aunt Marilyn today. We are all in for a treat!"

"Let's sit in the parlor for a few minutes before we go to the dining room table," says Hattie. She waves her arm toward the center of the sofa, and Octavia walks in a studied manner between the sofa and the coffee table. She cups her lavender and white flowered, crepe, church dress under her buttocks and eases down onto the powder-blue, cotton twill sofa. She shows her first sign of unease—with her dark eyes dotting furtively around the room—as she waits for everyone to claim their seats. Her salt-and-pepper hair is pulled back into a French twist with a white, bone clamp holding it neatly in place. She has large eye glasses that are overpowering her slim, oval face. They look to be well-worn and have thick lenses.

Jasper sits on one side of his mother, while Nora sits on the other side. Claudine sits in one of the single, cushy chairs, while Marilyn claims the other cushy chair which is close to the kitchen door. Hattie pulls up a chair from the dining room table which is set, not with the best family-treasured heirlooms, but still much prettier stuff than the everyday dishes.

"So, tell me Mrs. Martin," Claudine starts, "Jasper says your family is from Charleston, South Carolina. How did you get down to Macon, and how long have you been living here?" Claudine continues, leaning forward in her chair.

"I was born in Charleston," Octavia begins in a slow drawl, "but my family moved to Savannah when I was in the lower grades. Then when Daddy died, we up and moved out of Savannah to the country wit' his folks, but we did not like being around dem farm animals. So, my ma took me and my two brothers back to the big city. That's where I stayed 'til I finished my ten grades, so I went ta work for two years. Then, I courted a man that I ended up elopin' with. Don't know why, because I was of age by then. I really didn't have to get no permission from *nobody*," Octavia gabs on.

"Mama, nobody is expecting you to tell your life's story while the dinner gets cold," Jasper says, in a effort to sound light-hearted.

Chapter 3

Nora's Story

Mrs. Martin keeps talking nervously about her childhood and Jasper's creative talents while the aromas from the kitchen have me salivating. The entire parlor and dining room smell of Aunts Marilyn and Claudine's roasted pork shoulder with fresh rosemary, fried chicken drumsticks, wings and thighs, baked bourbon-laced yams, black-eyed peas with ham hock, smothered turnips with the leafy greens, macaroni and cheese with three different cheeses and bits of green "bell" pepper, pickled beets, Waldorf salad and, of course, buttermilk cornbread.

"And then, when I got Jasper's fifth grade report card with B's in most of his classes, but A's in arithmetic, music and art, I knew he had some different kind of talents. All he wanted to do was borrow one of those old beat up saxophones in Mr. Greer's band room and toot on that thing for hours after school and then come home and sing-song his timetables."

Octavia Martin reminisces and shakes her head, as if still puzzled by it all. She is wrapping her handkerchief around her left index finger as she talks and looks at no one in particular.

"Mrs. Martin, when did Jasper know he wanted to be a musician? And when did he get his first horn?" asks Hattie.

She is wearing her favorite mulberry skirt that gathers at the waist, and a pink cotton sweater tucking into the skirt.

Jasper chimes in, "Oh, I can answer that. By seventh grade, my daddy's father came to visit me in Savannah, and he bought me an old alto sax. After a couple of months I felt like I had found a long lost friend in that saxophone."

Claudine popped up from her chair on the opposite side of the coffee table.

"And I guess the rest is history. And the dinner is going to be history if we let it get cold and dried out.

Marilyn jumped at the opportunity to stand and walk back into the kitchen.

"We can finish talking at the dinner table," Marilyn says.

"May I wash my hands before I go to the table?" asks Mrs. Martin.

"Of course you can. Just follow me," *I say as I stand and stretch my arm out toward Mrs. Martin who is rising from the sofa.*

I lead Mrs. Martin down the short, hardwood-floored hallway to the small bathroom outside of Aunt Claudine's bedroom. The petal-pink, tiled bathroom is the bathroom my aunt has to share with visitors. She does a good job of keeping it company-ready most of the time, with its small green accent rug in front of the white porcelain basin adjacent to the white bath tub with its paw-like feet. The bathroom window facing out on the north side of our red-brick house is covered with venetian blinds and a white, cotton piqué curtain trimmed with green ribbon. Aunt Claudine has sewn them to match the room's color scheme.

"Just come on back into the dining room when you finish, Mrs. Martin," *I say as she steps into the bathroom and reaches for the door knob to close the door behind her.*

Aunt Hattie acts as the traffic cop directing Jasper and his mother to their seats at the dinner table, which is just about ten steps from the sofa through the door to the dining room. The table décor is a nod to the season with a red table cloth and white cotton napkins with pointsettias embroidered on them.

Hattie points to a chair on the far side of the table.

"You sit over there, Mrs. Martin. And Nora, you sit next to Mrs. Martin."

Hattie taps the chair right in front of her with the tips of her fingers.

"Jasper, this chair is yours, and I'll sit next to you."

Hattie's voice is uncharacteristically chipper.

"Marilyn and Claudine will sit in the hosts seats at both ends."

As if on cue, the apron-wearing Aunts, Marilyn and Claudine, march out of the kitchen, each carrying a serving dish or platter in each hand. I walk around the table.

"What can I bring out of the kitchen for you?"

"Nora, you can get the pitcher of iced tea and the small platter with the lemon wedges and mint leaves," answers Marilyn.

Hattie chimes in at that moment.

"You know I got two strong hands here, too."

Claudine admonished her in a rushed and distracted voice.

"Hattie, you just keep Mrs. Martin and Jasper entertained until we get finished here in a couple of minutes."

Mrs. Martin pans the room attempting to grab a second of eye contact with the three sisters.

"Before we go any further here, I want everybody to please call me Octavia. We don't need to be so formal, do we?"

Hattie is standing still, but Claudine and Marilyn are in and out of the dining room, back into the kitchen, and out again as they proudly place the food on the table. In the meantime, Mrs. Martin turns around in her chair to look at the two pictures on both sides of the curtained, double windows behind her. She speaks while waving her index finger back and forth in the direction of the pictures.

"May I ask who are the two people there in those nice antique-like frames?"

Aunt Claudine shouts from the kitchen.

"Those are our deceased sister and her husband."

Aunt Hattie responds in a rather somber tone.

"Oh, yes, well, those are Nora's late mother and father, who died much too young."

I feel a pinch of emotion.

"You see, I've been living with my mama's sisters since I was a toddler."

As if wanting to redirect a budding discussion about my early life, Claudine announces that dinner is about to be served.

"Come on Hattie. Take your seat and get ready to bless the table and food."

Mrs. Martin turns back from looking at the pictures and straightens herself in her seat.

Mrs. Martin responds with a little chuckle.

"Maybe once Jasper gets some food in his stomach, he'll start to talk. He's sittin' over there acting like the cat's got his tongue."

Jasper speaks up in an awe shucks tone.

"Mama, I just want you to be comfortable around Nora's family. I've been here many times and talked to them before. That's all."

A serious-sounding Aunt Hattie breaks into conversation.

"Let us bow our heads as we bless this food."

Hattie waits on everyone to shift their bottoms in their chairs and clear their throats before she begins.

"Dear Lord, we've gathered here this evening in fellowship and gratitude for the bounty you have provided for us. We want to ask you to continue to bless all of us and especially young Jasper as he heads out to train to serve our country. He needs your special favor as he may be headed into harm's way, if he is sent across the ocean. Bless our niece, Nora, who seems to be happy with this new friendship between herself and Jasper. May their respect and honor for each other remain steadfast in the weeks and months ahead. Bless Marilyn and Claudine who labored to prepare this good smelling food, which we are about to eat for the nourishment of our bodies. These blessings we ask in thy name. Amen."

A chorus of "Amen's" sounds around the table as Claudine began the chatter.

"Mrs. Martin, pass your plate and I'll put some pork and chicken on it so you won't have to lift these two heavy platters."

Mrs. Martin smiles and hands her plate over to Claudine who is sitting directly to her left.

"That's mighty nice of you, Miss Claudine."

She smiles as she gives a hint of a nod in Claudine's direction. Aunt Claudine chides her in a non-hostile tone.

"Okay, I'm going to get on you now. Don't you dare put a Miss in front of my name. I'm sure I speak for Marilyn and Hattie also."

Aunt Claudine stretches her arms as far as she can to reach the pork and chicken platters in the center of the table, then she is forced to stand and bend to get there.

"Hew, this table is acting like it's got rubber in it all of sudden, or maybe my arms are getting shorter."

Aunt Claudine chuckles. Jasper chimes in.

"You know most people's bodies do shrink when they age."

"Son, are you trying to stay in this lady's good favor, or are you going to stick your foot in your mouth?"

Octavia Martin and everyone at the table laughs hard at that question. Jasper has a rather sheepish look on his face.

"Miss Claudine and Miss Marilyn, you all sure are some fine cooks. These turnip greens and yams are some of the best I've ever tasted. Everything is just so delicious. This is a real skill, a real art form of sorts. I mean to cook so well!"

My sweet Jasper keeps going, as if he is trying to clean up his earlier faux pas. Then, Octavia looks up from her pickled beets.

"You can say that again, son. Oh, my goodness this buttermilk cornbread tastes like what Big Mamma used to whip up. Big Mamma was my grandma on my daddy's side. She lived way back up in da South Carolina country."

Octavia smacks her lips.

"Miss Marilyn, how long you had yo' buttermilk starter there in yo' icebox? This cornbread is so good, it'll 'bout make you grunt while yo' chewin'."

Her candor causes the Carpenter women to laugh so loud their bodies shake as they tilt toward their plates. My aunts relax more as the evening wears on.

When it is time to say good night, they all take turns hugging Jasper as he and his mother cross our door's threshold.

Hattie, puts her arm around Jasper's shoulder and pats his back with her hand. Then, Claudine preaches to Jasper giving him a soft bear hug.

"Nora will see you again before you leave on Monday morning, but we won't. I'm one of those people who believes you can find some good in most people you have to work with. You just have to look a little harder into some of their hearts. Stand your ground Jasper. Be a man, and don't let anyone make you lose sight of your good home training."

My Aunt Marilyn, though still wary of Jasper, has softened her early hostility toward him. The last one to speak, she tries her best to offer a softer side. Aunt Marilyn makes everyone laugh.

"Sure wish I could ship you some of my salmon croquettes out to Kansas, but you wouldn't be able to stay out of the men's room if you ate them after that many days."

On this rare occasion and for a few unguarded moments, my usually stoic aunt pats Jasper on one shoulder. I stand on my front porch as he and his mother walk down the front steps.

"I'll see you tomorrow right before eleven o'clock. Good night Mrs. Martin. I'm so happy you came over tonight."

Octavia looks back over her shoulder.

"No, chil'. I'm the one who's happy. You sure got an upstanding family."

After our talking for a couple of minutes, he and Octavia are on the path, leading out to the street. As the Martins walk toward Jasper's three-year old DeSoto—parked at the edge of the front lawn that abutted the street—he began to talk with his Mother.

"Mama, how did you like Nora's family? Don't you think they were really pleasant and genuine? And that food was so good and set out on the table so pretty. Don't you agree?"

"Oh, that dinner *was* mighty fine Jasper. They put a lot of work into fixin' it. But my Mother could cook as good or better than those two ladies. And she never had no ice box to keep her food in. You don't need no fancy ice box to be a good cook. Yeah, they were pleasant all right—in a put-on sorta way—and a little uppity, too, if you ask me, especially that Marilyn."

Jasper and his mother get into the car.

ଛୠୠ

Slowing his car only minutes after pulling into the street, Jasper turns and looks at his mother who is looking straight ahead.

"Mama, I thought you were enjoying them. Why would you sit there and pretend otherwise?" Jasper asks.

"I wasn't pretending. They were nice but..." Octavia trails off.

"But what, Mama? What are you trying to say?"

The pitch in Jasper's voice is rising.

"You could tell Miss Marilyn was playing nice and just tolerating me. By now, she might have warmed up to you, Jasper, but it ain't genuine. You watch what I say. And Aunt Hattie, well she's the most sincere, but they try to make her play second fiddle to them. Nora's Aunt Claudine, she' be the boss around them parts. She might as well be wearing some pants! And by the way, they don't have no men in that house. What happened to their husbands?"

Octavia looks at Jasper as if she has just come to the most important question.

"I don't know what to make of your summing up Nora's family in this way. Was there anything that was honest and enjoyable about the evening?"

Jasper bangs his hands on the steering wheel.

"Oh, yeah. Miss Nora was just as sweet and perfect acting as she always is. But them, Aunt Marilyn and Aunt Claudine, have the airs you get from some of our saditty, college-educated, colored folks. Some of them don't even know they got their noses so high up."

"Mama! I'm shocked that you could be so wrong about those

37

women. They are some of the most sincere and warm people I've met here in Macon. You need to look into your heart on this one! I just don't agree with you."

Jasper glares at Octavia, ending-the-conversation.

"Well, you, asked my opinion, didn't you?"

She snorted as she looks over at Jasper.

"I sure hope you will be gracious to Nora when she meets us for church tomorrow morning"

Jasper's exhausted statement was almost a whisper.

ॐ

I linger on the front porch just processing and savoring the events of the evening.

"I sure hope Mrs. Martin liked my aunts."

Aunt Hattie was the most friendly and engaging. Aunt Claudine was pretty friendly, but so busy trying to keep the food warm and help set the table. And Aunt Marilyn always uses her cooking as a barrier when she doesn't cotton to whoever might be sharing a meal with the family. So, her being a little stand-offish wasn't anything unusual. But she, like Claudine, always frets over serving the food at just the right time.

I go back into the house feeling anxious to hear my aunts talk about the evening. It bothers me how long it took Aunt Marilyn to warm up to Jasper and be half-way pleasant to him. I approach the dining room table.

"Aunt Marilyn, Jasper said he can't remember when he enjoyed a meal as good as what you and Aunt Claudine prepared tonight. And Aunt Hattie, Mrs. Martin says you are so charming and so good looking with your pretty hair in a bun."

While all of us are clearing the dishes from the table and walking the few steps back and forth to the kitchen, Marilyn steps into the conversation.

"Well, we got this evening out of the way, thank goodness! Now that Jasper and his mother can never say we didn't show any courtesy and respect about him leaving to go into the Army. They are nice and simple people, but you can tell she hasn't had any college training.

38

Jasper is a self-taught person. He's different from his mama."

Hattie points to one of the dining room table chairs.

"Marilyn. The lady's chair is not even cool over there and you're ready to start tearing her down. Everybody shouldn't have to be college educated before you are ready to consider them worthy of your time and effort."

"That's not what I'm saying. Stop twisting my words, Hattie."

Marilyn scrunches her lips together.

"It sounds like you have passed judgment on her value before you have even gotten to know her well. One night over a meal is not sufficient time to get to know someone, wouldn't you agree Aunt Claudine?"

Aunt Claudine carries a platter in one hand and perches her other hand on her hip.

"You all don't drag me into this. It's not a big deal. We had your gentleman friend and his mother over to dinner. He's leaving for the Army. And, both of you will probably find other mates before the springtime arrives."

"Wait one minute. You have no right to think you understand how strong or weak my feelings are for Jasper. I don't think any of you know how much I really care for Jasper and how much he cares for me. I'm hardly sleeping at night so worried about him going off to basic training and maybe going overseas. Did you invite the Martins over tonight just to pacify me. And then, you figure he and his mother will never come into this little house again?"

I felt like crying. Aunt Hattie walks toward me.

"Now sweet Nora, you know we don't think that or feel that way."

I am fighting back tears now. I don't want to break down.

"I'm sorry. I'm not a teenager, and I shouldn't be treated like one. I appreciate what you did tonight, even if your motives were not pure. Right now, I'm so hurt I can't even stay downstairs and help you straighten up. I'm meeting Jasper, my casual friend, at church in the morning, so I'm going to bed. Good night."

Chapter 4

Departure

Sunday morning comes bright and clear. The temperature is about sixty degrees. It is a perfect church-going day in Macon, Georgia and at Fernwood First Baptist Church.

The ladies wear their Sunday-best dresses which adorn the sanctuary with bright colored fabrics. They wear hats of various sizes and styles and white gloves. Always white gloves! The young and I-know-I'm-attractive ones would sashay down the aisle to maximize attention.

The older women—as brightly clothed as many of the younger ones—use their entrances to acknowledge others with a nod and be acknowledged, smile, and move in a practiced grace to the pew. These ritualistic entrances are most successful if one gets to church just about twenty minutes before the service starts and after the choir has stoked the ready-to-ignite embers of emotion.

These are the regular attendees and not the church's work-a-bees who come much earlier to prepare the sanctuary and pulpit—and usually wear the church's white uniform.

The young men are natty in their suits, with many of them wearing fedoras. Some of the older men are dressed in suits that maybe have been seen by two generations. When they come with their wives or girlfriends they often hang back—ever so slightly—when walking in to allow the attention to fall on the female.

"Good morning, Sister Martin. I see Mr. Jasper has his special friend with him today. This is your last Sunday with us for several weeks, right Mr. Jasper?"

Reverend Simpson raises his eyebrows.

"Yes sir, you remember Miss Carpenter, Reverend? She's attended Fernwood First Baptist with me before."

Jasper nods in agreement as the Reverend smiles as if to say he knows more than he shows.

Three of Octavia's lady friends approach us from behind as they walk into the church's vestibule. Sally Jenkins, one of the community's active members— active in ways too numerous to name—looks them up and down.

"Oh, I do declare. This young lady is a sight for sore, tired eyes. Jasper. How did you manage to find such a pretty lady friend?"

Octavia jumps in before Jasper can say a word.

"She's smart, too. She's a second grade teacher over at Fernwood Elementary school."

Clara Wilkins, interrupts, talking as though Jasper is invisible.

"Octavia, we are all going to send up some special prayers for your boy. We know he's been called into Uncle Sam's Army, and Lord have mercy, who wants to think long and hard about that one?"

Betsy Butler, the third friend is much more sensitive.

"Oh, stop talking so much Clara. You're going to cut a hog if you don't shut up."

"Ladies, this is my friend, Miss Carpenter. Nora Carpenter that is."

Jasper pulls himself up to stand taller.

"I'll be in training for six weeks in Kansas and who knows where or what my assignment will be after that."

Clara starts up again, with her hand in a wave-like gesture high in the air.

"You'd better come back and get Miss Carpenter wherever they send you. I know Octavia didn't raise no fool."

I just had to step in and stop all that mundane chatter.

"It's such a pleasure to meet all of you lovely ladies. I believe the service is about to start."

THE DEBT

Jasper spreads his fingers and holds his hands on both sides of his face.

"We all appreciate your good wishes and prayers. I'm going to be just fine."

All three of us step inside the sanctuary to walk to Octavia's long-held, self-selected pew near the front of the pulpit. I whisper to no one in particular.

"Let the good music begin."

ઠઈજ

And begin it did! The two-dozen choir members dressed in their magenta-colored robes started to sway in unison—left to right, right to left—as the organist took the chords up to a gradual pitch. The humming of the choir grew louder and after about five minutes, Reverend Simpson assumed his pious and statuesque pose on the side of the lectern. In one hand he held his bible; the other hand was raised upward, as if he had an offering for someone or something that the congregation couldn't see. He held his head, face up, and swayed along right in sync with the choir members.

I thought the service would never end as the message and music seem to all point to the theme of SACRIFICE. Reverend Simpson wove the sacrifices of people in Biblical times, to mothers and fathers who go without so their children can have, to church members who carve out precious hours every week to visit the sick and home-bound, to finally mixing in the young men—colored and white in our community—who are making the ultimate sacrifice by honoring their draft notices. I was enjoying the energy in the sanctuary and discreetly and periodically glancing over to Mrs. Martin and Jasper, on each side of me.

Then I noticed the "amens" were becoming louder and more frequent. The reverend realized he was striking an emotional cord when talking about how scary it would be for our young soldiers to be away from loved ones, whether state-side or oversees. At that point he deliberately ramped up his delivery. All of a sudden my emotions, which I had been trying to keep under control and hidden from Jasper and my family all these weeks, started knocking at the door to my heart. No amount of squirming in my seat, or reassurance from Jasper squeezing my hand, could keep my tears at bay. I snatched my hand from his and reached into my pocketbook for my hankie. There was one little tear….then three…then

43

six…all coming at a speed I couldn't keep up with. Mrs. Martin looked at me with mournful eyes, which themselves were beginning to redden. Jasper cleared his throat and put his arm around my shoulders with his elbow resting on the pew. I wept as quietly as I could, which seemed like an eternity. And in the middle of my "slippage," I heard muffled sobs from other women sitting in close-by pews. I kept saying to myself, "why won't he stop this clawing at our heart strings?" But I realized that's not what most lively Baptist ministers do. They don't backtrack or abandon ship when they can get the congregation whipped up! My stoic aunts, especially Marilyn and Claudine, would shake their heads at me and wonder, "what has come over that child?" Aunt Hattie's softer side would understand me at this moment. None of them realized how much I cared for Jasper. Could I love him and not even know it myself? We had come so close to being intimate on two occasions, but like a gentleman, Jasper had restrained himself. I went along with his stand-offish attitude, but it left me frustrated and wanting. That is why I was so looking forward to going to Atlanta to hear him play and lodge at the Y.W.C.A. We could have easily found a way to be together there. Now, there is no time for any of that. My thoughts were jolted back to reality when I heard the coins jingling in the offering trays as the ushers handed them from pew to pew.

∑ℂℂ

"Nora, I didn't mean to surprise you with this last minute, pop-over visit, but I had to see you alone before tomorrow morning," Jasper explains. He has driven over to the Carpenter's home to ask Nora to go for a short ride over to his friend Eugene's house to get his clarinet. Jasper has loaned the instrument to Eugene, but now he is retrieving it to leave in his mother's possession. Octavia already has his saxophone in their house. These two instruments are valuable to Jasper, and he knows they will be safe with Octavia.

"Well, at least my aunts got a chance to step out on the porch and wave good-bye to you. They weren't expecting to see you, either. They thought Saturday night was it—as far as goodbye," says Nora, as she sighs a deep sigh.

Jasper's DeSoto heads to Eugene's house about five blocks

away. Nora has on wool slacks and a soft knit sweater with buttons down the front. She is fresh, but dressed very casual because she is not expecting to leave home.

She and her aunts have finished a later afternoon dinner, cleaned the dishes, and are sitting at the kitchen table when Nora hears the motor of Jasper's car. It is pulling up in front of the house as the women are talking about what, of noteworthy interest, had occurred at Fernwood Baptist Church during the service. They are chatting and fishing for juicy tidbits of gossip. Nora is short on information because she was unusually disconnected—today in church—from what others around her were doing.

"It won't take me but a few minutes to run inside, say good-bye to Eugene and grab my clarinet," says Jasper, as he pulls his car into a bumpy, graveled, side-of-house driveway. "You just keep yourself entertained with thoughts about our future after my basic training," Jasper says, in an exaggerated deep and sexy tone.

ଛଡ଼

"Hi, Nora, how have you been lately?" Eugene asks. "If you or Mrs. Martin need any help with anything around your house while Jasper is away, you know you can call on me," he says, as he comes out of the house with Jasper and walks to the passenger side of the car to bend and talk through the open window.

"I know you are honest when you say this. But one of my aunts can fix and do, by herself, what you two would have to figure out together," chuckles Nora. "I'm not trying to mess with you guys' confidence, but my Aunt Claudine is a jack of all trades."

"Well, you can check with my Mama a couple of times if you want to, while I'm gone," adds Jasper.

"Are you sure you all packed and ready for tomorrow morning?" Eugene asks.

"Nora you hurry and let Jasper get on back home to get his rest so he won't make a bad impression on the first day in Uncle Sam's

Army," Eugene dead-pans, as he stands and does a clumsy salute. Then walking around the front of the car toward Jasper, Eugene puts out his right hand for a solid handshake. "Take care of yourself, my friend. The music won't sound the same with you gone, but me and the orchestra guys will see you in six," declares Eugene, in an authoritative manner.

ೋೀ

"Nora, let's just stop here on the back side of Hanson Park where all the pretty weeping willow trees just were swaying and flowing to their own internal music last summer. It's so relaxing to watch," says Jasper, who sounds like he is releasing all his tensions of a hectic, last day. "Besides, it's really quiet behind this path. Very few people walk here in early evening," Jasper says, with a confident tone.

As Jasper moves over from under the steering wheel toward Nora, she stiffens and blurts out, "My aunts are going to wonder what's taking you so long to get your clarinet."

"You can just tell them I remembered my mother asked me to run an errand for her while I was out, so that everything would be finished once I drove back to the house," says Jasper, in a nonchalant voice. He then puts his left forearm across Nora's chest to gently pull her, at an angle, toward him.

"I'm so sorry I never got a chance to come and hear you perform in Atlanta so we could spend some quiet, private time together. And of course, we would have had to figure out a way to work around whoever my traveling companion would have been—and how many days I could board at the Y.W.C.A.," Nora rattles on, in a fast-talking, nervous way.

"My sweet Nora, you are as soft as cotton and smell as fresh as a bunch of honeysuckle twigs," says Jasper, as his breathing deepens.

To her surprise and weakening defenses, Nora finds her upper body loosening its resistance to Jasper's embrace. She wiggles her hips and torso closer to Jasper's body as he places a warm, moist kiss on her left cheek. Jasper speaks first, as he alternates softly kissing her cheek and the lobe of her ear.

"It will be only six weeks and a couple of days before I return. We are both committed to each other so there's no restlessness to worry about. You know you can trust me, and I sure know I have nothing to worry about with you, my sweetness. It's a shame we are this age, all grown up and just finding each other."

With her right hand, Nora slowly lifts Jasper's left hand from her shoulder and places it on the top of her right breast. He then angles around to look into Nora's face, waits on her to open her eyes and then gives her a soft, full-mouth kiss. He begins to fondle her breast and to compete with the obstacle, which happens to be a button on Nora's sweater.

There is silence and heavy breathing as Nora tickles the side of Jasper's face with soft finger strokes, and he continues to kiss her and gently massage her breast.

"Jasper, we need to be cautious. Somebody might be walking through here and wonder whose car this is," whispers Nora. "They may call the authorities, and—and," Nora stammers, as she tries to complete her thought.

Jasper quiets her as he again fumbles with one of the buttons on her sweater.

"Shhh, Nora. It's a Sunday and almost dusk. This town is about ready to go to sleep. Nobody is out walking in this area."

Nora has moved her hand to Jasper's chest and is rubbing his chest in a circular motion through a flannel shirt. They both enjoying their above-the-waist, anatomical exploration and relishing the warmth and feel of each other's embrace. This type of front-car-seat caressing is inherently awkward and uncomfortable, but hardly noticeable in the throws of passion.

"Nora, oh , I wish I wasn't leaving in the morning. I feel like we are just getting to know each other on another level. I am going to miss you so much. I promise to write you so many letters. You will be tired of reading my letters. Just you wait and see," Jasper talks, as if he has taken a brief, cool-off period.

"Why are you talking so much right now?" whispers Nora. She initiates a kiss for the first time, as she moves her hand down lower on Jasper's upper torso.

"Oh, my goodness. I guess I'm trying to slow us down," says Jasper, taking a deep breath.

"Yeah, and you're over there trying to school yourself on how to unbutton my sweater like a gentleman," Nora teases Jasper.

They both are giggling and resting in their embrace when there is a faint *tap, tap, tap,* on the driver's side door. Jasper's body gets rigid, he looks at Nora, who is wiggling her hips to straighten herself on the seat while trying to press her sweater back into position. Then Jasper turns to where the sound came from, looks out the car window. When he doesn't see anything, he opens his door.

"Young man, what are you doing here? Was that you who was hitting my door?" asks Jasper, in a firm and angry voice. "Stand up, stop squatting down near the ground," he demanded.

"Yes sir, yes sir. Mr. Jasper. I am on my way home and I thought I knew this good lookin' car that is sometimes parked in front of my use-to-be-teacher's house," blurts Buster Brown, who is genuinely nervous.

"Do you know this boy?" asks Jasper, looking over quickly to Nora. "I certainly don't know who he is," Jasper states, unapologetic in tone.

As Buster Brown stands, Nora can feel the anger and rage building in her belly. "Do I know him?" Nora asks, rhetorically.

"Heeyyyy, Miss Carpenter. Nice seein' you on a Sunday evenin' on my way home and taking this short cut through the park. I'm late and my mama and daddy gonna be mad with me. I might not get my Sunday night san-mich if I don't scoot along. It's almost dark so I might be in big trouble. You all have a good evenin'. And I hope you don't get hurt in the Army, Mr. Jasper. And Miss Carpenter I hope you don't have to pine too much over the winter 'cause you can't go dancin' with them ladies," Buster rattles in a jittery way, as he backs away from Jasper's car.

While Nora sits stunned and speechless, Jasper is standing outside the car and begins walking toward Buster.

"Listen to me little boy. You are headed for a lot of trouble if you don't mind your manners and keep your nose out of grown folks' business. You had no right to sneak around my car, listening to my conversation with my fiancée and pretending it was all an accident. You just happened to be passing this way and had no control over your feet. You couldn't keep walking home. If I wasn't leaving town tomorrow, I would be over to your house asking to speak with your folks. From this point on, I'm going to make it my business to find out every time you do something wrong in Fernwood. I have a way of knowing. Do you understand me?" Jasper asks, as he realizes Buster is slowly backing away from him. He walked forward with him, eye-ball to eye-ball. He was a bit surprised at himself for letting this young boy get under his skin.

Nora is torn between being embarrassed, angry with herself and Buster Brown, wondering how much Buster Brown heard and saw and if he would blabber all her and Jasper's business to his playground buddies.

She doesn't speak very much to Jasper as he drives her the few blocks back to her home.

"Let's not have this spoil our good-byes to each other tomorrow morning, my sweet Nora, okay?" says Jasper, as he kisses Nora on her cheek while walking her to the front door.

Chapter 5

The Sad Goodbye

"Mr. Willie, you can stop right here," Nora says. She leans forward in the make-shift taxi and opens her small billfold to get her fare.

"I got you here in plenny time, Miss Nora," says Mr. Willie. He turns his head slightly to see the pretty little school teacher in a navy coat with an open, velveteen collar, accented by a sterling silver necklace with a silver heart that Jasper gave to her as a gift. The aunts are unaware of this very personal gift. This taxi service comes in very handy for the residents of the colored neighborhood. Macon's handful of Yellow Cabs with their blinding, bright-yellow paint do not go into the Fernwood section of town.

"You are a God-send, you know that?" Nora asks while counting her coins.

"Oh, look-a dere. Dere's Mr. Jasper dere walkin' toward us. He lookin' like a man on a mission. You better hurry up to keep him from waitin'." Mr. Willie has that wise look in his eyes.

"Don't wait on me. I will take the street car back across town. I don't know how long I will be," Nora says, as she reaches over the front seat to hand the coins to the driver.

Extending his arm to open the taxi's door, Jasper stoops to wave to Mr. Willie.

"Thank you for picking Miss Carpenter up this morning. I had to come a bit earlier. Uncle Sam's orders," he said.

"You manage to look pretty, no matter the time of day," Jasper beams, as he reaches for Nora's hand to help her to the sidewalk. He leans down and quickly brushes her mouth with his lips. He gently sweeps the heart on her necklace with his small finger. He had given her this symbol of his love.

There is *not* a wide margin of tolerance for public displays of affection, especially among the colored people in the city. The standards for them are always different, and Nora and Jasper know well the social norms of their small, southern town.

Jasper leads Nora toward a large group and thanks a man for keeping an eye on his well-worn Pullman piece and duffel bag. He then turns back to Nora with a bit of sadness in his eyes.

"Don't forget this is only temporary. These six weeks will pass before we can finish a package of writing paper. Mark my words," Jasper assures Nora. "I now know that I want a future with you, and we are going to find a way, somehow, to be together," Jasper says, in a lowered voice as he puts his second arm around Nora's other shoulder and leans in to kiss her cheek. At this point he feels the moisture on her cheek that could have only come from tears.

"Where is your hankie? Let me have it so I can wipe away those happy tears. You are happy about my plans for our future, aren't you?" Jasper leans back and asks.

Nora has her hankie twisted around her pinkie finger, which seems to be an unconscious sign of anxiety for many females. She chuckles as she unwraps the now, less-than-fresh handkerchief and reluctantly hands it to Jasper.

"Miss Carpenter, you have no idea how much I care for you and how vivid my dreams are of us being together and starting a family. You just wait and see what I have in store for *us*."

His eyes dart around the crowd. His words and his physical being are not in sync at that moment.

The sidewalk leading to the bus station's large, circular entrance is swarming with colored and white draftees. There is an invisible, but understood, line of demarcation on the paved entranceway. The whites are gathering several yards away from the cluster of colored people. From both sides of the color spectrum, their mates—wives, fiancees or girlfriends—their parents and other family members—are laughing, talking, and even weeping while trying not to show it.

Holding Nora's hand now, Jasper leads her a few steps away from the center of the colored draftees.

"I should know where I'll be assigned after basic training. If I go overseas, you will not be able to join me. If I get a state-side assignment, we can make plans to get married."

"Wait, wait, you're talking so fast I can't keep up!" Nora has her index finger twisted around her necklace's chain by now. "I have to think about my students and school, too! You haven't thought far enough ahead on these things, Jasper."

Just as Jasper is about to offer a mild rebuttal, an attractive, young woman in the crowd peeps around her male companion's shoulder, points to Jasper and states so everyone can hear, "Look! there's the saxophone player over there who's gotta' go into the Army, too. Ain't nobody spared, I guess."

"What saxophone player?" Her companion wants to know. He spins around and shoots Jasper a menacing glare.

"Oh, please, no more *here's the musician* kind of discovery," Nora mumbles not noticing the man's expression.

A handful of people turn and look in Jasper and Nora's direction. Jasper smiles like a courtly, country preacher and nods.

The male companion walks over to Jasper and asks, "You got some business over here with my lady friend?"

"No, I don't know your friend. She just looked over with a friendly face, and I acknowledged her," Jasper says, looking down at the shorter man.

"Just because you some kinda horn player, don't think you got a right to flirt with my girlfriend. I know you think you special and everything, but in this man's Army we all got the same color blood. It's red. So you ain't no better; you ain't no different. Don't you forget that, chump!" The man finishes with a scowl on his face.

Just as Jasper is about to respond to the put-down, Nora steps between them. Looking straight into the colored man's face, Nora says in a firm and confident voice, "You think my gentleman friend would be standing here with me and trying to entice your friend?" Nora fumes. "You need to find another outlet for your anger and frustration. Everybody who has to leave today knows he's not going on a grand vacation. So, let's just be pleasant and courteous to each other, okay?"

"Oh, you a fancy talking lady, ain't you?" the guy continues. "Well, you better tell that boyfriend of yours, music man or no music man, if he so much as look at my girlfriend again, he gonna need a doctor before he puts his big feet on the steps of one of these buses.

An older woman who probably has come to see a son off, steps up next to Nora with her hand on her hip.

"Percy, everywhere you go you want to always start some mess. Talking crazy here—talking crazy there. I don't see how you gonna last one week in Uncle Sam's Army. You 'bout as crazy as a betsy bug. Shut your mouth up, talk to *your* girlfriend and mind your own business. We all tryin' to cheer each other up and you want to act a fool!" says the woman, in a matter-of-fact tone. Tilting her head in the opposite direction, she continues her scolding of Percy, "If these other folks can be decent and courteous around here this morning, I know you can treat *your own* better than this."

The colored on-lookers are whispering among themselves, and a few mumble their standard word of affirmation, "Amen!"

Percy is left speechless as he backs up and rejoins his lady friend.

"Miss Mary, I know you from Walton's grocery store. You once worked there, right?" asks Jasper. "I wasn't offended by this man's nonsense. Different people have different ways of dealing with nerves. I'm happy you were able to make him see he was mistaken about my motives. He took the simple courtesy of acknowledging another human being as being flirtatious with his friend. By the way, is your son going off to Kansas too, or is he headed to basic training in New Jersey?"

"My son is going to New Jersey. He'll be a little closer to home than if he was going to Kansas. Good luck to you, Mr. Jasper," Miss Mary says with a smile.

"Good luck to your son who I see standing across the sidewalk," Jasper says, as he waves in the direction of her son, who looks to be about nineteen years old.

A portly man in the official green uniform of the United States Army comes out of the station with a bullhorn in his hand. He raises it and begins barking orders.

"At this time I want all you colored inductees to grab your gear and move to the rear of the bus terminal where you will be processed onto your buses. Say your last goodbye to your gals and families and haul ass, right now!"

Jasper grabs Nora for a final squeeze and quick kiss, and when he turns back for a final wave, he sees her sobbing with her now very wet little hankie in a ball and dabbing at her eyes.

Chapter 6

The Letters

In short order, Nora has mailed six letters to Jasper—he gave her his post address before he left. She doesn't forget to sprinkle a couple of drops of her cologne on each one. She has gotten four letters back from Jasper.

His letters are sweet, short and to-the-point. The point being he is still talking about marrying as soon as possible.

> *If I get an assignment on home soil, maybe as a Corporal, I can be assigned to base housing. I understand it's easier if you have a spouse. I know timing is everything, so we're just going to have to pray and keep our fingers crossed.*

Nora's letters speak of wanting many of the same things Jasper wants. But her letters also ramble on in a chatty, nervous-energy type of style.

> *For the first time since I began teaching, I am not as excited about going back into the classroom. I've got stars in my eyes and a big ache in my heart. I miss you so much my sweet, handsome Jasper. My busy work days are just that—trying to stay busy.*
>
> *Aunt Hattie seems to be the only one who understands my state of mind. Oh, by the way, she cut about eight inches off all that hair of hers. The church ladies just about had a fit! They have always made a*

fuss over her long, Indian-like hair. They realized her bun at the nape of her neck was much smaller. That's how they discovered what she had done.

And Aunt Marilyn is as negative and sarcastic as ever. She still has that nervous tick of clucking her tongue at the back of her throat. A strange sound, but she doesn't even know how many times a day she does it. She did do a nice thing yesterday and gave me four-dozen of her delicious sugar cookies to take to my school children. That's the nicest thing she's done in a long while.

Old Aunt Claudine has started another campaign to save money for some work around the house. The kitchen floor linoleum is wearing thin in spots, and Aunt C. said she is tired of waiting on the landlord to do some patch work. She wants everybody to throw left-over money in the household fix-it-up jar, as she calls it. So, now we are saving for another project. I don't know who appointed her the Lord and Master of the universe!

I went to see your Mother yesterday. She was sitting on her front porch with Sally Jenkins. They were chatting and drinking apple cider with a nip of her special spirits to warm them up. Your mom said she got her only letter from you last week. She was glad to know you had settled into the barracks so fast. Jasper, your mother has a spirit and a resilience to be admired. She truly is calm and at peace. Don't worry about Octavia Martin. We should all be so blessed.

"Lordy, here comes another one of those letters from that Jasper man out there in Kansas," Aunt Marilyn says. Nora, hearing the postman greet Marilyn, walks up to the front door, but stands behind it in the vestibule.

"The post office is going to start charging you a tax for having to deliver so much mail between the two of you. Here Nora, here's your next chapter."

Marilyn hands Nora the letter through a slight opening in the screen door.

"Sure thought that by now this foolishness would have been out of your head. That man is out there in those music halls near his Army post dancing and cavorting with all those women who hang around those military bases. Those loose women are just looking to have a good time and make those fools spend all their pay checks on them. I've heard those stories about what goes on. Then the wives and girlfriends back home pine over them like some sick puppies," Marilyn concludes.

"Aunt Marilyn, what in the world has made you so bitter and hateful toward people who love each other?" asks Nora. "You haven't had a kind word to say about Jasper and me since he left."

"You are just young and an easy mark. We don't want you to be hurt, that's all," Marilyn says, and then clucks her tongue almost simultaneously.

"There's no *we* here. You're the only one who tries to hurt my feelings about Jasper. Aunt Hattie is so kind and thoughtful in asking about how he is getting along. And Aunt Claudine, while she doesn't say much about Jasper, it is always much nicer than what you are constantly spitting out," Nora says with a frown on her face.

"You are going to be jilted by that man. Just mark my words," Marilyn says, then turns on her heels and walks inside to go to the kitchen.

About this time Aunt Hattie, overhearing the pithy conversation between Marilyn and Nora through the cracked bedroom window upstairs, rushes down to the vestibule.

Nora can feel her ears burning, and she knows the top rims are turning red. Her tear ducts become full, and she wipes her cheeks with the back of her left hand. Aunt Hattie takes one look at Nora, then rushes into the kitchen to confront Marilyn.

"You ought to be ashamed of yourself. You are just angry because Jonas was unfaithful to you. You couldn't stand that he didn't come home some nights. This is why you are so bitter toward men, and you hate to see anyone happy in a relationship. You ought to be pleased Nora and Jasper are thinking in a serious way about marriage," Hattie concludes, in a winded huff.

"Listen who's talking," Marilyn drawls. "You are so full of yourself and so smug because you never experienced a divorce. Oh no, Mr. Theopoulis was the perfect husband. Did you ever realize he was just henpecked? Did it not occur to you he wasn't the smartest cookie in the jar? Yeah, he had a decent job, but he was about as boring as an ironing board. So much for hitting the jackpot and ending up a young widow."

By now Nora, who has been standing at the kitchen door listening to her aunts rehash old animosities, turns on her heels and rushes out the front door. With the letter firmly in her right hand, Nora sits on the stoop like a wounded kitten and gingerly opens the bulging envelope.

All of Jasper's letters have been the same size. But this one, in his third week of basic training, is heavier and thicker. On this chilly late January day, Nora pauses a second to bounce the letter in her wide-open palm as if calculating its weight and content. She then rips the envelope at the back flap, almost tearing the corner of the first page.

With a faint smile of contentment on her pursed lips, Nora begins reading Jasper's much anticipated letter.

Hello my sweet Nora. I never knew how few words I command in my vocabulary until I start trying to describe my longings for just the sight of you—you with your big, bright smile, warm brown eyes, cute little button nose, perfectly curved and inviting lips all properly arranged on one of the most beautiful, almond-complexion faces I've ever seen. Seeing you will just be the beginning of our long-delayed opportunity to acknowledge just how deeply we love each other. I don't think I'm taking anything for granted when I say "we," am I?

I don't mean to shift gears so fast but look at around page five of the letter. This is such good news! I just inherited some money! I can hardly control my excitement and the daydreams this stroke of luck is bringing on. More than a year ago—before we met—my father's brother died in Memphis. My mother and I paid our respects. We went to the funeral. My uncle Ralph never married, but had a daughter who died from tuberculosis when she was about eighteen. He didn't keep in touch too much after that but was pleasant when we saw him every now and then at a family reunion. Just about all his folks, and everyone, are gone. He was my father's only remaining sibling. Aunt Gertie, my dad's sister, died a year after dad. Those three sheets of paper are so important so PLEASE put them in a safe place. I know in my heart I can trust you with this document. In his will he left me three thousand dollars!

Can you imagine what this means to our future together? We can make some solid plans once I know what my assignment will be and where I will or we will not go. Things are looking up Missy—up indeed! I can't wait to let your aunts and my mother know our plans.

Nora's attention turned from the remainder of Jasper's letter, and she began imagining herself, "Mrs. Martin." As if adopting the gesture of an older person with an achy joint, Nora begins rubbing her left knee as she continues to hold the letter in her right hand. She simultaneously shudders and smiles at the thought of marrying—a swirl of thoughts in a jumble of emotions. Her thoughts are racing now.

Oh, my goodness. Am I this close to making a decision to spend the rest of my life with Jasper? I know I love him, but I sometimes worry that his feelings for me are stronger than mine for him, and I don't quite understand why. Mrs. Martin has to be told about what we are planning—or what I think we are planning. Oh dear, I have to tell my aunts. Aunt Hattie will be so pleased and supportive. Aunt Claudine will probably be happy for us, but she will be stingy in her good wishes and praise. But I can just hear Aunt Marilyn now!

Are you sure you know what you are getting into? You have

never been away from home, and that Jasper is a worldly man—sure
is. He's been around the corner too many times—traveling and playing
in all those clubs and masonic halls. The situation will be just ripe for
breaking your heart.

Nora is deep into meditating about her future when Bubba Brown, the peripatetic neighborhood kid, pops out of nowhere and stands next to Nora—half on the front walkway and half of his chubby frame on the edge of the winter lawn.

"How you doin', Miss Carpenter?" Bubba Brown asks.

Nora angles her head up to see the wide-eyed, smiling boy.

"I'm doing fine young man. What are you doing with your time after school these days?" Nora asks, while methodically folding the letter and document. She then turns her attention to the precocious eight-year-old who is wearing a heavy jacket over a checkered, flannel shirt.

"Well, my mama and daddy tryin' to keep me busy so, as they say, I'll stay out of devilment, but there's not much to do other than play over in Hanson Park. We try and play ball out in the field some days after school, but the junior high school boys chase us away. They act like they own the park," Bubba Brown says in resignation.

"Have you thought of borrowing a couple of books to take home to read so you get smarter fast?" asks Nora as she looks up to see a calculating expression in Buster Brown's squinting eyes.

"Extra reading is for slow kids. I don't need that help," Bubba Brown says in a proud, big-boy's voice. "Just like you probably want to find some place to keep that letter. Whatever you were reading looks to me like it was real important. I'm not being disrespectful or nothin' Miss Carpenter, but I waited before I said anything to you because I could tell that was some serious reading," the kid says, as he checks Nora's facial expression.

"Little boys should not concern themselves with grown folks' business, do you hear me?" asks Nora in an incredulous tone. "And, don't lose what you've already learned, you understand?" Nora says in her school-teacher tone.

"Well, I just know that your friend, Mr. Jasper, is away at the Army, and I heard my mama say women folks with their boyfriends gone just pine the days away waitin' on letters and stuff," says Buster, as he tries to feign innocence.

"Young man, I think this is a conversation that's inappropriate. Does your mother know you eavesdrop when she's talking to other grown folks about things that are not her business anyway?" Nora asks. "You owe me an apology, and I think there's an empty ball field in the park waiting on you to show up," she concludes, in a disbelieving tone.

"Miss Carpenter, I didn't mean no harm. I just want you to know that you are not alone in your pine-in' for your friend. That's all I was trying to say to cheer you up," Bubba says, as he slowly backs off the lawn and scurries down the street.

Nora shakes her head as she stands, with an expression of disbelief and as if she has the weight of the world on her shoulders. She goes inside the house mumbling in a low tone, "Was I that brazen when I was eight years old? I know not!"

ഇരു

Nora's friend, Geneva, comes by the Carpenter home the very next day. She has on a long wool coat and laced up shoes. Her hair is coiffed in a fresh "do" and she looks like someone heading to the dance hall. She and Nora would often go to the dance halls together when Jasper was performing. Geneva sashays up the walkway and through the front door like a peacock.

"Hey, Honey. How are things going? You heard from Jasper lately?" she asks in rapid succession as she walks to Nora in the vestibule and gives her a quick hug.

Passing through the living room and leading Geneva back to

the kitchen table, Nora responds.

"Geneva, Jasper is fine, as far as you can be in basic training. He says it's hard, physical work, but you endure because you know it won't last for long. We write each other quite often," Nora says, while grinning like a young child.

"Girl, I hit the jackpot when I introduced you two. Both of you are kind-hearted people and both smart as a whip. You would never know Jasper hasn't been to college because he knows so much about a lot of stuff. And he knows how to speak the good King's English, as my grandma would say. Jasper's so good to his mama, too. You can go to the bank on a man who's good to his mama. That tells you a lot about how he's gonna treat his wife. Yes, mark my word on that one. I know you miss going out dancing since he's been away. Why don't you get dressed and come go with me in a little while down to the Elks Hall. You'll be safe. Everybody knows you're Jasper's lady. The guys will respect you as they always have. No one will make a pass at you. You know that you can just dance and pretend Jasper is in the orchestra as usual," the long-winded Geneva concludes.

"You know it won't be the same," Nora says wistfully.

"Velma and I don't want you getting into a rut these days. You can't turn into an old, settled schoolteacher before you get a ring on that finger. We *will* be seeing a ring before the year is out, won't we?" presses Geneva.

"Did Velma enjoy her recent trip to Charleston?" asks Nora, changing the subject. Staring toward the kitchen door leading out to the side yard, Nora says in a trance-like state, "I hear that's a pretty city, with all the houses along the river. Of course, I bet you none of the houses along the river belong to colored people. You know they got our folks living close to the railroad tracks, if they don't have a decent community carved out for themselves like Fernwood here," Nora concludes.

"My folks took me to Charleston when I was knee high to a

bull frog. I don't remember a single thing about the place," dead-pans Geneva.

"Lord, where are my manners?" snaps Nora, out of her trance-like demeanor. "Please excuse me for not pouring you up a cup of hot tea,"says Nora, jumping out of the chair in her red peddle-pusher pants. She looks a few pounds thinner since Jasper left.

"Aunt Marilyn got up early and baked some short bread squares. They are good and buttery. You want to taste one while you sip your tea?" Nora asks.

There is a brief spate of silence as Geneva drinks the hot tea.

"All right girl. I see you don't want to have a serious talk about what you and Jasper plan to do when he gets back. I'll leave it alone. But just remember, whatever you tell me is safe. You can go to the bank on my silence. Don't you ever forget that." Geneva studies Nora's face, as she finishes the sentence.

"Oh, Geneva, there is so much to think about. How can I talk about stuff that I haven't sorted out myself yet," Nora says in a half-whiny voice. She begins to circle the small kitchen table in the middle of the floor. While pacing and rubbing her palms together, she starts up again.

"You will always be my main confidant. It's just that I don't have any answers at this time. But it seems like I got to have some very shortly. Jasper is pressing me a bit. But, I just don't know with one hundred per cent certainty. Am I crazy or what?" Nora asks, in winding down her quasi-soliloquy.

"Honey, you are now twenty-three years old. I honestly think you love the man. I *know* he loves you. Neither one of you is getting any younger. What's the turtle waltz about?" Geneva asks, with a quizzical look on her face.

"You're a fine one to talk. Look at the many suitors you've chased away. Do you think you're approaching sweet sixteen on your next birthday?" Nora is becoming more energized.

"No and yes. No, I'm not getting any younger. And yes, I have turned down many suitors. But no one has come close to sweeping me off my feet. It may never happen, but I think I will know if it does. I should be so lucky as you," Geneva says, with a flurry of finality in her voice.

৪ঌৎ৪

"I'm so happy you decided to drop by for a visit," says Octavia. "Sure wish you would come and go ta church wit' me sometimes, too. There ain't no pressure. No strings or obligations ta me or my son by going ta church. The music is still good. The peacocks still stroll down the aisles every Sunday like the Easter parade forgot ta leave town. Damn near looking like the circus too, what with some of them young folks wearing those loud colors," Octavia Martin says, chatting on in a full conversational tilt.

Nora steers the conversation to Jasper's letters home. "Do you have any idea where Jasper might be stationed after Kansas?" Nora asks. "Has he said or even hinted about where he might be transferred?" she continues.

"No, sweetie. His letters are basically about him doin' just fine in basic training in spite of them sergeants working 'em like dogs from sun up ta sun down. He said a couple of times he hoped you and me was stayin' in touch and checkin' on each other. This is why I'm so happy ta see you today," Octavia chuckles.

"Gettin' down ta what's on my mind t'day. You know my boy is real sweet on you. You do know that, don't you?" Octavia asks, while staring Nora down.

Feeling the glare, Nora shifts her hips on the soft couch.

"Oh, Mrs. Martin, he's real special to me, too. I've never met a nicer, smarter man than your son. And he works so hard to be the best musician in this part of Georgia. He is ambitious all right about being hired by the best orchestras. That's what I admire about him so much," says Nora, with rising inflection in her voice.

"That boy is all I got since his daddy went and died on me. I have tried hard ta make sure he grow'd up like a man and understand what he needs to do ta make it in this here world. I made sure he stayed with his books and got his lessons. But when it came time for him ta go and grad-jate, I didn't have no money for him ta go to no college. Like a man before his time, he told me not ta worry. He would make good money playing his saxophone and clarinet, and that he wanted me to stop working shortly because he would be able ta take care of all our bills and needs. Well, you know he worked all the while he was in high school making chump change here and dare an playing a few gigs. I'm still workin', part-time now, however, so I don't have ta depend on him too much. Yeah, I been cleaning folks houses for many, many years now. It's just my way of life. Most of them folks have been half-way decent—a couple of them really very good to me—but oh, Lawdy, I done had a few dirty, lowdown snakes I ended up workin' for. But not for too long. The good man upstairs always helped me find another job when I needed ta get myself better situated," Octavia reveals, as she looks off in the distance.

"You're a fine and proud woman, Mrs. Martin," Nora says softly.

"No, Honey. I just tried ta make it the best way I could for me and my Jasper," she counters. "But my boy is special. *You* hear me?" she asks, with her eyes fixed straight on Nora again. "He don't deserve ta be hurt or toyed with. No, no, he's too good-hearted and kind ta not be with the right person," Octavia loudly clears her throat.

Nora is not prepared for Mrs. Martin's directness. She struggles momentarily for the right response. It doesn't take a genius to know this wise woman could sniff insincerity a mile down the road.

"Mrs. Martin, I have the utmost respect and affection for Jasper."

She measures her words so as to not offend.

"He *is* very special, and he means the world to me, just like he does to you," Nora's cadence quickens. "I would never think of being dishonest with Jasper, not for a minute. I've practically done nothing but write letters to him every other day or so," her response coming at a clip. "You know, we're being real serious with each other, and we'll talk more about our dating when he returns." Nora's tone becomes a little chipper.

"Listen chil', my son is ready ta ask you ta marry him. Are you as serious as *that*?" Octavia asks, without hesitation.

"Mrs. Martin, how do you know that? How can you be so sure Jasper is ready to get married?" Nora asks. She is surprised with Octavia Martin's omniscience.

"Don't ya' think I know my son's heart after all deez years?" Octavia asks, disbelieving.

"I, I, I'm not saying you don't know your son, but," Nora's voice stalls.

"Young lady, you need ta search *yo'* heart…way down and with a big dose of truthfulness. Jasper will be home in 'bout a month," Octavia says, with an end-of-conversation hint in her voice.

Nora stays another five minutes or so and makes light conversation about canning the fruits with her Aunt Hattie in a few months, the kids who are in her class, and then she makes a graceful exit.

"Mrs. Martin, thanks for such an enjoyable visit. You make a good apple cider too," Nora chats, right up to the front door.

"Your visit was a good surprise. You think *real* hard 'bout some of the things we done talked about, all right?" Mrs. Martin asks, as she closes the door behind Nora.

₨₧

Walking home after the visit, Nora is quite relieved to be away from Mrs. Martin and from the low-grade tension she felt rising in her chest. She is in deep thought as she walks along the uneven, sometimes-jaggered sidewalks and the well-worn dirt trails that lead her back to 1966 Magnolia Street.

I knew Octavia Martin was wise, but how had she sensed my fence-straddling about my true feelings for Jasper? And it is obvious Jasper hasn't told his mother about the inheritance. Or has he? Maybe I'm being too jittery about all of this. She's no mind-reader, but she is right about Jasper being home before you can bat an eye. I need to get serious about what I want in my life. I need to get on my knees and ask for some help!

ℂ℃

Over the next week, Nora becomes introspective and withdrawn around her aunts.

"The cat's sure got your tongue lately, Miss Nora," Aunt Marilyn says. Marilyn is cooking breakfast sausage that Nora says she doesn't have an appetite for, but Marilyn loves cooking, so, she ignores Nora's claim. The two other aunts, Claudine and Hattie, have the same schedule at Cloverdale Hospital this morning so they have already left for work. Marilyn has not been called as frequently to be a fill-in nurse at the hospital.

Marilyn tries to break the ice again, "Don't tell me you and your friend been squabbling in those letters you get just about every two to three days. You've had that hang-dog look for a while now," Marilyn says, as she turns her head to look back at Nora sitting absentmindedly at the table. "I sure hope this isn't the beginning of him trying to pull away from you, now that he's almost finished with his training," she says, focusing on the stove again. She was back to her usual snorting sound as she finished what she thought was a zinger of a comment.

"It's nothing like that," Nora says assertively. "Jasper and I are getting along fine. He's a really good man, Aunt Marilyn. You just can't seem to see the good in him or anybody of the opposite sex. You're going to miss out on a lot of pleasant friendships with some of these eligible gentlemen around the community. Besides, you could fix yourself up to look a little snazzy in about twenty minutes.

You still have your good looks hidden somewhere behind those negative thoughts. Why don't you relax and enjoy life a little?" Nora asks, as she snaps back to full consciousness. "Going back to church would be a good start at meeting some nice gentlemen your age," Nora says.

"Oh, you stop talking silly, girl," snaps Marilyn.

"This is not silly talk. I'm serious. You need somebody to take your attention away from this house, your garden *and* this kitchen," Nora says with a tone of finality.

ॐ

Nora attends church with her Aunts Claudine and Hattie. They, too, have asked her why she has been so quiet around the house. Walking to church Hattie even suggests maybe she needed to get out and go places with Geneva and Velma.

"Why don't you go out with your girlfriends anymore?" Hattie asks. "You did when Jasper first left, but it wasn't to go dancing. You all went to Sampson's Grill and had some ribs. I remember you saying how much you enjoyed catching up on the gossip and laughing out loud at their antics. You probably should go over to the Elks Lodge with them and dance a little bit. You have always loved to dance to good music," Hattie reminds her. "What is eating at you?" Hattie asks.

"Oh, I'm just thinking ahead. Jasper should know where he will be stationed soon, so I'll be memorizing a new mailing address for him," Nora says, in a matter-of-fact manner.

"Stop trying to fool us. You know everything is not normal with you. When you are ready to talk, we will listen, okay?" Claudine says, in a very frank tone.

Nora doesn't respond. She keeps, walking slightly ahead of her aunts as if checking the pathway for minor debris that could cause the two, older women to stumble or lose their balance.

To please Claudine, Hattie and Nora are wearing dresses

Claudine sewed for each of them as gifts for their last birthdays. Nora has a robin-eggs blue, cotton piqué dress that is fitted at the waist. The darts are neat around the bust line and the hem comes right below the knee. Hattie's dress is marine blue with small, white polka dots. It is a soft, chiffon-like fabric that flows to mid-calf. She has a two-inch, patent-leather belt at her waist. All three of women are wearing coats over their dresses.

"You Carpenter women look might pretty this morning, if I have to say so myself," Claudine boasts. They know this wouldn't be the last reference to the dresses. Claudine would claim all bragging rights when pointing out her sewing skills to the church women.

Nora's penchant for mumbling little near-silent prayers throughout the day heightens. She is on her knees much longer each night also. Here in church her attention is riveted on the service, especially the minister's prayers. As she sits in "Claudine's pew" between her aunts, her mind goes straight to Jasper.

What will be his expectations on return, and just what does she want to do. These questions and thoughts keep nagging her.

Dear Lord, give me the wisdom and insight I need to make the right decision. If I marry, I want it to be for a lifetime. I'm living in the shadow of two queens of divorce, and I can't see that it's made their lives any happier. Like his mother said, Jasper deserves someone who would make him a good wife. He is a good, solid man who has earned your attention and blessings. Am I the one who can honestly give him what he wants and needs? Will he love and honor me in the way you say husbands should do? I have dreams too. Can he help me be a better person? Lord I need some answers and I know you've got them.

Nora's daydreaming is interrupted by the choir standing in its pit to sing "Hold on to God's Unchanging Hand." It is a lovely, but low-key song.

Shucks, I need to hear something that's going to make my scalp tingle and my heart leap with joy!

Chapter 7

The Visitation

Nora becomes more quiet and introspective in the days following her last church service with aunts Hattie and Claudine. She is praying harder and longer than she ever has in her life, but it occurs to her that maybe she really doesn't know how to pray in a meaningful way. Her skills have not matured much beyond the juvenile style she adopted under the watchful eyes of her aunts when she knelt at her bedside. Those prayers were for her family, and at the coaxing of her aunts, for her deceased parents, her teachers, the preacher and other people important enough to mention.

Now Nora is thinking out loud as she sits in the parlor with a cup of tea.

Am I sounding sincere enough in asking God to help me search my heart for my true feelings about Jasper and marriage and babies? Does God think I'm being honest with him and myself? What was the good in attending those Sunday school classes growing up if I'm behaving like a fake as an adult?

Nora tells herself that, yes, she does love Jasper as much as he loves her. And no, she is not about to back out of the courtship. On those whispered declarations, she stands and walks outside to a large magnolia tree, leans in on its sturdy trunk and meditates. She decides she will be Jasper's wife if that is what he really wants, and she will move with him to his army assignment. She will be the brave military spouse who will hide her fears about war and death and loneliness. It didn't matter she has not been gushing about Jasper when talking with Mrs. Martin or her girlfriends, Geneva and Velma. It doesn't matter if they think she is lukewarm in her feelings for Jasper. She knows where her heart is, and this is all that she and Jasper need to know!

∞〇〇〇

Aunt Hattie comes rushing into the kitchen with *The Clarion Call,* Macon's main daily newspaper.

Out of breath, she blurts out, "Miss Mary's son was killed in New Jersey in basic training!" Pointing to the obit insert, she says, "It's right here in the colored section of the paper. It says he was accidentally killed by one of his trainers. He died from a rifle shot to his chest."

Nora sits motionless as she absorbs the information. Her large brown eyes doubled in size. Marilyn jumps up from the chair at the table and grabs the four-page rag from Hattie.

"Let me read what it says," she insists. "Joseph Hutchinson, son of Mary Hutchinson, was killed Monday at U-S Army base, Fort Dix, New Jersey, by his training officer. He suffered a fatal wound when the mistakenly fired bullet entered his chest. This is classified as a death by friendly fire. The colored enlisted boy was nineteen years old and lived in the Fernwood section of Macon," Marilyn slows to a monotone.

"How could this happen?" Nora stirs from her aimless gaze. "Jasper and I just saw him at the Greyhound station with his mother when they were shipped out. His Mother and Jasper exchanged pleasantries after she fussed at a man who accused Jasper of flirting with his girlfriend." Nora shakes her head in disbelief. "He looked like a sweet and nervous little boy."

After standing and walking slowly to the screened, kitchen door, Nora says, "Nobody is suppose to die in basic training. Only those who go overseas to fight the war are the ones killed."

With her eyes welling up and her body bending forward, Nora

begins shaking and sobbing. "This could have been my Jasper. This is not supposed to happen on American soil. I thought basic training was safe and secure. Oh, Lord, let Jasper come back home, and I'll marry him and love him with every nerve in my body."

The usually heartless and stoic Marilyn approaches Nora at the same time Hattie does. Marilyn puts her arm around Nora's waist and says, "Oh Nora, you're just upset at the moment and going overboard in how you think you feel about Jasper. You'll calm down shortly and see that you are reacting way out of proportion to the situation. Shhh, now, just get control and let your nerves settle," Marilyn whispers.

"There is nothing abnormal about her being upset on hearing such sad news," Hattie says. "Besides, she now realizes training in wartime is no child's game. The man she plans to marry could easily come home in a body bag, too."

"Who said anything about marrying?" asks Marilyn, turning to face Hattie.

Moving toward Marilyn with an expression of disbelief, Hattie says, "Have you been walking around with your head stuck in the sand, Marilyn? Don't you realize the three of us—you, me and Claudine—ought to be helping to make wedding plans?" sasses Hattie.

"Nora, have you been talking to your aunts about marrying that Jasper man and not telling me?" Marilyn scowls, while in essence talking to Nora's back, as Nora still stares through the kitchen door screen.

With an incredulous look in her eyes, Nora spins around and catches her second wind.

"No, I haven't said anything right out, but they understand me and my feelings about Jasper in ways you never will. They know my heart because they don't put up walls in their thinking and observing and understanding how I have moved toward being a woman in love," Nora says, in a let-it-all-hang-out tone.

"I don't want to talk about this right now. I need to start planning the full meal I'm going to cook for Miss Mary and take over to her house tomorrow—the mourning food," fumes Marilyn. "Since there is so much love in the air around this house, let's spread a little of it to that grieving mother tomorrow," Marilyn concludes.

"Marilyn, you always luck out when it's time to have an honest discussion about anything," Hattie says. "You're off the hook at the moment about Nora and Jasper because we do need to get the meal together. But don't think we won't pick this conversation up again, especially when Claudine can be in on it, too," Hattie glares in Marilyn's direction, with one hand on her hip.

Nora looks at the two older women as if she is battle-weary—a battle of words, not guns. She circles the table to walk toward the kitchen door that leads into the hallway and stops to look back over her shoulder.

"I have a headache so I'm going upstairs to lie down for thirty minutes," she sighs. "I'll help with the planning when I come back down. Will you need me to run over to Walton's grocery store to buy anything?" asks Nora, as she pauses briefly before walking out of the kitchen.

"I'll let you know later," responds Marilyn.

Hattie then walks to the kitchen door and gazes out to the side yard. She shakes her head as she talks out loud, but not necessarily to Marilyn, "Mary Hutchinson sure was a good worker when she was over at Walton's grocers. She knew how to keep up with everybody's credit sheet. And she didn't make anyone feel bad if they were short on money after she figured out the food bill. She would put it on their credit sheet and tell them to make up for it the next time. Yeah, she up and quit one day when she found out she was going to have that late-in-life baby. Word had it then, she was afraid to tell her husband they were about to be old parents. That's the boy that just got killed. Her only child. So sad. So, so sad."

"That is so true," says Marilyn, as she kneels to look into the ice box.

☙❧

The misfortune of death in small, southern communities affords most people the chance to show their sympathetic and generous side. The best show of caring and sympathy is to appear at the home of the deceased with your prized dishes—the dishes your family brags about. This gives the grieving family a break from mundane cooking chores. It also allows them to offer food to the stream of visitors coming to pay respect and to express their sorrow.

By mid-afternoon the day after word got out about Miss Mary's son being killed, the women of the community started making a bee line to Mary Hutchinson's small, bungalow home. Some of them had to walk back and forth from their homes a couple of times, over rough sidewalks and patchy grass trails, to deliver the mostly-hot food. Much of it was right off the stove, out of the oven or off the back-yard smoke pit. These community mourning rituals were devoid of complaints about cooking or stretching the already tight food money.

"Sure wish your Jasper was here with that car of his. Sho' nuff would be handy now with us carrying all this hot, heavy food two blocks over," huffs a tired Marilyn.

Nora hesitates before she responds. "Yes, people can be conveniently likable when they got something that's needed at the moment. I'm so glad the principal let us out of school an hour early."

"Oh, I didn't mean it the way it sounded," says the irritating Marilyn.

"I'll go back and get the blackberry cobbler. Maybe Claudine and Hattie can bring the big pan of short bread when they come over after work," Nora says.

While Nora knows coming to pay her respects to Miss Mary is

74

the proper thing to do, she is not looking forward to the face-to-face meeting. She hadn't slept well overnight because she was projecting her emotions about Joseph, or Little Joey as he was called, to her new-found fear for Jasper's safety. She was weepy, off and on, most of the previous evening, but she was careful not to let her aunts see her so unsettled.

"I've been on my feet getting this food together since six-thirty this morning. I appreciate that you washed the tomatoes and that we had enough jars of blackberries from last summer for a cobbler. Also it was a big help for you to wash and stalk the collard greens before you left for school," Marilyn says to Nora. "Sure hope this food is eaten up today because it won't hold fresh for long, plus folks will be bringing food right up until time for the funeral—which I hear is going to be Sunday. That's kind of quick if you ask me, but the sooner he's put six feet under the quicker his mother and rest of the family can begin to heal," Marilyn rattles on, as they slowly make their way to Mary's front stoop.

"Come right on in with those vittles, good sisters," Reverend Simpson says as he holds the screen door wide open. "I've been here a stretch already, just pitching in where I can—been sampling some of this good food that's passing by me too. These mourning meals hard on a man's waistline, sure are," chuckles the Fernwood First Baptist minister. "What you got there, Miss Marilyn?" asks the minister, as he tries to peep under the cheese cloth covering the two-pound meat loaf. "By the way, you haven't been to church in a month-of-Sundays. When you coming back to hear the Lord's good words?" he asks, trying to capture eye contact with Marilyn.

"All of us are here at Miss Mary's on a different mission," Mr.— oh, excuse me—Rev. Simpson, she says in a syrupy tone. "This is not the time for you to try to ratchet up church attendance," she warns.

There doesn't seem to be an inch of space anywhere to place more plates and platters of food. The small sideboard in the cramped dining room is taken with casseroles, two platters of yams, a still-warm and aromatic pound cake, fried chicken pieces, deviled eggs and big jars of tea, just waiting on a chip of ice from the big ice bucket out on the sagging back porch. Two, short kitchen counters are crowded with donated food, also.

"Where can I put this pan of mashed potatoes?" Nora asks one of the church members. "I helped my aunt make the potatoes to go with the meat loaf," she proudly announces. "Little Buster Brown is coming up the stoop now with the pot of collard greens. I told him I'd give him two cents to help get this over here. He popped up in front of our house at just the right time today," she says, as the lady moves serving dishes with food closer together to try and make room.

"I'll ask Buster Brown to go back and get the blackberry cobbler from the kitchen cupboard," Marilyn suggests. "You need to stay so you can speak with Miss Mary, when she finishes talking to that Sally Jenkins lady." Staring from the dining room into the adjacent parlor, Marilyn keys in on the lady seated next to Miss Mary. Marilyn asks, "Isn't that one of Octavia Martin's good friends?"

Looking in the same direction, Nora says, "Miss Jenkins does go to church with Mrs. Martin sometimes, and I think they visit back and forth." Nora turns to look at her aunt, "How do you know who Mrs. Martin counts as a friend?" she asks.

"I know more than you think I do, niece Nora," Marilyn whips. "Remind me to tell you something about that Sally Jenkins that will make you raise your eye brows to attention."

"Honestly, Aunt Marilyn, you have too much time on your hands since you haven't been called to fill-in at the hospital recently," Nora says, in a regretful tone.

Just as Nora and Marilyn are working their way into the parlor by squeezing past people in the home's small, cramped hallway, Sally Jenkins is standing and patting Miss Mary's shoulder in a consoling manner.

"You just hold on now and be strong," she says. "You've got this whole neighborhood here to help you, if need be."

"Nora, hurry and move in before somebody else sits to talk with Miss Mary," Marilyn says, with a gentle nudge to Nora's back.

"Oh, hello there, Mr. Jasper's friend," says Sally, in an affected drawl, as she turns on her heels and sees Nora tip-toeing toward her and Miss Mary.

"Excuse me, I didn't mean no disrespect. I know you are Miss Carpenter, the special friend of Octavia's son and all," she says, trying to disguise her patronizing tone. But this doesn't stop the neighborhood busy-body. "How have you managed to keep your nerves about you—with all this sadness going around about this war and your love interest being in basic training? You know two white boys from here were shipped home dead yesterday, and one the day before from somewhere over there in Europe. Honey, I tell you, it's just too much to think about," concludes Sally, as she shakes her head as though she can't believe the realities of soldiers' lives.

Nora's already raw emotions are stirring and threatening to dance down her face in the form of crocodile tears.

"How are you Miss Jenkins?" asks Nora. "If you don't mind, I'd like to speak with Miss Mary for a few minutes," she continues.

Mary Hutchison has been fairly composed until Sally's booming voice rattled her, too. She dabs her already-damp handkerchief to her eyes as she looks up at the elementary school teacher who nervously displays a half-smile. Mrs. Hutchison pats the cushion of the sofa with her other hand gesturing for Nora to sit down. There are three women sitting on a second sofa across from the grieving mother, and they are whispering in low tones as they nod their heads in acknowledgment of Nora. Mr. Willie, the neighborhood taxi driver, is sitting in a rickety folding chair eating some of the kitchen bounty.

"Hello, Miss Carpenter. Sho' is good to see you, but not under these tryin' times. Hello to you too, Miss Marilyn," Mr. Willie says in his lowered, best-manners voice.

Easing down onto the sofa, Nora leans into Miss Mary and begins her monologue.

"I—I—can't tell you how sad I—I—am to hear about your boy, Miss Mary," she starts. "My whole family wishes we could offer you more than just nourishment for your body. We wish we had the secret to help mend a broken heart. Little Joey was not yet a full-fledged man. He had his whole—whole—I mean he was still your baby boy. You and your late husband worked hard to make a gentleman out of him, and by all accounts he was moving in that direction. What an honorable thing to do—to go to learn how to fight for your country. So many men from our little town are trying to do—to do...." Nora's voice trails off. She then lowers her head, bites her bottom, quivering lip and begins to wipe tears with the back of her left hand. Miss Mary pats the back of Nora's right hand.

Betsy Butler, one of the women sitting on the sofa with a glass of lemonade in her hand, begins rocking back and forth, as she inserts her voice.

"Yeah, and they are talking about an accident! Your boy was shot by accident by one of the people who was suppose ta help him learn to be a good soldier. It don't sound right to me," no sir-ree, Betsy says.

Hearing the talk from the kitchen, Sally Jenkins pushes past Marilyn and the others crammed shoulder-to-shoulder and comes back into the front room.

"And you think anything is going to be done to that man who killed Little Joey?" she asks, rhetorically.

"Now as sad as it bees, my grandfather told me dat dis kind ah thing always go happen in da war. That why they got to say it be a accident," says Mr. Willie. "You got ta take the military man word for it."

Marilyn, who had coaxed Nora into offering condolences for

the family, jumps into the conversation unexpectedly. "Don't you think it's sad enough around here not to go and rub any more salt in this family's wound?" she says, looking around the room. " I know Miss Mary has family here from down in the country and close by so let's stop trying to figure out what did or did not happen. That won't bring Miss Mary's child back," Marilyn says firmly.

A little girl sitting off the end of the sofa on an upturned fruit crate, says to the old lady next to Betsy Butler, "Grandma, what they mean about dyin' in the war?"

"Pearly, you just keep on eatin' your pound cake and let us grown folks try to figure this out," says the grandmother.

"Excuse me please. I need to go in the back for a few minutes," says Mary Hutchison as she rises slowly from the lumpy-cushioned sofa. The tight cluster of neighbors in the cramped hallway move out of her way as if parting the waters. Miss Mary disappears down the short hallway and enters her small bedroom.

Mr. Willie rests his plate on his lap and says, "Sally, you and 'yo friend, Miss Betsy, always be talkin' so much, you don' gone an' upset Miss Mary talkin' 'bout somethin we ain't got no say over— can't do a damn thing about that boy dyin."

Rev. Simpson reappeared out of nowhere and says, "Mr. Willie, you know you shouldn't be using no curse word in this house where we got the spirit of the deceased amongst us."

"I can say damn all the day long and it ain't goin' to help nor hurt that dead boy," Mr. Willie, says in a huff.

Clara Wilkins, another one of Octavia Martin's church-going friends, struts into the front room with three more ladies crowding behind.

"If you all would come and eat some of all this food coming into this house, you mouths would be so full, you wouldn't have time to cut no hogs," she chides the parlor "squatters."

Some of the people beginning to stir will be going to fill a full plate of food for the first time. Others will be on their second gluttony tour—to the kitchen counter, to the dining room table and the side board. As they absorb Clara Wilkins's words, some of the older neighbors mumble their customary word of affirmation.

"Amen."

ℬℭ

A day later Nora gets another letter from Jasper. Nora could just imagine his excitement as she sits on her bed and reads his words—excited because he has just two more weeks before he would be able to leave Kansas.

I'll be home around February 20ᵗʰ or 21ˢᵗ my sweet Nora.

With a racing heart, Nora puts the letter down, smiles broadly, looked upward and mouthed a silent, "Thank You."

Send your principal your letter now telling him you won't be back for the next school year. We can get married right away. We don't have to have a big wedding. We can go to the court house, or have a very small ceremony with a few people in my or your church. I understand that I have a good chance of getting assigned to one of the enlisted men's houses on base, IF I have a wife—children even sweeten the request. How does this sound, Sweetie, for future planning?

Nora's head is spinning. She almost puts the letter down on the bed just to catch her breath. But she keeps reading.

I've got to write to my uncle's insurance man and ask him to mail me my inheritance check. You did put the insurance form in a safe place like I asked, didn't you? Do you know how many colored people have $3,000 to their name in this day and time—1944? This money can go a long way, but we've got to use good common sense in our saving and spending habits. We are starting out with a big leg up!

On about page four, Jasper gets around to asking how much Nora had told her aunts about their future plans.

Do they know we're talking marriage? My mother sure knows what I want to do, and I really didn't have to tell her. She always could

80

read my mind before my mind was even made up. My mama will be so happy for us. She thinks the world of you, Nora.

Jasper went on for another page-and-a-half. There were eight pages of this letter about their future. Nora knew, *finally*, that she truly wants to be Jasper's wife no matter how her aunts feel about it. Her uncertainty is scrapped with war's mounting death toll on just the colored and white men from Macon, let alone the fatalities in other cities she has been reading about. It seems she has matured and become more decisive a few days after the death of young Joseph Hutchison. Her personal rainbow appears in the same sky that beckoned Little Joey home to the angels. Such a loss, such a gain—all in the span of a few days!

ဆာလ

All the Carpenter women are eating dinner at the kitchen table when Claudine asks abruptly, "When is Jasper coming back from basic training? His time should be coming to an end soon, shouldn't it?"

"Yes," Nora says, as she exhales like a bellows blowing out a fire.

"Do you have a firm date yet?" asks Hattie.

"You've been mighty closed-mouth about Jasper in the last week or so. Can't tell if your sail is up moving with the wind, or if a storm is brewing close to the love boat and about to take that sail down," says Marilyn derisively, at the same time she let out one of her weird grunts.

"Jasper will be home around February 20th," Nora says right away.

"Oh, my goodness, that's right around the corner," quips Claudine. "When did you plan to tell us?"

"Everybody is being told, starting right at this moment," says Nora, with a hint of defensiveness. "And tomorrow, I'm giving my letter of resignation to my principal, Mr. Sanders, because I won't be starting the school year after Labor Day."

On that last statement, Marilyn drops her fork out of her hand and it hits the linoleum floor. Hattie snatches her glasses off and leans, wide-eyed, into Nora sitting next to her. Claudine jumps up and puts her hands on her hips and is the first to speak out,

"You giving what to whom? Nora, do you know what cockamamie statement you just made?" she asks loudly.

"Lord, I just about heard everything," Marilyn says, with a loud snorting sound. "You're about to give up a good teaching job, with good pay because you want to cavort with your soldier boyfriend when he comes home?" asks Marilyn, disbelieving the words.

"Let's let Nora finish talking. She must have good reason to want to stop teaching," says the ever-patient Hattie. "You know how level-headed this child has always been. Let's hear her out."

"Well—well—Jasper and I are planning to get married, and I will be going to his next assignment with him," says Nora, in a rehearsed tone.

"Will wonders ever cease?" says Claudine shaking her head.

"When did all of this thinking and plotting happen?" asks Marilyn, now standing with her buttocks resting on the stove's oven door.

"Nora has been living with us ever since she was a baby, practically. Don't you know and understand anything about her. Haven't you been seeing her changing right before our eyes?" Hattie asks. "Or maybe, you didn't want to admit that she was falling in love with Jasper. And we've sure always known how he feels about her," she continues.

Claudine sits back in her chair slowly and watches Nora as Nora straightens and closes her fingers above her pressed palms.

"Now, Nora. We know you are thinking you're getting up there in your twenties, and the pickings for male friends might seem slim around Macon. But you ought to spread those pretty little wings a bit—just close to home, however. Why don't you plan a trip to Atlanta with Velma and Geneva. You never know what new boyfriend might be on the horizon—just right up the road. Jasper won't mind. He's had almost six weeks now to spread his wings. And you know he has been doing that, out there in Kansas. It won't hurt to let yourself have some wholesome fun in the big city for a few days. Now will it?" Claudine asks, as Nora's clasped hands are now pressed against her lips.

"With all due respect, I have been thinking and praying for months about my feelings for Jasper. He is a good man. He is probably one of the finest men I could ever meet. He's honest— he's hardworking—he's responsible—he's good to his mother—he's has a pleasant and steady personality—he's going to make a good husband, and I've decided that's exactly where I'm headed." Nora stares at them with determination.

"Honey, we don't want to lose you. We are all so close here—us Carpenter women," says Claudine. "You and Jasper can get married. You just don't have to leave the fold. We can make your bedroom into a lovely husband and wife nest, and every time he has to leave he can come back to be with you. You can even visit him during your school breaks," Claudine suggests, in a sweet and supportive tone.

Hattie jumps into the discussion. "What kind of set-up would that be for newlyweds?" she asks. "Here is this house with three aunts—one widowed and two divorced. No, that's no way to start a new and fresh life together. They need to be away and on their own."

"Nora is just so sweet and soft. That Jasper just wants a wife he can control and have as a work mate. He has figured this thing all out to his best advantage," Marilyn chimes in.

"Just stop it, all of you!" Nora snaps. "I've made up my mind. Unless Jasper is struck by lightning or killed by friendly fire in the next few days, we are going to be Mr. and Mrs. Jasper Martin!"

"But—but Nora, you are not giving us time to plan a

wedding—a small one or whatever," protests Claudine.

"My dear aunts, I will be happy just going down to the court house. You don't need to plan anything for us. Honestly, just give me and Jasper your best wishes and your blessings. Is this too much to ask of good people who have given me a good life for almost twenty-four years?" Nora asks in earnest.

As Nora turns on her heels to leave the kitchen and her nearly-full plate of food, she looks back over her shoulder at the trio. Aunt Hattie has a smile on her face like a Cheshire cat. Aunt Marilyn looks sick to her stomach. And Aunt Claudine's brows are so scrunched they could have made a clapping sound.

"I'll see you in the morning. I have a very full and busy day tomorrow," Nora says, as she practically skips out of the kitchen.

After a full Sunday which includes going to church with Aunts Hattie and Claudine, getting emotional during church service, still having ambivalent thoughts about marrying Jasper, having dinner with the aunts, Nora is unusually exhausted when she finally goes to bed.

Nora drifts off to sleep eventually but not before sensing she's about to get some dreaded news. She tries to figure out what is bothering her, but there are no answers. Nora falls into a fitful sleep.

No, Mrs. Martin, tell me there is some mistake. You got the wrong Western Union Telegram. Tell me it is not our Jasper who has been seriously injured. Jasper has mentioned in several letters how cautious he is. He double checks all his ammunition and is very careful about unloading and locking his issued rifle.

The telegram said you will be getting any new information if Jasper's condition becomes more serious. Did they say there is any way to call the base switchboard?

Oh, no! I can't take this sad news. Will Jasper be coming home in a body bag just like Little Joey Hutchinson? Mrs. Martin is going to lose all her strength and optimism. Jasper is her only child. She and I will become the pity of the

Fernwood community with all those sympathy visits and plates and pans of food. Lord, I decided that I do love Jasper, and I want to marry him. If you will forgive me for being so wishy-washy and indecisive, I will make Jasper the happiest man in these United States. I promise you this.

I gonna stop crying like some wounded little girl and show you I know how to be a mature woman. If you just let Jasper come back home, I'll nurse him back to good health. You know my aunts can help me, too.

Please, please hear my humble prayers. Let Jasper come back to me!

The alarm rings and jolts Nora awake.

Chapter 8

Common Ground

Nora comes into the kitchen wearing a thin cotton gown. Her soft, easy-to-manage hair is unusually disheveled, and she has a somewhat dazed look in her eyes, which are darting around in a furtive manner. Nora rushes over to the ice box to pull the milk bottle out.

"Good morning, Aunt Marilyn," she says. "I've got a bunch of things on my to-do list, and now—" Nora stops in mid-sentence after noticing her aunt has her white nurse's dress on.

Walking around the kitchen table closer to Marilyn, she asks, "Are you working at the hospital today? You didn't mention last night that you had to go in this morning."

"I didn't know it then. A little after six this morning the scheduling supervisor came rushing over here to say I was sorely needed today," Marilyn says. "The nurse who was scheduled to work must have a real emergency to back out at the last minute," she continues, with a tone of mock irritation. "Anyway, I'm glad to earn some money for a change. The fill-in calls have slowed down over at the hospital, but this one, this morning, is putting too much of a rush on me. I'm going to miss the seven o'clock sign-in. Claudine and Hattie left over twenty minutes ago. I wasn't quite dressed then," she concludes.

"When I heard you moving around upstairs, I thought you were dressing to do some early-morning household chores. That can wait.

Money is more important," Nora says, in a lazy, still-waking-up voice. She eases down into the chair, placing a glass and the milk bottle on the table in front or her.

"I hope it won't be so hectic at the hospital this morning," Nora says, as Marilyn rushes out of the kitchen and heads toward the front door. "See you after four o'clock this afternoon," Nora calls out.

"Dinner will be late tonight," shouts Marilyn, as the screen door closes behind her.

"What a lucky break," Nora says to herself in a whispered tone.

"With everyone out of the house this morning, I can try to sort out that God-awful nightmare I had during the night. I feel like I've been through a washer tub wringer. Oh, my Lord, in my nightmare I saw Jasper in a hospital bed after being badly burned on his leg.

"Seems as though Mrs. Martin appeared out of thin air and said something about the Western Union telegram she got from Jasper's unit chief. Looking a little bit wild-eyed, she said, 'Nora, I can't make hide na' tails out of what they tryin' to tell me.'"

"Did she say the chief said something about hot powder from a canon shot? I could swear I heard Jasper cry out like a young child because he was in so much pain. 'Mama—Nora, I've been burned! Oh, it hurts so bad. Come here and help me.' I tried to talk to him but no words would come out of my mouth—wide open mouth—with lips moving—but no words! I mouthed, 'Jasper, don't worry, we are here to help you. I love you and will marry you when you come home. Your Mama and I will nurse your burns until you are well again just like nothing ever happened.' That must have been when I woke up and was soaked in perspiration and wiping tears from both sides of my face. This is why I have on a different gown this morning. I guess I went to my chest of drawers and pulled out a fresh, dry gown—the one I have on now. I think I remember not being able to stop crying, and then I must have cried myself back to sleep. Because when the nightmare came again, when I started to ask Mrs. Martin more questions about Jasper, she was gone. She was gone away as fast as she came to me. Then I remember shaking and being cold in bed and feeling like I needed my chenille robe in spite of being in this warm, spring-like break from winter. That damn nightmare back in my brain, I remember I wanted to talk to Jasper, but no one would let me in his hospital ward. I started crying, beating on the wall in the hospital corridor and calling his name. The nurse said I needed to go home and wait until I got word to come and visit. I told her I lived hundreds of miles away. How was I going to get home. I didn't even remember how I got to Kansas and at the base hospital in the first place. I asked her where had Private Martin's mother gone. She looked at me with a funny look and said she had not seen anyone there asking about a Private Jasper Martin."

"Come on Hattie. We're going to miss our bus if we don't get out of the house," shouted Aunt Claudine.

"This is when I came back into the real world. When I heard my aunts making noise and rushing off to work," Nora whispers.

⁎⁎⁎

"Lord, Marilyn, you look worn out," says Hattie. Claudine and Marilyn joined Hattie in taking off their white uniforms right past the front door's threshold.

"Well, you know Marilyn hasn't been in that kind of go-go work mode for a while. The patient load sometimes keeps us running for a couple of hours before we can catch a break," puffs Claudine. "It takes getting back in the swing of things at the hospital."

"You can say that again," sighs Marilyn, as they all walk back to the kitchen with their full, under slips on.

"It's been almost two months since I last filled in for an absent nurse. I need to get in the bathtub and soak in tepid water with some bicarbonate of soda added to it. I don't want to feel achy tomorrow,"

Marilyn concludes.

The front screen opens and the sound of soft footsteps in the hallway precede Nora's entry into the kitchen.

"How's everybody doing after a full shift at the hospital?" asks Nora.

"The full moon must have affected a couple of dim-witted people I had to attend to today," says Claudine. "These patients are not operating on a full deck to begin with, and then they get liquored up over the weekend and that makes them more dizzy, if you know what I mean," grumbles Claudine.

"Oh, you know they come from the other side of the neighborhood where they don't care how crazy they act once they start jookin' over at Maurice's Place. And with drinking Johnny Mack's kitchen–sink corn liquor, no telling what may come marching into the emergency room early Monday morning," Marilyn says, followed by one of her annoying snorts.

"Well, if you listen to some of the talk from the white nurses while they're waiting at the front of the line to grab their fresh linens, they come across some of the worst from their neighborhoods too. They march in there, also, on Monday mornings," says Hattie. "They drink and carouse just like our folks, but one of the things we don't do like them, we don't have those cock fights on the outskirts of town. I hear from just a little eavesdropping that there's gambling, with some sore losers, and then fist fights. Some of the fist fights get out of hand, and then a few rough guys pull out their pocket knives. So, those white nurses see knife slashes on the arms and sides of the face that folks have tried to nurse on their own all day Sunday."

"Don't forget the ones—colored and white—who get drunk and want to beat up on their wives and girlfriends," adds Claudine, like a clever Miss Know-It-All.

"Well, what about the people who come into Cloverdale Hospital on a Monday morning with just plain and honest ailments," queries Nora. "Don't they get some good citizenship appreciation?"

"Of course they do," says Hattie. "Like little Rodney Tucker, who broke his arm last night. He suffered all night, but his mother waited until a little after eight this morning to bring him in. He was in pain, but he showed his good manners and home training."

"Oh, my goodness! Rodney was one of my students last year. Will he be okay ?" Nora asks, with pity in her voice.

"He will be just fine." Hattie says.

"What's for supper, Aunt Marilyn. Do you need help preparing it?" Nora asks, changing the subject.

"Nora, why don't you and I prepare supper. Let's give Marilyn a rest," Hattie injects.

"To spare both of you some trouble and us waiting to eat, there are enough left-overs from Sunday dinner to fill all of us up," Marilyn says, with pride. "I'll quickly warm up the food around a quarter after five.

"Hey, Marilyn, did you get filled up with Arnold's compliments today?" Claudine asks, instigating a reaction. "He was so pleased when I told him first thing this morning—after I got to the hospital—that you would be working the seven to three shift. You know he asks me about you all the time."

"Claudine, if you don't quit talking silly, you'll be warming this food by yourself," Marilyn threatens.

"You all leave Aunt Marilyn alone," Nora suggests. She is not the girlfriend/boyfriend type! Maybe in the spring, right Aunt Marilyn?" Nora teases.

"Stop talking all crazy about Arnold," Marilyn says in a huff. "Everybody needs to take care to mind their own business."

She looks from woman to woman, with squinted eyes. The niece and two sisters all howl and leave Marilyn pouting in the kitchen, with wind in her jaws.

"Miss Carpenter, are you sure you have thought about this carefully?" asks the elementary school principal, with a stern facial expression.

"Yes, Mr. Sanders. I know a letter of resignation is not something to be taken lightly. I do, however, expect to be married soon, and I will be following my new husband, Jasper Martin, to his military assignment. But please, Sir, this is not for anyone else's ears, just yet. You know how people in this community love to talk about other people's affairs whether they have permission to or not," Nora says, in a half-pleading voice.

"I will hold your confidence, Miss Carpenter. And I will also hold this letter just in case you have a change of heart. I will need to think about filling your position when the time comes. There is a new crop of teachers in Macon and surrounding counties who are dying to get a teaching contract. They have graduated from good schools like your alma mater, Tuskegee Institute. Yes, they are from Spelman and Morehouse in Atlanta, from Valley Forge State College down the road there and Florida A & M—you name it. Just pray on your decision a little longer. Make sure you and Mr. Jasper are of the same mind about getting married," Mr. Sanders concludes, in a paternalistic tone.

"When I get to my new home, wherever that will be with Jasper, and I want to apply for a teaching position in the colored system, will you consider writing me a recommendation?" asks Nora. "I have loved my job here in my hometown, and I love young children. Heavens knows I've tried hard to be a good teacher to all of them. It's my wish to continue shaping and molding young minds."

"You have come a long way in your three years at this school," says the bifocaled Mr. Sanders. "Yes, you have developed into one of my finest young teachers, and there was a great expectation that you would be moved to maybe the sixth grade classroom in another year or so. This profession doesn't need to lose capable, young teachers, and I'm happy to know you aren't planning to leave the classroom all together."

"Oh no, I can't think of anything else I'd rather do than teach school. Maybe I will go back some day to work on my second degree, but it will still probably be in education," says Nora.

"If everything works out for you the way you hope it will, Mr. Jasper will be a very lucky young husband, and some school system will have hit the jackpot with their new elementary teacher," concludes Mr. Sanders, as he rises from his desk chair.

"Oh, thank you for your kindness and support of me while I was here and for your hope for my future. I'll be lucky if I can land in a good school like Fernwood Elementary and with a kindhearted leader like you, Mr. Sanders," Nora says, as she extends her hand for a handshake.

"Oh, come here little lady and give me a big hug," he says, facing Nora with his arms outstretched.

Nora walks slowly toward Mr. Sanders with a little girl's smile and reluctance. "You *have* seemed like an uncle, Sir," says Nora. She stands erect as the towering principal bends and wraps both his arms around the five-foot-three-inch teacher's shoulders. He gently pats her back below the nape of her neck with one opened palm and then releases the young woman.

"I wish you all the happiness and good fortune in the world, Miss Carpenter. And remember, if you plan a wedding here in town, I want an invitation—okay?" Mr. Sanders announces, as he looks down at Nora with a smile and raised eyebrows.

"Oh, you *will* get an invitation if we throw a wedding instead of going to the courthouse. We haven't decided yet which one it will be," answers Nora. At that point Nora smiles and eases toward the office door. "Thanks for everything, Mr. Sanders," she says, as she opens the door to leave.

Once outside she realizes her hair has the scent of the shaving cologne Uncle Hempstead had used. When bending over, the side of Mr. Sanders' face had brushed the top of Nora's head and now she smelled like Old Spice, the popular men's shaving cologne.

ഇ⊙രു

"Well, how did it go over at the school with the principal?" asks Hattie.

"He says he is sorry to have me leave, but he truly understands. But he also offered to hold my resignation letter in case I change my mind," says Nora, with a hint of surprise in her voice. "I don't know why everyone is acting like this is a hasty decision. A decision that I just might back out of—on a whim. Why am I, at almost twenty-four years old, not capable of knowing exactly what I want?" asks Nora, and not necessarily of her Aunt Hattie.

"Well, Nora, sometimes you have to show people what you're going to do, rather than tell them what you're going to do," Hattie says. "Everyone is not a believer. But they will see when you have that marriage certificate in your hand. Even your two aunts will then be believers!"

"Isn't there someone knocking on the door?" asked Nora.

"Yes, I'll go and answer the door. Are you expecting a visitor, Nora?" asks Hattie.

"No, I'm not. It's almost four o'clock. Only nurses on the early shift are finished working this time of day," answers Nora.

Hattie quickly leaves the kitchen and heads to the front door. "Well, what a surprise. Come on in," Hattie says. "Nora, come and see our surprise visitor," she calls back over her shoulder.

"Ssshhhh," said the visitor, with her finger pressed against her pursed lips.

Putting down the tomato she is slicing and taking off an apron, Nora rushes through the dining room toward the front vestibule.

"Oh, my goodness. What a pleasant, drop-in visitor you are.

93

I haven't seen you in a couple of weeks. How have you been Mrs. Martin?" gushes Nora.

"Oh, I can't complain. As long as the good Lord lets you get out of da' bed every morning, you don't have nothin' to complain about. That ain't saying I don't have plenty to *talk about*," chuckles Mrs. Martin, tickled by her own sassiness.

"Starting with that marriage you and my boy been planning, I hear tell. He's as happy as a hog in you know what. He's been writing about your decision to go to the military base with him after you marry and—" Octavia Martin stops mid-sentence, looks from Nora to Hattie with a questionable expression, and blurts out, "Am I talking in front of the good aunt or are you one of them that don't particularly like the idea of your Nora marrying my Jasper?" she pauses and waits, with a stern look on her face.

"Oh, I'm the one who has always welcomed Jasper with open arms, Mrs. Martin," insists Hattie.

"I thought we decided some time ago, that I'm Octavia and you're—you're—which one are you anyway?" Octavia asks, impatiently.

"Mrs. Martin, all of my aunts adore Jasper. Aunt Marilyn and Aunt Claudine are just slow to warm to new friends. They take longer," she says. "Aunt Hattie and I are a lot alike. We warm up to people quickly. We seem to be able to just know, right away, when we've come across decent, honorable and caring people like you and my Jasper. My other two aunts want to wait and see, and wait and see, until they can make our new friends uncomfortable. That's all. It's real innocent and not mean or anything. That's just how they are," Nora says, in a pleading tone.

"You could have fooled me," Octavia says, with a smacking sound.

"Come on, let's go into the kitchen," says Hattie.

Nora, puts a kettle on the stove for tea and brings three cups to the table.

THE DEBT

They sit around the table and talk about when Nora and Jasper are going to marry—right away, after he arrives back from Kansas to Macon to marry.

Nora jumps in quickly, "Oh, Mrs. Martin, I'm so excited about Jasper almost being done with his basic training, and getting married, and moving away with him." She is almost out of breath, but she adds, "And I gave the principal over at my school my letter of resignation today. I told him I might leave before the school year is over."

The conversation flows from whether it should be a small, albeit hastily planned, church wedding or a go-to-the-courthouse and get-it-over-with event.

෨⃝ශ

Just as the three women are relaxing and enjoying the tea, Marilyn and Claudine struggle up to the kitchen side door with two heavy bags of groceries.

"Nora, come and help us with these two bags," shouts the out-of-breath Claudine.

Nora jumps up and takes the few steps around table and with two more steps is opening the door.

"Here, Aunt Claudine, let me take that heavy bag for you," Nora says, stretching her arms out the door.

"Hurry up, and close the door you all so we keep the heat in," says Hattie.

"Oh, be quiet, Hattie. "You claim you couldn't go over to Walton's grocers with us because your muscles started tightening at the hospital," chimes in Marilyn, who is struggling to get through the door.

"I did feel my back muscles pull when I was helping lift that heavy patient from one bed to another," Hattie says defensively.

Standing and walking toward Marilyn, Octavia says, "Let me help y'all ladies. I'm as strong as an ole' mule."

"It's nice to see you again, Octavia," Marilyn says.

"See there. She is not so formal with this name calling. You remembered what I said when I was over fa' dinner before my Jasper left, didn't you Aunt Marilyn?" Octavia asks slyly.

Marilyn ignores her question, but allows Octavia to take the bag from her and sit it on the end of the table close to the ice box. Marilyn gingerly lifts out a small basket with fresh eggs wrapped in newspaper and places it on the table. She takes three items wrapped in brown butcher's paper from the large hemp bag. Then, three canned goods and, finally, a bottle of milk. After everything is at the edge of the table, she opens the ice box and quickly finds space for the items. Then she slams the door.

Watching Marilyn's swift and deliberate moves, Octavia says, "You can't tarry when ya' open that ice box door. No sir. Your blocks of ice will melt and ya' vittles will spoil."

"That's right, I heard Jasper bought you an ice box before he left for basic training," says Claudine. She is putting non-perishables in the cabinet over the sink as she looks back at Octavia, who is sitting again.

"When do we get another block of ice?" asks Nora.

"Mr. Willie will bring some tomorrow morning. By the way, you don't need to lock the side door. He knows how to let himself in," says Marilyn.

"I get my ice from Mr. Willie, too. He's usually dependable, but sometimes he got ta drive somebody somewhere, then go ta da ice house to fetch his blocks afterwards—in order ta make his rounds. He sho' has figured out how to make a living a lot of different ways. That's bein' smart in ways other than book learning, sho' is," Octavia concludes.

"Well, to what do we owe this nice visit from you?" asks Claudine.

"I was 'bout to say I come by to visit Nora and all y'all. Excuse my manners for just walkin' up ta your door, but I'm betting everybody has got use to the idea, by now, of Jasper an' Nora marrying and of her going to live on da base wit' him," Octavia says, in a non-stop manner. "She even say she done gone and give the principal a letter today—explaining that she might leave before the end of the year."

Claudine looks around the table with a sullen expression on her face, and says with exaggerated restraint, "Nora, dear, I thought you said you would wait a few days to make sure you are making the right decision about leaving your good-paying teaching position. You know good jobs are hard to find, and we talked about making a little marriage nest upstairs out of your bedroom."

"*You* talked about that Aunt Claudine, *not me*," Nora reminds her, without hesitation.

"Nora, I told you not to put too much stock in your friend still being serious after he will have been away for six weeks and around all those bar women who hang around soldiers. He might be saying anything in those letters just to keep from hurting your feelings. You better be sensible and listen to what we're trying to help you with," pleads Marilyn.

"Wait 'ah minute here," Octavia says, as she sits up in her chair.

Hattie pops up out of her chair and walks over to Mrs. Martin.

She begins, "Octavia, they are just so sad about the idea of Nora leaving home for the first time that their imaginations just cook up all these silly excuses and reasons she should wait before marrying—not only Jasper—but this would be about marrying *anyone*."

"This is our dead sister Clementine's child, and I have sworn on my sister's headstone that I'd take care of her baby," says Claudine.

"That's just it. She *ain't* no baby! And my Jasper ain't no crib robber! Dey got the good sense ta make up their own minds and ta know dat they love each other." Standing and walking over to Marilyn, Octavia puts her hand on her hip and says, "And fa' you ta talk like *my* Jasper could be lyin' to Nora an leadin' her on. I won't let *nobody* run my son's good name through da mud. If you got a nerve to say 'dis to me—to my face, you sho' must be gossipin' 'bout dis and spreadin' false em-formation ta other people 'round these parts. You best be glad I done gone and mellowed out in my sunset years, 'cause you might be getting up off dat floor by now," Octavia concludes.

She walks over to Nora who has a shocked and saddened look on her face. Octavia grabs Nora's hands in hers and looks her straight in her eyes. She speaks in a very earnest tone, "Nora, I sus-speck there mo' evil thoughts widin these here walls dan you could ever reckon wit. Now, let me talk saditty-like. Yo' Aunt Hattie seem to be da only one wishing you and my Jasper the kind o' happiness you deserve. I don't know what happened in Marilyn and Claudine's love life with them men friends or husbands, but they be all confused about what true love look like and feel like," she says, in exhaustion. "I'm going to mosey on home now and pray for everybody, 'cause somethin' is way off track here within these four walls. I *will* figure out what's really behind all this ugly talk to try and keep you under their thumb. Lord, help my son around deez women!"

"Mrs. Martin, I won't change my mind about marrying Jasper, no matter what happens here at home. I love him too much. My family is going to have to come into their straight minds about my right, as an adult, to make my own decisions. Please don't worry about me. I have found a new strength—just this afternoon. It's a strength I've never felt before. Try and have a good evening," Nora says, with pleading eyes.

"Come, Octavia. I'll show you out the front door," says Hattie, as she gently cups Octavia's elbow in her hand.

෧෬

There is an atmosphere of a wake around the Carpenter house for the next few days. Nora is fairly silent with sleepy-looking, downcast eyes. Hattie acts as the go-between passing curt messages along from niece to aunts and vice versa.

By Friday, late-afternoon, Hattie broke the ice with her two sisters saying, "It's time we all start acting like sensible adults here. Jasper will be back in Macon in less than a week and, whether you like the idea or not, there's going to be a marriage taking place soon. I'm not saying there has to be a wedding—but I put my money on them getting married. So, we need to come together and have like minds about how we plan to support our niece and let the community know, when the time is right. We need to talk now before Nora gets back home. She left a note on my bed saying she had gone over to Geneva's house and would be back in time to help with dinner."

"We *still* don't know if *that boy* is serious about marrying Nora, or if he's setting her up for heart break," says Marilyn. "She'll always be going to those clubs and Masonic Halls to follow his playing, and sometimes he may be taking her to work with him in some old dives, with loose women, too much liquor-drinking where squabbling and fighting are always going on. And that's where the devil lives in all those no-good places."

"His name is Jasper, Marilyn. Funny you didn't forget his name when you were talking to Octavia a few days back. You knew better than to refer to her son, in her face, as *that boy*," Hattie points out.

"Let's not get tacky here and lose track of what the real issues are," Claudine says.

"The real issue is that I genuinely feel Nora has belief in her heart Jasper loves her and intends to do right by her," says Hattie, as she paces around the kitchen. "We have given her our love and guidance and all the good moral teachings we got from our parents and grandparents. She knows how to judge people and decide if they meet her—and our—high standards. Let's stop this foolishness and trust her judgment and instincts. After all, she has made us extremely proud these twenty-three years and has never given us pause to be embarrassed about anything."

"Yes, and she needs to stay right here so she can continue her good deeds, in her own community," injects Marilyn, in a strong voice.

"Another issue is that we have always pulled together, as a family, and it has taken *all* our earnings to make a comfortable life here. It's been a wonderful thing how we have prospered when we have worked together on improving our home by saving as a group so we can buy the big things like our ice box and all of our bedroom furniture pieces. Three and a half salaries are better than two-and-a-half. I say half because we can't always know what Marilyn may bring in," reasons Claudine.

Marilyn snaps her head around to look at Claudine. She then hits the table with her opened hand and says, "Yeah, it's Marilyn who keeps this house going, in between my filling in at the hospital. The majority of the time you don't have to worry about what's for dinner, is the garden being tended, the bathroom downstairs and upstairs spruced up. I sure do more than my share to make up for what may be missing in green backs. Don't you ever play my part short."

"You know I didn't mean it the way it sounded," Claudine says, half-cooing. "But listen, do you think Nora is going to want us to spend a lot of money on a wedding?" Claudine asks, with raised eyebrows. "Whether it's little or medium-size, families—that is families without a dead, rich uncle somewhere—come up short on their regular bills for months and months after the love birds have traipsed off somewhere. Excuse my English, but, we 'go be in a pinch for money, if we have to go through with the expense of a wedding," she sighs.

Hattie, still standing, continues with her arguments for support of Nora. She is trying to understand why her two sisters keep resisting what is, to her and Nora, inevitable.

"Now let me get this straight," Hattie starts, in uncharacteristic bluntness. "Marilyn, you are still claiming Jasper a liar about his intentions and motivations. You claim you don't know if he's serious. Have you noticed how often he has written Nora in these almost six weeks—not just one page letters, mind you. So what if he plays his saxophone and clarinet in high-brow places or low-brow place? Why is that a threat to our niece? Is it because your ex-husband was known to sneak around those places when he thought no one was noticing? I trust Jasper's judgment in those matters as well as Nora's judgment. And let me remember your *other* reason for wanting our niece to stay put. No one else in the community does as many good deeds and is as respected as this one, little elementary school teacher, the always-willing Vacation Bible School teacher, arithmetic tutor, science club sponsor—do I need to keep going?" asks Hattie.

"Ooh, I never heard such exaggeration, sister," scoffs Marilyn.

"And who gave you the big crystal ball so that you know everything about Jasper *and* Nora in this very delicate and serious situation. This situation which just may be a grand mistake almost!" questions Claudine, who then gulps water from a mason jar.

"Oh, you just wait, Miss self-appointed pack leader," Hattie snaps. "Your reasons or excuses are even more troubling. About a week ago you said if Nora and Jasper get married, Nora wouldn't have to leave Macon. We could decorate her bedroom as a love nest or some other description and when Jasper visited Macon on leave from the post, this would be his home too. I said then that was a cockamamie idea. No young newlywed couple wants to live in the bride's home with three of her single aunts. Not if they can help it. Besides, the Army post will give them their own temporary living quarters. Then you claim we are too poor to have a simple, but pretty little wedding. Claudine, you can sew her a beautiful dress in no time flat. Wouldn't cost much at all. And you know it. Still, we don't honestly know if they want to have a wedding. But if they do, then what?

"I bet Miss Scrooge here—motioning toward Claudine—has Nora's late mother and our sister—Clementine—turning over in her grave! The idea that her big sister would deny her daughter, who she tragically left at an early age, the dream of a wedding ceremony must have her weeping in heaven," Hattie sermonizes.

"Just wait a minute, Hattie. I didn't know you have so much pent up resentment for me and Marilyn. You are twisting everything we have said and are continuing to say," Claudine protesting in a loud voice, standing eye-ball to eye-ball with Hattie.

"I'm not finished yet," insists Hattie, backing up a few steps.

"You sure as hell need to be," growls Marilyn.

"Here—right now—within the last five minutes, you now are saying this tight-knit family needs to stay a tight-knit family. Look, we all had our chance at marriage. My husband, Theopolis—a wonderful gentleman and provider—died," Hattie says, with a mix of regret and pride.

"You're entitled to stretch the truth, but time does dim a widow's memory, miss perfectly married lady," huffs Claudine.

"Marilyn, your ex, Jonas, never was much of a husband to you, especially after you suffered your miscarriage. And Hempstead tried to make you happy, Claudine, but you were so head-strong about everything—still is, by the way. But let us give Nora her turn at trying to build a solid and happy marriage. We owe her that," Hattie demands.

"How can you claim to know anything about my and Jonas' marriage. You and Theopolis were living in your new house, and you were acting like "Miss Ann" during that period. You don't know a thing about what was going on in my life then," Marilyn says, in a quivering voice.

"I'm still not finished," says Hattie. "Now Claudine is claiming we can't do without Nora's paycheck in this household. Since when do we own each other's paychecks. Yes, we put money in the big jar, over time, to save for expensive stuff, but we also help each week with the groceries and other bills. But after that, there is always our left over money that is ours to keep, to save, give away or do what we want. It's never a whole lot, but it belongs to us—free and clear.

So now, we'll have one less person eating, one less person burning the couple of light bulbs around here and using the Borax and Ivory soap so we should be able to adjust. I just *know* this is not about wanting to keep Nora here for her paycheck," Hattie ends, on an incredulous note.

Claudine nervously rubs her hands together as she walks toward the kitchen door. "I'm going to check for premature buds on the peach tree out back. Seems like they're early," she says, walking quickly out of the kitchen.

"Hattie, I've never seen your dandruff so worked up! You have hurt both my and Claudine's feelings by misreading our sentiments about Nora. You have made us feel that we've never loved that child. And Lord knows that's not the case," sighs Marilyn.

"Yes, and I was born yesterday," Hattie says, as she leaves the kitchen.

೮೧೦೪

"Aunt Hattie, where are you?" shouts Nora, from the stair landing. She has gone into the kitchen, and it is empty. No sightings of Claudine, Marilyn or Hattie. What a rare occurrence—a seemingly empty house at 1966 Magnolia.

Nora runs up the stairs to the upper rooms, and there she hears water running through the bathtub pipes. At that moment, Aunt Hattie comes out wearing a bright, flowered duster.

"How long have you been home?" she asks Nora.

"Oh, I just got here. Where are Aunt Marilyn and Aunt Claudine?" asks Nora.

"I believe they're in the backyard looking at the fruit trees," Hattie responds.

"I'm getting back later than I had planned," Nora begins. "But I sat and talked with Geneva for a long time. Then her friend Sarah came by. I had not met her before. She lives on the outskirts of Macon. She's somewhat a newlywed—been married about nine months now. It is so comforting to talk with someone who is still excited about marriage and is feeling her way with her new husband. She gave me some good pointers."

"Nora, your aunts and I had a serious and heated talk about you and your plans for marriage. They are still not believing it's very likely to happen. I guess they want you to be an old maid," Hattie chuckles. "But—just be patient and be yourself. We all need to start talking to one another again. I hope like everything that what I said to them this afternoon will make them start to come around and be rational about your and Jasper's intentions. Just understand I'm in your corner. I hope they will be too, very soon. Let the two of us continue to pray and think positive thoughts. Come on, let's go downstairs and see if we can be useful in the kitchen," Hattie says, in an up-beat tone.

&)(&

"Claudine and I thought we would have to send Mr. Willie out looking for you," Marilyn says, in an effort to be light-hearted.

"The time just got away from me this afternoon. It was good to visit with Geneva. She asked me to say hello to all of you," Nora says, softly.

Claudine jumps the gun on the conversation, saying, "I suppose you and Geneva talked about Jasper coming home and you wanting to marry him."

"He wants to marry me, too!" snaps Nora. "*We* want to get married. He's as excited about it as I am."

Hattie shoots Nora a calming, half-smile, adding, "Now Nora has to decide if the love birds want a small, but very lovely, wedding ceremony, or do they want to just go before a Justice of the Peace at the courthouse."

"We can have the wedding right out back in the yard," Claudine suggests. "We have those two large, white trellises all covered in those white dahlias come Spring, and the other pretty flower beds around

104

the edge of the yard. All of us can decorate folding chairs we will borrow from the church—and—and Marilyn and I can cook up the most delicious food—or maybe we just want some fancy cakes or petit fours," Claudine continues, with mounting enthusiasm.

"And it would not cost so much money as a church wedding," Marilyn blurts out. "We could ask Rev. Simpson to officiate—oops, I mean y'all ask Rev. Simpson to officiate 'cause I ain't one of his favorites," Marilyn adds, in a mocking speech pattern.

"Also, if this is what Nora would like, she can ask Velma and Geneva to be her attendants, and, of course, Jasper would choose a couple of his buddies to stand with him," Hattie adds.

"Wait one minute, please," suggests Nora. "Jasper and I are not all hot to have a ceremony of any kind. We are happy to keep it as simple as possible. Let me ask him when he gets here.

"Nora, let me just say this in all sincerity," Claudine begins. "It has taken me and your Aunt Marilyn a while to get used to the idea that you want to marry and follow Jasper on his military moves. We were slow to understand that your happiness is what is most important now—not our love for you and our stubborn, clinging ways," Claudine concludes, in a syrupy voice.

"No, we are just trying to make sure of your course in life, just like your mother, Clementine, and your father, Horace, would have done," asserts Marilyn. "You know they loved you so much, and you came to them after she lost two earlier babies in the womb. We are just trying to do the right thing by you."

"And, Lord have mercy, if you had been in that car with them that night. I shudder every time I think about us not having a sweet little girl to bring joy to this household," Claudine chimes in.

"And this little girl is doing what comes natural—grow up, get an education, fall in love, and *begin to* create her own life. Make her own decisions as an adult!" Nora says, with conviction.

"Let's set the table and get supper going, while everybody's all agreeable," Hattie chuckles.

Only Nora notices the quick, sly glance Claudine throws Marilyn's way, as Marilyn begins humming when she leans into the opened ice box.

༄༅

All weekend, between other chores, Nora organizes her clothes by seasons. She doesn't have an extensive wardrobe, but what she owns is of very acceptable quality and in good taste. At least half a dozen of her nicer outfits have been expertly sewn by Claudine. One or two are a little matronly for Nora's taste, but it doesn't matter when she wears them to church. She hums as she examines each outfit and thinks through the sorting process.

I could never wear this to one of the clubs or ballrooms, it's just not stylish or snazzy enough. If I get a teaching position, even if I can substitute teach, that will give us more to spend and then maybe I can buy a couple of new things. Wonder if the military will allow Jasper to play his instruments in the city— away from the base. He probably will have to get some special permission to do that. Anyway, it won't be cold for months, but it will get cool earlier there than here, since we're moving northward.

It is late afternoon on Saturday when Hattie calls out from downstairs, "Nora, what are you doing?" she asks, with a raised voice.

"I'm still messing with my clothes, trying to organize things," she shouts out from the bedroom.

"Come downstairs for a minute, there's someone here to see you," Hattie says, cheerfully.

"Oh, my goodness," Nora mumbles, "I look a mess! Okay Aunt Hattie, I'll be right down," she answers.

Nora quickly puts on a fresh, white blouse but doesn't change the powder blue peddle-pushers. She takes the rubber band out of her pony-tailed hair, rakes the comb through it, and twists the band again around the neatly combed pony tail. She runs down the stairs and, to her surprise, is this hulk of a man she hasn't seen since she

106

graduated college almost four years ago.

"Uncle Hempstead, oh, my goodness. What are you doing here?" she asks, giddily. "I'm so happy to see you. I didn't hear you come in," she continues, as she rushes to him for a big bear hug.

"You are as pretty as ever, Nora. Didn't mean to come unannounced but saw your old childhood friend, Velma, over at Sampson's Grill. She told me about your upcoming marriage to this impressive young soldier. I just had to come by and give you my best wishes," he gushes. "Hattie was standing on the front stoop when I drove around the corner, and she almost twisted her ankle running out to the edge of the yard. I knew, at that moment, one of the Carpenter sisters is happy to see me," he chuckles.

"Are you still living in Atlanta? How long will you be in Macon? Do you want some cool ice tea?" Nora asks, in rapid-fire fashion.

"Slow down, Miss Nora. I've got a little while before I have to take off," he says. "I guess I'd better ask—where is Claudine?" he says, looking toward the kitchen. "I haven't seen her in some years. Sometimes, I run into her when I come here on business. One time, she was half-way cordial and the other two times chilly as the north wind. Can never figure her out," Hempstead laments.

"Claudine and Marilyn just left for Walton's grocery store. They'll be gone a while. Let's sit here on the sofa," Hattie says. Hempstead smiles as she leads him toward the parlor.

"Is it all right for me to still call you Uncle Hempstead?" Nora asks, in a child's voice.

"I would be insulted if you didn't. You know you will always hold that special place in my heart," he answers.

"You haven't told us why you're in Macon," says Hattie.

"I'm here to check on that parcel of land I own right outside the city limits. You remember those thirty acres where I had planned to build Claudine a big spread?" asks Hempstead. "Well, I've got the best offer yet for that land, even in this war-time, penny squeezing period. I need to decide if I want to keep it or sell. Rumor has it that some big-heeled contractors want to build some duplexes out there, right after the war is over, whenever that happens. If that is true, my price tag will automatically go up. Those white land speculators been trying to get me to sell for some time now. They even tried a trick or two to cheat me out of my land, but I know where to find some good lawyers when I need one, oh yeah!" he concludes.

"Have you ever thought about marrying again, Hempstead?" asks Hattie.

"Nah, I'm having too much fun just visiting friends in different cities and keeping my rental properties up in Atlanta. That takes all of my time. I do drop in for Sunday services at my church from time to time. Never got into that every Sunday mode, like you good church sisters. What about Marilyn?" he asks. "She still won't go to church with the family?"

"You know some old folk tales claim we were all some animal in our other life. Well, Marilyn was certainly the most stubborn mule in *her* pack," chuckles Hattie.

Hempstead and Nora join Hattie is a good, belly wash of a laugh.

"Hattie, how have you been?" Hempstead asks. "What about *you* finding another mate. Theopolis passed on many years ago. I remember him well. Yes, he was as solid as they come."

"It's remarkable how happy memories of my husband have kept me going all this time. It's left me with a mood of contentment that surprises me. I am blessed to feel so comfortable with my life. Oh, don't get me wrong. Being in this house with my two sisters can be thorny sometimes, but all in all, I can endure it. Nora has been the light of this household," Hattie says, with a smile.

"You know Velma can talk, so I got an ear full about Jasper from her. But you give me your version of this lucky feller. And I do mean *lucky*," Hempstead emphasizes.

Nora gave Hempstead all the pertinent details of Jasper's life. His childhood. A strong, widowed mother who is extremely protective. Smart, college material, but didn't graduate college. Excellent musician on two instruments. Hard worker. Good earning potential. A soldier by draft. A gentleman's gentleman. And his love for her, and her for him.

"I'm sorry I won't be here when he returns on—did you say the twentieth?" asks Hempstead.

"Yes, that's about right," says Nora.

"Well, your aunts must be so relieved that you have such a solid, honorable young man who is going to sweep you away," Hempstead says.

"Don't you kid yourself, Hempstead," Hattie blurts out. "Claudine and Marilyn have been plumb fools about Nora wanting to marry and leave home. We have had many a-go-round in this house over their courtship—even before the marriage issue. It's all settling down now since they realize there's not a damn thing they can do about it—at this late date," she concludes.

Standing up to leave, Hempstead walks over, hugs Nora and kisses her on her forehead.

"If there is ever anything you need, please let me know. No request is too much. You understand me?" he asks. "Now—here. I want you to have this and use it any way you see fit."

Nora looks into her hand where her Uncle Hempstead has pressed a folded bill.

"Oh, my goodness!" she squeals. With eyes stretched as large as a saucer, she pitches her voice high, "This is too generous! Aunt Hattie, he has given me 100 dollars!" Unfolding the bill, she says, "You don't know how touched I am. Oh, thank you, thank you, thank you," she repeats.

With that she steps close to him and this time, she tip-toes up and kisses him on his plump, moist cheek after he bends down to her small frame.

Chapter 9

Jitters

Moving toward the front door, Hempstead beams, "That Jasper sounds like a fine young man. I'm so happy for my little Nora." He then eases his six-foot-one, approximately 250-pound body down the front stoop.

Standing on the small porch Nora and Hattie smile and take turns bidding him farewell. "Be careful driving along that old country road by yourself," Nora warns.

"Yes, you know how jealous those white folks can be when they see a colored man in a shiny, new car like yours. Is that one of those Buicks?" Hattie asks.

As he stops and looks back over his shoulder, Hempstead says, "Yeah, it is. It's a smooth ride, too. It's called a Roadmaster. It's my best car yet. I figure as hard as I been working all my life, I deserve it."

He eases on toward the large, maroon-colored car sitting at the edge of the street. The sun's reflection off the rims of the big, white-walled tires enhances the car's impressive profile.

As Hattie and Nora wave their hands in the air for their final good-byes, Hempstead turns and continues ambling forward. He suddenly straightens his back and stops in his tracks. What Hempstead sees coming around the corner of Magnolia and Crescent are Claudine and Marilyn struggling in the unusually warm late afternoon with heavy knap sacks of groceries Hempstead picks up his gate and moves toward the ladies, "Claudine—Marilyn, let me give you a hand with those bags. My goodness, it's so warm out here. You must be worn out."

Hattie and Nora rush across the yard. "Hempstead just happened to stop by to say hello," Hattie blurts out.

"Yes, he heard about Jasper from Velma," giggles Nora. "And he came by to give me his blessings."

Hempstead reaches to take a heavy hemp bag from Claudine's forearm, and they lock eyes for a couple of seconds.

"How you been Claudine?"

"Oh, I can't complain. Nothing much has changed around here except Nora's news about her boyfriend," Claudine says, in a monotone.

"And good news that is for my little Nora," Hempstead gushes.

"There's nothing *little* about her anymore—at twenty-three years old. She acting like she has the wise mind of someone much older though—rushing into marriage and wanting to leave Macon," Marilyn says, in a huffed voice. They all move toward the front door with grocery bags in tow.

"That's the most natural thing for a young woman to want. To start her own life with someone she loves and build her own little nest with that person," Hempstead adds.

"You tell them, Uncle Hempstead," Nora says, in an emphatic tone.

"He's got no say about what should and should not happen around here," asserts Claudine, as she stops dead in her tracks.

"Now Claudine, you don't have to be so quick to try to put Hempstead in his place. We all know he's not the man of the house anymore," Hattie snaps.

Walking the few paces down the hallway toward the kitchen, Hempstead mumbles to no one in particular, "Claudine is the same Claudine, nothing has changed."

"Let's just all be pleasant with each other," Nora suggests.

"I don't know any other way to be, ladies," Hempstead says, with resignation.

Everyone puts their items on the kitchen table as Marilyn and Claudine begin to sort and put them away.

After an awkward silence, Nora takes Hempstead by the arm and leads him from the kitchen.

"Thank you for stopping by this afternoon. The money will come in so handy. You have no idea all the little details I'm working through."

"I didn't ask you earlier, but are you planning a wedding of any kind, or will you go to the courthouse?" asks Hempstead, looking straight at Nora.

"We haven't really decided yet. I still have your old Atlanta address and the phone number you gave Aunt Hattie over a year ago. They haven't changed, have they?"

"No, they're the same. I sure wish you all had a telephone in the house though. That would be much faster."

"Our neighbors, the Jenkins, have one. We have used it on two very important occasions. Maybe I could offer to pay them the price for the call. Will calling up to Atlanta be more expensive than calling a number here in Macon?" asks Nora.

"You bet your bottom dollar it will be," Hempstead declares. Reaching into his back pants pocket, Hempstead pulls out his wallet. "Maybe I need to give you a few bills to tuck away in case you want to call and let me know your plans."

"Oh no, you don't give me another penny, Uncle Hempstead," insists Nora.

"Baby cakes, you know I won't miss this money, but you might miss yours if you have to pay for the call," Hempstead chuckles.

"I refuse to act like a *kept woman* any more today. Besides, Jasper and I won't be starting out as paupers. Don't know how we may end up, but the beginning should be pretty solid. You've done enough already. Please, put your wallet away," Nora concludes.

"Boy, you might not have *all* the Carpenter women's traits, but you do have that overdose of pride like them. You women just confound me!" Hempstead says, in exasperation.

Standing for the second time with Hempstead on the front porch, Nora says, "You'll be hearing from me in about two weeks, after Jasper and I have discussed everything. Look for that phone call, okay?" Nora says, as she waves good-bye to Hempstead a second time.

෨෩

"Girl, are you ready to move all your things out in a few weeks, if you decide to marry right away and follow Jasper?" Geneva asks Nora, as she and Velma sit on the side of Nora's bed. Velma is Nora's second-best girlfriend, of the two.

"You can see the edge of my footlocker there," Nora says, pointing toward the foot of her bed. "It has all my heavier, dressy clothes, a few pairs of shoes and a couple of pocketbooks. I can still fold some of my lightweight outfits in there, too. I also have a Pullman piece which I can use for my summer clothes. Don't forget, Jasper's car has a large trunk, but I don't want to start out irritating him because of lugging around too much junk," chuckles Nora.

"How many thin nightgowns do you have?" asks Velma, looking toward the chiffonier. "Honey, that's all you gonna need for the first two weeks," says Velma, with a single cackle at the end her statement.

With a smile on her face and a mischievous twinkle in her eyes, Geneva asks, "You still claiming you have your virginity, right, Miss Nora?"

"Ooooh, don't start no mess, Geneva," Velma coos, as she stands and puts a hand on one of her hips.

Nora stops in her tracks in the small, somewhat cramped bedroom. "Look, you two are my closest friends, and good or bad, you know all my business. With these hawks as aunts, I couldn't have gotten away with anything if I had wanted to. Besides, I never dated anyone I felt strong enough about to go all the way. You two know that. Stop trying to get my dander up," she says, in mocked irritation.

"You know you've always shied away from uncomfortable girls' talk Nora, but now you can square up with us about those college dalliances," Geneva says, egging Nora on. "You know Velma attended Savannah State, and I went to Morris-Brown so we don't know exactly what *Miss Carpenter* was doing over at Tuskegee Institute," Geneva says, in a messing-with-Nora manner.

Tilting her chin down and looking up and out of upturned eyes, Nora says in a slow and lazy manner, "Miss Carpenter was going to class faithfully, joining some campus organizations, and having fun dating a few, *very nice* class peers. Also, Sunday church services were a part of my routine," Nora says, in an even slower, somewhat reflective tone.

"Let's cut the small talk," chimes in Geneva.

"You've got that right, Geneva," says Velma. "Because Nora, if you are a virgin, you have to be ready for the pain and discomfort on your wedding night," she says, with authority as she paces in a small circle.

"Who says she has to wait on her wedding night. Is she marrying Jasper thirty minutes after he steps off the Greyhound Bus?" asks Geneva, still sitting on the edge of Nora's bed. "Otherwise, why should two adults in love with each other have to torture themselves and wait for a wedding two or three weeks away?" Geneva asks, this time in an incredulous tone.

"Since I've gone all these years not experiencing any intimacy with a man, I might as well be a virgin on my wedding night," says Nora, analytically. "Why not exercise a few weeks of celibacy and have a good old virtuous, traditional, southern, Sunday-school-teacher-type-of wedding night?" Nora asks, as she bobs her head for emphasis.

"Oh, aren't we being smart-alecky," Velma shoots back, as she stops pacing.

"No, I'm not. If I dated Jasper for almost six months before he left, and we were able to forego intimacy, what will a few more days or three weeks matter?" asks Nora, still trying to sound convincing.

"Remember our talks after you had been seeing Jasper for about three and a half months, and you were frustrated because there was never any alone time for the two of you. And how we laughed about the missed opportunity the early evening before he left for Kansas?" Geneva asks. "Well, what happened to Miss Hot Panties. Huh?" she asks.

"Maybe Miss *Hot Panties* collided with an iceberg," Nora sasses back.

"No, maybe she is running for the hills because she's scared," Geneva offers, in a consoling tone.

"Or maybe, she's been around her celibate and strict aunts for so long she can't quite see herself being carefree and intimate with her future husband," adds Velma.

Nora's lips start to quiver as she begins to weep softly and struggle to talk, "I don't know if I can be a good wife because I don't know what a strong, loving couple looks like. My Aunt Claudine was never warm or relaxed around Uncle Hempstead. She made him so unhappy. And I don't remember Aunts Hattie and Marilyn's husbands because I was so young. How will I know if I'm making Jasper happy, or if I'm doing the right thing as a new bride?" Nora asks, as her girlfriends have already stepped closer to her to offer comfort.

80CR

My dear, dear Nora, I hope this letter is reaching you before I get back. I did try real hard to write you as soon as I got your letter. It's going to be so good to hold you in my arms after almost seven weeks. I can't wait! As to whether we should have a small wedding or not, I think you might have more beautiful memories of our marriage if we go ahead with a lovely little garden wedding in your backyard. Can your aunts pull this off from this point, or will we have to give them a month or so to get things ready? My Mother might want to help in some small way. Will this cause some friction? Let's not cause any problems between the women before we can get started on our new life together.

'So, you see Aunt Hattie, Jasper is not opposed to a small wedding," Nora says, as she finishes reading and folding a portion of Jasper's just-delivered letter this Saturday afternoon—just a few days before he arrives back in Macon. Nora knows her true ally, Aunt Hattie, will hold her confidence about her back-and-forth thoughts on whether or not to have a ceremony.

"But if you wait until Jasper gets to Macon, that's going to cut down on your planning time," Hattie warns.

"I know, I know," Nora sighs. "I must decide in a day or two."

ഐൠ

"I can't believe this Greyhound Bus is already thirty-minutes late," Nora mumbles as she paces on the sidewalk on the side of the station like a cat on the prowl. She can hardly wait for Jasper to descend the steps of the bus. Holding an opened parasol overhead, she also finds herself replaying what had occurred around the kitchen table at home last night—two days after the one-sentence Western Union telegram stated:

I'll be home Monday around 12:30 p.m.

ഐൠ

Nora's mind goes back to Sunday dinner with her aunts on the eve of Jasper's return.

While Marilyn was scooping the mashed potatoes from the pan on the stove— and with her back to her sisters and me seated at the table—she could be overheard talking to herself in a barely audible whisper.

"I wonder if Jasper is bringing an engagement ring with him?"

116

I was already hyper-sensitive and not knowing what Aunts Marilyn and Claudine might have up their sleeves, and discerning Aunt Marilyn's mumblings, I stood up and blurted out, "You don't have to wear a ring to be engaged and on the verge of getting married. I'll get the ring, the marriage certificate and the whole deal in one fell swoop," I finished in an angry tone. "And by the way, I've decided I want to have a garden wedding right here in our backyard, at this home where I've grown up. And if it's going to be too much work for all of you, I'll ask Mrs. Martin to come over and help," I said, conscious of the discomfort the statement would cast over Marilyn and Claudine.

Aunt Hattie was the first to react. "When did you decide on the garden wedding here as opposed to going to the courthouse?" she asked. "Don't get me wrong. I think it's the best decision. And we'll welcome Octavia's help, won't we?" asked Hattie, while expecting her question to be ignored, as it was.

Aunt Marilyn then replied in a calm and innocent tone, "Don't be so defensive about the engagement ring. It would show his honorable intentions, you know. Of course it seems it doesn't matter now. You've already decided to put the cart in front of the horse—marrying with no engagement ring first."

Aunt Claudine, cleared her throat and squinted her eyes while looking around the table. "I can see right now you're expecting us to kill ourselves rushing to have a wedding here in a couple of weeks. What about a guest list, getting out invitations, setting up the backyard with decorations and some borrowed lawn furniture, planning the food, and, Oh Lord, do you have enough money for some kind of wedding dress?" Claudine asked, in an exhausted tone. "I'm already tired from thinking about what we are going to go through to show our community how much our dead sister's child means to us and how much we think of Mr. Martin," Claudine concluded, trying to amend her earlier, negative tone.

While Aunt Marilyn's breathing became audible, Aunt Hattie chimed in, saying, "Can't we all start to eat in peace and leave the dinner table without causing each other to have indigestion?"

Nora recalls not saying much after that, but she takes solace in the thought that it would not be long before she would be living on her own.

೫⌘೩

With her mind transitioning back to the present, Nora starts noticing other families—colored and non-colored—standing around and shifting their weight from one exhausted foot to the other.

She finally walks toward a young colored woman she had not remembered seeing in the community. "Are you here waiting for a returning soldier too?" she asks the petite woman. This striking lady doesn't have Negroid hair or features but Nora, like all people of her race, could easily spot her own, her kind.

"Oh my goodness, yes," comes the lady's rapid reply.

"I am too," says Nora.

"My husband, Harrison, has been in the Army for six months now," states the woman, without hesitation.

"Where is he coming from?" asks Nora. "And let's move closer to the people standing right over there," Nora says, pointing in a discreet manner. "We don't want anyone to think there is a mixing of the white and colored race here."

"Oh, I know how to handle other people's confusion about whether I'm white or colored. By the way, I'm Abigail. My husband is coming from Fort Craig in Selma, Alabama," says Abigail, speaking in a confident and assured tone.

"So, he's coming from Alabama, huh?" asks Nora, as if confirming the information.

"Where has your husband—it is your husband isn't it, Honey—where has he been?" queries Abigail, in a pronounced southern drawl.

"It is my intended or fiancé who is coming from Fort Leavenworth. That's in Kansas. Sure wish I could say he is my husband," moans Nora.

"Was he stationed there?" asks Abigail.

"Oh no, or I guess I should say, yes. He just completed six weeks of basic training," says Nora, with more energy.

"Does he know his next assignment?" asks the inquisitive

young woman.

"No he doesn't. We're praying it's stateside," Nora answers in an instant, almost clipping the woman's last word.

"We're?" she says, with raised eyebrows. "I thought you weren't married."

"Oh, there's a marriage on the horizon," gushes Nora.

"There is? Well, how soon?" Abagail asks, now more engaged in the conversation.

"As soon as we can get our license and decide on a garden wedding in my backyard or just a stand-up at the courthouse," Nora says. "By the way, "I'm Nora Carpenter."

"I'm sorry, I'm just chatting away and forgetting my manners. My full name is Abigail Carrington Stewart," Mrs. Stewart says, with a healthy dose of pride.

"Nice to make your acquaintance," Nora says, at the same time she offers her gloved hand for a handshake. Her new acquaintance is also wearing white gloves. "I haven't seen you around Macon. Are you from here?" Nora continues.

"No, I'm from Atlanta. I'm meeting Harrison here because this is where the route led from Selma. We are going to spend a few days with my Grandma and Grandpa Carrington in Forsythe before heading back up to Atlanta."

"I hear Atlanta is a good city to visit," says Nora, in a wistful voice.

As if on a one-track thought, Abigail continues, "Getting back to the subject of whether or not a wedding—let me give you a bit of advice. Little wedding or huge wedding, they can be a headache!"

"Why do you say that?" asks a surprised Nora, about Abigail's bluntness.

"Well, I've been married almost a year now, and my mother insisted on this *grand* show. If I had to do it over again, whew, I would go to the courthouse!" Abigail says, as if fatigued by the memory.

"What was wrong with the wedding, which was big, right?" "Was it real expensive and a strain on your family?" Nora asks, with heightened interest.

"Sweetie, it was big and a *lot* of work, even though Mother had hired people to help her plan and do most of the running around," says Abigail.

"When you say big, how big?" Nora pumps for details.

"I had nine attendants, and Harrison had nine groomsmen," says Abigail.

"Oh, I could never afford anything like that. My family is worried about what a small wedding will even cost, if we decide to do that," Nora says softly. "And I told my family last night I'm thinking of a small garden wedding in our backyard—in maybe three weeks.

"My goodness! In three weeks?" Abigail asks, as if not believing what she just heard.

"Nora, you are not going to get much sleep if you have only three weeks to plan," counsels Abigail, with an air of wisdom.

"I know, I know, but I've got three very hard-working and organized Aunts who can move mountains when they need to," chuckles Nora, which belies her serious concern.

Still fixated on her own, year-old, wedding, Abigail says, "I've got beautiful pictures and mostly beautiful memories, but I broke out with the hives days before, and my complexion was looking a mess. My nerves—everybody's nerves—were on edge. My skin cleared up just in time, but one of the bridesmaids almost didn't make it. She came down with a stomach problem the night before, you know—the runs," Abigail says, in full, tell-all mode.

"I suppose your family could afford to give you a big, expensive wedding," Nora says, in a speculative tone.

"Honey, I'm the only girl my mother and father have. There's an upside and a downside to that distinction. I have a brother who is younger," says Abigail.

"My situation is totally different. I was reared by my late mother's sisters. My mother and father died in a terrible crash when I was two years old," says Nora, all emotion long past dissolved.

"Oh, how tragic!" Abigail gasps.

"They have been wonderful in most ways, but there's been that upside and downside and even a sideways in my life, too," Nora chuckles, at her witty comeback. Abigail snickers at the description and then they both began laughing out loud.

After the moment of humor fades, Abigail says, "Getting back to the decision about a wedding, I still say don't take on that headache."

"That's good to hear because I don't want them to sacrifice too much to pay for something that I can live without. I hope I'm not being too personal, but were your parents paying for your wedding months afterwards?" asks Nora, in a delicate manner.

"Honey, *no*. Father owns two of Atlanta's largest colored funeral homes, and he has been awfully successful. All the old folks in our A.M.E. church keep reminding me and my brother, Sunny, of how blessed we are. I get tired of hearing them," Abigail says, with an air of resignation.

"Abigail, since you're already married, why didn't you go to your husband's base with him?" asks Nora.

"If you could see that base housing for colored soldiers, you might think twice about going, too," Abigail speculates.

"I don't care what it looks like, I want to be with Jasper," Nora says, in a down cast tone.

"Besides, father put a down payment on a lovely little home for us in Atlanta, and I decided to stay in Atlanta and keep my teaching job. Besides, Atlanta is much more exciting than Selma," concludes Abigail.

"Oh, my goodness. I'm a school teacher, too," Nora says with a pitch in her voice.

"You are? What grade do you teach?" asks Abigail.

"I've taught third grade for the past three years," answers Nora.

"And I've taught third grade for two years!" says Abigail.

"Where did you go to college?" asks Nora. "Don't tell me Spelman in Atlanta."

"Oh, no. As good a college as Spelman is, I had to get from under my parents for a couple of years and get out of Atlanta. I chose another private female college. I went to Bennett in North Carolina," says Abigail, with pride in the announcement.

"I've heard about Bennett. Is this why you know a little bit about the Army base in North Carolina, because you went to school in the state?" asks Nora.

"Yeah, I suppose that had something to do with it," says Abigail, shrugging her shoulders.

"What is North Carolina like?" Nora asks.

"I'm no authority on the state. The college is in Greensboro, and that big base is in a town called Fayettesville. Greensboro is a bit countrified compared to Atlanta. It's a pretty little college, however. As for the other town, I hear it's all about the military," she says in a nonchalant tone.

Nora looks back toward the road and down at her watch. "I've been out here almost an hour and there's no sign of the bus. We would be so much more miserable if we didn't both have parasols," she says.

"I parked my car under a shade tree down the street there. Would you like to go and sit in it? That would be more comfortable than standing out here," suggests Abigail.

"You have a car that you drove down here—from Atlanta?" Nora asks, in disbelief.

"Yes, father sent Chester with me. He's one of my father's employees. He did the driving. I could have driven my own car myself, but my parents would have been worried with me driving the distance alone," Abigail says, in a no-big-deal tone.

"Is Chester light skinned like you? Otherwise, there might have been some trouble on the road. What with people *thinking they are seeing* a white woman in a car with a colored man," asks Nora, sounding like a quizzical child.

"I sat on the back seat, and father had Chester wear a chauffeur's hat so no one would be the wiser," says Abigail, as if stating an old routine.

"So, where is Chester now?" asks Nora, looking down the street where Abigail had gestured a moment ago.

"He parked discreetly down the street. I got out of the car and walked casually up the sidewalk until I reached the outside of the station here. Then Chester waited a while and walked right up to the ticket window and bought a ticket to return to Atlanta. He's already gone. He left the hat wrapped and placed in a shopping bag on the floor of the car. We know how to operate like this when necessary," Abigail says, casually.

"So, is your husband as fair-skinned as you are?" asks Nora, in an incredulous tone. "And as handsome as you are pretty?"

"Who are you calling pretty? You're about as pretty as a ready-to-eat Georgia peach, with your beautiful, light brown skin, your soft rosy cheeks and those sparkling brown eyes. You must turn heads on the street every time you hit a new block," chuckles Abigail.

"Tell me about Harrison. Is he light-skinned like you?" Nora repeats her earlier question.

"Yes, he is. So, we have no problem when we're together. We just let those other people assume what they want. Of course, we would never betray our heritage and pretend otherwise. And our people know us, just like you knew me," Abigail says, in an all-too-familiar explanation.

"You could get by much easier in life—some situations, if you just—" Nora starts saying, and then hesitates and catches herself.

"Please, don't ever say that. Harrison and I would never—" Abigail, too, starts to respond, but does not complete her sentence.

"I'm so sorry—I didn't mean any disrespect. Please forgive me for speaking out of turn like that," pleads Nora.

"You are forgiven. You are not the first one of *our* people to suggest that. It's like they think they are trying to help me make my life easier, since it would be so easy to do. Now, do you want to go and sit in my car?" asks Abigail, with no irritation in her voice.

"Are you kidding me? I might have to end up pretending to be the maid!" Nora speculates.

This produces the second, good belly laugh of the afternoon between the two fast friends.

ಬಂಡ

Buses arrived and buses pulled away. With each new arrival, a station attendant would call out the bus's originating routes.

Nora and Abigail chat on for a while longer and then they hear the attendant's loud, sing-song voice echoing from his bull-horn. It reaches their ears the short distance down the road.

"Buses fifty-four, fifty-five and fifty-six arriving in aisles two, four and six—rolling in from Fort Hood, Fort Leavenworth and Fort Craig. Y'all stand back now—from the steps of the bus—so every man can manage his gear," the station attendant barks his message, as if he's a military person giving out an order.

Abigail looks as cool as a cucumber to Nora. But Nora can feel her heart racing and can detect little beads of perspiration forming on her forehead. She pulls a second handkerchief out of her small purse and starts gently patting her entire face.

The families—all the colored families—know the routine. The Negro soldiers have to sit in the back of the buses so they will naturally be the last to get off.

The attendant has sheets of paper on a clip board and starts checking off names from each soldier's name tag. They are coming off the bus at a pace that would let everyone waiting think they had time to stand in place and catch a little shut-eye.

"Don't be nervous, Nora," Abigail says.

"I can't help myself. It seems he's been gone for such a long time," says Nora, sounding nervous.

"By the way, what's your best friend in the world's name?" Abigail smiles, with the question.

"His name is Jasper—Jasper Martin. And I'm soon to be Mrs. Nora Carpenter Martin," she says, with strong emphasis.

"I just know things are going to work out for the two of you. What do you say, let's stay in touch with each other. I'll be anxious to hear about your marriage. I have my name and address on this little card from my purse. I have an extra, clear one that you can use to give me your information," offers Abigail.

Both women are silent as they take off their gloves. Nora gets a pencil from her purse to scribble on the card. Nora finishes writing.

"I can't stand this waiting. Can't stand it," Nora barks, softly.

"You would think they'd have the sense to look for us from their windows, all of which are wide open. We could at least wave," says Abigail.

"Maybe that's against the rules. My Jasper says there are rules and rules and rules to follow. Here's my address—for the time being," Nora states, as she hands the card to Abigail.

"Here's my Atlanta address," says Abigail, as she hands Nora an off-white card, from expensive stock and engraved with her name. She has written something on the back.

As Abigail hands Nora the card, Nora catches sight of her wedding rings which are blinding in their brilliance.

"Oh my goodness! What lovely wedding rings," Nora gasps.

"Thank you. Harrison does have good taste, if I say so myself," Abigail says. "I generally only wear them on special occasions. Like meeting Harrison today. Otherwise, I wear a simple wedding band."

"My rings from Jasper will be pretty, I'm sure. But they will be very modest.

Abigail gives Nora a reassuring smile, and says, "It's not the ring, it's what the ring stands for."

"You're so right about that," says Nora, in a soft and sweet voice.

"Oh—my goodness, here comes Harrison struggling with his big duffel bag. Harrison, Harrison," Abigail softly calls out. Bouncing on the balls of her feet and waving her gloved hand in the air, she continues, "I'm over here sweetheart—I'm over here." Turning to Nora, Abigail says, "Jasper should not be far behind."

"As brown as he is, they probably sat him on the last row," Nora chuckles.

"Oh, don't talk silly like that," Abigail says casually, while turning back to see Harrison make his way through the crowd.

At that moment, Harrison spots his wife about three rows back in the concentrated huddle of colored people on one side of the pathway and the white family members on the opposite side. Two of the white women standing at the head of their pack, step back to allow Harrison to enter the huddle. He ignores the gesture and walks straight into his group. The women look at each other with surprise in their eyes, shrug their shoulders then turn to watch Harrison make his way through the anxious and excited crowd. Everyone knows their place, and without even a parting of their lips, the two ladies' unspoken question is immediately answered. Harrison gingerly pushes his way between *his* people saying "Excuse me," as he advances. Abigail presses forward leaving Nora still standing back.

When Abigail and Harrison come face-to-face, he leans down and scoops her slightly off the ground.

"Harrison, I'm so glad you made it back. It's been a dull, slow winter—" At that point, mid-sentence, their lips meet and silence bowed under their tender embrace. No one pays attention to each other's greetings because the entire crowd engages in copy-cat-like behavior. It seems everyone in the crowd is either hugging, kissing or weeping with joy.

Nora, still waiting, can feel her heartbeat accelerate. She worries about remaining calm.

Locked arm in arm with Harrison, Abigail looks back at Nora's anxious expression and projects her voice the short distance, "He's coming—hold on," Abigail says, with a wide grin on her face.

Nora acknowledges her with a closed-mouth, half smile. After their momentary eye contact, Nora glances up and looks slightly over the heads of the crowd. Jasper is just turning at the top of the bus stairs to make his way down. Nora leaps into the air and, to her surprise, begins to rapidly wave her hands and shout out his name in a too-loud fashion. Jasper sees her immediately and flashes his pearly white teeth in that all-over-his-face smile. His press through the crowd is more aggressive, and Nora begins to giggle and hop up and down like a teenager. She realizes her behavior and quickly reigns in her excessive excitement.

As Jasper comes closer, Nora runs ahead and beyond where Abigail and Harrison are standing. "He's here, he's here," she announces, as she rushes past them. She stops short of Jasper and bounces as if she has a bathroom emergency. Jasper throws his two bags on the ground and hoists Nora in the air and does a 360-degree twirl two or three times. On putting her back on terra firma, he leans down and kisses her with such passion until her aunts would have almost fainted had they been present.

"Oh, Jasper, I have missed you so much. You have no idea what it's been like these last six weeks," Nora says, with a mix of excitement and self-pity.

"Shhhhh, shhhhh, " Jasper encourages. "You don't have to tell me what I already know. Let's just enjoy the moment," he suggests, as he holds her tight and close.

Jasper has a new fragrance on his face and neck, and while Nora doesn't know its name, it makes her feel light-headed. It is the kind of light-headiness that makes Nora's legs feel wobbly and causes a smile to come across her face. This is an aura she has never felt before.

"Jasper," Nora said dreamily. "I've met a new friend here at the station. Her husband has been in the Army for six months now. She's over…"

As Nora turns to locate Abigail and her husband, they are walking toward them, smiling and holding hands. Harrison has left his luggage on the grass unattended.

"Look, who's smiling now," Abigail teases. "I brought Harrison over to say hello, and, of course, I want to meet Jasper. This is my husband of almost a year, Harrison Stewart,"

Abigail gushes.

"So happy to meet you, Mr. Stewart. I'm Nora Carpenter, and this is Jasper Martin,"says Nora, with a renewed sense of contentment.

"Oh, please, please. I am Harrison. And may I call you by your first names?" he asks.

"We wouldn't have it any other way," answers Jasper, in an up-beat tone.

"Nora and I have been carrying on like we have known each other for ages, haven't we Nora?" Abigail asks, with such familiarity.

"Yes, and it's because you're so easy and pleasant to talk with. I knew you were friendly and had a pleasant disposition before I even said hello," Nora claims.

"Tell me Harrison, did you just finish basic training, too?" asks Jasper.

"No, I've been in for six months now," says Harrison.

"I was drafted. What about you?" asks Jasper.

"Yeah, they got me too, dog-gone-it," Harrison admits, in a grudging tone.

Nora and Abigail have moved a few paces away from the men as they begin to talk. The two ladies start up their own conversation when Abigail says, "Nora, Jasper is so tall and handsome. You all will have some pretty children one day. Please don't be suspicious of me when I say this, but it seems as though I've seen or met Jasper before. I felt this way immediately when he rushed over to you. Has he ever lived in Atlanta?" Abigail asks.

"No, I don't think he has," Nora answers.

"This is going to nag me to death until I can figure this out," Abigail says, as she purses her lips.

"We need to get going because Jasper's mother lives here in Macon, and she's anxious to see him, too," says Nora.

Abigail is not listening to Nora at all. She has turned and is looking over at the men who are deep in conversation.

"You don't mind my asking do you, but what type of work was Jasper doing before he was drafted?" Abigail asks, with her brows furrowed.

"Well, Jasper is a professional musician. He plays saxophone and clarinet," Nora says, in a casual tone.

"Does he ever play in Atlanta?" asks Abigail, still looking toward the men.

"All the time. That's where he makes the best money," Nora says, with pride.

"I am still trying to place where I know him from," continues Abigail.

"Oh, it really doesn't matter," says Nora. "He just has one of those familiar faces, maybe."

"Where in Atlanta does he play music?" Abigail asks, becoming more anxious to solve the where-do-I-know-this-face-from puzzle.

"Wherever his orchestra performs," Nora responds, with a bit of annoyance building.

"What's the name of the orchestra he performs with?" asks Abigail.

"For God sakes, Abigail. It's the Ellis Walker Orchestra," Nora says, flabbergasted.

Abigail's eyes stretch wide and a look of incredulity comes across her face. She runs over to the guys and shouts, "Harrison, Jasper played at our wedding! He's a member of the Ellis Walker Orchestra! I knew I had been in his company before," Abigail gushes, like a school girl.

"Oh, man! We had the best wedding and reception. And people are still talking about your wonderful orchestra and all that good music. You guys are some hellava musicians," Harrison says, now as pumped up as Abigail.

"I have this little negative side to my personality where I can't let a puzzle go until I can solve it. Nora, please forgive my 100 and one questions. I know I can be a little pushy," Abigail says, apologetically.

"You're forgiven. But you wore me out!" Nora admits.

Jasper jumps into the conversation. "Well, to close the chapter on this little inquisition, you two had one of the most beautiful weddings I have *ever* attended. And I have played at big and fancy white weddings *and* colored weddings. No detail was spared. And you were the loveliest of brides, Miss Abigail. Now when is that first anniversary coming up? I might need to moon light if I can steal a few hours away from Uncle Sam's Army."

They all get a big laugh out of Jasper's humor at trying to fly the coop or go AWOL.

Chapter 10

The Big Plan

"Lord have Mercy!" Octavia Martin shouts as she rushes to her front door. Nora and Jasper are getting out of Jasper's car, after Mr. Willie helped Eugene deliver it to Jasper and Nora at Hanson Park.

"Lord have Mercy!" Octavia repeats, even louder this time. She rushes down three uneven steps with outstretched arms. "My Boy done gone and come back healthy—and in *one* piece. Oh, my God. What a sight for sore eyes!" Octavia says with a crack in her voice.

Jasper rushes to meet his mother halfway down the unpaved path to the unpaved street. He bends down and raises her off the ground, and she dangles her feet like a young, giddy child.

"Mama, I told you I was going to be okay. You had to know I would make it back to Macon to you and Nora," he says, with a mix of strength and little-boy emotion.

Nora hangs back beside the car with a warm and loving expression on her face. She soaks in the full display of love between a man-child and his mother. As Jasper motions Nora to come up the walkway, he continues to embrace his mother, but now with one arm around her shoulder.

"Isn't this a wonderful day?" Nora asks Mrs. Martin. Octavia Martin can only smile and nod in agreement. Walking closer to the two of them, Nora continues, "Jasper, your mother was stronger than all of us while you were in Kansas. If I can only find half of the determination and guts in my lifetime as Mrs. Martin has, I'll be a rich woman, emotionally," Nora concludes.

"Let's go and sit in the front," Jasper suggests. "Momma, do you have some hot water for some tea? A cup of tea would surely be relaxing," Jasper says, as the three of them enter Octavia's front room.

"Jasper, why don't you go and change out of your uniform?" Nora asks. "You must feel like you're out of place in civilian life," she concludes, as they walk into Octavia's small kitchen on the back side of the small house.

"Now you know old Private First Class Martin want them aunts of yours to see him in his uniform—or as the old folks in the country would say, his Uncle Sam's issued clothes," chuckles Octavia.

"Momma, Macon is about as close to being in the country as you can get," declares Jasper. His stark reminder generates a quick burst of chuckles.

"Nora, you and Momma chat at the kitchen table, and I'll go back and get my bags out of the car to carry them to my bedroom. You women can start to talk about how we're going to get hitched," Jasper says light-heartedly, as he looks at Nora with a mischievous twinkle in his eyes.

☙❧

"Lord, Jasper, Miss Nora here has already been cookin' up y'all's wedding plans," says Octavia, with a tone of surprise in her voice.

Jasper sits between the ladies on the sofa and picks up his cup of tea. He has taken his uniform jacket off and put it over the back of the chair. Now his buffed, six-weeks-of-training biceps are bulging beneath his short-sleeve uniform shirt.

Nora looks down at Jasper's exposed arm as he sits beside her. "You must have done a million push-ups to get those big, new muscles," Nora says, in a tone of amazement *and* appreciation. She, then, immediately begins to unravel her thoughts on the wedding plans.

"Jasper, while you were inside the house I told your mother we are going to get married in my backyard. It will be a small, but pretty, little garden ceremony. We should wait until the beginning of Spring, it will only be four to five weeks, that way the grass and trees with be at their early stage of turning green. The buds will be out, and I'm thinking of a late afternoon wedding. My family will invite about a dozen or so people, and you and your mother can do the same.

My aunts will plan everything, with Mrs. Martin's help—if she wants to lend two hands and two, strong legs. My Aunt Marilyn will be in charge of the food planning and cooking. And she'll make sure her flowers beds are well tended before the big day and the grass has been mowed. My Aunt Claudine will organize the details about how we will seat everyone in the borrowed, white folding chairs from our church. And, of course, she'll ask Reverend Simpson to officiate. And she'll decide the number of tables, white tablecloths and all the little details that will make everything picture perfect. We, you and I, will help Aunt Claudine decide our wedding colors and flowers for those who will need them. My Aunt Hattie—and maybe Velma and Geneva—will help me pick out a pretty, but reasonably priced, wedding gown. Aunt Hattie will also choose pretty plain, white cards with matching envelopes to write out the invitations. She has the most beautiful Palmer method of handwriting. And she will gladly hand deliver the invitations to the front doors of the people here in Macon. So you, see, I've just about figured this whole thing out," Nora concludes, almost out of breath.

Then she remembers. "Oh, by the way, the most important detail is the date. Today is Monday, February 21st," Nora says, in earnest.

"Yes, and I just missed Valentine's Day," Jasper says.

"Mrs. Martin, where is your church calendar?" asks Nora.

"Wait just a minute. It's on my wall in my bedroom," says Octavia.

Nora asserts herself again. "Now, to get back to the date of the wedding. Saturday, March 25th seems the perfect day. This gives all my *loved ones* one month and four days of planning—counting today. The wedding will usher in the beginning of Spring and my 24th birthday," Nora says, in a triumphant tone.

"Chil', what day is your birthday?"

"Mrs. Martin, it's April 4th."

With a probing expression on his face and squinted eyes, Jasper stands, turns around and looks down at Nora.

"I see you have given all of these suggestions a lot of thought," says Jasper, seeing a side of Nora that is more revealing.

"Sounds like a sergeant barking orders to me," says Octavia, with a loud clacking sound and a deep chuckle. I don't mean this as no disrespect for your ideas, but you sure yo' aunts gonna be dictated to like this?" Octavia asks, with her eyes opened wide and her brows raised.

"No, Mama, Nora sounds like she knows her own mind and what she wants for our ceremony. Also, she sounds like a military wife who's already up to speed on making firm decisions and dictating orders. That's what I'm seeing in this sassy little lady," Jasper states, with pleasure and surprise in Nora's assertiveness.

"How much all this go cost?" asks Octavia.

"Well, we need to write it all down in columns, add a couple of things Nora maybe hasn't thought of, and then maybe take a couple of ideas out. Then we have to plan a sensible budget," Jasper says.

"Well, I'm not like a teenager marrying right out of secondary school and with no small nest egg. So maybe I should offer a contribution to my aunts," Nora speculates.

"Ohhhh, no you're not going to think you have to help pay for your wedding," says Jasper in a strong voice. "Let's just see if your aunts are going to need any help. Besides, I believe the tradition is for the bride's family to shoulder the cost, right? Not the bride-to-be herself," Jasper concludes.

"Hey, I done squirreled away a little bit of save-in's over da years. I reckon I can help," Octavia chimes in.

"But I don't want them paying for our wedding months after it's over. That would be too much of a strain because, I'll be taking money out of the household when we marry and I leave to go with you," Nora sighs, as if exhausted over the discussion and the festering feeling of abandoning her responsibility to her aunts.

"That's what you s'pose to do," says Octavia. "It natural—part of Mother Nature for a woman ta want ta marry, get her own place and have some babies. You gotta walk away from yo' family to do *that*. But this is what the Bible supports between a husband 'n' wife. Buildin' yo' own nest and not havin' to hang around with yo' family if you can afford otherwise."

"I am able to help with some of the expenses if I need to," says Jasper, in a stress-free tone. "Nora, this is the last thing I want you to concern yourself with. Where the money is going to come from is not one of your problems, sweetheart," Jasper assures her.

"Please treat me like the adult I am, Mrs. Martin," Nora says in a firm tone.

"Honey, you go 'preciate the good attention my son go give you when you marry him. I 'speck you go have a pretty good life 'cause he loves you and you won't want for too much. Mark my word," Octavia says as she stands up. "Y'all best get goin' over to Nora's house so you can say hello ta Miss Nora's three aunts, Jasper. They go just *love* to hear all them wedding plans. So you two love birds be brave now and stand yo' ground."

"Oh, Mrs. Martin. Please be a little more understanding of my aunts. They are good women who have come to adore and appreciate Jasper. Just you wait and see how they will embrace our union. Jasper can have dinner with us so don't worry about cooking extra food for him. I promise not to keep him all to myself over the next couple of weeks. I'll tell my Aunt Hattie to let you know how you can help with the wedding ceremony plans," Nora says, as the three of them head for the front door.

"Mom, I'll see you later. I have my key so don't concern yourself about having to let me in," Jasper says as he walks back to the kitchen to take his uniform blazer off the back of the kitchen table chair.

"Good-bye, Mrs. Martin. You'll probably see my Aunt Hattie walking up to your front door in a few days. I sure wish both of our houses had one of those new talking phones. It sure would make everything happen faster. Take care of yourself." Nora walks ahead of Jasper and pushes the door open.

"Good-bye y'all. How the car workin' Jasper? Did Eugene take proper care of it?" Octavia, asks as she leans out against the door frame.

"Everything is fine, mother," Jasper assures Octavia.

ၷჾრ

"Here are Nora and Jasper pulling up out front," says Hattie, in a raised voice as she looks out the front door. "Come on Claudine and Marilyn. Come and see Uncle Sam's new Private First-Class in his uniform. He's walking around his car now to let Nora out. Looks like that training buffed him up quite a bit."

"We're coming now. How can you see all of that before they even come up the walk?" asks Claudine, walking up behind Hattie, with a lukewarm tone in her voice.

"All this rushing and pretend excitement is not my cup of tea," mumbles Marilyn, who is on Claudine's heels.

Nora is smiling as she approaches the stoop while holding Jasper's hand and pulling him along behind her.

"Isn't Jasper handsome in his uniform?" Nora gushes. "I asked him to keep it on so you all could see him in it."

"Oh, look at you, in your Army green!" says Hatti with enthusiasm.

"Hello to you three nice ladies. You are looking well indeed," says Jasper, in an upbeat and complimentary voice.

"Hello, Jasper. Good to see you back in Macon so Nora can calm down and relax her nerves," says Claudine, with a slight chuckle.

Without directly saying hello or welcome back, Marilyn again goes to her emotional shield, saying, "I put your name in all my pots today so just come on in and let's get ready to eat. I cooked up some salmon croquettes," she emphasizes, in a prideful and braggadocio tone.

"Should we sit in the parlor here?" asks Hattie, as they all—one-by-one—cross the door's threshold to start to walk back toward the kitchen. "This will give Marilyn a few minutes longer to set the table."

"I wish you had thought to bring some more comfortable clothes to change into here at the house, Jasper," Nora says.

With Nora's statement, Claudine becomes visibly tense as she straightens her back and Marilyn loudly clears her throat.

"You could have changed in the bathroom or gone up to my bedroom," says Nora, seeming to enjoy rubbing the discomforting thought into her Aunts' skin.

Ever the peace maker, Hattie closes the short uncomfortable subject with, "Jasper will be just fine in his uniform."

ଛୁଙ୍ଗ

As the sisters, their niece and her intended enjoy the croquettes and fresh root vegetables, the subject of planning a wedding goes into full tilt. Nora outlines the same details she shared with Jasper and Octavia an hour or so earlier.

"And remember, Aunt Marilyn said she would do the food planning and cooking. Geneva and Velma will stand-up with me, and Jasper will ask Eugene and a second friend to be what is called groomsmen. Aunt Claudine could ask Mrs. Crenshaw—the church's best singer—to be the vocalist, and Jasper will ask three or four of his musician friends to play for the ceremony," Nora says.

Nora is almost out of breath by the time she gets to the zinger. "And oh, don't let me forget. Aunt Hattie, you can ask Mr. McKinney, who has that little print shop over on Sewanee Street, how much would a few dozen invitations cost, just to save time. And do you know who has offered to work with you on delivering the invitations to each of our guest's front door? Mrs. Martin says she would be so happy to be your second set of legs. You two could put on one of your Sunday dresses and get the deliveries done in no time. Mr. Willie could even drive you in his taxi to a few of the houses that may be a little further out," Nora concludes, with a flourish of confidence.

As Nora finishes her recitation of plans, the sisters come out of their trances when Jasper speaks first.

"Nora sure has thought out all the planning for our wedding day, hasn't she?" asks Jasper, not sure of what the response will be. "Whether Nora realizes it or not, she is planning with military-like precision," Jasper chuckles, nervous-like.

"Yeah, and she is giving us our marching orders, like we are just coming out of basic training," quips smart-tongued Marilyn.

"Girl, you got me tired just listening to all those details," sighs Claudine. "You probably got my dead sister meaning your late Mother, Clementine, turning over in her grave. Whew!" Claudine exhales with exaggerated energy.

"If we all draw down on our saved-up energy, we can pull this wedding off. How many weeks away, Nora? What day are we talking about?" asks Hattie. "And how do we know Uncle Sam is going to let you, Private Martin, hang around in Macon long enough to say, I DO?" Hattie asks, as she looks back and forth to Nora then Jasper for answers.

Nora says in a flash, "It's going to be Saturday, March 25th. That is thirty-four days from today."

"Good God 'a Mighty! You are going to kill us Nora. We're too old for this kind of rushing," says Claudine.

"No, we're not. We all do whatever we want to and when we want to. No matter how physically hard it is," says Hattie, in defense of Nora's timetable.

Hattie says, "Nora, I need you to go upstairs and get a wedding invitation out of my keepsake drawer in my dresser. You know where it is. I want to see if you like the invitation enough to use it as an example of what you may want. It was Martha Jenkin's oldest daughter's wedding. Make sure you get the right one. I have a few other saved invitations in the drawer.

"Okay, Aunt Hattie. I'll be back as soon as I find it. Hold the conversation," Nora says, with a burst of excitement in her voice as she goes through the dining room and toward the staircase.

৪৩৵

Hattie begins talking in a low voice so Nora won't overhear the conversation from the kitchen while she is upstairs searching for the invitation.

"I sent Nora up there so we can get ourselves together on these plans. This child deserves whatever is going to make her happy. She is not shooting for the moon here. And yes, it will be a fast turn-around. But we can do this. Claudine and Marilyn you need to stop hemming and hawing about everything. We need to quickly figure out how much we think this will cost. Let's all do some figuring on paper, fold your piece of paper, and we'll put each in a small, brown paper bag. Jasper we need you to do some figuring with us too. Why don't you come by tomorrow afternoon with a small jar of your mother's fruit preserve that you say she wants Marilyn to taste. If Nora is here and sees you hand the bag to Marilyn, she won't be suspicious. Have your folded calculations in the paper bag. We can sum up what each of us calculates to give us some idea. We're not asking you to put your money in the pot, but just help us since your mother says you're so smart in mathematics. Is this a plan we can all

139

agree on?" Hattie asks, still whispering

"Yes, it is,"says Jasper. "But I insist on helping with the expenses. Nora doesn't have to know."

"We are not on welfare or anything like that, Private Martin," snaps Marilyn, in a too-loud-voice.

"Marilyn, stop being so sensitive," Claudine, says in annoyance. "It's just an offer that we all know we can't accept because we can manage this wedding on our own."

"I think I'm ready for some of your banana pudding Miss Marilyn," Jasper says, as they hear Nora talking to herself approaching the dining room and on to the kitchen. "That mess hall food is nowhere close to this good home cooking."

⁞

"I found it Aunt Hattie. But it wasn't easy because you've got more than a few programs and invitations you're keeping," teases Nora.

"I'm sorry it took longer than I thought. I hate that your food is not even warm anymore. We were impolite and kept eating," Hattie concedes.

"Hold the invitation up so we can at least see the front to remember what it looks like," says Claudine.

"Why did she decide on light pink as the color of her invitation, I wonder?" asks Marilyn.

"Don't conjure up anything negative about the color choice here, Marilyn," says Hattie. "I know how your mind works."

"Lighten up on Miss Marilyn, Miss Hattie," Jasper says, laughing softly.

"Well, Jasper, since Miss Marilyn's mind is so negative, do you think it's negative of me to ask if you ever considered giving my niece an engagement ring *before* the wedding?" asks Marilyn, stunning everyone at the table.

"Ah, ah, Nora and I are more interested in carrying a small nest egg into our early marriage. I don't think it is too wise to spend on an engagement ring and then matching wedding bands in the span of a few months. I know it's nice to see a little diamond and everyone can comment on it, but I want to continue to save something on the side for a mortgage on a house in a couple of years."

"Aunt Marilyn, you certainly didn't mean to hurt Jasper's feelings and embarrass him here at our dinner table. I think we are going to act like you never asked that question. You are forgiven," says Nora, with an awakening and new-found maturity that stuns everyone at the table.

Marilyn purses her lips and with a sheepish look on her face, jumps up, and begins taking up the empty plates.

"The banana pudding is coming right out," she says, without emotion or apology.

Chapter 11

All Loose Ends

Jasper's DeSoto pulls up to the Bibb County Courthouse.

"You're not *fixin'* to change your mind about me, Miss Carpenter, are you?" Jasper asks, as he drives up on one of the raised patches of worn grass. Across the graveled road stands hitching-post for riders to secure their horses. "You've been mighty quiet over there—this short distance from your house." Jasper glances over to see Nora gazing at him in a child-like manner.

"I'm just daydreaming about my new name, Mrs. Nora Carpenter Martin. A few more years and everyone would be calling me an old maid," Nora chuckles. "Now, I'm about to hush up the neighborhood busy-bodies."

"Do you have any idea how long it's going to take to fill out the papers for our marriage license?" she asks. "Are the rules different for us coloreds?" Nora lowers her voice with this unsettling question.

"Well, we won't know the procedure or the clerk's attitude until we get inside. But, I think it is wise for me to wear my uniform, don't you?" asks Jasper, as if fishing for reinforcement.

"If the clerk is a white man he might be jealous because you're so handsome in your uniform," Nora asserts.

"Well, you know, since the war's been going on, some of these jobs have been taken over by women because so many men are on military duty, here around the states or overseas," Jasper reminds Nora.

THE DEBT

"Well, let's just go on inside and see if all this military pride we read about in the *Macon Courier* is shown to us too," Nora says, exuding new-found energy.

ഓരു

"You don't have to tell me why you standin' there in that uniform with that girl by your side," says the bifocal-wearing male clerk. "Everybody's tryin' to get hitched—especially you lower ranking soldiers. But ain't too many of your kind come up to my window this winter. I guess making it *legal* ain't at the top of everybody's list," Clerk #3 declares in a slow drawl, while standing behind his grill encasement.

"Well, in my family…" Nora's response is spontaneous.

In the split second that Jasper's lower leg nudges Nora, Jasper jumps in. "Well, in Miss Carpenter's family *and* my family, getting a marriage license and having a Christian ceremony is high on our list, sir," Jasper says with stilted deference.

Ignoring Jasper, the clerk leans closer to his grill, looks out and slightly downward to Nora and says, "Girl, what's your first name so I can type y'all's stuff on my form?"

"It's Nora, sir. Miss Nora Carpenter," answers Nora in a firm voice.

"Your soldier-boy there already told me your last name," Clerk #3 barks back. "You sure you of age? You look mighty young to me," the clerk says, then purses his lips tight.

"I got my papers in my pocketbook with my birth date on them if you need me to show you," Nora says, in an anxious tone.

"Naw, don't bother. You will be the one in trouble if you ain't telling me the truth about your age. It ain't going to be me in trouble down the road," he says in a dismissive voice.

With a slight, side tilt of his head, the clerk looks straight at Jasper and says, "Now soldier-boy Martin, I see your name tag on your chest there, but I reckon I need a first name too," the clerk says in a fatigued voice.

"My first name is Jasper—that's J-A-S-P-E-R, sir," Jasper says in a monotone.

"I know how to spell. You don't have to school me on how to spell that colored-folks name," the clerk says to Jasper.

After the clerk finishes asking questions and typing the information onto the form, he begins to wrap up the process.

"Well, I have what I need here. You can just give me the five-dollar fee now. And you can pick up the license this coming Tuesday at that room over there," concludes Clerk #3, as he points in the direction of "the room."

"Oh, by the way. When you come back on Friday, Betty Jean is going to appreciate two dollars for her time in processing y'all's stuff. Make sure you give her the money. Ya hear me?"

"I understand. And thank you for your time," Jasper says as he and Nora turn cautiously to walk toward the side, colored-exit door. It's the same door they had to use to enter the courthouse once they climbed the stairs and took the turn to the side of the building.

ॐ

After stopping by Sampson's Grill for their second cup of coffee after their breakfast coffee—Nora at her house and Jasper in his house—Jasper drives Nora over to see Geneva.

"Oh, my goodness! Look at you, all dressed up in Uncle Sam's stuff," gushes Geneva, as she answers her door in casual, around-the-house clothes. "Velma and I, as well as them Aunts, thought we were going to have to lasso Nora a day or two before your bus arrived back here in Macon. Missy was so excited. She was climbing the walls over there—and here, too. Come on, let me get my hug in," says Geneva, grinning from ear-to-ear and with her arms opened wide.

"It sure is good to be back, for the short time I'm here," says Jasper. "Of course, I still have my fingers crossed for a state-side assignment—hopefully at Fort Bragg in North Carolina. You look well," says Jasper in a complimentary tone.

"Geneva, I'm going to have to bring you up to speed on our wedding date and plans," Nora joins and redirects the conversation.

"Hey, look! Why don't I go home and change out of these clothes into something cooler and more comfortable. Nora, I can come back in an hour or maybe ninety minutes and pick you back up. And I'll make a quick stop over at Eugene's house to see if there are any gigs I can squeeze in on in the next week or so. You ladies can talk just fine without me accidentally eavesdropping—right?"

"Yes," agree both of the young women as they laugh at Jasper's eavesdropping comment.

☙❧

After telling Geneva about all the latest wedding plans and solidifying Geneva's commitment to be one of her bridesmaids, Nora begins to tell her friend about her *new* friend she met at the Greyhound bus station. Nora spares no details about Abigail's seemingly charmed life and her prince-of-a-husband, Harrison. She recounts how Abigail reconnected the dots to knowing Jasper, because he was a member of the band that played their wedding reception in Atlanta.

Nora concludes the conversation saying, "Abigail also has one of those new talking contraptions in her home, just like Uncle Hempstead and the Jenkins family around the corner from her house. She says it's called a telephone."

"Girl, you sure are impressed with Miss Abigail," Geneva says, in an effort not to sound too judgmental or envious. "You know you may, or may not ever hear from her again. She is existing on another level—in another world from us."

"I told you we did exchange addresses. I'll see," Nora concludes, sounding deflated.

Geneva immediately picks up on Nora's altered mood and says, "Girl, we had better set a time to go downtown to Marguerite's

Bridal Shop to look at gowns. We can go over to Dempsey Wedding Emporium first to see their more expensive and wider selection of gowns. You don't want to pay their higher prices *and* you certainly are not going to buy a gown you can't even try on. They don't let us try on anything, but they sure want us to buy it without the benefit of knowing if it will fit properly. And of course, you can't take it back. That's for the birds! We'll act interested at Dempsey's and then we'll say we need to think about the purchase for a day or so. Then we'll try to come close to matching their more expensive cost and style at Marguerite's. Let's go on Saturday. Do you have to ask one of your Aunts to go with us?" Geneva asks, as she winds down the wedding gown discussion.

"Aunt Hattie wants to go. She says she will pay for the gown. Marguerite will let her buy it on installment payments, if necessary. I have some money I've saved up. I can pay for my own gown if I need to," says Nora, in a defiant voice.

"No, you're not going to pay for your own gown—unnnh-uh!" Geneva shoots back.

"Okay, let's not waste any time on this argument," Nora says, sounding like she's running out of steam.

"You're right. Let's go sit at my little table in my sun nook off the kitchen. It's coming up on lunch time. I made some fresh chicken salad this morning. I'm going to make each of us a sandwich or would you rather have yours on a small bed of lettuce?" Geneva asks.

∞∞

After Jasper changes into cooler, street clothes, he decides to go to pay his respects to Mrs. Hutchinson, who weeks earlier lost her only child, Joey, to friendly fire at his New Jersey Army base while going through basic training. He realizes not showing up in his uniform is the right thing to do.

"Good afternoon, Mrs. Hutchinson. I'm Jasper Martin, the man who's squiring Miss Carpenter over on Magnolia Street. I saw you, ah-ah, and your son Joey at the Greyhound station," says Jasper, before Mrs. Hutchinson cuts him off.

"I know who you are, son. Care to come inside, if you have a minute?" says Mary Hutchinson, as she opens her door wide for Jasper to pull his tall, slim body inside her home.

Jasper is a bit anxious and jumps at the chance to steer the conversation.

"Mrs. Hutchinson, my heart brings me here to your home to let you know how very sad I was to hear of Joey's death. Nora, Miss Carpenter, wrote me the same day the Cloverdale community got the awful news. I can't say I know how you feel, but I can only imagine the pain and sorrow," Jasper's voice trails off, as he looks down and sees Mary Hutchison wiping away tears with the hem of her apron.

"I bet your Mother would know my kind of sadness and how 'ah empty heart feels. You yo' Mama's only child, ain't you? I know because I remember when y'all moved into this colored part of Macon. I can't figure out how an empty heart can feel so heavy. Lord knows I can't figure out nothin' these days. Why God took my only child. He know he done already took my husband. I'm all by myself now and wondering if I even believe there's somebody in heaven who even cares about what's go happen to me! Lord have mercy! Lord have mercy!" Mary sobs now as her emotions veer into full-throttle wails.

Jasper, at a momentary loss for words, eases a few steps forward to reach Mary Hutchison. He says nothing as he puts his arm around her, and she leans into his chest. Her body begins to shake from the force of her unbridled crying. Jasper feels warm tears tip-toeing across his jaws, and he is grateful Mary Hutchison does not see this. His unsummoned emotion catches him off guard, and he feels a twinge of embarrassment for his need to conceal it.

After a few seconds of silence and as both regain their sense of the moment, Jasper, stepping back from Mrs. Hutchinson, picks up his message of condolence.

"I understand your sadness. You know, Mrs. Hutchison, this is a crossroad in your life where you are going to have to reach way down in your gut and find the strength you don't even know is there. God gives it to us to use in these moments of our lives. You are stronger and more able to cope than you realize. Plus, you've got a whole little hamlet here to help you through this rough period. My Mother and the other—"

"No offense, Mr...ah, ah." Mary jumps in with a tone of anger and frustration. "Excuse me forgetting your name. But your Mother ain't loss you. She don't know how to help me. And these ladies around this community will bring you food and cry wit you for a few minutes, and then they sashay on home and go 'bout their business. And them Army people claiming in that Western Union that it was a mistake that his training boss shot him. I don't even know if they tellin' me the truth! God Almighty, how am I suppose to get out of my bed ever 'day and put one foot in front of the other? Who can walk in my shoes—right now—at 'dis time in my life? Can you answer them questions?" Mrs. Hutchison sighs, after her moments of rage.

"While I'm just twenty-four years old, I couldn't give you any good answers if I was a wise old man of ninety. You have got to find your trust again—trust in the Lord, trust in your own strength, and trust the good deeds of the people around you, especially your minister at your church," counsels Jasper.

Mary Hutchison raises her brows and creases her forehead, "You mean that old jack-leg of a minister of mine over at Morning Glory Baptist Church?" she scowls. "That's why I took my Joey back down to the country—my family's home spot—and had the service and burial at my old home church. That was where I buried Joey—. right there by his Daddy's grave. I need to find me another church here in Cloverdale. Yes siree, I need to find me a new "Man of God.""

The clock done run out on that greedy, connivin' preacher I got now. I ain't stuttin' that man no 'mo. What church do you go to in town?" asks Mary, after her noticeable mood change.

"Please don't ask me to recommend a church or minister to you," says Jasper, in a firm voice.

"I know you must go to some church, with "yo' lady friend," Mary probes.

"Miss Carpenter's family has gone to Cloverdale A.M.E. for years. My Mother and I joined in more recent years," answers Jasper.

"Oooooh, I know 'yo minister over there—a Reverend Simpson. He came to my house when Joey died to help out, and he took over like I belonged to his church. That didn't matter to me. I was in such a daze and dizzy with sadness then. My 'ol scoundrel of a minister came by for an hour on the first day of community visits, but he didn't tarry. Then he never came back. The church members came from Morning Glory, though, and your church too with food, flowers and stuff to drink. But I didn't see old, no good Reverend Brooks again. And if my memory still working right, I believe Reverend Simpson said something to me on one of those days he came by about coming to join y'all's church. I'm go give it some studyin'—some thought. We'll see," Mary concludes.

"Mrs. Hutchison, it was my pleasure to come to visit you. Joey's short life was a blessing that God gave you, so keep him in your heart and honor his memory always. He did the right thing by answering the call to serve his country, our country. You should be getting a flag of the United States soon from the Army. I don't think they make a difference between colored and white soldiers who serve and pass on honorably." Jasper, on uttering those last words, regretted he might have triggered, again, some sadness in the grieving Mother.

"You don't know how much this visit 'go help me Mr. Jasper. Please don't hold it against me that I ain't using your military name. I can't be comfortable with that, just yet. You may be young, but you sure got some 'ol folks sense—like talkin' strong and tryin' to encourage me. Sho' nuff appreciate it! You run along now. Take care of yourself and be careful. You don't want your Mama goin' through this kind of torture with you bee-in in the line of that friendly fire," Mary Hutchinson says, as if spitting out those two nasty words.

ଛଠ

"Come on in, door is unlocked," Eugene says, in a loud voice.

"Hey, my main buddy! What you know that's good?" Jasper asks, as he walks into Eugene's small, front room.

"Look who's back in Cloverdale. As if I didn't know you got back," says Eugene.

Eugene gets up from his couch, and the two men embrace quickly, then back away.

"Nora has kept our little group buzzing about your return. She has been so excited. Say man, how was Kansas? Did they kick your butt in basic training?" Eugene asks.

"Man, I was able to hang with the program and pass muster at every point. That's all I wanted because I knew I had a rainbow back here at the end of that temporary cloud," chuckles Jasper. Eugene joins him in an all-knowing laugh.

"I suspect you and Nora have gotten to know each other better with all that letter-writing I been hearing about. How serious is y'all's courtship, buddy?" asks Eugene, as he leans against his wall.

"It's serious enough that I'm looking for a Best Man for my wedding, which is in less than three weeks. Are you still game for this high honor?" asks Jasper, with a sly grin engulfing his face.

"Watch out now. I'm not in the mood for no horse shit," says Eugene, shaking his head in mocked annoyance.

"Naw, man. This is for real! Nora and I have decided to jump the broom. We decided before I finished my stint in boot camp. She and them Aunts are buzzing like drunk bees planning the ceremony in her back yard. They're calling it a garden wedding. I'm just trying to make sure I show up on Saturday, March 25th." Jasper exhales.

"Yeah, I'll be your best man if you need me to come to your rescue. Am I going to be by myself—standin' next to you?" asks Eugene, in a tentative tone.

"I need two hard legs. I'm told the other one will be called a groomsman. But you my main man, Eugene—my best man. I don't have time to try and get one of my old, hometown friends from my childhood. I need one of the boys from the orchestra. You know the ones, other than yourself, I enjoy being around. Give me your best suggestion," Jasper says, pressing for a timely decision.

"You 'go put some unwanted pressure on me. I'll still be in the shrinking ranks of the unmarried around here. Don't leave me hanging out like this," whines Eugene.

"Come on Gene. I need you to be serious," insists Jasper.

"What about trumpet man, Tommy Collins—young 'June Bug?'" asks Eugene. "We always have more fun when he hangs with us after our gigs. The trouble is, will we two be booked to perform somewhere on that Saturday night?" continues Eugene.

"If 'June Bug' agrees, the two of you should ask Ellis for the night off. Give him your request now so he'll be able to find two sit-ins—if need be," Jasper suggests.

"You 'go upset the apple cart so much in the Ellis Walker Orchestra that weekend until Ellis ain't gonna want to let you do some stand-ins with us—before we even get to your wedding day," Eugene speculates.

"Yeah, I love to play my horns, but I ain't pressed for green backs during this stretch. But man, I have missed gigging with you guys over the past seven—damn near eight weeks!" Jasper moans.

"Well, it's been our loss too. You 'bout the best damn alto sax and clarinet man around this part of the country. We can hear what we've been without. No shit man!" Eugene says, with hyped enthusiasm.

"You're in man. You don't have to pump me up to be in my wedding. Stop this kissing up, and stop talking so damn much," laughs Jasper.

Eugene enjoys the comical moment but gets serious again. "One of your problems, man, is that you are too modest. You don't know what a musical star you are. You are a stand-out, but refuse to really claim it. You can blow your ass off, man," Eugene concludes.

"All right, all right, whatever you say. Now is June Bug still living in that little apartment over on Hamilton Street? I need to nail down a commitment from him. I hope he will accept my request," says Jasper, as he gets up off the couch and prepares to leave.

"He'll be happy to. I'm willing to put some money on that," Eugene says with certainty.

℡™

"Good Afternoon, Miss Marilyn. How you doing today? You holding down the fort all by yourself?" asks Jasper, as Marilyn comes to the screen door and steps out on the front stoop.

"I'm just fine this afternoon. How you think you know I'm the only one here?" Marilyn snaps.

"Well, Miss Hattie, especially, is the one who usually rushes to answer the knock," says Jasper.

"That's because she thinks she's the greeter around here," Marilyn snaps back.

"No comment on that, Miss Marilyn," Jasper says, in a polite tone.

Jasper raises his hand to show the brown paper bag he is holding. "Nora is visiting with Geneva so I didn't have to be sneaky about getting my wedding expenses estimate here to the three of you. Have you ladies had a chance to talk about what you think everything will cost?" asks Jasper.

"Yes, we have talked a bit about everything. We are going to have to figure out another time when all four of us can talk—without

Nora being around," Marilyn says, in a curt manner.

"Let me leave this bag with you. I know you will keep the note inside out of Nora's sight. It sure would help if our two houses had one of those telephones. It would make planning a lot easier," Jasper speculates.

"I don't know if I'm ready for one of those. I heard they are not too private. You can hear other people's conversations, and they can listen to yours. That's for the birds. I don't want no one being nosy about my talk with my friends," Marilyn concludes.

"Well, just a thought, Miss Marilyn. I'll see you later, after I pick Nora up and return her home," Jasper says, in a winding-down voice.

"See you later Jasper," says Marilyn, as she reaches for the brown paper bag.

Chapter 12

The Wedding Gown and the Guests

"I sure wish I had taken Jasper up on his offer yesterday to drive us downtown this morning. That old slow, bumpy trolley ride was no joyous event," says Nora, who is leading the trio on the sidewalk.

Aunt Hattie, Geneva and Nora head to the country-ritzy Dempsey Wedding Emporium to look at its collection of dresses. It is possible for Geneva to find something she likes also and, like Nora, look for a copy-cat version at the colored-owned and operated, Marguerite's Bridal Shop. Dempsey is Macon's best. It is not in the running with any of Atlanta's bridal shops, but it would like to think it is.

As the three ladies approach the entrance to Dempsey, Geneva rushes ahead to open the door for Aunt Hattie and Nora. "You ladies first," she says, as she holds the door wide.

As they stroll under the arched entrance into the softly-lit parlor, a middle-aged woman approaches them.

"Good Morning and welcome to Dempsey's. How you girls doing this morning, and what do you think I can help you with?" asks the tall, perfect-posture sales lady.

Before Aunt Hattie or Nora responds, Geneva says, "We ladies would like to look at your wedding gowns." Without moving one foot, she turns her head and upper body toward Nora, thrusts one arm in Nora's direction and states in a no-nonsense tone, "Miss Carpenter would like to see your selection of wedding gowns. She is to be married in less than a month."

"Oh dear, well I'm Mrs. Elizabeth Dempsey, the owner of the emporium. I had better assist you, Miss...what is that name again? At any rate, are we talking about a wedding with a little chickadee in the oven? We have some lovely little off-white gowns that are quite reasonably priced. You have that adorable, young person's waistline so I can easily find something for your occasion AND your budget," gushes Elizabeth Dempsey, in a triumphant tone.

All three ladies stare her down as they try to steer the conversation. Nora jumps in ahead of the ready-to-pounce two other women.

"Excuse me, ma'am. I have you know I am not *with child* as I stand here looking at you. I am a citizen of this town and, more to the point, a respected member of the Cloverdale community. My occasion is a first marriage to a never-before-married colored, Army private, and I do plan to wear white," Nora unfortunately pauses to catch her breath, and Aunt Hattie snatches the opportunity.

"I have you know, Miss Carpenter is a highly regarded teacher at Cloverdale grade school and a four-year, college graduate. Money is not one of her problems either. As a matter of fact, we would like to browse through some of your gowns on our own, if you don't mind," Aunt Hattie asserts, with a phony smile directed straight at Dempsey.

"You ladies from your community always come into the boutique with a chip on your shoulder. All of us here bend over backwards to show you respect and the same courtesies we show our other customers. And since money is not a problem, I can bring you some of the better gowns from the back room we don't ever put on the floor. Those gowns are our little secret for our upstanding customers like you Miss...ah, ah. Please forgive my memory lapses this morning. I'll be in the back office getting another cup of coffee."

Backing away slowly, Dempsey continues, "Please look around

and *please* call me if you have any questions. Y'all understand I truly welcome your business. All we ask for are clean hands and a soft touch in handling the merchandise," Dempsey turns and walks toward the back of the boutique.

"I didn't get my turn to let that arrogant witch have a piece of my mind," Geneva says, in a whispered, regretful tone.

"Let's just look at a few of these gowns and walk out without saying a word," says Aunt Hattie.

"You two know I am not interested in spending a lot of money on a gown or even on the entire wedding. We don't have to stay in here a minute longer," adds Nora.

"No, please let me call her back with a question. I didn't get a chance to say anything," Geneva whines.

"You always want to have the last word, Geneva," Nora reminds her.

Before the ladies can decide on an exit strategy, Elizabeth Dempsey approaches with a fresh smile on her face and a more conciliatory demeanor.

"Well, I'm ready to pull out a few of my more pricey gowns from the back room. You ladies want me to get my Annie to bring some out. I think Annie probably lives over in your community," says Dempsey, in a milky, sweet voice.

Geneva is determined not to lose this second chance to speak directly to Elizabeth Dempsey.

"You know, we think we are just going to pass on seeing anymore merchandise in here. Miss Carpenter's intended has a very nice car, and she has decided to have him drive her to Atlanta to buy her gown. You may or may not have heard of the colored business area in Atlanta, known as sweet Auburn Avenue. There is a wedding gown "boutique" there that sounds like it would leave Dempsey's in the dust. It is known as one of the state's finest, ladies' dress shops, and it carries many fancy labels of wedding gowns. It is owned by a colored husband and wife team. I'm going to make sure I tell all my friends to shop for their wedding gowns in Atlanta where the prices are not hiked and half the dresses are not hidden in a back room," Geneva says.

Walking toward the entrance with Nora and Aunt Hattie, Geneva says with a sly smile on her face, "Now you make sure you have a good day, Miss Dempsey." She smiles again, as if in competition with Dempsey's fake smile.

"I am *Mrs.* Dempsey, thank you. I am seeing more of you people acting uppity these days. Too bad. And sadly, grandma here is not able to reign you in. You don't know how good you coloreds have it here in Macon," huffs Dempsey. And on that note she walks ahead to open the front entrance to her boutique.

Old Grandma—Aunt Hattie—with her head high and her pocketbook firmly under her arm pit leads the trio out. Geneva gladly exits last, so as she passes Elizabeth Dempsey, she can softly grunt, "Huh!"

ഇരു

The ladies were almost at the end of their four-and-a half-block trek over to the second, downtown bridal shop. "Let me open the door this time," Aunt Hattie says. "I want to be the first one to greet Marguerite's daughter. I've only seen her a couple of times since her mother passed last year."

As the door opens to the small, but neatly arranged bridal shop, Joycelyn Turner, Marguerite's daughter and present owner, greets the trio.

"Hey you ladies come on in," says Jocelyn. "I figured I would see you this week or next. You know how talk travels in this town. Miss Nora, everyone has heard you are getting married near the end of next month. Congratulations to you and your intended, Private Martin. Now that you have probably been to Dempsey's, I can show you my dresses that are *almost* a dead ringer—a little fewer frills, less heavy material and expensive lace and a *lot* less money," announces Jocelyn, without apology.

Nora smiles politely and asks, "Where is the Ladies Room? And when I get back, may I please have a drink of water if you have some?" Nora asks.

"How have things been going in the shop, since you're now the owner? Has business slowed down with many of our Cloverdale boys away and serving in the military?" Aunt Hattie asks.

"You know, I miss my Mama. She ran this shop for so long and kept building it up with more merchandise. She had started to make a pretty good profit in the last five or six years of her life. Business has slowed down a little, but I'm hopeful more people will start to come back soon," Jocelyn says, with her voice trailing off. "Miss Nora, you asked for water, but I can give all three of you some sweet tea if you'd like. I now have an ice box and Mr. Willie was here this morning with two blocks of ice. How does that sound for trying to relax?" asks Jocelyn.

"You can just call me Nora, Mrs. Turner," says Nora, in her usual sweet tone.

"Oh no, Honey. Where I come from you respect all teachers and principals with a Miss, Mrs. or Mr." Jocelyn announces. "But one thing that's not too respectful is that I have to give you the tea with the ice chips in Mason jars. I haven't brought my Sunday-best drinking glasses back from home. The minister and a few church people came over to my house last Sunday so my good drinking glasses are still sitting clean on my sideboard. It's not fancy around here like Dempsey's, but I try my best. The good Lord knows I do," says Jocelyn, raising her clasped hands to her just-closed mouth.

ಬಂಞ

"Those last two gowns you tried on fit you just right. You are a dead-ringer size four, and the gowns add a little *umpf* to those curvy little hips I see trying to peep out from under the fabric. Or maybe

158

you want a gown with a fuller skirt and more body. What do you think, so far?" asks Jocelyn.

"Well, I think Jasper may want to see a bit more of the chest area and curves around the hips," says Geneva, circling around Nora. "And aaaah—"

"Just hold up Geneva," says Aunt Hattie, trying to tamp down on Nora's opinionated girlfriend. "Nora is a bit on the conservative side when it comes to showing off cleavage and hips. She already has a husband-to-be waiting on his curtain call. She is not still casting her net—if she ever was in the first place," Aunt Hattie says in a defensive tone.

"I think I asked Miss Nora to give *her* opinion about what she has tried on so far. I know you ladies are anxious and want to help her make a good decision here. But she is the one walking across that new green grass. Not either one of you," says Jocelyn, in a firm and authoritative voice.

"No disrespect toward you Mrs. Turner, but I'm not putting this much stock in selecting a gown. I just want to get married, not spend too much money on a dress or the ceremony, and leave and go to my new husband's military assignment with him. You all don't get too worked up over this selection," says Nora, almost sounding embarrassed over her mild indifference.

"I am not taking this personally, believe me. You are not the first bride to come in here and want to be finished with the whole drill in an hour. I like your honesty and your sense of what is most important to you. I was about to say we can try to order a gown from a shop I do business with in Savannah. This would be cheaper than me having my son drive me to Atlanta to look for a reasonable gown there," says Jocelyn.

"Nora, you have always been the easiest child, now young adult, to please. You go out of your way to be reasonable about things. Let's make a decision about one of the pretty dresses you have already tried on. We don't have to spend all afternoon here if it's not necessary. You know I am paying for it, and no, no objections, please!" Aunt Hattie says in a close-the-book manner.

Geneva is sitting down during this brief give and take of a conversation. She looks a bit deflated and stunned.

"Girl, I thought I knew you. You have surprised me with how level-headed you are trying to be at—what's your age, huh? You suppose to be all excited, and giving everyone a fit, acting like 'Miss Ann' on her throne. You're about as cool as a cucumber. We can't argue with what you want. You love Jasper so much, this little show we're all excited about is almost a distraction to you," Geneva analyzes, in quick fashion.

"Well, what do you want to do Miss Nora?" asks Jocelyn. "You know Lucy Rivers does all my alterations for me. She is so good ,she should be working in one of those big shops in Atlanta. If you want to make a decision today and it needs to be altered, Lucy will start to work on it Saturday when she comes in. Of course, you'll have to come back in to be fitted," Joycelyn states.

"Let me try on the pretty little gown you brought out last, the one that's hanging on the hook on the side of the long mirror," says Nora, with a bit more energy in her voice. "If it fits me just fine, I might walk out of here today with it in a box," says Nora.

"No, no you won't take it out of here today. Jasper can drive you down to pick it up in a few days. Because it will be in the box, he won't see it. So you don't have to worry about having bad luck because the groom saw the bride's dress before the ceremony," preaches Geneva.

ଚେଠ

The wedding plans go full tilt in the next two weeks. Lucy Rivers begins altering Nora's wedding gown she chose before the three ladies left Marguerite's. While Nora is being fitted, Jasper visits the Carpenter women to talk about the wedding expenses. Then he goes to visit Tommy Collins, "June Bug," who agrees to be Jasper's second groomsman. Geneva and Velma go to Marguerite's, without Nora, to shop for their soft pink dresses. Jasper begins to explore the process of how to buy and get a telephone put in his Mother's home, as well as the Carpenter's home.

ಇಾಡ

Sunday morning rolls around and it's church-going time. Jasper drives to pick Nora up at her home. Octavia gets out of the front seat and moves to the back seat of the 1940 DeSoto.

"Good Sunday morning, Mrs. Martin," says Nora, as Jasper holds the door for her to get inside the car. "We haven't seen each other in so long. Seems like an eternity right now," Nora giggles.

"Honey, it's 'cause you are impatient 'bout everything these days. You and my Jasper are hot to marry. Lord have mercy. Where the hose pipe to cool y'all down?" Octavia cackles out loud at her perceived cleverness.

As Jasper pulls away from the house, Octavia asks, "You know people been asking me if they go get invited to the garden weddin'. What am I suppose to tell them? Too many of 'em think they go be invited."

"We all know this is going to be a problem. We are going to have to be honest and say there can only be family and very close, long-time friends invited because of the small back yard. All of the fruit tress and rose bushes take up so much of the space," says Jasper.

"Let me handle some of the people at church. And Aunts Hattie and Claudine will be there, too. They already had left the house, Jasper, before you came," Nora says.

"Reverend Simpson go say all the good stuff 'bout how we should love one another and do God's good deeds and so on and so forth, then the devil's gonna come out after the service when the women start asking about who's invited and who is not invited. Mark my words. Just wait an see," says Octavia, in a foreboding tone.

"I feel like going back home," says Nora.

"Too late. We're already here," responds Jasper, as he steers his car onto the grassy lot behind the church.

୨୦୧

"Good Morning, Good Morning and Welcome to Cloverdale A. M. E. Church this good Sunday morning!" bellows Reverend Simpson to all the attendees climbing the steps to enter the vestibule.

"Good Morning Reverend," says Octavia, with a broad smile and walking ahead of Jasper and Nora.

"Pleased to see you again, Reverend Simpson," says Nora, flashing her pretty teeth behind a broad smile.

"Good Morning, Sir. It's good to be able to worship with you and the congregation today," Jasper snaps, as he takes his uniform hat off.

Reverend Simpson smiles, tilts his head up and down while saying, "Oh, aren't we looking spiffy in that uniform, Private Martin. So honored to have you with us today. And to have you re-commit yourself to the Lord as you're about to enter yet another phase of your manhood."

Jasper's facial expression does not change. But Nora has a look in her eyes, at that moment, that says, *don't say more than you need to say.*

The smiles, the gawks and the not-so-subtle waves and whispers follow the trio down the sanctuary's aisle to Octavia's end of *her* pew.

୨୦୧

Reverend Simpson's sermon, AVOIDING THE REGRETS, is a potpourri of themes and warnings. First, not to forget about honest worship as springtime is fast approaching the Cloverdale community. He called that slippage into lax behavior *The Sins of Spring.* Second, not to slack up on tending the crops and livestock during the "fun period" of the year. Third, avoiding the ravages of weather, when possible. Fourth, warning that heat strokes are no laughing matter.

162

Fifth, trying to maintain an even temperament, saying the heat makes your brain do crazy stuff, and when you add too much of that bug juice, or corn liquor, to the high temperatures, you invite the Devil to come into your heart at full speed. Sixth, he warns *you pretty little young girls out there* that there's a time to procreate, but it ain't before you finish your education and get married.

The minister acknowledges the two uniformed military men in the sanctuary and thanks them for their service.

"The 'white man' here on earth may not be giving you all your proper recognition and respect, but the Man Upstairs appreciates you loving your country."

The Reverend says the Spring is the season of a lot of weddings and courthouse marriages. He reminds the congregation that marriage is suppose to be forever. It should be taken seriously, and "It ain't no escape hatch from what you think is your ho-hum life. You think your mama and daddy are mean and hard on you. You ain't seen mean until you marry a mean snake of a woman or man. Let's be real now," he says to the congregation. "A mean and miserable partner can be a man or a woman."

Sprinkled throughout his message, is a mixture of Amens, laughter, shout-outs of "Tell it," "Praise the Lord," You got that right," and occasional bursts of soft clapping. There were only a few occasions where Reverend Simpson read relevant verses from the Bible in this unusual, freelance style of preaching.

As the Deacons are passing the offering plates through the pews and the choir is trying to raise the roof, Octavia, sitting at her end next to the aisle, leans toward Jasper and whispers, "My goodness, he was all over the place in that sermon."

Nora, overhearing the whisper, smiles that let-Mrs.-Martin-speak-her-mind kind of smile. Nora says nothing to Jasper who is seated between the two women.

శంౚ

The vestibule of the church is becoming crowded as people leave the sanctuary. Some of the overflow is outside on the front landing of the church, standing under an aluminum awning.

Aunts Hattie and Claudine have joined Nora and the Martins in the stuffy vestibule, and there is suddenly a five-person "family cluster."

Before the niceties and greetings are over between the ladies, three of Mrs. Martin's friends saunter up to the group.

"Good afternoon everybody," says Sally Jenkins. "Octavia, I know you are so proud of your handsome son in that uniform. You too, Miss Nora," says Sally, as a throw-away acknowledgment of her.

"Hello, ladies. Miss Carpenter and all my soon-to-be-family have given me their complete blessings and approval," Jasper says, smoothing over the intentional or unintentional slight.

"Octavia, have I met your three friends before?" asks Claudine, with a hint of skepticism in the question.

"Well, I reckon not. But they might as well be let out of the bag today. Better now than later, I guess," Octavia says, with an amused look in her eyes and fanning her face with one of the church fans.

"I'll do the honors," says the aggressive Sally Jenkins.

Before Sally was able to continue, another voice interrupts.

"No need for all this fanfare. I'm Clara Wilkins and this is Betsy Butler on my left. And Miss Chatterbox, here on my right side, is Sally Jenkins," says Clara in a calm and more dignified manner.

"I'm Nora Carpenter's Aunt Hattie and standing beside me is her Aunt Claudine," Hattie says, while scanning the huddle to try and gain eye contact with the three newcomers.

"We're so happy to make your acquaintance, Miss Hattie and Miss Claudine," says Betsy Butler, the last of Octavia's friends to speak.

"I know all y'all over there in that nice old house at the corner of Crescent and Magnolia. Yeah, everybody knows that house is full of you educated nurses," says Sally, in a dismissive tone

"Excuse me, Mrs. Jenkins, but my fiancée is a school teacher. Nora graduated from Tuskegee Institute in Alabama," Jasper says in a proud voice.

"Octavia, just how are y'all deciding who to invite and not to invite to the wedding of these two love birds?" asks Sally, with intended bluntness.

"Hold your horses, Sally," says Octavia. "It ain't my decision about no invitation list. I been told dat's up to the bride's family."

The church's stuffy vestibule is clearing out because more parishioners are leaving. Reverend Simpson is standing close by and clearing his throat. Whether he is suffering from the ill effects of prolonged talking or he is hinting for the Carpenter-Martin-three-ladies' ensemble to leave is anyone's guess.

"Excuse me, Mrs. Jenkins," says Nora, in a firm voice. "My Aunts Claudine, Hattie and Marilyn are deciding on the invited guests. Mrs. Martin will give us her and Jasper's list, and then the final decisions will be made."

"Jasper, your mother has been acting like the cat's got her tongue about who is coming. She ain't usually never able to keep her lips so tight," says Sally, in a frustrated tone.

"Mrs. Jenkins, Mrs. Jenkins. You must realize we are all trying to ensure that first, Nora is pleased with the list of wedding guests and, two, the back yard will not be crowded with too many people," says Jasper. "After all, we are trying to make Nora happy. This will be *her* big day. We want people there who have a special place in my and Nora's hearts," concludes Jasper.

"Jasper, I think we all understand what you are saying, right everyone?" asks Claudine, in an effort to sound pleasant.

"Of course, we do. Don't we Sally and Clara?" asks Betsy.

"Just wait a minute. Speak for yourself, Missy. Octavia, what about all your buddies. What about our small Bid Whist group of ladies?' asks Sally, in a surprised voice.

"Our card-playin' friends ain't got no connection to Nora and Jasper. I have ta add a few family names from back down home, from Savannah. That's where my head count gotta be," says Octavia, without hesitation.

"Octavia, am I hearin' you say WE three may not even get to the wedding?" huffs Sally.

"I ain't sayin' yea nor nay. It's comin' down to the numbers— down to the numbers," Octavia says, in a tone of now-leave-me-alone.

Jasper looks in the direction of where Reverend Simpson is nodding to the last two church members.

"I think the church doors are about to be closed and locked so we had better move on out," he announces.

There is an awkward silence among the eight people left in the vestibule.

Then Sally, in characteristic fashion of wanting to have the last word, says, "Octavia, I just knew you'd stand up for us. You are showing me a side of you I ain't seen before. You have got all mealy-mouth in front of your soon-to-be new in-laws. Lord have mercy!" Sally blurts out.

"Sally Jenkins, I ain't stuttin' you at dis moment. Go cool yo'self down. Keep talkin' and yo' name may not even make da *first round* on da list—let alone bein' crossed off later!" Octavia ends her message and looks up to the vestibule's ceiling while pursing her lips.

Chapter 13

A Bundle of Nerves

Before heading to school, Nora is busy going over her to-do list to accomplish what's left to prepare for their wedding. Lucy Rivers has completed altering her gown. Geneva and Velma found similar pink gowns for the wedding. Marguerite says the style with the length below the knee is known as opera length. She gave them a deal on the price. Nora needs to buy white shoes to wear. She and Aunt Hattie need to design the single page wedding invitation and go to the stationer's shop downtown to buy the card stock. Nora and Aunt Marilyn need to buy flowers to help design a larger bouquet for the three women and a flower girl. Jasper is taking care of the details for the men's wedding suits. He, Eugene and Tommy Collins will wear rented black suits.

All three of Nora's aunts are working at the hospital, and Nora is enjoying the quiet of the morning and her rambling thoughts. She almost told Jasper she would have the house to herself for about an hour. But more and more she is feeling a very strong urge to remain celibate until her wedding night. Jasper has put no pressure on her, and the decision seems mutual and the agreement tacit.

After eating a piece of fruit and one of Aunt Marilyn's biscuits, Nora hears a knock at the front door. She is dressed so there is no hesitancy about answering the door. A young white man is standing there with a Western Union envelope.

"I have a Western Union Telegram for a Miss Nora Carpenter."

Nora, now anxious, says, "That's my name."

He hands her the envelope after she signs a page in a small tablet. With her heart racing and her hands trembling, she slowly opens the envelope not knowing what the urgency could be or who may be sick, or, worst yet, dead or dying. The top of the page saying where the message has come from is Atlanta, Georgia. She quickly looks down to find a name, and, to her surprise, it is her new friend from the bus depot—Abigail Carrington Stewart. Nora is mumbling in a soft whisper, "What could be so urgent?" Nora doesn't even make it back to the kitchen table with the Western Union. She detours into the dining room and pulls a chair out from the table to sit and read the message.

Dear Nora,

Even though we just met, I feel such a connection to you. I had to tell you Harrison received orders to ship back out after being home for less than a week. He had orders to leave last week. I have been crying my eyes out. He had to get up to Charleston, South Carolina. He has been assigned to a unit that is shipping out to Europe this week. The message said the war is heating up, and more US troops are needed to help. Has your Jasper received word on getting a new assignment? To go to Europe or out of the country? What about your wedding plans? I wish you had a telephone. The out-of-town calls cost a bit, but I would ask Daddy to let me make a couple of calls. You would be one of them. This Western Union is not cheap either, but I just had to let you know. I am so sad.

Your new friend,

Abigail Carrington Stewart

Nora presses the page to her chest as if her empathetic heart could send a message right back to Abigail.

With a total lack of control her mind begins to rattle off a litany of the "what-ifs." *What if Jasper gets orders this week to go to Europe? Or somewhere else out of this country? What if he hears nothing for ten or eleven days and, two days before the wedding, he gets notice to leave in two or three days like Harrison? What if all our plans and family money go down the drain.... at the very last minute?*

Not knowing where to turn, Nora grabs her small pocketbook and the door key and rushes out of the house. She decides Geneva's house is closer than Jasper and his mother's house. Plus Geneva is more likely to be home.

୫୬

"Hey, Nora. Girl, aren't you supposed to be going to school? Why are you so out of breath? What's wrong, Honey?" Geneva asks as she swings her door open to let Nora enter.

"I, I didn't know who to talk to. I'm so upset," Nora says, as she hands Geneva the Western Union.

"Wait, wait. Let me read this right quick," pleads Geneva, as she feels a bit of tension about to grip her.

Nora just stares at Geneva like a fawn caught in headlights.

"I understand why your friend is so upset about how quick her husband's order came and he had to leave. But why are you letting this upset you so? You barely know her," says Geneva.

"But this could happen to me and Jasper. This could be our wedding plans flying out of the window, just like him flying over to Europe or somewhere. I couldn't take this kind of disappointment, not on the horizon of our wedding," whispers Nora, as she begins to weep.

"Don't start this unnecessary speculation," says Geneva, like a much more mature person.

"I don't know if I should tell Jasper and my family about how so-out-of-the-blue these military orders can come and turn your world upside down," says Nora.

"Honey, this is nothing new or wouldn't be a big surprise to Jasper. He has to know how fast your plans can be interrupted by Uncle Sam's business," says Geneva, in a comforting tone.

Geneva puts her arm across Nora's back and steers her to the living room sofa where they both sit down.

"You have to brace yourself for the sudden changes and

169

disrupted plans if you are going to be a good military wife. You're going to have to tell yourself life sometimes will mean just going along to get along," sighs Geneva. "Now, get yourself together and go to school and teach those kids."

"I'm not sure I can go on planning for an event that may not even happen. This seems so unfair to have you and Velma spend money for my ceremony that may have to be called off. My aunts are going to be disappointed too. You think so Geneva?" Nora asks, but not sure she would like to hear the honest answer.

"We can finish talking about this later. Here's a washcloth to wipe your face, pull yourself together and get yourself over to your classroom," Geneva asks. "Besides, I've got to get to my job around 9:00am. Let me finish dressing right quick and this will give you time to calm your nerves," Geneva says, as she rushes back to her bedroom.

"Calm my nerves," Nora says out loud. Then she burst into a loud laugh. "Geneva, you are making me sound like an old woman."

ೲღ

In the early evening hours, Nora is invited to eat dinner with Jasper and his mother at their home. She barely says anything to Jasper as he drives the short distance.

"Hey, the cat's got your tongue, huh? I'll give you a penny for your thoughts, Miss Nora," Jasper says, in a light-hearted way.

"Oh, Jasper. I'm just feeling drained. It's been a strange kind of day," Nora's weary voice reveals.

"You really are not acting like my bubbly little lady. Come on, tell me what's eating at you?" he asks, as he cuts the car's motor off in front of his home.

"I don't know if I should. You're going to think I'm being silly and pessimistic," Nora says.

"Try me. Just give me a chance to hear what's bothering you," Jasper says, in a big brother manner.

Nora begins to unload her fears on Jasper about sudden military orders. Up to this point he's been mostly silent. At a faster pace now, Nora continues to talk, starts to weep, starts to hyperventilate and, then, talks some more. Jasper moves as close as he can to Nora and angles her torso toward him to try to embrace her.

"Nora, my sweet princess, please don't allow yourself to become upset over the workings of military assignments and orders. You're smart. You know what my life, our life, may be like as long as I'm serving our country. This is something we will be facing while I'm in uniform. What smart military folks do—until they get an official re-location order in hand—is live their lives as normally as possible. Wherever in the world they may be. As long as we are able to move around together, that is all that should really matter to us.

"But Jasper. You're glossing over the point! What if you have to leave right before our wedding day? All this planning, the money we are all spending—even though I'm keeping everything modest. Will we just throw everything aside and shrug our shoulders? Will we have to wait for God knows how long—your first leave maybe— and then rush down to the courthouse and marry right on the spot? If you get sent overseas, you may be gone for a year with no leave time." Nora is almost breathless, again.

"I didn't tell you that on Friday I went to the recruitment office here in Macon and talked with the Lieutenant in charge. There is some funny French name for his title. But nevertheless, he says it's impossible for him to know if I might have a fast turn-around. He still thinks my paperwork stating my interest in Fort Bragg, North Carolina may have a little influence, if I am stationed state-side.

"The Lieutenant says the fighting is still going on and our side is going to try to get the upper hand on Germany. Just as I was about to leave heading back here, the enlisted guys at Fort Leavenworth had wind of this, and they were trying to sort out the information. The officers don't pass all the detailed information down to the foot soldier. That's just how that pecking order works," Jasper concludes.

As if a light bulb goes off in Nora's head, she looks straight toward Jasper and says, "That's why Abigail's husband, Harrison, is being shipped over to Europe. Her Western Union message says something about war gearing up. My goodness, I didn't bring the Western Union letter with me. I'll show it to you when you drive me back home after dinner."

Just as Nora and Jasper are refocusing on Octavia waiting dinner for them, Octavia rushes out the door and shouts, "Okay now, this dinner in here getting' cold while you two out here pattin' and rubbin' on each other. Uh, huh. I know what time of day it is. Come on in and wash dem hands and get to my kitchen table. You young folks—hot as one of 'dem firecrackers!" Octavia says, as the door slams behind her.

"Well, Nora, you sure won't have to do too much to figure out your future Mother-in-Laws' personality," Jasper says, in a resigning tone.

Nora presses the back of her head onto the car's front seat and lets out a howl.

Chapter 14

Another New Girlfriend?

Nora, her family and the few members of the wedding party continue doing their part to move the planning along for the big day, Saturday, March 25th.

Two days after Nora receives the Western Union from Abigail Stewart, and because she can't seem to get this new friend out of her mind, Jasper tells Nora he will pay for a two-line response Western Union. Nora is giddy about Jasper's offer. Once at the downtown Macon location, which on the inside is smaller than Nora's kitchen, Nora writes her message on a piece of paper to hand to the machine operator. Jasper speaks to Nora in a calm voice.

"Just take your time and choose your few words real careful," he tells her.

"All right, young girl. Hurry up. I ain't got all day," the operator says to Nora. He ignores Jasper standing beside her. Jasper has to resist the urge to point out that Nora is not a girl, but a young woman. A middle-aged white woman comes in and hands the operator her message already written out.

"Oh, good. I see you know how to come prepared. I wish everybody would respect my time like you," he said, looking in Nora and Jasper's direction as they stand at a very small table with a sign above on the wall that says, "Colored."

Nora rushes to complete her message.

Dear Abigail, So sorry about Harrison's orders. I understand your sadness. Wedding set for Saturday, March 25th at 4pm out in my backyard. I'm excited and nervous! Please write again. Nora Carpenter

As the operator examines the message, he mumbles. "Writes real good." Out loud he says, "I see you have the Atlanta address and the recipient's name here, so I don't have to wait on that. Abigail should get this later today. This'll cost you two-dollars," he says, to Nora.

"I'm paying for this," says Jasper, as he takes his wallet from his back pocket.

"Nothin' like an old sugar daddy," says the clerk, with a sly smile directed at Nora.

"I beg your pardon, Sir. Miss Carpenter and I will be married in less than two weeks. And she is a fully grown young woman," Jasper relates in a calm and intentionally respectful manner.

"Coulda fooled me about her age," the operator smirks.

"Since I'm downtown, where do I go to ask some questions about one of those new tella-fones?" asks Jasper.

"Boy, I see you got a little money to your name. You coloreds want everything that somebody else has. I guess that's the new sign of coloreds making baby steps of progress," says the operator, with an air of surprise. "What's your job?" asks the man.

"I'm a Private 1st Class in the US Army and on active duty. I'm also a professional musician," says Jasper, with a bit of pride and a tinge of disgust in his voice.

Nora has become impatient at this point and has raised one foot on its heel and is swinging it from side to side.

"Go on down the street to the Macon Electric and Light building. There's an entrance around the back. They can talk with you," the operator says, as he studies Nora and Jasper's appearance for the first time, as they head to the door.

THE DEBT

SOCR

"I told Eugene to meet us for lunch at Sampson's Grill," says Jasper.

"But I have so much to do at home. Why didn't you tell me we were stopping here?" questions Nora, as Jasper pulls his car up to the popular grill in the colored section of town.

"We won't stay long. This is just a quick pop-in for a fast sandwich or bowl of gumbo," says Jasper.

They are not sitting for five minutes before Eugene comes in with a very attractive young lady by his side.

"This is my friend, Cynthia. She and I met a year ago in Atlanta. She is here visiting her aunt for a few days. I didn't even know she had an aunt here in Macon. And Nora, this is going to knock you off your feet. Cynthia told me yesterday her aunt is Mrs. Turner, who owns Marguerite's Bridal Shop. Is this world not small?" asks Eugene, all excited about his friend's local family.

"Well, it's good to meet you, Cynthia," Jasper says, standing, as a gentleman would, to let her slide into the booth seat across from him and Nora.

"And this is Nora. I'm sure Eugene has filled you in on our connection. Welcome to Macon," Jasper says with a smile.

"Hey, partner, Ellis wants you to take a vacant alto sax chair at the Elks Club this Friday night. Are you game?" asks Eugene, with excitement in his question.

"You bet I am," says Jasper. "You don't know how I have missed my playing dates. Nora, we don't have any other plans for Friday night, do we?" asks Jasper.

"No, not that I recall," says Nora. "Hey, Cynthia, if you're still in town, we can make this a two-couple evening. If that's okay with you."

"I would love to join you, if Eugene doesn't already have another lady friend waiting in the wings for the Friday night jam

175

session," says Cynthia, almost guaranteeing he won't disappoint.

"Oh, it's a deal. It's a deal. Cynthia, you owe me for coming to Macon and messing with my social calendar. I might never recover after you return to Atlanta," Eugene says, as he leads the laughter all around the booth.

ഇൽ

As the two couples stand to leave the grill, Nora looks over at Jasper and says, "I've got an idea. Why don't you drive me over to Marguerite's and let me see how the alterations on the gown are coming along? I won't be long and you can wait in the car as I run in for a few minutes. I shouldn't have to try it on again at this point," Nora speculates.

"Look who claimed earlier she has to rush back home to attend to other wedding details," Jasper reminds Nora, as the four of them slowly approach the door to leave.

"You know, we ladies have license to switch gears as our mood dictates. Besides, Cynthia can go in with me to maybe peak at my gown," Nora says, as her eyes sparkle with enthusiasm.

"Oh, this is so exciting! You two are about to be married! Are you sure you're not doing something that's taboo as far as me sneaking a peep at your gown?" Cynthia asks, in an earnest manner.

"I really don't know. Your aunt can tell us when we go in. I'm not one of these types of women who has read ten books on wedding do's and don'ts," giggles Nora.

"Let's get out of this hot sun," Eugene suggests, as they are paused on the sidewalk.

"Man, no one asked you if you have time for this unannounced detour. If not, I can drive Cynthia back over to her aunt's house when we leave the shop," Jasper offers.

"I'm good," says Eugene. "Just plan to clean and polish my instruments later this afternoon and get ready for Friday and the rest of the weekend."

176

ഇൗരു

Nora and Cynthia are standing in front of the check-out counter waiting for Jocelyn to answer their question.

"Too many connections to try to figure out," says Jocelyn Turner. "I should have put two and two together and realized your friend Eugene and Nora's intended both play in that wonderful Ellis Walker Orchestra."

"Aunt Jocelyn, is it okay for Nora to let me see her gown?" asks Cynthia, in a tentative voice. "I won't be here when she gets married."

"Well, there are mixed opinions on that. If you have a leaning toward being superstitious, you won't let anyone other than the women in your bridal party see your gown. But Miss Nora here impresses me as a bit of a free spirit. She won't be hunting for you later to throw some voodoo dust on you if there is a little hiccup in the ceremony and early marriage," says Jocelyn, like an old sage.

With that assessment from the older woman, Nora and Cynthia just bend over laughing.

"Cynthia, I ain't trying to get into your business 'cause you a grown young woman. But if you and Mr. Eugene are cooking up a close friendship, why can't you be his date for the wedding and plan to come on back down to Macon for it. This way, we don't have to find no voodoo dust and you don't have to look at this gown today!" Jocelyn states, in a no joking voice.

"Aunt Jocelyn, please don't try to rush me into a serious relationship I may not be ready for yet. Since Peter and I broke off our engagement almost eighteen months ago, I'm being very careful. You see how I've been able to put that part of my life on the shelf and keep moving forward.. I don't want Eugene to think I'm suggesting anything serious because I'm fishing for an invitation to Nora and Jasper's wedding. I just met them two hours ago. There's no way I would be on their guest list otherwise. You understand what

I'm saying?" Cynthia asks her aunt, in a very serious tone.

"You sound like you still pretty sensitive to me about the break-up. Hell, I was ready to have my son Henry drive me to Atlanta to take measurements of all eight of your attendants so I could start ordering bridesmaids' dress samples. Then like overnight, you and Peter just called the whole thing off. My sister, your mother, Muriel, still talks about that disappointment to this day," concludes Jocelyn, as her voice begins to fall.

"Well, that's Mom's headache and not mine anymore. Nora, I'm sorry you had to hear this tale about a near-marriage that ran off track two-hundred yards from the station, so to speak. I've gone beyond it. Peter and I are cordial to each other because we still maintain mutual friends. I am not on the hunt for another soul mate. And all is well. Eugene knows an itsy-bit about my broken engagement, and that's only because I chose to tell him few details. We really are just good buddies at this point—and no more. Nora, I'll be happy to see your wedding pictures after they've been processed. You are getting a professional photographer, aren't you?" asks Cynthia, casually.

"Oh, my goodness!" says Nora. "I haven't even thought about that little detail."

ഇരൽ

The next day Aunt Hattie and Nora have Jasper drive them downtown to the stationery shop. Nora, while eating breakfast earlier, thought about Cynthia's aborted wedding. It occurred to her, briefly, that Cynthia probably is knowledgeable about invitation-quality stationery, and she could have helped her and Aunt Hattie this morning. Nora quickly cast that thought aside. There is no reason to stir up old, sad emotions in her new acquaintance.

"Good Morning, you two. What can I help you with today?" asks the mature sales lady.

"My aunt and I are here to look at your white card stock for wedding invitations," says Nora.

"Yes, we want the plain cards, and I plan to write the invitations in cursive with my calligraphy pen and ink," says Hattie, in a confident tone.

"Do you have experience with this type of writing?" asks the formal-speaking woman. "Mistakes can be painful with this costly paper. And how many cards do you need?" And do you need matching envelopes?" the clerk keeps asking.

Nora speaks up again, "We want to see your selections, please."

"My name is Mable Maxwell and your names are?" she asks, in a polite manner.

"I'm Nora Carpenter and I'm the one getting married. This is my Aunt Hattie," Nora responds.

"Come on over to this display case and you can see what we offer," says Miss Maxwell. "It's rare to have a customer who knows the cursive writing style, uses the correct writing instruments—and is comfortable tackling such a delicate job. I learned the technique when I took a class in writing styles when I lived in New York. It truly has become a dying art form. Not too many people, outside of art students and graphic arts types, even bother anymore," Mable Maxwell concludes.

"I spent a summer working in Philadelphia some years ago, as a visiting nurse, and I took a couple of classes in things I was interested in at the time," says Hattie. "I practice and keep my skill level up when it comes to my calligraphy," Hattie says,

After looking at their options, Hattie and Nora pick fifty classic white cards with matching envelopes. They are about 5 x 7 in size and will demand carefully worded and spaced composition.

The sales lady tells them each card with an envelope is fifty-cents." The total comes to twenty-five dollars plus tax," says Mabel Maxwell.

After Miss Maxwell wraps the cards and envelopes in soft tissue paper and delicately places them in a box with the name, Crane, on top, she leads the Carpenter women to an antique secretary's desk. Aunt Hattie pulls a weathered, letter pouch from her purse and begins to unfold bills in denominations of five's and one's.

"It's been a pleasure helping you ladies today. And Miss Carpenter, I know you will be one of Macon's prettiest brides this season," gushes Miss Maxwell, as she ushers the Carpenter women out of the shop.

ᘛᘚ

Cynthia, driving her Aunt Jocelyn's Ford-model station wagon on Friday night, picks Nora up at her home.

"So, Eugene tells me you live with your three aunts," Cynthia casually states.

"Yes, since I was a toddler. My parents died together in a car accident, and they adopted me," Nora responds, with no hesitation.

Shifting the conversation, Nora asks, "Eugene told you how to get to my house, huh?"

"Yeah, it wasn't hard to find. Driving here in Macon is so much easier and less complicated than driving in Atlanta. Do you drive?" asks Cynthia.

"No. Neither do any of my aunts. I guess we're in a time warp here in Macon concerning certain things," Nora responds in a lazy voice.

"Don't put yourself down like that. More ladies, in the larger cities, are slowly learning to drive. I bet your Jasper is going to teach you how to drive soon after you all are married. Want to put some money down on that?" chuckles Cynthia, in a light-hearted tone.

As Cynthia and Nora reach the Elks Hall and Cynthia eases into an empty space on the lot behind the building, the women emerge from the station wagon. They both get a chance to assess each other's appearance.

"Oh my goodness," Nora says. "What a pretty dress you have on, with those big, colorful flowers printed on that beautiful yellow background. That looks like something you see in one of those fancy ladies' magazines," she says, as she practically circles Cynthia's body.

"Girl, I'm looking at that hot pink skirt with so much body to it. Do you have crinoline under it? And that black eyelet, puff-sleeve blouse. You look like a little China doll who is ready to show out on the dance floor. Eugene told me you are a superb dancer," Cynthia is rattling on non-stop.

Nora doesn't respond to Cynthia's compliments, but instead tilts her head toward the building and says, "Let's walk around to the front entrance where our tickets are waiting for us with our names on the envelope. The guys can't break away at this point to meet us at the entrance. They know we're coming, and they've notified the greeter. Nobody will look at us as unattached women," Nora explains.

Chapter 15

The Elk's Club

"Hello, Miss Carpenter and Miss Sinclair," says Clarence Crenshaw, or "Cee Cee," the Elks Club's affable manager and greeter. "Jasper and Eugene are waiting for you. If you'll follow me, I'll show you your table, right up front."

"Hi, Mr. Crenshaw. This is Cynthia Sinclair, Eugene's friend from Atlanta. Thanks for always being so helpful and courteous," Nora responds, as she follows Crenshaw around the outer edge of the tables circling the dance floor and with Cynthia close on her heels.

Crenshaw turns back and says over his shoulder, "The orchestra members have already warmed up. Your timing is almost perfect. I don't think any of the guys can walk down from the stage now and come over for a quick chat because they are about to get the show started."

Nora and Cynthia see the guys as they approach one of the front tables. Nora says, "There they are on the front saxophone row." She shows Jasper a full-face smile followed by a gestured kiss formed with her puckered pink lips.

"Oh, my goodness, don't Eugene and Jasper look good in those tan, tuxedo jackets with the honey-colored lapels. I like this Macon-styled tuxedo with its different twist," says Cynthia, in a sassy tone as she and Nora quickly claim their chairs. They don't wait for Crenshaw's too slow movements as he attempts to hold their chairs for them. "Thank you, sir," a smiling Cynthia says, looking up from her seat.

The Ellis Walker Orchestra kicks off the evening with Ellis Walker himself coming to the microphone with a broad smile on his face, "Hey, hey, hey ladies and gentleman! Welcome to the Elks Club here in the Fernwood community. What a show we have for you tonight! I'll introduce the orchestra members in our first intermission, but one person I want to acknowledge right now. Back with us tonight, after returning from basic training, is our premiere alto sax player Mr. Jasper Martin."

"Stand up Jasper so everyone knows who you are, man," Walker proudly suggests. Jasper pops out of his seat for a few seconds to the sound of heavy applause and a couple of "my man Jasper" cat calls from the back of the club.

Nora looks over to Cynthia and winks her eye as she, too, joins in the applause for Jasper. Another couple has joined them at the table for six people. Nora and Cynthia, so wrapped up in the moment, didn't see them quietly tipping up to the table.

In a quasi-hyped, carnival barker's tone, Ellis Walker loudly proclaims., "We're going to get this show on the road tonight by getting you in the mood with—Fats Waller's *This Joint is Jumpin'*. Come on out of those seats now and don't return to them anytime soon," Crenshaw booms with great enthusiasm.

One of the disadvantages of sitting in front of a performing orchestra is how difficult it is to start a conversation with someone and even be able to hear a response. So Nora and Cynthia acknowledge the young couple with inviting smiles but realize they need to wait on a pause in the music to strike up a conversation.

Nora is also trying to size up who will ask her to dance. Jasper enjoys seeing his former girlfriend, now fiancée, accept offers to dance from male patrons in the club. Their lady friends, or wives, politely tolerate the attention the skilled, fast-paced jitterbugging partners attract. The three men, well-known neighbors, who usually ask Nora to dance are Bernard, Chester and Jerome. Nora is so natural as a nimble and sure-footed dancer until she causes others to stop to appreciate her skill. Occasionally, an unknown gentleman will approach Nora. She very casually obliges and enjoys the subtle differences in movement and style they usually display. Nora, a quick-study on the dance floor, loves a hint of a challenge.

As the patrons start to sway to the music in their seats and others move onto the dance floor, Nora sees Chester coming over to her table. Chester reaches the table right in front of the orchestra, and he turns to offer a perfunctory bow in front of Jasper and his sax line. Chester, a Fernwood neighbor, is married to Lorraine. Chester turns to Nora with a big smile on his face, bends over slightly to hold out his hand and asks, "May I have this first dance my-lady?"

Before standing, Nora looks up and says, "Hi, Chester, so good to see you. Of course, we can get out there and get our blood circulating. Nora stands and her hot-pink skirt seems to shout *'Let's go.'* She looks up toward the stage in Jasper's direction to gauge if he sees her and Chester moving toward the center of the other dancers.

With his voice elevated, Chester competes with the music as he leans into Nora and asks, "How you been doin' and how are those wedding plans coming along?"

He grabs her right hand and swings her in a half-circle movement before they both jump right into the rhythm of the song. Nora's black patent heels and Chester's white spats covering his black shoes become a blur as they move to the song's fast tempo. He swings her in fast spins. He joins her, at intervals, and they both spin. Nora gracefully and intuitively follows his lead. So, there is no surprise when his opened hands lock Nora's waist and lift her off her feet to swing her from one side of his body to the other side while he's doing nimble foot movements. Their turns are so wide and so frequent until other dancers just give them more space. Chester's exuberance causes him to let out a soft "Yeah" or a light-hearted tease directed to Nora such as, "Watch out now, don't show me up."

Cynthia, still seated, cranes her neck to follow Nora and Chester on the dance floor. She is smiling, giggling and clapping her hands as she enjoys the artistry of the two stand-outs.

As the music and vocal selections continue, Nora gets other offers to dance. Cynthia dances two or three times to fast-paced tunes. The men know it's best not to ask to dance a slow number with another man's wife or girl. Harmony and goodwill are social notes in this climate of high spirits and musical notes.

At the intermission, Jasper and Eugene step down from the stage and approach the table. There are smiles all around as Jasper hugs Nora and quickly brushes her lips with his. "I see you're having a good old time dancing, Miss "Twinkle Toes," Jasper says to Nora. Eugene and Cynthia hold hands as they watch the two lovebirds.

Interruptions are frequent as neighborhood people and Elks Club regulars engage in fleeting compliments about the performance. The young couple who sat at the table earlier introduce themselves as residents of Valley Forge. They are visiting family in the country, outside of Macon. They said they had heard from friends, in other parts of Georgia, about the Ellis Walker Orchestra. And a few people pausing at the table mention Nora and Jasper's wedding, which the colored community is buzzing about.

"How are you going to keep peace among your friends here in Fernwood when you can only invite so few of them?" asks Cynthia.

Eugene butts in, "Don't you worry about Nora and Jasper's guest list. I've got my problem solved, I think, because they are inviting you to be my date for their wedding. Are you on, Miss Sinclair?" asks Eugene, in a rushed and pressuring tone.

"That's right Cynthia," Nora says. "Eugene beat us to the question. But will you honor us as one of our guests at the wedding?" Nora asks. "Oh, my goodness, I can't believe it's just nine days from today," sighs Nora.

Cynthia gushes, "Yes, I will come to your wedding. Thank you so much! I feel as though I've known you two much longer than one week."

Cynthia looks straight at Eugene and says, "You know I'm going to have to return to Atlanta to make some wardrobe changes. I'll probably take the Greyhound back mid-day tomorrow and drive back down maybe on Thursday."

"Whatever you have to do Cynthia so my buddy and best man won't have that hang-dog look on his face next weekend," teases Jasper.

The quartet of friends laugh out loud.

ῼ´

"While you two wet your whistles and stretch your legs, Cynthia and I will head to the ladies' room," Nora announces. "We'll try to be in our seats before the second set starts." In a tease of self-importance and blinking her eye toward Jasper, Nora says, "But don't let them start before Nora Carpenter is in place." She then playfully sashays away with Cynthia walking by her side.

As the ladies are powdering their noses and reapplying their lipstick, Cynthia finds herself staring at Nora's mirror image in a wistful way. She slowly turns her head to look at Nora's side of face closest to her. Feeling Cynthia's glare, Nora turns to meet Cynthia's gaze.

"You and Jasper are going to have a good marriage," says Cynthia. "It's so obvious how you both care for each other, are relaxed around each other and have so much basic, simple, silly fun together.

"Your observations are interesting," says Nora. "You are talking like a wise, older person with experience," she says with squinted eyes and a quizzical look.

"No, I see many characteristics in your relationship that my mother and father had. They had a strong marriage that lasted almost thirty years. My father died suddenly almost two years ago. My mother misses him so much. My younger brother, Michael, lives in Chicago. He means well but, you know, boys are not as attentive to their mothers," Cynthia chronicles, in a near-monotone voice.

"So, your father's death was close to the time you broke off your engagement and wedding plans, yes?" asks Nora.

"Everybody says I was grieving over my daddy's death, but there was something about Peter that was becoming more unsettling. I couldn't quite put my finger on it," Cynthia says, as if she is still searching for more clarity.

"I can tell you are college-educated. Were you and Peter college sweethearts?" asks Nora, without hesitation.

"No, Peter graduated back in his hometown of St. Louis. I graduated school in Nashville, at Tennessee Agriculture and Industrial State College. He was a third-year medical student at Meharry Medical College in Nashville. I stayed in Nashville after graduation to become a social worker. I was from Atlanta, and he was from St. Louis. We both felt we were hip, big-city kids who knew how to show off and act sophisticated. We had many good friends. He studied hard, but we were very social too," reminisces Cynthia.

"What caused you to fall out of love with him?" asks Nora, who, like Cynthia, has become oblivious to the ladies coming in and out of the restroom. No one bothers to interrupt their conversation because the seriousness of it is quite apparent.

"We both had big plans after we married. We hoped Peter would get a good medical residency in a mid-sized city. We talked about what he might want to specialize in as a doctor. We delighted in the idea of having maybe two kids. He didn't want to talk about kids too much. We talked about eventually building that big home and entertaining on a large scale. He was causing me to be more excited about what we could get with a doctor's salary. How we would stand out in the community and be liked, and envied," Cynthia keeps going into more details.

"Let's walk out in the hallway so we have more privacy," Nora suggests.

"Ladies, Ladies, the second set is about to start. You don't want to miss any of it. By the way, Jasper was looking around for you, Miss Nora," Crenshaw says to her, as if he's just remembering.

"Thanks Cee-Cee. We lost track of the time. My goodness, this girl talk can take your mind in a whole different direction " Nora says, shaking her head, as if clearing the fog.

"But wait," Cynthia says, as she gently grabs Nora's forearm.

As they very slowly walk back toward the ballroom, Cynthia finally reveals the volcanic eruption. "More and more Peter's conversation became all the wealth he wanted to accumulate, the fine cars, the diamonds I would get. He became obsessed with having these material things," Cynthia sighed. "And then, the straw that broke the camel's back came, when a couple of months before the wedding, and after Dad had died—when all of us were just trying to put one foot in front of the other—Peter revealed his true stripes. He sat me down and showed me how we could use my inheritance from my father to jump-start OUR lavish lifestyle. He was telling me how to spend my daddy's money before the soil had even settled around his coffin," Cynthia says in a quivering voice.

"Oh, no!" says Nora. "I am so sorry your heart was broken twice in such a short period of time. Your father passed on and then your fiancé tore your heart out again with his greed."

Pulling her handkerchief out of her small clutch, Cynthia begins to cry with such force her shoulders are shaking. Nora turns around and says, "Let's step out the back door for a few minutes." She puts her arm around Cynthia's shoulder and pulls her new friend into her body. The two young women passed the restrooms and Nora unlatches the back door that leads them out into the dark night.

Crying and heaving at the same time, Cynthia manages to surprise Nora even more, "I've never told *anyone* the real reason I called off my wedding. The hurt and disappointment were unbearable. And to think I was such a poor judge of his character. What does this say about my level of maturity? Oh, Nora, please don't tell anyone—not even Jasper. Please!" Cynthia begs. "To this day, only Peter knows the real reason we are not married. And now you know," Cynthia exhales, as if a ton of bricks have been lifted off her shoulders.

"Don't worry Cynthia. Your grave misfortune is safe with me. I promise," Nora says, with sincerity.

"I know my judgment is right—at this moment! I have found a new and very dear friend in you, Nora," Cynthia announces, then gently wraps both her arms around Nora.

80)08

It's a good thing the club-goers are up and dancing to the lively first selection in the second set, because Nora and Cynthia are not as visible tipping back into the ballroom.

"I can't believe we talked so long," says Cynthia, still sniffling softly as they take their same seats.

Nora is reluctant to re-establish eye contact with Jasper because she feels like a kid who stayed on the playground—the primping room—too long. He has no idea what a wrenching conversation she has had with her new friend. Not even Geneva or Velma will be privy to this secret. After all, Nora feels her word is her bond. No if, ands and buts about it! Subject closed and hopefully forgotten.

"I haven't upset you, have I Nora, or messed up the spirited mood of the evening?" asks Cynthia, in a raised voice.

"What are good friends for?" asks Nora, as she winks in Cynthia's direction.

No one else is at the table when the two return, so they are able to keep taking a few deep breaths.

Chapter 16

Checking the Lists

Hattie is heading over to Octavia's house early Saturday morning —around eight-thirty—to collect her and Jasper's combined guest list for the wedding. She has asked Jasper to tell his mother she would be coming by. Hattie is mindful of the unsolicited interference from her sisters, especially Marilyn, if she and Octavia would do this work around the Carpenter's kitchen or dining room table.

Along the patchwork of dusty lanes, poorly maintained walking stones and cement blocks, Hattie begins mumbling to herself, "No one can say I'm not giving my leg muscles a good work-out today. I'll need to eat another light breakfast if I burn too much more energy."

Hattie sees a neighbor approaching on the path.

"Good morning, Martha. How are you doing?" Hattie asks, as both women stop to face each other. "It's good to know you agree with Claudine that your granddaughter, Candy, will be the perfect little flower girl in Nora's wedding. We plan to have a brief wedding rehearsal out in the backyard Friday night. You and Candy can come over around seven o'clock. Also, Nora is going to need to pay you to make a call to Atlanta on your phone. I hope you don't mind her setting a time over this weekend to come over to make that call to her Uncle Hempstead."

"Oh, that's going to be just fine. After I get back home this morning, I don't plan to get out in the mid-day heat anymore. Like you, this is why I run my errands early. Nora can come over at anytime. Just tell her that," Martha Jenkins continues. Then Martha's facial expression changes and she raises her brows. "You're talking about Hempstead, Claudine's ex ? Is this who Nora is calling? Is he coming to her wedding?" Martha unloads the questions, non-stop.

Hattie takes a deep breath, looks Martha straight in her eyes, and says, "My niece, Claudine's niece, still loves Hempstead. He was like a father to her. Just because the two adults couldn't make a go of it, doesn't mean Nora's feelings or Hempstead's feeling have to go up in smoke. Let's not read anything else into this situation," Hattie says, with a stern now-mind-your-own-business look.

"Honey, you don't have to tell me twice," says Martha, in an expression that conveys she's not offended. Then relaxing her facial expression, she asks Hattie in a sugary tone, "When you Carpenter ladies going to go on and get yourselves a telephone?"

Hattie, completely ignoring the question, says, "Hope to see you and Candy Friday evening."

"Okay, you will, Hattie," Martha practically sing-songs the response.

As the two ladies continue on their way, Hattie, after walking a few yards, again begins to mumble under her breath. She caps the encounter off with an audible, "Huh!"

₧₧

"Good morning, Hattie. I've been waiting on you," says Octavia, as she holds her screened door open.

"It's good to see you, Octavia. You're looking well. It's easy to see the joy and contentment in your face. Something really special is about to happen between our two families," Hattie says, smiling while entering Octavia's compact entryway.

"Oh, you sho' right about that! Of course, it ain't a done deal until Reverend says, 'You may kiss the bride'," Octavia chuckles.

"Let's get right down to work with compiling the master guest list. We need to start and finish delivering the invitations tomorrow after the churches let out," Hattie says, in a sped-up voice.

Octavia darts into her kitchen and returns with a round, woven basket with four warm cinnamon rolls. She goes back for two cups of coffee and a small glass of cream she has just taken out of the ice box. The sugar cup, already on the table, holds two spoons.

"Is Mr. Willie gonna drive us, like we talked about a while back?" asks Octavia, as she leads Hattie to her small, dining room table with its four chairs.

"Yes, he is. He will stick with us until we finish. All our guests realize we planned this wedding unusually fast because of Jasper's basic training and his pending new orders. We had to throw most of those wedding planning rules that Emily Post talks about by the wayside. Our timetable has been too short," Hattie sums up.

"Who is that Emily Post lady? I done heard that name somewhere before. Don't know where. What she got ta' do with everybody's weddin' bizness, anyway?" asks Octavia, in a mildly irritated voice.

"Well, she is somewhat the authority on wedding manners and other social graces, if you want to follow what many people think are the standards for good manners. People all over the country follow her rules and suggestions. Her advice columns are in some of the big newspapers and in *Collier's* and *Good Housekeeping* magazines," says Hattie, in her brief summary.

"You talkin' 'bout all those fancy magazines with them white folks on the front and inside? Who don' gone an' give her that kinda permission?" asks Octavia, her interest now piqued.

"Oh, Octavia…I don't know. Some people just see what they think is a need for rules about certain things. Some people have a less bossy way of thinking of it. They call her suggestions, guidelines. Some mothers of brides-to-be follow her suggestions or guidelines exactly. Others pick and choose which ones they want to follow," Hattie says, with more finality to her voice, with this expanded discussion.

"I don't know who all go' want some white lady telling them

how they got to do it this way—and not that-away. Too much say-so from one aw-atha-raty for me," complains Octavia.

"I'll just probably say quickly to our invited guests that I know we should have given them the hand-written invitation about three weeks ago, but we were not working from that same time-line, or Emily Post's time schedule. They will understand," says Hattie.

"Oh hell! Excuse my language, but my boy and his intended had ta' work from Uncle Sam's orders. 'Nuff said," Octavia concludes.

"You're right!" says Hattie. "But we have to be a little polite about it all," Hattie suggests.

"Ain't no need to apala-gize. These folks 'go be glad ta' see a pretty bride an' handsome groom, eat Miss Marilyn's good vittles, see her pretty yard, see Claudine's lay-out of 'da plates and table linens, hear that good, soft music some of Jasper's musician friends go play. It's go be a grand day if the rain holds up! Yes sir-ree," Octavia concludes, in a trance-like gaze.

"Let's see who you and Jasper have put on your list," says Hattie, as they sit at the table with her organizing tablet and a couple of pencils.

"Ain't nobody here on our list that's a big mystery, 'cept maybe my sister, Fannie. I went on an' wrote her when Jasper first left for Kansas. Told her then I 'speck there was gonna be a marriage in Jasper's future. She wrote me back shortly after sayin' she been ailin' a bit and her legs not movin' too good. We go mail her invitation to her, and Jasper already done sent her a short Western Union. We don't know, yet, if she go make it from Savannah or not," Octavia explains.

Looking at the list, Hattie asks, "Who are Vaughn Griffin and Albert Hall?"

"Oh, I guess I was wrong when I reckoned you done heard of them. Vaughn is Jasper's school buddy from when they was in secondary school. He went off to college somewhere in South

Carolina. Nora know who he is. Albert is the porter at that music store downtown, where they sell all them fancy and expensive pianos, horns 'an drums. He been so good to Jasper since he first started tootin' them horns—telling him when they put them reeds and stuff on sale. And asking his white bosses to hold stuff for Jasper until he comes back to Macon. They like Albert 'cause he been there so long, workin' so hard and is as honest as they come. They know the Ellis Walker folks, too," Octavia concludes her identifying the unknowns to Hattie.

"Yes, I see your friends here—Sally, Clara and Betsy. And I know Clarence Crenshaw, who manages the Elks Club," Hattie says, as she looks over the rim of her glasses toward Octavia.

"Do I need to okay you Carpenter sistas' list, too?" asks Octavia with a straight face, followed by a long pause. "I need ta make sure 'yo people meet the Martin family's high-on-the-hog standards—ya' know?" Octavia's stern look gives way to a sly smile and then a full-blown, belly laugh. Octavia slaps the table with her opened hand, saying, "I got you Miss Hattie. That was a good one—a good tease… if I have to say so myself," Octavia concludes, as she reins in her "tickle bone."

Hattie, momentarily thrown off balance, again looks over her rims and says warily, " A good, clean tease never broke anybody's law."

✿❧

After ten minutes more in Octavia's home, Hattie stands to leave. "I'm going to work on writing the invitations all day today. Mr. Willie and I will pick you up around two o'clock tomorrow. Most folks should be arriving home from church around that time. Are you going to church tomorrow?" Hattie asks.

"I don't reckon I will. Ain't no fun in having people eyein' you and ready to pounce about who go get one of them envelopes," Octavia says, in a weary voice.

194

"Neither Claudine nor I will be going to church. We will stay home to work on the dozens of small wedding details around the house," Hattie says, sounding like she's being imposed upon. "I'm not sure what Nora and Jasper are planning for tomorrow," Hattie adds.

"Now ya' know I can come over yonder to help all y'all, if 'ya need me. This is one of deez times in life when we all need one of 'dem tella-fones, so we can talk right-a-way," concludes Octavia.

"We'll be fine, Octavia. Thanks for the offer. I know it's genuine. I'll see you tomorrow afternoon," Hattie says in a very sincere manner.

"Thanks for coming over," Octavia says as she walks Hattie to the front door.

"No, thank you for your help and for the hospitality, and say hello to Jasper." Hattie throws one hand up in a good-bye gesture as she heads to the path at the edge of the small front yard.

Chapter 17

❧☙

The Carpenter Family
Claudine, Hattie and Marilyn
Requests your presence at the marriage of
Nora Norton Carpenter
To
Jasper Leonard Martin

❧☙

Saturday, the twenty-fifth of March
One thousand nine hundred and forty-four
at five o'clock in the afternoon.

❧☙

The Carpenters' Home
1966 Magnolia Street
Macon, Georgia

❧☙

Cocktails, dinner and dancing to follow.

After a late-morning nap and a light lunch around noon, Hattie begins setting up her work space on the covered, dining room table about one o'clock Saturday. Like a surgery room nurse carefully placing a doctor's tools at the ready, Hattie lines her pens in a row and places extra paper under the bottle of ink. The blue box of Crane cards with matching envelopes rests in front of Hattie, who sits mid-table.

Claudine and Marilyn walk back and forth to the kitchen then other parts of the house. They keep asking Hattie if she needs any help.

"You haven't had this much delicate writing to do in a long time. This is going to wear you out," says Marilyn.

Claudine chimes in, "She set herself up for this punishment."

"Consider this my labor of love for *our* deserving niece. Now if you two would stop so much stomping around and talking loud, my level of concentration will stay elevated. Please," sighs Hattie.

"We're going to try our best even though we aren't allowed to ask about a few of those strange people on the guest list," complains Marilyn.

"Please may I get started now—without any interruptions?" asks Hattie.

෨෬

Around four o'clock on Saturday afternoon, Nora, Geneva and Velma rush into the Carpenter home giggling and moving toward the stairs to go up to Nora's room.

The young women's greetings to Hattie get eclipsed with all of them practically speaking at once.

"Hi, Miss Hattie."

"So good to see you Miss Hattie."

"We'll talk in low tones, Aunt Hattie," as they all rush upstairs.

Hattie barely raises her head to acknowledge their presence. She is totally engrossed in completing as many invitations as she can in this first round of the tedious work.

Once upstairs, the two wedding attendants begin nudging Nora on, in a lighthearted way, to let them see her wedding gown.

Outspoken and sassy Geneva says, "You haven't been so picky about wedding traditions up to this point, why are you acting all by-the-books now?"

"Yeah, we need to see if you are really going to look like the Nora we know, or are you going to try to sneak and look like a lady of the night?" Velma asks, in an effort to get Nora to cave.

"Honey, we got to know if we need to put you on a diet for a week so you will still fit into, what I hear, is a gown that shows your little ass and those healthy tittees," Geneva says, also trying to provoke Nora.

"And yeah, we need to know should we bring some of that smelling salt stuff in case Mr. "Ain't seen nothin' Jasper" gets light-headed, and his knees start to buckle," Geneva continues, in an exaggerated drawl.

"Well, we might find out that Mr. Jasper and Miss Nora here are not as innocent as she is pretending. Maybe he has seen IT ALL… ALREADY," Velma says, while forcing her eyes to bulge for effect.

Nora's girlfriends push her over the edge with their wise-cracks, and she falls to her knees with out-of-control laughing.

"Enough, enough! We must be about to drive my Aunt Hattie crazy with all this noise. I give up. I'm on the verge of changing my mind, just to shut you two up," Nora says, as she tries to catch her breath.

"Okay now, I see that big white box on top of the chifferobe armoire. We'll tip downstairs to the kitchen for five minutes or so," says Velma.

"Yes, and when we come back up, we expect to see you modeling for us and showing us how you plan to walk like a lady across the lawn next Saturday, see?" says Geneva, walking and swaying her hips as they turn and walk out of the room.

Nora pivots and looks at the chifferobe. She pulls a chair over and steps up on it to bring the box down to the bed. She opens the box, smiles, and looks at the dress. She shakes her head and says, "Unh-unh."

෨෬

"So, no one from this house is going to church this morning?" asks Nora.

"Unless we have a family member who's coming down from heaven to shame us, we've made our decision," says Claudine.

"Claudine and I are making final selections about the menu. It's going to be real tricky because just about everything has to be prepared on Friday and Saturday morning. I have some of our friends agreeing to store the food in their ice boxes, but this means they have to hold off buying some of their own food until Monday. Because it's going to be warm outside still, I don't plan to be pulling anything out of neighbors' ovens. We'll have three or four large fresh salads—green salads and fruit salads—taken out of the ice boxes at the last minute. I will have small, fancy sandwiches using chicken and pork. It's too hot for any kind of fish. Fish will spoil too fast, plus the odor is not that pleasant. I'll have two platters of pickled vegetables, a big bowl of my peach preserve, fresh pecan halves, small tea cookies and small yeast rolls, which can be made ahead of time. Of course, we'll have the wedding cake to serve. Mr. Joseph is baking and decorating the wedding cake. The heat is going to be a bit scary as far as the cake icing. There will be plenty of lemonade and sweet tea. Hempstead told Nora when she called him yesterday that he is bringing down two cases of champagne from Atlanta. I sure hope the police won't stop him because of his good-looking car and find out he has that good champagne in his trunk," Marilyn concludes her plans for the food.

"And I've got all the borrowed extra glasses and serving pieces under control. Jasper will be picking many of them up and driving them here, as well as the folding, white church seats. Curry's yard service from down in the Pickinsville area will be plucking out the new weeds and trimming the edges of the yard, as well as giving it a fresh cut. Did I get all of that right, Marilyn?" asks Claudine.

"Well, Jasper and I are going to talk with little Mister Busy-Body, Buster Brown. We know he's too grown for his age, but there's a cute quality about him that's endearing. That's why I think he'll be a good ring bearer. Besides, Martha Jenkins suggested him to me because she says he and her granddaughter, Candy, get along quite well. We're going to make sure his Mother wants him to participate. If she says yes, that's two more invitations for Aunt Hattie to hand out later today—or tomorrow," Nora says, as she finishes her contribution to the final wedding details.

"Child, if every bride-to-be was lining up all her people at the last minute like you, the family members helping to plan everything would be having nervous breakdowns by now," Claudine says, in a I-give-up tone.

"Y'all please don't worry. My spirit tells me everything is going to work out fine because my favorite people—*all y'all loved ones*—are so involved," Nora says, in her best affected, southern drawl.

⊰⊱

"Mr. Willie, we can't thank you enough for agreeing to drive me and Octavia through the community to hand deliver these invitations for next Saturday," Hattie says to Mr. Willie as he drives away from Octavia's house. "Everybody who is getting one already knows they are invited. It's just a good manners formality," Hattie continues.

Octavia cuts her off, "You know what I think about dem too many forma-lalities, or however you say it, from that Post lady. I ain't stuttin' her."

In a very slow drawl, Mr. Willie says, "I don't know what y'all talkin' ah-bout."

"It ain't worth repeatin' Mr. Willie. Sho' ain't," Octavia says, as she looks out the car's window.

෫෬

"Oh! Stop here Mr. Willie. This is our first house. It's where Clarence Crenshaw, the Elks Club manager, lives. Come on, Octavia. You can walk up to the door with me," Hattie states, in a commanding voice.

"Okay, if you say so," Octavia says, as she wiggles along on the back seat to exit the car behind Hattie.

Octavia looks toward Mr. Willie as she passes the driver's side and whispers, "Here we go."

Mr. Willie chuckles and says, "Hush 'ya fuss."

෫෬

"He must not be at home," says Hattie, in a tone of disappointment.

"We knew that a minute or so ago," says Octavia, as she and Hattie walk back down the rocky driveway. "We were actin' like peepin' toms trying to see through his front window and that window around the side of the house. We can't lose too much time wit' that kind of patience, that ain't producing no results."

Hattie ignores Octavia's assessment of the ill-fated delivery attempt.

"Well, he'll see dat little white invelope bee-tween his screen an' front do', where we lef' it," says Octavia.

Climbing into Mr. Willie's old, but proudly maintained car, Hattie gets back on point with, "Our next stop, Mr. Willie, is Sally Jenkins' house. You know where she lives, right?" Hattie asks.

"Oh, yeah I do. I'll get you dere right direck-ly," he says, in a confident voice.

"Ooh, Sally is going to love gettin' this fancy writin' invitation on dat pretty and expensive paper. She know'd she was on my list, so

201

it ain't go be no surprise. But she go' be tickled pink," Octavia says, as if she already knows her good friend's reaction.

"We are so happy to have her among the guests at Nora and Jasper's wedding," says Hattie, in her most sincere and genuine-sounding voice.

ᔥᦒ

"Hello, you two Sunday, best-dressed ladies," Sally greets the ladies with a wide smile, as she leans out her screened door. "To what do I owe this friendly visit?"

"Good afternoon, Mrs. Jenkins," Hattie says.

But before Hattie could say another word, Octavia jumps in. "Sally, you don't have ta put on no airs fa' us, or try to remember yo' good speech. Miss Hattie here is Nora's understanding and kind Aunt. She sho' different from dem other two."

Sally quickly asks, in a somewhat rehearsed manner, "May I invite you ladies in for a glass of lemonade or tea?"

"No, thank you, Mrs. Jenkins. We must try to stay on schedule this afternoon. Don't you agree, Octavia?" Hattie says, looking straight toward Octavia.

"Yes, I guess you are right. How many of these invitations we tryin' to hand out today?" asks Octavia.

"The number is not important. We just want to make sure our friends in the community who are invited get these lovely, hand-written invitations as a memento or keepsake item. Both of you understand, I'm sure," says Hattie.

"That sounds like some mo' of that lady's rules—that Post lady. Sally, I'll have to tell you later who she is. It's a mess, how she don' set down all the "you cans" and "you can'ts" for everybody's weddin' and other uppity society stuff. It's like it's all a big secret. I ain't seen no final guest list or nobody don' told me how many," huffs Octavia, in a hint of frustration.

Hattie hands Sally Jenkins the invitation and turns to leave.

"Mr. Jasper has seen the guest list. Please enjoy the rest of your day, Mrs. Jenkins. We hope to see you on Saturday, the twenty-fifth," says Hattie as she walks back to the waiting car.

Octavia smiling, with a mischievous twinkle in her eye, looks back at Sally and says, "I'll have to tell you later more about that lady whose last name is Post. I reckon by that time I'll be able to remember her dag-gone first name."

ﮡﮥ

"I heard you were coming through the community today to hand-deliver the wedding invitations," says a smiling Jocelyn Turner, as she answers her front door.

"Good afternoon, Jocelyn," Hattie greets her, in return. "This is Octavia Martin, Jasper's mother, who is helping me spread the official good word. You know we are so behind schedule getting these invitations out."

"Hello, Mrs. Martin," Jocelyn says, displaying a warm smile. "Do you ladies have time to come inside?"

Octavia jumps into the conversation with, "It is sho' nice to make your acquaintance, Missus Turner. I ain't never had no reason ta' come into that fancy shop of yours, but I hear'd it is sooo nice."

"Oh, thank you for the compliment," says Jocelyn. "Let me step out here on the front porch with you ladies so I can pull my door to keep those pesky flying insects from getting inside."

Hattie reaches inside her crocheted tote to pull out two invitations.

"This is for you and your niece, Miss Cynthia Sinclair. Nora sure took an instant liking to her. I'm happy Nora is meeting more nice young ladies. And I know Eugene is a very respectable young man, so you should be comfortable about them getting to know each other, too," says Hattie.

"Oh, Honey, I try to stay out of my niece's business. My sister, Muriel, did a pretty good job rearing her, and she is a wise young lady with very good judgment, " says Jocelyn, with a tone of finality.

"Dats what I'm talkin' 'bout. Stay out of these young folks bizness," asserts Octavia.

Hattie smiles uneasily as she looks over to Octavia and says, "I think we should keep moving along our planned route to finish getting these invitations out. Don't you agree?"

Octavia offers her best effort at a courtesy nod, accompanied by a forced, closed-mouth smile. She doesn't utter a word.

"I know you are going to love the beautiful dress Nora chose. Lucy did a superb job with the slight alterations to the gown. It's just the right length so it's not hitting the grass too much. We adjusted the length with her high heels she is wearing. I know all of us are praying for no rain on the twenty-fifth," Jocelyn concludes.

"I say Amen to that," Octavia blurts.

"You have a wonderful Sunday afternoon, Jocelyn," Hattie says, as she turns to take the three steps down to the lawn.

Octavia follows her, then turns around to give a silent wave and warm smile to Jocelyn Turner.

෨෬

"We are making pretty good time, Mr. Willie," says Hattie.

"Yeah, this is one interestin' day all right. I'm meeting some new folks here in da community," injects Octavia.

"Our next stop is the Brown's home over on Scotts Road," Hattie says. "You do know the family don't you, Mr. Willie?"

"Yeah, they my customers too," says Leroy Willie. "They done gone and got der ice box a few weeks back. I carry dem their ice twice da week also.

"I hear'd they are coming 'cause you just want dat little cute and devlish man-chil' of theirs to be the ring boy. Otherwise, the parents wouldn't be on no-body's society list," blurts Octavia.

"Mrs. Martin, please," says Hattie, with a hint of exhaustion in her voice. "Please don't ever give that impression or support that kind of gossip. You know Joshua and Hortense Brown are our good neighbors here in the Fernwood community. They are well liked. And everyone adores that little precocious boy of theirs, Buster Brown. By the way, his role in the wedding will be the ring-bearer. He and the little flower girl, Candy Jenkins, are the only children in the ceremony."

"Yeah, well Martha Jenkins is everybody's friend in the neighborhood. She go and let every Tom, Dick and Harry come in her house to pay her to use that tella-fone of hers. Of course, everybody go like her, ha, ha," chuckles Octavia.

"Octavia, no one is pretending to like certain people because they need a favor or service from them. Let's not think in that way, please," Hattie says, sounding more and more weary.

"My lips are sealed—as I always try ta keep 'em. Sometimes is ain't so easy—'cause it be hard not to call a spade a spade!" asserts Octavia, sounding like a minister at the pulpit.

"Here we go. Here be da Brown house," says Mr. Willie.

"Let's go Octavia," Hattie says, as she opens the car door to the sound of that single, always-noticeable loud squeak. "Here's the home of Joshua and Hortense Brown."

"Okay, let's get dis dog and pony show revved up one mo' time," chuckles Octavia.

"Hello, hello," says Hattie, in her most pleasant and almost sing-song voice, as Hortense Brown surprises them by walking around the side of her house and up to the front door.

"How ya doin' Miss Hortense?" asks Octavia.

"Hello and welcome ladies. Everybody been buzzin' about y'all comin' through the neighborhood today. It's been like, who's going to win the prize," says Hortense, with a smile and an up-beat manner.

"We are so happy to have your family attend Nora and Jasper's wedding and to have your little eight-year old son participate. We are having a rehearsal out back, on the lawn, Friday night at seven.

Please bring Buster over. It will be short, and we won't keep you long," Hattie concludes, as she hands Hortense Brown the invitation.

"We are so excited. We can't wait. And Junior, or Buster, has promised to be on his best manners and not act up or try to understand and comment on gown folks business. This child has been a handful all his life. He's too old and wise for his age. I'm glad we only have the one," Hortense admits.

"Jasper told me your husband gave him Buster's measurements last week so he can rent the black suit for him and then return it with the rest of the guys' clothes," details Hattie.

"Yeah, Miss Hortense. We all expectin' a might fine weddin' between Miss Carpenter and my Jasper. Yes, in-deedy," says Octavia.

"Do you need an extra pair of hands or two extra feet in the next week? I am real handy in a lot of ways. Just let me know or grab Buster if you see him in the neighborhood and tell him. He'll get the message to me before you can say, 'Jack Rabbit'. He's real reliable in that way," assures Hortense.

"Where is yo' youngin' today?" asks Octavia

"He and his daddy went to visit a cousin out in the country," says Hortense. "They'll be back later with their second full stomachs for today. I won't have to serve up a meal when they return. You know how the kin folks feed you, down home," reminisces Hortense.

"We're going to keep moving on our delivery schedule," says Hattie. "It's been nice talking with you, Mrs. Brown. We'll see you at seven o'clock Friday evening."

"Bye, bye ladies. What a lovely Sunday afternoon it is. God bless you," says Hortense as she walks down the small front lawn toward the unpaved street.

"Good Sundi' afternoon, Miss Hortense," says Mr. Willie as he steps out of his car and stands at his driver's door.

"You doin' the Lord's work today," says Hortense, with a chuckle.

"I sho' is," says Mr. Willie.

∞CR

"With those two invitations we've left at the front doors of the people not at home and the others we've delivered, we should be finished in another thirty to forty minutes, Mr. Willie," says Hattie.

"Do you have any of those invites still hangin' on?" asks Octavia. "I can walk them through the neighborhood tomorrow mornin'."

"The ones I'll have left over after this afternoon will be the ones I have to put in people's hands—when I see them—like Hempstead when he arrives from Atlanta, Geneva, Velma, Eugene and a few others who will come by the house tonight or tomorrow. Thanks for the offer, however," says Hattie.

As the women conclude their neighborhood odyssey, Mr. Willie says, with great deference, "I'll drop you off at your home first Miss Octavia, then I'll take Miss Hattie on home."

"Mr. Willie, we couldn't have done this without your help. You are such an asset to our little hamlet here, that we call Fernwood. You are always so willing to make yourself available to everyone—with your ice service and your jitney service. We just appreciate you so much. On behalf of the Carpenter and Martin families, we want you to be one of the guests at the wedding on Saturday, the twenty-fifth," says Hattie, almost as if she is about to hand him a special, written proclamation.

Mr. Willie tries to contain his emotions as he reaches for the invitation Hattie is handing him over the front seat of the car.

"Oh, Miss Hattie. I be so honored to git this im-ba-tation. This go be so special ta' me ta' come to de weddin'."

There is silence between the three of them as Mr. Willie opens the envelope. He says nothing. He mumbles to himself as he observes and attempts to read the fancy calligraphy writing that tells every recipient, YOU'RE INVITED.

207

Chapter 18

Last Minute Oddments

Early Monday morning, March 20th, even before Nora has come downstairs dressed and ready to go to Fernwood Elementary School—after taking a week off to attend to the wedding—Claudine and Hattie are in their nurse's uniforms and preparing to leave for the day.

Claudine reminds Marilyn, "Don't forget Hattie and I are taking Thursday afternoon and Friday off. We put in those requests when Nora and Jasper told us their wedding date. I pray there won't be any community emergencies, and we get bogged down on Thursday." Then she and Hattie gather their purses to leave the house.

∞Ωβ

Marilyn opens a cabinet drawer and pulls out a handmade binder with a jagged-edged hole on one of the top corners. The binder has lined cornbread paper held together with a piece of thin, rolled hemp running through the hole and tied in a knot. She eases herself into one of the kitchen table chairs and begins to read in a soft whisper the writing on the second page. It really is what she told Nora and Claudine last week about how she plans to manage the food preparation and presentation. Marilyn is anxious for everything she is responsible for to come off without a hitch. She is expecting all helping hands to follow her lead in the two to three days leading up to the wedding ceremony.

Marilyn's concentration is broken when Nora sits at the table to quickly finish the last of a biscuit and the last gulp of coffee. Grabbing her jacket, her purse and her school satchel she takes an apple from the fruit bowl on the table.

Marilyn, talking to herself, says, "Oh, these are my notes or directions to keep all my one-hundred and one details sorted out. It's a lot to remember, and a lot of folks offering to do little tasks here and little tasks there. It's enough to make you dizzy."

"This is your strong suit, Aunt Marilyn. I mean managing all these serving details to get your delicious food into everyone's stomach. People pay good money to outside helpers to work with them to pull off pretty weddings. My new friend, Abigail, who lives in Atlanta says her mother had a lot of help with her wedding and she still could have used more. After you show out on Saturday, folks may want to hire you to help them with a family wedding. Who knows?" asks Nora, stroking her aunt's ego.

"All of us aunts may need to check into Cloverdale Hospital's basement after Saturday. We will be worn out," sighs Marilyn.

"You don't know how much I love what you, Aunt Hattie and Aunt Claudine are doing for me, or better yet for us—me and Jasper," Nora says, in an endearing tone.

"Honey, you are our sister Clementine's baby. This is what we are suppose to do. This is what we want to do for you," says Marilyn, in a soft and out-of-character manner.

"How can I ever repay my three wonderful Aunts?" asks Nora.

"Who is saying anything about pay back?" Marilyn asks, with furrowed eyebrows as Nora waves and steps out the door.

೩つೞ

"Eugene, do you think I can survive the cost of this wedding ring I'm about to buy?" asks Jasper, as they approach Goldstein's jewelers in downtown Macon.

Eugene, with an uncertain expression responds, "Do you think Geneva is right when she says she and Nora have the same size hands and she gave you the right information about Nora's ring size?"

"I sure hope so. Maybe I should have brought Geneva down here with us to try it on," Jasper says, in a tentative tone.

"Naw, man. You don't want the bride's best friend to wear her ring before she does. That don't seem right to me," Eugene speculates.

"Do we know what the hell we are doing, as far as picking out a small diamond ring?" asks Jasper, sounding confused.

"You know old man Goldstein. He's a jeweler. He might try to take us on a ride," Eugene says as if he's talking to himself.

"I probably should have bought this darn ring in Atlanta," concludes Jasper, as he warily reaches for the door.

ৡৃ০৪

"What are you two colored gentlemen interested in seeing today?" asks Silas Goldstein, looking over the rims of his glasses.

"I want to see some of your not-too-expensive wedding rings," says Jasper, in a not very confident tone.

"Is this an engagement ring or a first ring for the bride to be?" asks Goldstein, having not moved one step.

"I did not give my intended an engagement ring. We decided to wait and be able to afford to pay a little more for a ring closer to our wedding day," responds Jasper.

"I see. Well, what is your budget? And do you know your lady friend's ring size?" asks Goldstein, as he looks over at Eugene who is gawking at the ring display cases.

"Well, I want something pretty, but kind of small—a small diamond that is. She is young. Her ring size, for the ring finger is a size four. We are more interested in trying to save for a home in a short period of time rather than spend too much on a ring," says Jasper, as if reciting a rehearsed script.

"Let me show you what I have that is moderately priced. What kind of job do you have?" asks the jeweler.

"He's in the Army," blurts out Eugene.

"I was drafted, Sir. I recently finished basic training and I'm waiting on new orders. And I'm also a professional musician. I play in large and small orchestras here in Macon, and in cities like Savannah, Atlanta—ah Birmingham," says Jasper, with his voice trailing off.

"I see," says Goldstein. "Can you pay me the full price today? Once a soldier leaves town on new orders, we jewelers get nervous if he still owes money. Of course, I have a very fair payment plan for Uncle Sam's folks. And I don't charge the colored more interest than I charge the white boys. And that's the honest truth," states Goldstein, in a very assertive fashion.

"Let me see what looks pretty to me in my price range. Then you can tell me exactly what each set costs," says Jasper.

"Okay, let's walk over here to this case," Goldstein says, as he leads Jasper across the small store, with Eugene following close behind.

At this point, a younger white man comes from behind a draped door to stand beside Goldstein.

"What about a silver band with a small diamond in the center and two little diamonds on each side? If your eyes are not so strong, you may miss the two little ones. But it's a pretty little ring. There are other styles, for instance, such as three pin-head diamonds of equal size. The first set will cost you ninety-five dollars. It's total diamond weight is about .025 carats. The second set will run you about sixty dollars," advises Goldstein.

"Let me walk around for a few minutes," says Jasper. "Would you have most of these rings in my price range in a size four and I could walk out with the set in a pretty ring box this afternoon?" Jasper continues inquiring.

"Oh yes, you can walk out with the rings today. Just asking for cash on the spot. The best way to do business. No strings attached, no dust left on the floor," Goldstein says, now more animated.

"Marion, get the polishing cloth out and my sales receipt book from the desk. Would you, please?" Goldstein asks of the assistant, who looks to be about twenty-five years old.

Eugene and Jasper circle two small cases of rings as they talk in low tones, occasionally pause to point at a set, then repeat the process.

"My friend thinks he has made up his mind," Eugene says, after they've spent about thirty minutes in the store.

"Yes," says Jasper. "I like the very first set of rings you showed me—the set right there, he says, pointing to the rings in the case.

Chapter 19

The Countdown

Jasper drives to the Carpenter's home a few hours after purchasing the wedding rings and after Nora gets home from school. He doesn't tell Nora the good news. They sit in the parlor, holding hands, talking and giggling and occasionally sneaking a kiss as if it's a taboo act—just days before marrying.

"Nora, I have some good news to tell you. I got the three thousand dollars my Uncle Ralph willed me. It has been a bit of a struggle. The Atlanta bank, where I had to draw on the funds, didn't believe I was legitimate, even with the document I sent you from Kansas. They didn't have a picture of my Uncle Ralph so they jumped to conclusions before reading the fine print. It said clearly *'a colored man of fifty-seven years old'* and so on. My full name was clearly written in as the beneficiary and my kinship to Uncle Ralph stated," Jasper concludes, without realizing Nora is dabbing tears as he tells her of the entanglements.

"Jasper, this means we don't have to start out worrying about financial struggles or emergencies as newlyweds. But, of course, your inheritance is nobody's business—other than your mother knowing," Nora suggests, between sniffles.

"Ellis Walker put me in touch with a good lawyer in Atlanta, a Jewish man. He helped me get through the red tape. His fee was reasonable, too. He also helped me set up a savings account that helps our money earn what is called compound interest. And we're going to try to save on top of that money too. He immediately suggested I add an extra statement about you being the sole beneficiary. That's the key word—sole. That's if I should die before my time," Jasper says, in a military-type of cadence.

"Oh hush, Jasper. You're going to make me start weeping again. I don't know why my emotions are so delicate these days," says Nora, in a puzzled tone.

"Oh, I know why," Jasper says in an authoritative voice. "It's because you are about to become Mrs. Jasper Leonard Martin and that means your heart, your mind, your baby-making engine and all that other stuff is getting revved up. Miss Carpenter, in only a few more days, you are about to go on the ride of your young life. We are going to have such a good life, full of fun and babies and our own nice home—and—and—you just wait!" Jasper says, as if running out of good things to suggest.

"First of all Uncle Sam needs to let us know if we're going to be lucky enough to be assigned stateside. This waiting is working my last nerve," Nora chuckles. "I've heard your mother use that phrase."

After talking a bit longer and embracing while watching the setting sun from the front window, Jasper stands to leave. "Why don't we go out to the country for an early dinner tomorrow. I know this little shack of a restaurant where the owner can give your Aunt Marilyn a run for her money when it comes to rattlin' those pots and pans. What you say?" asks Jasper, looking down as Nora remains seated on the sofa.

"What day is tomorrow?" asks Nora.

"You've got to be pulling my leg," chuckles Jasper. "I know you are in the countdown phase, Miss Carpenter. Just waiting on Saturday to come. Tomorrow is Tuesday!"

"Is four in the afternoon a good time to pick me up?" asks Nora.

"As good as any," says Jasper, in an upbeat tone.

‮ℬℭ‭

"I'm here to ask for the hand of Miss Carpenter, to be my dinner companion this evening," says Jasper to Aunt Hattie, as he stands on the front stoop shortly after four o'clock Tuesday afternoon.

"Won't you step inside for a—

"Oh, here I am, Jasper!" says a bouncy and bubbly Nora, cutting Aunt Hattie off mid-sentence.

"Nora, girl, you are getting prettier by the day. Ain't no more pretty to find between now and Saturday. You have just about emptied the bank's 'pretty vault,'" says Jasper, as he eyes Nora in her cardigan and corduroy pants.

"Oh, my goodness. You two love birds go on out to the country. Now Nora, don't you brag too much on Miss Lizzie's cooking when you come back. You know how Marilyn thinks she's the queen of cooks in these parts," Hattie reminds Nora.

"You know I'll be tongue-tied about that when I get back," laughs Nora.

‮ℬℭ‭

It's a beautiful afternoon for a drive out in the country. Jasper and Nora pass few other cars, but they do compete with some horse-drawn carriages crossing from one stretch of farm land to another stretch across the roadway. Courteous drivers, of autos or carriages, know to be sensitive to horses being spooked by sudden loud noises.

"Oh, this air is so refreshing," says Nora, as she leans out the open window. "It does make me keep my kerchief tight under my chin, however."

"We're almost there. I can't quite remember the name, but it's right around the bend about a quarter of a mile further up the road," says Jasper. He is enjoying the fresh breeze as much as Nora on this mild afternoon.

"Is that it?" asks Nora, pointing out the windshield to a slightly-faded, Robin's-egg-blue hut. On the front of the structure a sign reads *Miss Lizzie's Food Shack*.

"Yes, that's the restaurant if you want to call it that," says Jasper as he puts his left arm out to turn up the bumpy lane.

"Whew, we made it," says Nora.

"Let's roll up the windows before too much dust settles inside the car," says Jasper.

There is an old bicycle leaning against the base of a large tree, a carriage with a horse hitched to a post, and an old Model-T looking car. Jasper holds the car door for Nora as she steps out and smooths the front of each leg of her pants with one hand. "This looks like an adventure to me," says Nora, in a young girl's voice.

"Oh, you'll get a kick out of this," says Jasper.

⁎⁎⁎

"Hey, how you been, Mr. Saxophone man? Ain't seen you in these parts in a month of Sundays," says a stout, aging beauty with her silky hair pulled up in a bun.

"Hey, Miss Lizzie. It has been a while. You're looking well. This is my fiancée until this Saturday when we tie the knot."

"Oh my Lord! Child, what's yo' name? You 'bout as pretty as they come. And you go give your life to this roving musician who barely got roots in Macon?" pumps Miss Lizzie, with a mouthful of questions and opinions.

"I'm Nora Carpenter, Miss Lizzie. And I feel so blessed to be able to finally get this man to cut his Mother's apron strings and ride into the sunset with me," chuckles Nora, in a good natured tone.

"No, I'm the one who's blessed. Miss Lizzie, you don't know that I was drafted back in January and just finished my basic training earlier this month. Nora's sweet letters and our blooming romance kept me going while I was in Kansas. I'm waiting on my new orders which should come any day now," Jasper concludes.

"I'm certain you didn't drive out here only to tell me about your wedding this weekend. Folks comin' this way want to eat some of my vittles. Come on back here close to the kitchen so you can see me take two fresh muffin pans of corn muffins out of the oven and serve up a delicious dinner for just the two of you. My other customers are about ready to pay up and leave," notes Miss Lizzie, as she looks back and scans the booths they just passed.

"We'll just sit right here where the aromas are making my mouth water," says Jasper, as he points to a booth for Nora to slide into.

"Lucy, come on out from back there and work the register for a few minutes. A couple of the customers are about ready to leave," shouts Miss Lizzie, to one of her kitchen employees. "I got a special engagement dinner on order."

ℰℴℭℛ

"Miss Lizzie, if you bring another plate with hot muffins on it, I'm going to pop. I've had three muffins already along with your pork chops, corned beef hash and mashed potatoes. And your fried apples were just right. I know why Jasper was anxious to come back out here," explains Nora, after raving over the delicious dinner.

"You can see why your Aunt Hattie doesn't want you to upset Miss Marilyn. You can't brag about this food when you go back to the house of the Carpenter women. Nora was reared by three of her deceased Mother's sisters, Miss Lizzie, and one of them is a fine cook herself," says Jasper, forgetting his manners and talking with a half-full mouth.

"Oh, I understand, and I think I remember hearing about those Carpenter ladies—all of them nurses in Macon—who adopted their niece some twenty odd years ago. Oh, I know your story Miss Nora. You know how good news—mixed with a little sad news—gets talked about 'round these parts. So you really grew up with *not one*, but three mothers," concludes Miss Lizzie, as if she has unearthed, for the first time, some long-lost secret.

"Tell me about trying to listen to three would-be Nuns as a

217

young child. They loved me too much at times and would hardly let me breathe. But I think I turned out all right because everything they tried to do was for my benefit," Nora says, in reflective appreciation.

"You turned out perfect," says Jasper, with an enough-is-enough expression in his eyes.

He is so relieved when Nora asks Miss Lizzie where the ladies' restroom is located.

ဆဩ

"I'm so happy Nora left the table. I've been trying to see how I could quickly ask you if you still have that pretty little cottage, further back on your property, you rent out as a romantic get-away. And, if it's available, can we come here on Saturday night after our guests leave the wedding reception?" asks Jasper, in a hushed, but brisk, manner. "I need to know quickly before Nora comes back to the booth," he says.

"Boy, why you waitin' until the last minute? You must be livin' right, because you have just lucked out! The little cottage is vacant this weekend. It's all clean, pretty and waiting for the next guests. And now it's going to be Mr. Saxophone Man and his new bride. Hot Dog!" says Miss Lizzie, with excitement and in a too-loud voice.

"Do you want me to pay you in advance?" Jasper asks, in a hurried manner.

"Naw, you can pay me on your way out on Sunday night or Monday morning," she smiles, in a wicked half-smile. "I love seeing the groom leave after a day or two of honeymooning. I don't always see the new bride, some are still a little shy about the goings-on and already in the car or carriage. But the groom has to settle up the bill and hand over the key. I wouldn't miss seeing that look. Funny thing though. You can sometimes feel when the marriage ain't going to settle in too good. It's just a gut feeling after bein' in this business for so many years, yes sir-ree,"the old, owl-of-a-businesswoman says.

ဆဩ

"I'm sorry. I decided to take my hair clamp out and do my hair over. The wind got in it a bit on the drive out. Plus I needed more color on my lips and my nose dabbed with my puff. I didn't mean to take so long," Nora apologizes.

"Oh, sweetheart, you don't need to apologize. Miss Lizzie and I had a chance to talk about a few years ago when she had time to come to the Elks Club more often. She says she misses hearing the music and seeing the guests dancing. This was before your aunts let you out of prison to come to any of the fun spots," Jasper says, with a chuckle.

"Don't rub it in Mr. Martin," Nora warns.

"Well, we'd better pay up and get on back to town," says Jasper.

"Oh, no. This dinner is on the house," says the restaurant owner. "I think I see a match made in heaven," Miss Lizzie continues, as she nods her head.

‽)(‽

"Hi, Mrs. Martin. Jasper says you want me to see your dress you bought for the wedding. I hope I'm not surprising you by coming unannounced," says Nora, as Jasper holds the door for Nora to walk into the parlor.

"Hey, Miss Nora. No, you not surprising me. Jasper kind-a hinted you two might come by after drivin' back to Macon. I know you don't need no food since you just ate dinner. So ain't no reason for me ta' act all phony and say, can I get you somethin' ta eat?" Octavia says, with no apology. "Honey, come on back to my bedroom where I have the dress hanging," Octavia instructs, as she gestures the direction with her head.

"I'll read the newspaper I picked up this morning as you two ladies do what you need to do," says Jasper, as he heads to the kitchen table.

"Come on in, this bedroom that ain't too spay-shus, but I manage to move around in it okay. Now you know'd Jasper wanted to drive me to Atlanta ta look for a dress. But I went to Marguerite's, and she had this light lavender dress that I liked right off the bat. She say it's a pretty com-pa-liment to the shades of pink your aunts go wear—and them two bridal maids. I hope you like it 'cause it be a tad late now to change it," Octavia says, as she rotates the dress on its hanger, 360-degrees, a couple of times.

"Oh, Mrs. Martin, it's perfect!" says Nora, in an indisputably truthful tone.

"Do you *really* like it?" asks Octavia, with uncharacteristic humbleness.

"Yes, I would not be dishonest about something so important to me and Jasper. The style and the color will look wonderful on you and are so complimentary of your smooth, pretty skin tone and your nicely shaped figure," Nora assures Octavia.

Octavia's eyes brighten and she displays a toothy grin, which is rare for the take-no-prisoner personality she often engages, with honor.

"You don't know what a relief this be to me. I don't care 'bout nobody else and their opinion—not even my know-it-all, nosy lady friends. You hear me?" Octavia asks, triumphantly.

"I'm so pleased about your good taste and judgment," Nora continues to emphasize her pleasure.

"Hey, Jasper," Octavia calls out in a loud voice. "She like my dress."

Jasper rushes into the bedroom with a closed-mouth smile, but beaming eyes. He looks at Octavia's dress as she continues to hold it aloft. "I told you Nora would really like your dress. Mother, don't you think I know a thing or two about the lady I'm going to marry in four days?" Jasper asks.

☙❧

"Jasper, you know Mr. Saunders, my Principal, gave me the next three days off as well. So, Velma and I need to go to Marguerite's to

220

pick up a couple of items for Saturday. Miss Jocelyn ordered them from Atlanta. Velma is expecting me over to her house sometime this morning so why don't you just drop me off there. After Velma dresses we can walk downtown," Nora concludes, outlining her rest-of-the-morning itinerary.

"Nora, why don't I drive you and Velma the six to seven blocks downtown? You know her house is closer than your house to Marguerite's shop. I don't want you wearing yourself out before Saturday," Jasper says, with genuine concern.

"You know how strong and steady I am on my feet. Plus, I need to walk off that huge dinner we enjoyed last night at Miss Lizzie's place," Nora says, as if Jasper has forgotten about their over-indulgence.

"Okay, if you insist. I can use my morning to try to catch up with my second groomsman, June Bug or Tommy Collins, as you know him," Jasper says. "Also, I need to swing by little Buster Brown's house to make sure his Mama has everything under control for this weekend."

"Buster Brown is the person to worry about controlling. That kid just has old folks' opinions and ways," Nora sighs. "And don't forget to remind them, and everyone in the wedding, to come to Friday night's seven o'clock rehearsal in our backyard," Nora reminds Jasper.

"What else can I help with later in the day, around three or four o'clock?" asks Jasper.

"Aunt Hattie has a few people who keep asking her for an invitation to the wedding. I think she wants to deliver four or five more to some last minute people the family is inviting. Why don't you drop over to the house and ask if you can drive her," Nora suggests.

"It's a chore I would love to take care of," answers Jasper, in an upbeat tone.

Chapter 20

The Rehearsal

"Oh, my goodness! Look at these heavy rain showers this morning," says Claudine, in apparent alarm. She is standing and looking out the kitchen window at the backyard. "I was here at the kitchen table and in my bedroom at my sewing machine until about 1:00 AM, trying to put the finishing touches on our dresses for the wedding. So glad I started sewing time Nora hinted at a wedding on the horizon," Claudine says.

"This Wednesday morning rain is good for today. It will give the grass and my budding, young flowers some much needed water," says Marilyn. "But, Lord forbid, I don't want to see a drop of rain on Friday or Saturday," she sighs.

"Hattie, come on down here," Claudine shouts up the stairs from the short hallway, where she has walked from the kitchen. "You're not going to even have time for your coffee and a couple o' bites of fruit or a biscuit," she says, in a half-scolding voice.

Marilyn, mumbling under her breath, says, "She and her determination about them fancy invitations. Heck, she's all worn out and frazzled."

Hattie rushes into the kitchen right on Claudine's heels, "Whew, I had to wake Nora to tell her about handing out yesterday's last invitations. I'm a bit tired this morning. But after we rush through the rain and get over to the hospital, I'll be fine," Hattie announces, sounding a bit winded.

THE DEBT

Nora comes downstairs two hours or so later when Aunt Marilyn shouts up to her, "You've got a Western Union that just came."

In an excited, but first-words-of-the-morning raspy voice, Nora says, reaching for the telegram, "Who in the world would be sending me a telegram?"

"Open it and let's see," says Marilyn, in a rushed and curious voice. She hands it to Nora.

Tearing the envelope open, Nora reads in silence.

"Well, who is it?" barks Marilyn.

"It's Cynthia Sinclair. My new friend who lives in Atlanta. She is Miss Turner's niece," says Nora, in a slow and contemplating manner.

"Well, what is she saying in that telegram?" asks Marilyn, with some urgency.

"It's nothing earth-shaking. She's saying and apologizing at the same time. Her mother wants to come with her to my wedding," says Nora, sounding a bit surprised.

"Oh, here they come! The last-minute people, inviting themselves to a wedding they really have no business coming to," says Marilyn, almost sounding happy to have something to complain about.

"Is this going to be a problem with the food or the number of chairs? If so, Jasper and his friend, Eugene, can help you figure it out," responds Nora, in a that-solves-that tone of voice.

"Oh *now*, I remember what's going on. This Cynthia lady is Eugene's new girlfriend. The one who got *herself* invited at the last minute," says Marilyn, in a caustic voice.

"Oh, Aunt Marilyn. Can we not be so negative this week—the last few days leading up to my wedding?" asks Nora, wearily.

"Honey, you're just young and don't know nosy, colored women like I do. We got her, on top of Octavia's three nosy friends and a few other busy-bodies," says Marilyn, with some resignation in her voice.

ℬℭ

The items on everyone's previously written to-do list are being checked off all over the community—the last three days—as those involved prepare for Nora and Jasper's big day.

Nora has everything she needs for Saturday. Geneva and Velma are shampooing and styling her hair Friday night after the wedding rehearsal. They are as good as the top, colored stylist at Carol Jean's Beauty Salon. Geneva and Velma's pink dresses have been ready for a week or so.

The flower girl, Candy Jenkins, who will be coupled with Buster Brown has her white dress at the ready.

Jasper and his groomsmen are ready with their attire. Buster Brown's mother and father are excited about his participation so they have everything in order for him. Eugene is helping Jasper with some of the last-minute errands on Thursday and Friday that call for driving around to pick up borrowed items. They also have a trumpeter, a bassist and a flautist to accompany the soprano saxophone man. Ellis Walker is helping with rounding up the four musicians who have to leave the ceremony around 8:30 PM for the Elks Club show.

The aunts are excited and working and buzzing like bees in a bee hive. Claudine finishes all three dresses and the two sisters seem to be pleased—or so they are saying. They all plan to work with their soft and manageable hair themselves—a couple of hours before their guests start to arrive.

Octavia is getting her hair coiffed at Carol Jean's. She is allowing herself this rare grooming treat. Her friend Betsy Butler will clip and paint her nails and put a smidgen of make-up on her at the Martin's home.

Reverend Simpson has invited himself over to the Carpenter

home a couple of times in recent days to repeat, "I'm ready for the big day!" He also lingers to see if Aunt Marilyn will offer him a snack before he moves on with his duties.

And, as if Nora's cake needed more icing, her "adopted" Uncle Hempstead sent her a telegram on Thursday, saying he would be arriving in Macon on Friday afternoon.

ഇറ

Members of the wedding party start arriving at the Carpenter's home around 6:30 PM on Friday evening. It has not rained since mid-morning Wednesday, and the lawn with its bordering shrubs and newly-planted flowers is in tip-top shape.

Claudine has borrowed a second, tall, curved trellis to serve as the side-lawn entranceway to the backyard. It is draped with long, green vines. She will have some of the church volunteers place long-stemmed white and pink flowers purchased from the colored florist all through the vines. This is to be done about an hour before the ceremony is set to begin on Saturday. The Carpenter's own identical white trellis—Nora's wish—will be decorated with white flowers and streamers. Jocelyn Turner is helping with the planning and ribbons.

As the rehearsal crowd has gathered, some begin commenting on how lovely they know the back will look come Saturday afternoon. It is obvious Claudine has put a lot of thought and effort into the backyard decorations. The white church chairs and a half dozen circular tables are in place. About four lovely, white wicker chairs have been strategically placed.

Mrs. Martin's friends surprised the Carpenter sisters by announcing on Tuesday they would bring fresh baked cookies and jugs of lemonade for the rehearsal crowd. Marilyn couldn't miss the opportunity to say, "They just want to see what the rehearsal will tell them about the wedding." Of course, she was reluctant to admit this was a big help to her.

THE DEBT

Claudine walks out back from the kitchen door with her tablet in hand and loudly greets the people gathered. Nora and Jasper come out behind her, smiling and holding hands. The wedding party participants begin to say hello—almost in unison.

The family martinet, Miss Claudine, begins. "What we are going to do tonight is just run-through what everyone is suppose to do tomorrow and where you should be standing when you perform your duties," Claudine says, in a firm voice. "Thank you all for coming over. This won't take long at all. I see you've been enjoying the nice refreshments donated by Mrs. Jenkins, Wilkins and Butler. I and my sisters appreciate the kind gesture," she says, in a genuine tone.

"A small riser for the four musicians will be over to the side of the wedding party," begins Claudette, as she points to the spot. "They will serenade you for a short time before the ceremony begins. Then the last bit will be Reverend Simpson coming and standing in front of the altar as the flower girl and ring bearer come from the side door here. The flower girl will begin to drop white petals here around the altar, then with a second basket begin to drop pink petals on the ground between the chairs on both sides of the lawn. That will be the imaginary aisle where the married couple will walk to the back of the lawn at the end of the ceremony. The bride will eventually toss her bouquet to some young hopefuls from that position as she and Jasper greet all of you," says Claudine. "Are there any questions so far?" she asks. No one says a thing.

She continues, "Once the wedding starts, the two bridesmaids will be escorted out the side kitchen door by the two groomsmen, across the lawn to this point—several feet in front of the riser. They will walk to the left, around the curved trellis, NOT under it. That's your left—the guests' left."

"Then the groomsmen will walk toward the trellis then stop just right of it, where they will be positioned. The groom will also walk out the back door here. They are all coming from the kitchen area. He will stand in front of the first groomsman, but under the trellis. Nora will have been upstairs with her Aunt Hattie and her bridesmaids getting dressed. At *no time* will she or the groom come in contact with each other before they meet here at the altar—which is under this flower-decked trellis."

"Nora's *adopted* Uncle Hempstead will escort her here to meet the waiting groom. He will then walk to his waiting seat on the front row. He should be here with us now to rehearse, but he's running a bit late, it seems," Claudine pauses for the first time and puckers her lips with an expression of wonder in her eyes.

"Okay, let's have the entire wedding party go back in the house. Nora you, Geneva, Velma and Hattie go upstairs like you will be tomorrow as you get dressed. Lucy Rivers, from Marguerite's Bridal shop, will be with you tomorrow upstairs. Make sure you close those bedroom doors—tonight and tomorrow. All other participants will be in the dining room area and in the kitchen. Mrs. Jocelyn Turner will be in charge of having everyone lined up and coming out at the right time. Does everyone understand this?" Claudine asks, in a booming, but lady-like voice.

"Just for practicing the ceremony tonight, Henry Turner is going to hum and maybe sing a few notes of the wedding song. He has a strong and wonderful voice so you won't have trouble hearing him as he stands near the riser."

"Okay, Miss Jocelyn, your turn to do the directing. Follow her into the house everybody," Claudine says, in passing the torch.

The nine participants, minus the four musicians follow Jocelyn Turner through the side kitchen door.

ഇൻ

The wedding party goes through the paces three times, with a few glitches here and there. Everyone seems pretty relaxed and comfortable when Claudine says, "Okay, I think we got it down enough. We aren't trying to be all perfect and everything tomorrow. We want joy, happiness and fun to be the most important things in this union, starting out. Take some of those delicious cookies with you as you leave."

"I want everyone in place here in the house at a quarter of four—no later. Some of you will come just about fully dressed, others will have to change real quick in my bathroom here on the bottom level. Only Nora, and her two bridesmaids should be the people going through the entire dressing routine. It's been in the mid-seventies most of this week—so five o'clock tomorrow shouldn't be too uncomfortable inside the house. We borrowed two more fans to add to our one fan so we can circulate some cool air where you all in the party will be gathering. Sure hope we don't blow no fuses," Claudine adds, as an after-thought.

"You know the large trees outside will keep most of the seated area shaded so I'm hoping for a somewhat comfortable affair tomorrow. Thanks for coming everybody. See you tomorrow!" Claudine raises her forearm and sweeps it across her torso as she waves good-bye.

಄಄಄

Back in the kitchen Nora raises her concern about Uncle Hempstead's where-abouts. "I got a Western Union from him saying he would get in town this afternoon. He always usually keeps his word about important things, doesn't he, Aunt Claudine?" asks Nora, obviously perplexed.

"Honey, you are asking me about the attitudes of somebody I haven't been around in years," Claudine says, somewhat dismissively.

Jasper jumps in and tries to sound reassuring, "Nora, if he gave you his word, he'll be here. He's just hours off-schedule.

"Well who, at the last minute could we ask to step in?" Marilyn asks, with a snarled and disgusted look on her face.

"What about Deacon Jackson at the church. Nora loved his

Sunday school classes as a youngster and how he sometimes shared Sunday dinners with us before he moved away and then returned some years later," ventures Aunt Hattie. "I did add him to the guest list on my last hand-outs."

"I don't really know the gentleman," says Jasper, "but I'd be willing to drive over to his house if you tell me where he lives and ask him to be on stand-by. Miss Hattie would you go with me?" Jasper asks, as serious as he has ever sounded.

"Let's just wait a little longer and see if Hempstead gets here. I remember him as a truly dependable man who stands by his word," says Hattie.

"It's approaching nine o'clock and I know John Hempstead is real careful about being on the highway by himself too late, after it gets dark in these parts," Claudine suddenly recalls. "Of course, he's shrewd like an old, wise fox. He's fine. He's just operating on colored people's time tonight," Claudine smirks.

She achieves exactly what she intended. She gets a laugh around the kitchen table out of the "colored people's time" remarks.

Marilyn takes a large pitcher of apple cider out of the ice box and asks who wants some. Only Claudine opens her mouth to respond. Nora excuses herself and says she'll be right back. She runs up the stairs and closes her bedroom door. Jasper looks behind Nora and shifts in his chair.

"I think Nora is truly starting to worry about Mr. Hempstead," says Jasper. "She has told me quite a bit about how much he means to her, and her memories of him in her life when she was a child. I wouldn't be surprised if she wasn't on the verge of tears right now," Jasper surmises, in a low and serious tone.

"Oh she is just busying herself to be distracted while we wait. Nora is in a hurry for tomorrow to get here," chuckles Marilyn.

The three sisters and Jasper make rather uneasy small talk waiting to see if Nora will come back downstairs.

"Miss Hattie, let's just drive on over to Deacon Jackson's house. It's getting late and we are already half-way disrespecting him by asking him to be a last-minute stand-in tomorrow. What do you say?" Jasper asks.

"I'll go upstairs and get my purse and my tablet of addresses so we will drive to the right house. While I'm up there, I'll tell Nora what we plan to do. Do you have a good flash light in your car? You know how dark some of the streets are around this neighborhood at night," Hattie reminds Jasper.

Hattie rushes out of the kitchen, saying back over her shoulder.,"It won't take me but a couple of minutes, and I'll be back down.

Jasper stands and walks to the side door to look out on the dark and half decorated yard. It is awaiting the late morning rush of friends and volunteers to put the rest of the borrowed lawn furniture in place. The positioned tables and table linens will be covered with fresh, clean white sheets until the last minute—just to keep small flying insects at bay. Jasper stands silent as Marilyn and Claudine open and close cabinet doors and Marilyn peers into the crowded ice box.

Hattie rushes back down the stairs, slightly winded and says, "That child is up there on the verge of tears. She is so worried. Jasper, let's just go and come back quickly with an agreement from the Deacon to help. This will help calm Nora's nerves."

"But I think I should speak with her first," he insists.

"No, she knows we need to get going. She understands it's getting late," Hattie insists.

Claudine says,"Marilyn and I will go up there right now and reassure her. You two go, just go."

℗ℤ℞

Jasper's DeSoto pulls away from the front yard's edge as Marilyn and Claudine sit on Nora's bed watching her peer out of her

230

bedroom window at the car.

Before they can say anything, Nora blurts out, "Why would Uncle Hempstead leave Atlanta so late heading down here and miss the rehearsal? Now, we don't know whether to be angry or worried," Nora concludes, as she walks slowly toward her bed.

"Honey, most men are so not thoughtful when it comes to—" Marilyn stops abruptly as Claudine's elbow jabs her in her side.

"No bad mouthing anybody tonight, Marilyn," Claudine says forcefully, as if scolding a much younger person.

"Oh please, you two. Let's not make things any worst," pleads Nora.

"I sure wish I had some of Octavia's old bug juice by now," says Claudine. "It would calm my nerves right through here."

The three women are silent for close to a minute just trying to think things through when Marilyn asks, "Wait, wait, do I hear a car's motor out front?"

"Jasper and Aunt Hattie can't be back this soon," says Nora, rushing over to her window and pulling the thin drapes back.

"The car's lights are out and I can't tell if it's Jasper or, or maybe, maybe Uncle Hempstead," Nora shouts.

At breakneck speed, Nora bounds down the stairs with Marilyn and Claudine struggling to increase their speed getting out of the room.

Nora swings the wooden door open and then fumbles to pull the screen door hook up. "Oh, Oooooooh, it's Uncle Hempstead's car. He's here. He's here!" she exudes, like an out-of-control child.

"You wait on us to be sure," yells Claudine, as Nora races ahead down the few steps onto the walkway to the yard's edge.

"Uncle Hempstead, where have you been? Come on and get out of the car. We've been so worried," Nora's torrent of words flow non-stop.

Claudine and Marilyn join Nora at the passenger's door and

they all bend to try to see through the glass. Slowly the car's driver's side door opens, and there is a loud groan and some muttering.

Nora beats the older women getting around to the driver's side. "Uncle Hempstead, what the matter? Come on and get out of your car," Nora urges, innocently.

"Nora honey, something is wrong," says Claudine. "Are you hurt Hempstead? You know we don't have lights on this block yet. It's almost pitch dark out here. We can hardly see you."

"I have a cut over my eye. I can hardly see anything for the bleeding. Step back and let me see if I can get my footing," Hempstead says, slowly.

"I'll grab your arm Uncle Hempstead," says Nora , anxiously.

"No, he needs to have his arms for balance," says Marilyn.

"Oh my Lord. I didn't think I was going to get here tonight. I've been in a struggle with—ouch!" moans the husky and tall Hempstead, as he struggles to get out of his Roadmaster.

He slowly and wobbly stands to his feet. The two older ladies rest his elbows in each of their palms and slowly walk him around the back of his car.

Nora, hyperventilating at this point, sniffles, "I'll get your stuff off the front seat. Do you have your keys so I can lock your doors?"

"Take it easy, Hempstead," Claudine says, with a hint of tenderness in her voice.

"We've got to get you inside and sit you down to see what's going on with your eye and everything else," says Marilyn, with heartfelt concern.

Nora rushes ahead and holds the screen door open. She watches Hempstead move slowly with a slight limp and dried blood under one of his eyes. His sport shirt's top button is dangling and its placket ripped.

"Uncle Hempstead, what happened to you?" asked Nora, innocently.

Marilyn jumps in. "You know Claudine and I know the earmarks of what we're seeing. You ran into some Klansmen or crooked sheriffs on the road, didn't you?" she asked, in an all-knowing tone.

"I'm getting all three of our nurses bags so we can clean your face up and look for bruises and other broken skin," Claudine says, as she rushes off to her bedroom closet.

"They were crazy and as mean as rattle snakes. Two so-called sheriff deputies and then one of their buddies came along and—and decided to join in the fun of striking terror in my heart. They stopped me less than thirty minutes after I drove into Forsyth County. Dammit, I should have taken the longer route around the county," he stammered, with a mix of anger and survivor's disbelief.

"Here, Uncle Hempstead. Just rest your head on the back of this chair and I'll get a clean sheet so you can lie down on the sofa," whispers Nora.

"I am so lucky you women are all nurses in this house—except my sweet little teacher—ooh," moans Hempstead. "I think I got a cut on the side of my tongue."

As Marilyn and Claudine take Hempstead's torn shirt off and begin to gently clean the blood under his left eye and that side of his face, he begins to relax and regain a sense of security. They wash his wounds with iodine, clean three abrasions on a lower arm, determine what has been struck and is now about to bruise. They, together, raise each heavy leg to see if there is sensitivity or wounds beneath his pants.

Just as Nora is going into the kitchen to get a glass of water for Hempstead to dissolve the Bactine powder on his tongue, the ladies hear Jasper and Hattie rush up the pathway. Nora runs to push the screen door open and announces in a loud voice, "He's hurt!"

No one even thinks of asking about Deacon Jackson, but is interested in hearing, through Hempstead's painful recollection what happened to him.

As it turns out he was able to haltingly tell them he was pulled over, off the two-lane highway, in Forsythe County and asked where the hell he was going in his fancy "nigger, show-off" car? He politely told them of his niece's wedding in Macon, and that he had traveled from Atlanta. After showing his papers of ownership, he said he had worked all his life from fifteen years old and did not have to steal this Buick. They mocked and verbally abused him in more ways than he could repeat. One made him empty his pockets of small bills and a few coins. They made him get in the sheriff's car and one of them drove his car in a wild and reckless manner as he watched, handcuffed, from the back seat of the sheriff's car.

When they slammed the cell door closed at the jail house, that's when he started to silently pray. He heard them talking in low tones while he was languishing in the hot cell for over an hour. They were trying to decide what would be his crime. What would they charge him with? Would they keep him there all night? Or call some of their "friends" to come and take him on a joy ride and get him drunk on cheap corn liquor? Then would they leave him in the woods? How would they explain whose fancy car they had in their possession? Hempstead fell asleep on the cell's iron cot in the sweltering heat. But he doesn't know how long he slept because they had taken his watch before shoving him into the cell with one other colored man.

When his jailers finally opened the cell and told him to come on out, he asked about the facilities. They laughed and said, "Nigger, you know where you all go—to your stinking out houses, or are you too high and mighty up there in Atlanta? Huh, Mr. Colored man ? He pointed to an out-house some twenty yards from the jail's back door and said, "There you go."

The two deputies then drove him into the woods, tied him to a tree and took off in his car. "We go see how this here fancy car go handle on da road. Then old Mason here may go buy one of deez for the Mizzes—right Mason?"

234

Hempstead said Mason held his head down like a whipped dog. He was defenseless and subservient to the older, more cruel deputy. They took off in a cloud of dust and came back all juiced up and smelly. Hempstead, in his fear and confusion, could not figure how long they had been gone. They made Hempstead sit in his car for one last time before, "You go meet your Maker," said the senior deputy. He then ordered Hempstead to sit behind his steering wheel. Hempstead remembered him saying something like, "So you can remember da' feel of yo' fancy car when you get to hell." As Hempstead sat there trying to not show his creeping fear, he felt the barrel of a gun behind his head. The older sheriff said, "You know nigger, you got all your coon friends waitin' on your ass in Macon. You not showing up is gonna' cause us mo' trouble than your ass is worth. We just got off probation with the judge for bein' out of line with some of your stupid brotherin' over in the next town. Your number just ain't comin' up today. Lucky you! So you just go on down there and eat all that nigger food, fornicate with all dem' loose colored women and drink yo' seff cross-eyed. You better go the other way when you haul your black bottom back to Atlanta. We may not be so fa-givin' next time!"

Hempstead remembers the sheriff spewing his brand of verbal venom, while the younger deputy paced back and forth in a nervous manner, the menacing deputy leaned in close to the side of Hempstead's face and spat on his jaw. He then pulled his hand back and slammed the butt of the gun into the back of Hempstead's head with such force until his face went toward the steering wheel. His left eye just missed the steering wheel, but his forehead above took the brunt of the blow. Hempstead knew there would be some blood letting as he felt the dizzying sensation of a spinning earth. He sat there, dazed and in pain, for a long while before deciding to drive on to Macon.

"Oh, my Lord, Hempstead! You are a lucky man! Those red

necks could have killed you," Hattie says while audibly exhaling.

"I know, I know," says Hempstead, trying hard to control his emotions. "God was with me on this scary trip."

Marilyn jumps into the conversation and reminds everyone, "You know back about twenty-five years ago, a big mob in Forsythe County started a riot and ran about a thousand colored people clean out of the county. The mob hung about three young colored boys then on some made up charges of rape. We don't never need to forget that bit of sad history right here almost in Macon's backyard."

"This is why Ellis Walker is always reminding us to give ourselves extra time to drive up to Atlanta—so we can go around Forsythe. It's too dangerous!" Jasper says, with his voice rising.

‱

"Well, I'm going to let you sleep here in this front bedroom for tonight," says Claudine. "Is your head feeling any better since you swallowed two packets of the Bactine powder?"

"Nora, sweetie. I'm so glad I will still be able to walk you to the altar tomorrow. This will be my joy that will make me forget all the crap that happened to me today. Nothing else can erase today's nightmare but YOUR WEDDING. God spared me, and for his unbelievable act of mercy, I'm going to try to be a better man and the best Godfather any Martin child could ever have. Do I get an Amen to that?"

"Uncle Hempstead, you may be too sore to get out of bed tomorrow. And all this talk about a better man. You have always been the sweetest and most kind man I have ever met—well, I mean older man. Jasper has taken your place, of course," she says, smiling demurely.

"You truly did receive God's blessing today and we, too, are beneficiaries of his mercy. He spared a kind and decent man. Let us all say a prayer of thanks tonight. And we'll make a decision about who is fit and able in the morning. What do you say about that?" asks

Jasper, with an air of authority.

"Lord, this woman who used to be my wife is going to dislike me all over again for taking her comfortable bed away from her for even one night. You win and luck out in some tight squeezes and then you mess up in some other important areas. Life is so strange and unpredictable. It sure is!"

"Let's close shop for tonight everyone," suggests Jasper. "Tomorrow is a new day and a very promising one at that." Can I help get Mr. John settled before I leave?" asks Jasper.

"No," says Hempstead. "I'm about as happy as a bear about to go into—well, only about eight hours, but go into hibernation. But it will be like going to heaven and back."

ℴ∙ℴ

"With all this worry and excitement tonight, I'm forgetting I will be Miss Carpenter for only ten minutes or so after looking into Jasper's eyes at five o'clock tomorrow."

The aunts look surprised at Nora's burst of bravado. All three are exhibiting expressions of pleasure and long-delayed acceptance, however.

"And now, I'm going to walk my future husband to the door to say good night. It doesn't get any better than this," says Nora, with some sassiness in her tone..

As Jasper leans down to kiss Nora good night out on the stoop, he whispers in her ear, "Oh, you have no idea what *better* is like."

Chapter 21

The Big Day

Marilyn is the first person to stir around six-thirty the next morning. She tips into the kitchen to get the coffee percolator ready on this momentous day—Nora and Jasper's wedding day!

Her thoughts turn to waking everyone else up, but she then realizes maybe she should first tap on Claudine's bedroom door to see if Hempstead is awake. They all know Hempstead's condition will play a big role in Nora's joy. Hell, they even may need to have Hempstead go on the other side of the house and sit out in that big wash tub with some Epsom Salt to relieve his stiffness and sore muscles. Marilyn reminds herself that he went through quite an ordeal. His common sense and age-old survival skills had him fold and tuck his bills inside his socks flat against his arch. The sisters saw this after he struggled, with Hattie's help, to get out of his shoes, stand, put his thin robe over his pants, and wobble to the hallway bathroom. Jasper had thought to ask about Hempstead's luggage as he was about to walk to his car to leave. Everyone realizes the crazy and threatening deputies weren't really trying to steal a piece of luggage or rob Hempstead of all his money. They just wanted to terrorize him and go right to the edge of something more sinister.

Marilyn taps the closed bedroom door with her knuckles.

"Hempstead, oh, Hempstead. Are you awake?"

She could hear Hempstead's soft, non-threatening, pleading voice.

"You don't understand. My niece is getting married tomorrow. I have to walk her to the altar. Pleeeez, I have to get to Macon. Just let me get there for her," Hempstead whimpers, in a voice that exposes a loss of dignity.

"Hempstead, you're having a nightmare! Wake up!" Marilyn shouts through the closed door and rouses the still-sleeping household.

Aunt Hattie rushes to the top of the stairs, looks down and asks, "What's wrong Marilyn? Is Hempstead all right?"

Not stopping beside Aunt Hattie, Nora rushes down the stairs and joins Aunt Marilyn in urging Hempstead to arouse himself and open the door.

"Uncle Hempstead, please come out of the bad dream. It's upsetting you," Nora pleads, as she tugs at the belt of her thin cotton robe.

Hearing the ruffling of the sheets and the squeaking of the bed's foundation, Marilyn and Nora each press one ear to the door as Hempstead begins asking, "Where am I? I don't know whose bed I'm in. Somebody tell me what's going on?"

"Open the door, Hempstead!" Claudine commands, with a tone of impatience, after joining *the hallway club*.

"Oh, my arrrrrm, my leg, my aching face. I don't know where I am. I don't even know if I can walk," Hempstead moans.

"Put the darn robe on because we're coming in Hempstead," Claudine now barks.

The prude of the Aunts, Hattie, shouts out from upstairs.

"Make sure he's dressed before you open the door."

"What he's got, we've all seen before," says Claudine. "That's except our sweet Nora."

"I don't have to go in. I'll go to the kitchen," says an exasperated Nora and mumbling, "What a way to start *my* big day."

ℰℭℛ

Everyone ate a breakfast of hot grits with butter, pork sausage, fresh cut fruit and percolated chickery coffee. Marilyn quickly puts the food together then rushed everyone to finish eating so they could move out of the kitchen. Claudine and Hattie walked on each side of Hempstead, to steady him across the back lawn to the opposite side of the house. Nora had made several trips to the tub with hot water boiled on top of the stove. It was after eight o'clock, and a timeline had to be followed starting mid-morning.

"Aaaaah, this feels good," Hempstead drawls, in a lazy tone. He was talking to himself because the ladies had given him his privacy after turning their heads and clumsily holding each upper arm as he used the two-step utility riser to climb into the tub. He grunted and mumbled sounds of discomfort as he lifted his big hulk of a body.

About half an hour later Eugene is tapping on the Carpenter's front screen door.

"Good Morning, Miss, Miss," Eugene stutters in a juvenile manner.

"I am Nora's Aunt Hattie. I know you are Jasper's best man. What can I help you with this morning, Mr. Eugene?" Hattie asks in a surprised tone.

"Let me apologize for coming so early and unannounced. But Jasper told me, on his way home last night, about Mr. Hempstead's awful trouble driving down. He asked if I would come over to see if I could help you ladies with getting Mr. Hempstead out of bed and maybe helping him take a full bath. Jasper didn't want to risk coming himself. He wants to follow the custom of not seeing the bride on her wedding day. Also, he wants me to let him know this morning if we need to have Deacon Jackson perform Mr. Hempstead's duties," Eugene concludes, after talking non-stop.

"Hempstead is around on the side yard soaking in the big wash tub. He is pretty banged up, but you know he is pretending he's much better this morning. He is determined to try to function. Why don't you go on around the side here—across the back of the house—to the other side. The side you can't see from the street because of all the trees. You can measure his condition this morning and report back to Jasper. I think Hempstead would be ready to tussle with you two men rather than sit out his role as father of the bride," Hattie finishes, making an uncharacteristic smacking sound with her tongue.

ꕥ

Geneva and Velma shampoo and prep Nora's hair for her wedding "do."

After Eugene leaves, Hempstead ambles and limps around the periphery of the backyard, using a walking stick and putting Claudine's special liniment on his bruised and swollen face and stiff joints. Claudine patiently goes over Hempstead's role in the wedding ceremony. He listens carefully, but doesn't walk the paces.

Mr. Willie, Rev. Simpson, and Deacon Jackson stop by the Carpenter home to inquire about Hempstead. Claudine and Hattie politely talk to the concerned men, but they shield Hempstead from any direct contact with them. The sisters believe one of Octavia's lady friends is spreading the information after having heard—from Octavia, via Jasper—about Hempstead's ordeal. If Octavia is found to be the source of the leak, she will undoubtedly be forgiven. Who can suppress the retelling of such an awful and life-threatening drama? The colored community is ever vigilant about such dangerous encounters.

"Lord, have mercy!" pleads Marilyn. "We don't have time for all these well-meaning, concerned neighbors this morning. We've got to put on a wedding!" Marilyn shouts to "the heavens" or whoever is within ear-shot.

ꕥ

Mr. Willie offers to come back a short time later to thoroughly clean the wash tub on the side of the house. Close to the time of the ceremony the wash tub will be filled with some of his blocks of ice to keep large jars of sweet tea, lemonade and spiked punch chilled. Marilyn has given certain ladies money to purchase the items for the beverages, prepare them and deliver the jars at a designated time.

Claudine and Hattie pause to shampoo their hair and pin it up off their necks until it is time to dress for the ceremony. Claudine, whose hair is heavy and more coarse than her sisters' hair, sometimes uses her hot straightening comb to smooth around her edges. Also, she needs to hit the hair at the nape of her neck—which was known as 'the kitchen' in colored communities. Marilyn says the warmth of the day will dry her hair while she is dressing. She doesn't want to stop down for anything as she and Claudine orchestrate the arrival and placement of the extra folding chairs, the placement of the table coverings with clean sheets draped over them to guard against smudges and accidental stains. The vines will be laced through the trellises as they await the arrival of the fresh donated flowers and flower petals. These will come as late as possible and in buckets of cool water and the petals lying in flat white-wicker baskets with damp cotton rags to keep them from wilting. The staging area is the side yard where, earlier, Hempstead soaked undetected. The branches of the large trees create a canopy that shields perishable foods, for short periods, from too much sun.

Marilyn has calculated how much can be carefully placed in their ice box and when it can be taken outside. Quite a bit of the food has been prepared a day ahead, covered as air-tight as possible and waiting in neighbors' ice boxes. As guests, they will quickly go to their homes after the ceremony and return with the prepared food items, already on the designated presentation platters and plates.

⋙⋘

As three o'clock stares the Carpenter ladies in their faces, Claudine reminds everyone in the house that the wedding party has been told to arrive at three forty-five. The three sisters are in the kitchen. Geneva and Velma have been in the house and upstairs with Nora for about ten minutes.

"All right Hattie and Marilyn, you can't start dressing *after* the people get to 1966 Magnolia Street," barks Claudine. "Hempstead has had his bath. He's lying flat on his back on the sofa in the parlor. Poor thing is so tall his calves and feet are resting on the arm of the sofa. I have got to use my bedroom to dress so he can't rest there. If we had been thinking straight, we should have had Eugene drive him and his clothes over to Jasper's house. He could have stretched out and rested there. Jasper, Eugene and what's the other guy's name? They could have helped poor, achy Hempstead get dressed there," concludes Claudine.

Hattie, the ever-proper, social doyenne of the Cloverdale community says, "His name is Tommy Collins."

"There's no problem with Eugene helping Hempstead get dressed when he gets here," concludes Marilyn. "I don't want him dressing upstairs, however. This means he's going to have to get back in your bedroom., Mrs. use-to-be Hempstead," Marilyn chuckles out loud, to both sister's surprise and annoyance.

"Let's not get silly just because you are running on fumes about now, Miss Marilyn," Claudine hits back.

"All of us need to find our second wind so we can get through the rest of the day AND enjoy the festivities," Hattie says, in a calm and dignified manner.

"Okay, we know what we've got to do for our sister's Motherless child. Let's get in high gear—starting right now," Claudine insists.

"What do you think we've been doing for the last three or four weeks?" Marilyn asks, in an agitated tone.

Ignoring the back and forth between her sisters, Hattie says "I'm going upstairs to get dressed. Jocelyn will be here soon, and remember she says she will answer the door."

"I'm right behind you," declares Marilyn. "All is well at 1966 Magnolia Street."

୫୭୧

"You are so calm Miss Nora, which is a good thing, *I guess*, "says Geneva, as she circles around Nora slowly, assessing her demeanor.

"From what I can gather, this is working in her favor *and* our favor," says the less opinionated Velma. "You don't know how many crazy stories I've heard about difficult and demanding brides and how they can make everyone around them miserable."

"Yeah, so far, I guess we've lucked out, Velma," says Geneva.

"Oh, you two have about two more hours with me. There's no telling what kind of witch I might turn into before five o'clock," Nora says, in a teasing and half baiting tone.

"But seriously, I love Jasper so much, and I'm so sure of his love for me. This is why I'm so much at peace. You know this wedding is special and I hope it will be enjoyable for all of the people who are coming to share this day with us. But I could have gone on off with Jasper and not have my family and friends working so hard to do this for us. I'm just so full of gratitude," Nora says, with such sincerity.

"You deserve every bit of all our efforts. I , we—and I'm sure Velma agrees—feel honored to be your very best friends and to be members of the wedding party," proclaims Geneva, as she almost chokes on her words.

"I love you two like you are my sisters. We have known each other so long and even though I may not see you for long stretches of time in the years to come, we will always be bonded," Nora says softly, as her mood shifts and she has begun to pace around.

"Come on. Let's play with Missy's hair and see how we are going to place these fancy pearl barrettes in her up-do," says Velma, as she tries to lighten the tone of the conversation.

"Now you haven't gained four or five pounds in the last week-and-a-half have you?" asks Geneva. "We don't want to have to squeeze you in this dress because Jasper may not know how to get you out of it later," Geneva continues teasing Nora as Velma looks at the pretty white gown hanging on the chifforobe's door.

"Do you know where you guys are going tonight after the wedding?" asks Geneva, prying when maybe she shouldn't be.

"No, he says it's going to be a surprise," says Nora, in a I-give-up- tone. "You don't know how many times I've tried to tease it out of him," Nora chuckles.

Velma runs to the bedroom window. "Stay where you are Nora. It's Jasper and his mother at (looking down at her watch on her wrist) three-forty. Don't come to the window," she says, with a firm voice.

"You think I would deliberately jinx my marriage by disregarding this age-old myth?" Nora asks.

"We don't have much longer before you need to go and jump in the tub again—just to freshen up. Is the fan helping you to stay cool or are you getting warm because of the mounting excitement?" asks Geneva.

"The fan is doing its job. I am as dry as a desert. I hope I can remain this way tonight. I'm more worried about tonight than I am the ceremony," Nora admits.

"Remember what we've told you lately. Just relax. That's what I have read. And it won't hurt so much. Don't look at me like that, Nora. You know I've been a good girl," Geneva says, with a don't-push-me look.

All three of them just burst out laughing at Geneva's dancing around the virginity issue.

₨₩ℓ

Jocelyn Turner rushes to hold the screen door open for Jasper and Octavia Martin. Jocelyn smiles as she sees the excitement in Jasper and Octavia's eyes. She admires how Octavia is exhibiting a calm presence that few have probably seen.

"Mrs. Martin, you are giving that pretty violet dress its proper due. I am so happy you chose it because it's perfect for you. You will get so many compliments. Mark my words," says Jocelyn.

"Pvt. Martin, you look so handsome in your tuxedo and so amazingly cool and calm," says Jocelyn. "I need to bottle your secret for the unruffled husband-to-be. I could put it on the shelf in my shop and sell it. What I also see is a young man who knows his mind and is so firm with his decision. I don't always see this a few hours before a wedding ceremony," Jocelyn concludes, with such certitude.

"Why don't the two of you relax in the parlor, Pvt. Martin. Mr. Hempstead is sitting out back under the shade tree after lying down in the parlor for a stretch. What a horrible ordeal he went through yesterday in Forsythe County," says Jocelyn, who is pleasantly chatty.

"I'll go out and see if he is ready to put his suit on. My assumption is he plans to participate in the ceremony," says Jasper. "I say this because I haven't been told otherwise."

The unusually quiet Octavia chimes in, "It sho' sounds like he took a whuppin' from those two, mad-dog depa-tees. Sho' nuff does.

"Excuse me, I see Lucy at the screen door," says Jocelyn, her voice rising.

"Jasper, I want to go with you to meet Mr. Hempstead. Is this okay?" asks Octavia.

"Let me go and see if he's presentable," says Jasper. "I'll go and come back through the kitchen to let you know. It will take only a couple of minutes. We don't want him to feel uncomfortable or embarrassed," cautions Jasper.

ജ‍ഊ

"Lucy, just wait here in the parlor with Octavia Martin while I go upstairs to let Miss Nora know you're here. Her two bridesmaids are with her in the bedroom," says Jocelyn, as she rushes into the short hallway to turn and climb the stairs.

"Mrs. Martin, you hit the jackpot when you picked that dress out for yourself. It still has your name on it. Yes it does," Lucy says, approvingly. "And I didn't have to alter it or anything."

"Miss Nora and her girlfriends are waiting on you," says

246

Jocelyn to Lucy as she comes back into the parlor. "Nora is being very careful not to stick her head out of the bedroom door and risk the chance Mr. Jasper may be passing through the kitchen and back into the parlor. This house is not that large," Jocelyn announces, as a matter of fact.

Lucy picks up her alterations' knapsack, turns right out of the parlor and after about three quick paces forward, hits the staircase going up.

"Hello, Miss Nora and company," says Lucy, as Velma offers her quick entry into the barely-opened door.

"I'm here to get you ready to meet your groom, with the help of your two bridesmaids. You know you're going to be one of the prettiest brides this community has seen in a long time. You don't look like you don' gone and put on nary-a-pound," says Lucy, with an approving smile.

"Velma, let me go and see if Nora's aunts are done dressing," Geneva says. "If they are, we can slip into our dresses in that bedroom then come back over here where Lucy will already have helped Nora get into her gown," reasons Geneva.

"That's my girl Geneva," says Nora. "Always two steps ahead of everybody in figuring out the small details."

"Then all three of us can fuss over your hair style, help you with your face powder, rouge and lipstick and just keep the fan turned in your direction so you won't start to sweat—or as a proper lady would say… perspire," teases Velma, in a haughty, exaggerated tone.

⁂ψ⁂

As hard as they are trying, the four ladies—Nora, Geneva, Velma and Lucy—now alone upstairs, can't help but hear the front screen door open and close. These early guests are doubling as volunteers and their voices are alternating between excitable giggles, whispered conversations and an occasional full-throated belly laugh. While Nora isn't saying so, the ladies are probably thinking she is listening to hear the voices of Jasper, Octavia, Uncle Hempstead and a few others. The kitchen is humming with activity and low-level chatter as a few food items and beverages are being delivered and accepted.

ൠൠ

Claudine explained to the wedding party and the few on-lookers the night before that as the married couple walk from the flower-adorned, trellis-turned-altar and down the petal strewn aisle a few of the guests-volunteers will rush to their nearby-homes to retrieve the food platters and plates. The couple will be at the back of the decorated lawn greeting everyone as Mr. and Mrs. The four musicians will play soothing music initially and the bride will be priming the ladies for the bouquet toss. All of these traditional maneuvers and rituals will give Claudine, Marilyn and Hattie time to complete setting the tables for the reception. The guests will chat with their friends, church members and community invitees and no doubt gaze toward and approach some of the unfamiliar faces in the backyard.

ൠൠ

As the clock approaches four-thirty, the ladies upstairs hear Reverend Simpson's loud voice booming between the parlor and the hallway leading toward the kitchen. The Brown family can be heard arriving because Buster Brown is bubbling with excitement, and his mother can be heard coaxing him to speak in his Sunday school voice. Martha Jenkins and her granddaughter, Candy, have recognizable voices, and they are heard coming into the parlor. Candy, as the young flower girl, doesn't stir the low-level of apprehension Buster Brown does, as a wedding participant.

Claudine raises her voice to her volunteers who are among the people starting to crowd the parlor, the dining room, hallway and entrance to the kitchen.

"Don't forget, let's lead the arriving guests from the front yard—left side as we practiced—through the gate and into the backyard. Everyone is not suppose to pass through this house. Only the wedding participants are to wait here inside. You have to remember to seat the bride's guests on the left side of the altar and Jasper's guests on the right side of the altar," says Claudine, in a forced-nice voice. "In one more minute I want all of my greeters out on the front, left-side of lawn, waiting to escort the arriving guests. Those of you not in the wedding party, would you please exit out of the front door and walk through the side yard to the gate and follow the directions of the escorts. Five o'clock will be upon us before we know it," says the strong-voiced "wedding chief."

ℝ℞

Jasper, Eugene and Hempstead are coming out of Claudine's bedroom after Hempstead is given some assistance with getting into his black suit, white shirt, and black and white tie. The men were only in Claudine's bedroom because of Hempstead's bruised and sore body as well as his bandaged forehead.

"Everything okay?" asks Tommy Collins, Jasper's second groomsman. "I heard what happened to Miss Nora's uncle. You know how news—good or bad—travels around this community."

"He's going to be okay. Just moving slow and taking it easy," says Eugene.

Jasper is now in a somewhat quasi-pensive mood. After the unexpected stress connected to Hempstead's ordeal, Jasper feels he needs to refocus on the afternoon and evening ahead of him and his new bride. Jasper is sitting on the sofa in the parlor. Eugene walks over to Jasper and shows him the ring—*again*.

"You see it's still safe in the box here," he reassures Jasper.

"Miss Hattie has shown me the kitchen shelf to put the ring box on a few minutes before I come out of the door with Geneva on my arm.

Buster Brown's mother is lingering in the hallway with him. The father is standing outside on the side yard waiting on his wife to join him so they can be escorted to their seats. She seems hesitant to leave Buster on his own.

"Mama, I can stay in here by myself. I know how to act like a grown-up kid and use my good manners. Daddy is waiting on you. Y'all go be on the last row if you don't go on out there," counsels Buster, as if the mother is the child.

"You know better than to say y'all," she says, in a failed attempt to whisper the corrected grammar.

"I was just playing with you to see if you were paying any attention to what I was saying," Buster replies. Buster Brown's mother is barely out of the house when Buster Brown eases over to Eugene and asks, "Is that a real wedding ring Mr. Eugene or is it from the five and dime store from downtown Macon?"

"Young boy, don't get yourself in trouble before we can even hit the backyard. Mr. Martin bought his bride-to-be the real deal—a beautiful diamond ring. It will blind those old big eyes of yours," Eugene adds, in a now-be-quiet tone.

At this mild rebuke, Buster Brown seeks out Candy and nonchalantly saunters over in her direction.

ഇരു

Upstairs, Nora's mood suddenly and unwittingly seems to match her mate's mood downstairs. She has become quiet and a bit withdrawn.

Lucy has left Nora with Geneva and Velma after she easily zipped Nora into the white, pearl and lace, body-fitting gown with a modest four-inch train. The dress has cropped, laced sleeves with tear-dropped shaped pears on their bottom edge. The lace and pearl veil has a double layer of mesh. The hair is in a soft and feminine, French-style twist that the women have seen lately in a couple of the ladies' magazines. And the good quality, faux-pearl hair barrettes add a sophisticated touch.

"You look absolutely gorgeous my dear," says Velma.

"Yeah, somebody is going to have to bend down and pick Jasper's eyeballs up off the ground. They are going to come out of their sockets when he sees you in this new-fangled style gown. I know your Aunt Hattie thought the styling was a bit too modern, but this is made for a woman with your sculptured body," concludes Geneva, looking at Nora from all sides.

Nora is standing in front of a slanted, floor model, vertical mirror when there is a knock on the bedroom door.

"It's a quarter of five now," says Aunt Hattie, a bit winded from the last minute rush. "Jocelyn's niece and her mother, Muriel, just came up the side yard. I understand they dressed over at Jocelyn's home after they got off the road a couple of hours ago. You know Muriel is Jocelyn's older sister. Jocelyn will be up to get you ladies to come down to the kitchen in another five minutes or so. Nora you are beautiful. And your gown is growing on me still—these last fifteen minutes," chuckles her Aunt Hattie.

"Lord, we three aunts love you so much, it's as if the Lord let you come out of Clementine's stomach and eventually made us feel like all three of us birthed you too," Hattie says, fighting back her emotions. "Let me go before I mess up my rouge with these crocodile tears."

Geneva and Velma observe and soak in the emotional bond so obvious between Hattie and Nora. Hattie comes over to Nora and with a soft touch brushes Nora's cheek with her index and middle fingers she has pressed to her own lips.

Velma rushes over with one of several white hankies Hattie has purchased just for this day.

"Miss Claudine sure did a hell of a job sewing your pink dress. I can't wait to see the other two aunts' dresses," says Geneva, as she tries to redirect the tears' flirtation with Nora and Hattie's just-right rosy cheeks.

THE DEBT

೫೦೦೪

There's a urgent knock at the bedroom door, and Aunt Marilyn rushes in to announce an unexpected guest.

"I hope this doesn't upset you or surprise you too much, but your new Army-wife-friend, Miss Abigail, just waltzed through the gate. I know you sent her an invitation as a courtesy, but you didn't expect her to come down from Atlanta. Did you?" asks Marilyn, rhetorically.

"Oh my goodness. What a surprise!" Nora gasps. "I don't have time to greet her or Cynthia and her mother. But these are such wonderful additions to the guests list."

೫೦೦೪

"Okay, okay ladies. It's time for you three to make your way down to the kitchen. Jasper is on the side yard, and he won't be able to see you Nora. Eugene and Tommy will be in the kitchen with the ladies," organizing directress Jocelyn announces.

Chapter 22

The Nuptials

"Oh, my Lord! I can die and go to heaven tonight after my sweet Nora marries today. You are the prettiest bride this side of the Mississippi. Has anyone ever told you that?" Hempstead chatters and gawks in a nervous manner as Nora enters the kitchen.

"Hi, Uncle Hempstead. Hi, everybody," Nora says softly.

After staring at her beloved father-figure, Nora asks, "Uncle Hempstead, are you going to be able to manage me hanging onto your arm and you using your cane to steady yourself on the opposite side of your body?"

"Don't you worry about me. I wouldn't give away this honor for all the tea in China," Hempstead snaps back.

"Okay, Reverend Simpson," Jocelyn says. "You can walk out now and stand in front of the altar. We're about to get started. It's a few minutes before five o'clock."

"Oh, what a beautiful day in many, many ways. I agree with your uncle, Miss Carpenter. You are a beautiful bride and it's an honor to officiate today. Now let's all bow our heads for a prayer," he says, catching Jocelyn off guard.

"Make it quick, Reverend," Jocelyn strains to sound accommodating. "We've got a good crowd out back and they are excited."

"Our heavenly Father. As we come before you today for the express purpose of bringing these two young people together, let us pray for their happiness and longevity as a couple. Keep all evil spirits away from this gathering, away from their life and the children you will certainly bless them with. Keep Private Martin safe in Uncle Sam's Army and keep both of them healthy into their ripe old age. These blessings I ask in your name. Amen!"

"I'm going to say Amen a second time. Is that all right?" asks Buster Brown, out of the blue as he stands over by the door leading out.

"Young man, just follow your instructions from last night," says Jocelyn, in a dismissive tone.

"Okay, Reverend. You head out. Our sweet and cute little flower girl will come out the door close behind you—with her first basket full of white petals that she will drop around the altar. Then she will take a few minutes to drop pink petals—from a second basket she will be handed—on the lawn going all the way down the aisle. Just like we practiced last night," Jocelyn's more relaxed tone becoming apparent now.

"Here we go," says Reverend Simpson in a somber tone, as he establishes eye contact with Nora.

Reverend Simpson's exit out the kitchen door signals the beginning of the ceremony.

৪৩৪৩

A quiet hush comes over the wedding attendees as Reverend Simpson walks up to the flower-covered, circular trellis and looks out over a good portion of the residents of the colored section of Macon, known as Fernwood.

A few of the ladies collapse their parasols, which have protected them from the sun, but would now block the views of the people sitting behind them.

Candy Jenkins seems almost angelic as she tip-toes around the altar with a fixed concentration on her task. She gets the second basket of pink petals from her grandmother, Martha, then proceeds to drop them all along the lush green path which serves as the aisle between the divided section of chairs.

Peeping discreetly out of the cracked kitchen screen door, Jocelyn says in an upbeat tone, "Okay, Miss Geneva and Mr. Eugene, you're next."

From her position behind the screen door, on the kitchen side, she cracks it two times as a signal to her son, Henry—who is standing on the lawn outside of the hinged screen door. These two, slight openings is his signal to pull the door wide for each group of wedding party participants.

"Now, it's your turn Miss Velma and Mr. Tommie," Jocelyn says, after the two preceding attendants have taken their positions on both sides of the altar.

"Oh, we've got a lot of craning necks out there," says Jocelyn. She is able to see the seated guests each time she momentarily gives Henry his signal.

"Okay, little Mr. Brown. Mind your p's and q's now and be the best little ring bearer Fernwood has ever seen," advises Jocelyn.

"I promise I won't lose the ring Mr. Eugene gave me a few minutes ago. See, here it is—still in my pocket," says Buster Brown, as he pulls it out to show Jocelyn Turner.

"Put it back, put it back," snaps the ceremony directress. "Now go, please," admonishes the kitchen officiate, as she stands behind the screen so that Buster Brown can walk out to take his position, which is beside Tommie Collins, the second groomsman.

Nora and Hempstead come out of the dining room to stand near the now *closed* kitchen door. Everyone seated on the lawn waits in high anticipation.

Out of Nora's eyesight, Jasper walks from the side yard and takes his position in front of Eugene and near Reverend Simpson at the 'altar.' To everyone's surprise, Jasper is wearing his official dress, Army Private's uniform and not the black Tuxedo he had said he would be wearing.

THE DEBT

The flautist and the soprano saxophone player begin to play, in a soft and melodic way, the traditional Mendelssohn processional "Wedding Song."

The wooden kitchen door is opened, then the screen door is again held back from the yard side, by Jocelyn Turner's son, Henry.

Many of the guests start to wiggle to the edge of their chairs.

"Tell me when you're ready, Nora," says Hempstead, in a soft and loving tone.

"I'm ready now. I'm as ready as I will ever be," says Nora, looking her beloved, surrogate Uncle straight in his eyes.

After a thanks-for-everything comment to Jocelyn Turner, Nora turns to Hempstead and says, "This is it. Let's go."

Upon seeing the two cross the threshold of the kitchen door, the guests gasp and begin to stand to view the short procession from the house to the altar some twelve yards away.

Nora caters to Hempstead's slow and slightly shaky pace. She is smiling and, no doubt, silently praying as she exudes an aura of serenity and dignity.

Henry has switched his role from door holder to wedding photographer. He rushes to position himself near the altar as he holds his mother's 1930's model Kodak. Jocelyn volunteered him early on, after Cynthia reminded Nora she needed a photographer for the wedding.

Jasper's eyes widen as Nora and Hempstead approach the altar. He doesn't appear to try to suppress his full-tooth smile as she gets closer. Only when Hempstead momentarily stops in his tracks does

Jasper's demeanor change. The guests acknowledge the pause also with immediate dead-silence. Hempstead appears to recalibrate his gait for about ten seconds and then continues on to deliver Nora to her waiting prince.

The sense of relief is felt, by not only the wedding party, but every breathing guest on the lawn. Geneva moves gracefully toward Nora and bends straight down with an erect back and an outstretched arm to straighten her short and manageable train.

All of colored Fernwood has heard about Hempstead's Friday ambush in Forsythe County, so he has the full sympathy and understanding of the wedding guests.

After Reverend Simpson positions himself looking out at the guests and straight into Nora and Jasper's eyes, he begins.

☙❧

"Who gives this young woman, Nora Norton Carpenter, to be wed to Jasper Leonard Martin?" asks Reverend Simpson.

"I do," says Hempstead, in his booming and enthusiastic voice.

Hempstead takes one hobbled step closer to Nora to place her hand in Jasper's hand. He is careful when he leans over to kiss her on her left cheek. Hempstead then turns and slowly makes his way to the fourth seat on the bride's front row. The sisters, lined in the first three seats, are Claudine, Marilyn, and Hattie, respectively.

All eyes are on the altar as Reverend Simpson begins.

"Dear God, we are here today to bear witness to the marriage of Nora Norton Carpenter to Private Jasper Leonard Martin. We believe we are experiencing a true declaration of love and the promise of a life-long commitment to each other."

Simpson continues, "There are times when there is almost unanimous consent amongst family and friends that they are about to witness the consecration of one of the truest of love stories. Many have told me this is how they feel about this union. I have married many young and attractive couples, but, in my gut, I'm a' feelin' something truly unique and unusual about this pairing. Young Nora and her soldier boy beau have got that special magic going on. Truth be told, Miss Nora didn't come to church every Sunday, but in these last three to four months when she often came with her two aunts, I saw that glow and that halo around her temples get brighter and brighter. That signaled to me—watch out—this pretty and chaste young lady got somethin' stirrin' in her soul. And then, when Mr. Jasper—he wasn't Private Martin then—started showin' up some Sundays with her—Need I say anymore? You know what I'm talkin' about.

"I just told you their brief courtship history. Now, here we are today in the present time. In this year of nineteen and forty-four, on this Saturday, the twenty-fifth day of March, we are going to help them tie this knot so tight, no evil spirit will enter their homes. God will help the devil lose his road map to every house they will ever occupy, and they will be blessed beyond their wildest dreams. I'm telling you my friends and church members, I'm feelin' this union. Do I get an Amen?" Reverend Simpson pauses, to catch his breath.

"Amen, amen," chant the wedding guests. They seem as though they are forgetting they are in the Carpenter's backyard—and not Cloverdale Baptist Church.

Henry has been moving around trying to get good pictures of the wedding party and people sitting on both sides of the back lawn.

ഔൽ

After stirring the guests a bit more than intended, Reverend Simpson continues, "Not all couples, however, begin their lives with the type of uncertainty that Nora and Jasper will face. When you're in Uncle Sam's Army, you don't know where—in which city, state or country—your head will find its pillow every night. And your new bride may not be there with you. I say this not to alarm the almost-married man standing before me. But I want him and his new bride to know that trust and fidelity are big-time ingredients in a strong and long marriage. Do not forget your Bible School and Sunday school teachings from your early years and all the other Godly deeds you picked up in your adult life. Miss Carpenter, your three Aunts taught you well. Mr. Jasper, I haven't known you and your mother as long, but what I have seen, means you will honor your wife as the Bible tells you to do. Miss Octavia is a good woman too, although she may sting you with her witty tongue. Then she'll turn around and offer you some of her special tea to make you smile. Y'all know I know my community," says the minister, as he suppresses his own amusement.

"And when it's time to raise those precious babies, don't forget to introduce them to the Lord's good works early on," Simpson says, in earnest.

"Is there anything you want to say to Private Martin, Miss Nora?" asks Reverend Simpson.

"Yes," says Nora. "I want Jasper to know I never expected to feel so loved and so completely at ease and assured of my decision to marry him. He is about to complete my life for the moment, this is until we start our family," she concludes, her certitude unapologetic.

There is an unmistakable hum or sigh coming from many of the invited guests as they appear to sanction Nora's comments.

"And what about you Private Martin? Your words for Miss Carpenter, who has about five minutes left before becoming your beautiful wife," asks Simpson, as he good-naturedly baits Jasper.

"Nora, my love, you are a dream come true for me. I had no idea what true romantic love would feel like, until I met you. The speed of my drunkedness for your love still makes my head spin and my heart skip a beat. You are going to help me become the husband I want to be and the good father I know I can be," concludes Jasper, as his bottom lip quivers.

"OOOOOOh" is the lone murmur of a word heard from a small chorus of women.

"Is there anyone seated among us who objects to this marriage?"

asks Reverend Simpson. "If so, speak now, or forever hold your peace."

Approximately fifteen seconds feels like a long stretch of silence.

"Young man. Will you please hand the ring to the best man?" asks Reverend Simpson.

Buster Brown doesn't move, but he looks out at the guests, then at Tommie Collins, and then over to Eugene before he creeps over and looks up at the minister.

"What does *objects* mean," asks Buster, in his classroom-style inquisitiveness.

"Little Mr. Brown, Mr. Owens is waiting on the ring," the minister reminds Buster Brown.

"But, but sir," starts the man-child's appeal to the minister. "This wedding is too important for me not to understand if I should give this ring to Mr. Eugene or not. I don't want to be the one everybody gets mad at me if Miss Carpenter and Mr. Jasper go get their dee-vorce," says Buster, with genuine fear in his voice.

Eugene comes out of formation and walks up to Buster. With a low buzz of conversation from the seated guests creeping into the air, Eugene bends over and whispers in the boy's ear.

Buster Brown's large eyes open wide on his chubby face, and he reaches into his pocket and brings out the diamond ring and its matching band. His facial expression suggests his question is unanswered, but he doesn't open his mouth. His rather sheepish appearance says it's only a temporary pause, not an issue put to bed.

Nora has been determined not to turn around to stare at the brief stand-off. Jasper is gently rubbing the top of Nora's ring hand as if to keep it warm and supple.

"Children are always full of surprises, aren't they," says Reverend Simpson, in a controlled voice as he pulls the attention of the guests back to the ceremony.

"Private Martin, do you promise to love, honor and cherish Nora Carpenter Martin as your wife?" asks the minister.

"I do," says Jasper, with military-like crispness.

"To provide for her and your children and to allow the blessings of God to fill your home with love and charity?" he continues.

"I will," Jasper answers, in a softer and warmer voice.

"Will you be with her through sickness and in health and till death you do part?" continues Simpson.

"On my Father's grave I promise," says Jasper, in a saddened, but honest voice.

"Okay, Miss Carpenter. Will you love Jasper Leonard Martin as your husband and life's partner?" asks Reverend Simpson, looking at Nora with serious, unblinking eyes.

Nora's eyes widen also and she looks at the minister and answers in a raised voice, "I will."

"Will you be a good Mother to the children you have together and maintain a home in a Christ-like spirit?" continues Reverend Simpson.

"I will love our children unconditionally and always keep Christ as a companion in our home," Nora answers, with conviction.

"Will you stand by Jasper Martin in sickness and in health and till death you do part?" ask the minister in a gentle, but solemn manner.

"Yes. Yes," says Nora. "I will never be far, nor absent, in Jasper's life."

"And may I have the rings, Mr. Owens?" asks Simpson.

"Yes, you may," answers Eugene. He hands both of Nora's rings to the minister and backs into his position.

The minister looks at the rings then hands Jasper the band first.

Nora holds her left hand out and opens her fingers wide so that Jasper can place the band on first, then the diamond engagement ring goes on afterwards.

Nora smiles as she looks at the pretty but dainty rings Jasper has given her.

"Do you have a ring for Private Martin?" asks the minister.

"Yes, I do," says Nora, as she takes Jasper's band from Geneva.

Jasper smiles like a little boy on Christmas morning, as Nora puts the band on his left, ring finger.

"Now, if you will join the wedding party in prayer," says the smooth-talking and unflappable Baptist minister.

"Heavenly Father, we have witnessed the sacred matrimony of Nora Norton Carpenter to Jasper Leonard Martin on this day, in the year of our Lord, one thousand nine hundred and forty-four. May you shower abundant blessings on them and the children they hope to have. May you help them live a Christian life and spread love and charity to others. Keep these young people free from harm and allow them to enjoy the love of older family members for many years to come. With all the blessings you have for them, allow the waters of mercy to begin flowing now."

"I now pronounce you man and wife. Family and friends, please greet Mr. and Mrs. Jasper Leonard Martin. You may, now, kiss your bride," says Reverend Simpson, in a triumphant voice, as he concludes the ceremony.

Oblivious to all in their midst, Jasper raises Nora's veil, puts one arm around Nora's waist and a second arm curves her back from shoulder-to-shoulder. His lips meet her lips and everything disappears as they momentarily melt in a blissful embrace. He releases Nora, looks into her large, light-brown eyes and whispers, "Hello, Mrs. Martin. It's going to be so nice to get to know you."

While Nora and Jasper turn at the altar to face the anxious and excited attendees on the lawn, Geneva and Velma rush behind them to straighten the short train on her gown and fluff the tulle on her veil.

Buster Brown manages to escape the "line-up" and pounces in

front of the newlyweds to quickly ask, "Is that a real diamond there, Mr. Jasper?"

"You bet your bow tie it is," Jasper chuckles.

"Congratulations Miss Nora," says Buster Brown, as he rushes back to stand, again, behind Tommie Collins.

Chapter 23

The Reception

Nora and Jasper walk slowly down the petal-strewn aisle smiling to guests on both sides of the lawn as the guests clap, smile and wave to the newlyweds. A few women can be seen dabbing their eyes with their handkerchiefs. Others can be seen discreetly pointing to Nora's gown and whispering among themselves.

The flute player and soprano saxophone player softly render a commonly heard victory flourish as everyone's attention is focused on the slow, steady, steps and pauses that Nora and Jasper engage in until they reach the back of the lawn.

As planned, Marilyn has rushed some of the women to their homes to bring back the prepared and plated tea sandwiches, beautifully carved pork roasts, baked chicken drumsticks, the sliced, smokehouse ham, the cheeses, the fresh sliced and cubed seasonal fruits, and the green salads to be double-bowled with chipped ice upon arriving at the house. The fresh-baked, small, buttermilk biscuits, yeast rolls and corn muffins round out the spread. Saltine crackers compliment the assortment of pickled vegetables in small bowls dotting the long, feasting table. The table has been set up in front of the music riser and close to the shaded trees section of the lawn.

Once Nora and Jasper reach their destination on the back lawn, as expected, some of the ladies begin to move in their direction to get a closer view of the couple and offer their compliments.

Two chairs have been covered in white, poplin cloth with sky blue streamers on Jasper's chair back and pink ribbon wrapped and tied in a bow for Nora's chair.

Before Nora can decide whether to sit or continue standing, Abigail rushes up to her with wide-opened arms.

"Oh, aren't you a beautiful bride," she shrieks, as she hugs Nora. "And what a gorgeous gown to showcase your fashion-magazine figure," she continues. Looking to Nora's husband, Abigail gushes, "Congratulations Jasper—you handsome devil. You must feel like the luckiest man on earth to land such a stunning and smart bride. I told my mother and father I just had to get down here for your big day, and what a lovely setting for an early Spring, garden wedding."

Abigail sweeps her arm as she surveys the entire lawn. She continues chatting, oblivious to the people waiting to greet Nora, too. Among those standing and waiting are Cynthia Sinclair, Geneva, Octavia Martin, Hortense Brown (Buster's mother), Martha Jenkins (flower girl Candy Jenkins's grandmother) and others from the community.

"Oh, my goodness! I'm taking up too much of your time," Abigail finally realizes and blurts out apologetically. "I'm going to go and taste some of this delicious-looking food. Don't worry about me. I'll seek out your aunts and introduce myself to them and some of your guests. We'll talk later," are Abigail's departing words, as she politely excuses herself through the gathering cluster of people, who've been standing *and* waiting.

"Hi, Mom. Come on over here by my side," says Jasper, as he sees his Mother in the group of people. All of our attendants are welcomed to join us as we thank all of our family, friends, church members and neighbors," Jasper says, with excitement and reverence in his voice.

Jasper's announcement refocuses the cluster of people, whose eyes have been fixed on Abigail with stares of impatience.

"I didn't think we would get a word in edge-wise, with Miss chatterbox hogging all y'all's time," blurts Octavia, as she makes her way to Jasper and Nora.

Jasper, knowing his mother all too well, chooses to ignore her snide remark. Nora attempts to suppress a creeping smile.

"As many of you know, my mother has been my rock since my father passed on. But I'm so happy she eventually decided to move to Macon. Otherwise, I would never have met the beautiful lady who today became my wife," Jasper gushes, as he looks down to meet Nora's eyes and squeeze her closer to him.

"Ooooh," says a couple of the ladies standing in the cluster.

Geneva and Velma have come forward and are standing on Nora's other side. Geneva is holding Nora's bouquet of fresh flowers.

"I want to say what an honor it is to be a part of this lovely wedding. Please don't get worried. The bride will soon toss her bouquet for some lucky lady to claim," Geneva reassures the hopefuls in the crowd.

"Let me ditto what Geneva just said. Mrs. Martin deserves all the happiness she and her new husband have coming their way. It's a blessing to be a participant in this happy union," Velma concludes.

Stepping slightly forward and with a broad smile, Nora begins to speak. "We may have gotten out of the traditional order of comments here, but that is not important. I never felt the wedding and reception had to go by any strict rules set years and years ago. What is most important is for me to thank my Aunts Hattie, Marilyn and Claudine for giving me the love and attention of *three* Mothers. Is that not a blessing? Even though I don't remember them, I also feel the spirit of my birth parents today—Horace and Clementine Norton. I know they are proud of Jasper and their sisters. Mrs. Martin, my new mother-in-law, is a very special lady, so full of wit, wisdom and good common sense. Our children will just adore and love her as I have come to do. Geneva and Velma are my two best friends.

They are irreplaceable. Eugene and Tommie are Jasper's friends who I have claimed as mine, also. They are not standing here with us because they are also two of the musicians playing right now. Thanks to my adopted Uncle Hempstead, who has known me all my life. Thanks Reverend Simpson, Mrs. Jocelyn Turner, Mrs. Lucy Rivers, Mr. Henry Turner, Mr. & Mrs. Brown, for allowing Buster to be our ring bearer and, also, thanks to Mrs. Martha Jenkins whose adorable granddaughter, Candy, was our precious little flower girl. To all the family friends, church members and neighbors who have helped my aunts prepare the foods for the reception, gifted us with their fresh flowers, assisted in decorating the lawn here. A special thanks to Mr. Willie, who offered to drive my Aunt Hattie to deliver the invitations. No words are good enough to convey my gratitude to all of you," Nora concludes, as more people had come to the back lawn to listen to the bride, groom and members of the wedding party.

"Whew, it's time for us to rest our dogs. Ooops, I mean feet," Octavia says, as she corrects her speech.

Out of the blue, comes a familiar and disruptive, comical voice, "Do I get an Amen on that?" shouts Buster Brown as he runs around the edge of the gathering. His mother takes off after him as he scampers away toward his father, who is already sitting down.

"Please, please, we want all of you to eat, drink, relax and dance until you can't anymore. Nora will toss her bouquet soon so don't you single ladies stray too far. The four musicians will have to leave the reception around seven forty-five, but enjoy them until then," Jasper says, officially concluding the reception remarks.

‟ʠ

"May I have your attention please?" Eugene asks, in a pleasant, but loud and booming, voice. If Mr. and Mrs. Jasper Martin would grace us with their presence in this open area behind the altar, you will witness their first dance together."

Holding hands, Nora and Jasper walk from the back of the

lawn toward the altar area, smiling and surveying the guests scattered around the quickly arranged tables and chairs.

Eugene points to the area as the husband and wife reach the top of the lawn. "We hope you enjoy the tune we've selected for you," Eugene says, holding his soprano saxophone and counting down to the flute, trumpet, and cello players. "Three, two, one—"

The three begin to play in a soft and soothing tone, the love ballad, *I'll Be Loving You Always*. They play the first stanza with Eugene singing in a whispery manner, "I'll be loving you always, with a love that's true always..."

Nora and Jasper smile as he pulls her close and they slow-waltz to the popular song. The gathering becomes very quiet and attentive, with smiles and the sound of a few sniffles all around.

80QR

After detouring to the cleverly-decorated table and observing the bountiful display of foods and condiments, Nora and Jasper walk to their reserved table across from the food station and musicians' riser. Their table is adorned with fresh, white flowers and an abundance of fresh fern and greenery.

"Okay," says Marilyn, projecting her voice to the guests on the lawn, "Geneva and Velma will prepare Nora and Jasper's plates then all of you can form a line on both sides of the far end of the table and prepare your plates. Enjoy! There's more food where this came from."

Nora and Jasper can barely take in two bites before they are interrupted by well-wishers. They rest their flatware on the edge of their plates to accept the array of compliments coming from the attendees. No surprise, the ladies want to see Nora's rings up close.

Buster and Candy, who've been tagging each other at the back of the lawn, run up to the newlyweds' table.

"Mr. & Mrs. Martin, I waited until all the grown folks were through talkin' before I brought Candy up to see the rings I was scared of losing. And I want to see how they look on your finger Miss Carpenter—oh, I'm sorry—I said the old name," Buster Brown apologizes.

"Of course you and Candy can see my rings," says Nora, as she proudly raises her left hand and extends it over her plate.

"You proved to all of us that you were careful with the rings," adds Jasper.

"See Candy, you know they real, 'cause look how they shine," Buster tells Candy with his little boy's authority.

"Oooooweee! I want some rings like that when I grow up," Candy says, while giggling.

"You got to fall in love first," says Buster.

"How do you fall in love?" Candy asks, innocently.

"You have to kiss a lot and then I think, ahh, ahh," Buster hesitates, just long enough for an interruption.

"Why don't you two go and get something to eat. There's a lot to choose from over there," says Jasper.

"Okay Mr. Martin," says Buster as he turns to walk away. "Come on, Candy."

"Make sure you speak to Mr. Saunders, your school's principal," Nora says to Buster.

☙ ❧

Nora catches a glimpse of Abigail talking with Cynthia. They seem to be in deep conversation and oblivious to others around them.

Several people, stopping by the table for a minute, comment on how good the music sounds with just four people playing.

From the way Nora catches sight of her Aunt Claudine spinning around, she knows she is boasting about how she managed to sew three pink dresses for herself and her two sisters.

Geneva and Velma are helping with replenishing the platters on the table. People are eating, talking and laughing politely as they converse with others within their range. A few of the younger people are starting to dance to up-beat selections like, *This Joint is Jumpin.*

Jocelyn Turner and her son are still moving among the guests and taking pictures. She is answering a couple of questions about Nora's gown and some of the other dresses purchased at her shop for this occasion.

Octavia is circulating among the crowd but mostly talking with her girlfriends, Sally, Clara and Betsy. She is truly basking in the glow of her son and daughter-in-law's union.

Mrs. Hutchinson comes by the table and pauses to thank Nora and Jasper for inviting her.

"I can't thank you enough for allowing me to come out of my sad home to see all these people so happy for you. You are two of the nicest young people in this town. Everyone will miss you when you leave. My life has been so sad these last couple of months without Joey. You know everyone was so helpful and available when Joey first died. Now, they seem to feel uncomfortable to even mention his name. Maybe they think it's best for me that they don't talk about him anymore. But I need people to keep remembering him, not forgetting that he ever existed," the still grieving mother says.

"We are so pleased you accepted the invitation," says Jasper, standing in a gesture of respect. "Your son was an exceptionally polite and serious young man. He would have matured into a fine gentleman with a bright future. But being sad is one emotion. This will soften as the years add up. But guard yourself against being bitter and angry toward your son's commander who accidentally shot him. Hanging onto those two emotions will destroy you. They will sap your spirit and your will to live. Pray for strength and guidance to move forward in a way that helps you find new meaning and purpose for your life. Lean on your faith in the months and years to come," Jasper finishes, by patting Mrs. Hutchinson's shoulder.

"If Jasper and I leave the community on a military assignment,

I'll make sure to stop by and visit with you when I come back to Cloverdale to see my family," Nora says, to the mother, whose back seems to be straighter and her head held higher in just the brief span of their three-way conversation.

"How did two young people like y'all get so wise and caring so early in your life?" Mrs. Hutchinson asks.

"It's what we learned from both of our families," says Jasper.

ৠﮤ

"Are you itching to dance, Mrs. Martin, since the music tempo has picked up quite a bit?" asks Jasper.

"Are you kidding me? In this gown with a train on the back? You would be picking me up off the lawn and searching around for our wheel barrel to roll me away from the scene," says Nora, as they both get in a good full-belly laugh.

Uncle Hempstead limps over with the help of the walking cane. "I still can't believe you are jilting me, Miss Carpenter. I loved you first, before this frog, who is still green, hopped into your life. What am I to do without you?" asks Hempstead.

"You are to be patient until we start our family. Then you will have some little ones to fret over and spoil," says Nora, as if looking into her crystal ball.

Geneva comes over to the table and announces, "It's about time to get ready to toss the bouquet. I'll get it from out of the ice box in the kitchen. It's only been in there since they took out the last food platter. By the way, your new friend from Atlanta sure loves to talk—and I mean about everything," says Geneva, in a sarcastic tone.

"No gossiping today, Miss Geneva," chuckles Jasper.

ৠﮤ

"Have you announced where you're going on your wedding night?" asks Abigail, in her usual perky tone.

"Oh no. This is still my secret alone," says Jasper, as he and

271

Nora have left the table to stroll among the guests.

"We are doing just a little something this weekend, but I don't know anything about the surprise. We really are not planning anything serious now, as far as a honeymoon. Jasper may get new orders any day. I pray we can be together, starting out," says Nora, her voice fading near the end of the sentence.

৪৩৫৫

Geneva and Velma walk down the middle of the divided lawn, as Geneva announces, "Mrs. Martin is ready to toss her bouquet to some lucky young lady today. Let's all move into this area as Nora walks back toward the altar. She will toss it from that point back to here. We need the spectators to move toward the chairs and tables so there will be plenty of room for the single, young women in the group to chase the bouquet, if necessary," chuckles Geneva.

The guests start to chatter among themselves.

The young ladies congregate at the designated area.

Velma takes the bouquet from Geneva and walks it over to hand to Nora.

Nora giggles as she rotates the bouquet as if to give it one last look before the big toss.

Jasper stands with a cluster of men. They are amused by all the buzzing and anticipation.

All three of the aunts stand together near the food table. They present a palate of pink in their dresses.

The trumpet player offers a monotonous stream of flourishes that mock an "on your mark" sound.

Geneva and Velma rush to the center of the lawn to join the handful of hopefuls.

"Okay, here it comes," says Nora. "One, two, three and away!"

"It's coming toward me," one lady shouts.

"No, I'm about to get it," someone else squeals.

"Oh, you threw it so high Nora," complains another.

The ladies jump, squeal and nudge each other as they go after the bouquet.

It is caught and then dropped by a guest who lets out a heart-wrenching, "Oh no!"

"I got it! I got it!" shouts one lucky lady who swoops the dropped bouquet off the ground.

Everyone turns to see a beaming Cynthia Sinclair holding the bouquet.

Geneva and Velma have a look of disbelief on their faces.

Cynthia's Mother, Muriel, the last-minute invitation-requester, mumbles loud enough for others to hear. "Here we go with attempt number two. Oh my God!"

The on-lookers clap and cheer the ladies who are patting their hair back in place and straightening their dresses after the not-so-dignified scramble.

ഇൻരു

Hempstead creeps up to the spot Nora is still occupying and says in a loud voice, "I have the honor of announcing the bride's garter toss by her husband. Come on up Mr. Martin. Here's the chair that's just been put here for your bride. All you bachelors get right in the area where the ladies were just standing. All you single guys in the band, put those instruments down and come try your luck. Hurry up."

All the musicians rush off the riser to join the other men.

Jasper starts, with that mischievous look in his eyes. "I shouldn't be showing my wife's thigh like this, but it's nothing that hasn't been shown in the summer when women try to beat the heat in their shorts. So guys, one of you is going to be crowned as the next groom. If you're too chicken to say I DO in the near future, you got about thirty seconds to get out of the huddle. Okay, my lovely wife, here we go."

Jasper talks to the attendees as he performs the task. "I will carefully remove the garter, then turn to these anxious wolves in our midst, and with a flick of my wrist, I will let the garter soar toward you and—voila!"

The men are more calm, audibly, than the women were. But they still jump and reach high to try to get the garter belt.

"I got it! I got it, but I don't want it!" shouts a voice which is not that recognizable.

Everyone turns to see Mr. Willie holding up Nora's garter. He looks shocked. "I was sittin' rat at the edge of the mens and Private Martin throwed it so hard, damn if it ain't gone and fall in my lap!" he says with a look of disbelief.

The crowd starts laughing so hard, especially Jasper, until it is a minute before he can reign in the commotion.

"I ain't stuttin' bout marryin' nobody at my age. No sirree, I ain't," he blurts out, which brings another round of hearty laughs.

Jasper jumps right in, "Let's have a second garter toss. I won't add too much strength to my wrist this time," he says, still with some amusement in his voice.

A few of the women are still snickering when Jasper says, "Here comes Gertie the garter, a second time."

After a few grunts and a couple of the men jumping off the ground, there's a heavy voice saying, "The right person got it this time." People strained their necks to see Eugene raising the garter with a wide grin on his face.

"I knew my best man would want to be a copycat and follow in my footsteps," says Jasper, in a teasing tone.

Few in the crowd know Cynthia Sinclair, the lady from Atlanta who caught the bouquet, and Eugene seem to have a budding romantic interest between them.

☙❧

The dancing continues, the beautifully decorated cake is cut, Henry takes a few more pictures of the wedding party and Nora goes to change into a lovely pink, cotton jacquard dress that Hempstead asked Jocelyn Turner to order from Atlanta as a surprise to Nora.

While Nora is upstairs changing out of her wedding gown with Aunt Hattie's help—so Geneva and Velma won't miss any of the fun of the reception to come inside with her—Abigail unintentionally ruffles Geneva's feathers.

Abigail—still a new friend Nora knows little about other than her family is very wealthy and her handsome, Army-private husband comes from a solid, well-to-do family also—asks Geneva how long has she known Nora. She also is interested in knowing where did Geneva go to college.

"Excuse me," says Geneva. "You are inquiring about my friendship with Nora? It certainly is longer than three weeks, as the two of you claim," Geneva says, in a not so ingratiating way.

"I am just curious as to how far back you two go. That's all," responds Abigail.

"We met in the second grade, right here in the Cloverdale community. We were only apart during our four years of college," answers Geneva, in a more calm tone.

"I know Nora graduated from Tuskegee, and where did *you* go to college?" asks Abigail, not realizing she is being too pushy.

"I'm a proud graduate of Savannah State," snaps Geneva.

"And what about Nora's other girlfriend. Where did she go to school?" Abigail keeps pumping for more information.

"Look, why don't you ask the other friend, whose name happens to be Velma. Why are you so darn nosy?" Geneva asks, plainly irritated at this point.

"I just want to know who my other new friends are going to be here in Cloverdale. You can never have too much information, you know?" answers Abigail, with a little sass in her voice.

"Excuse me," says Geneva, who eyes Nora coming out the kitchen door with her lovely pink dress on. Abigail's back is toward the house so she doesn't see Nora.

"We're all going to have to share *our* sweet Nora," says Abigail, as Geneva walks away in a mild huff.

ℰᴑᴄᴙ

Nora walks out onto the lawn looking beautifully refreshed. She is gracious about the second round of compliments on how pretty she looks in her Atlanta, high-fashion-style dress.

She fields a few questions about where they are off to tonight. She is honest with those few inquisitors when she tells them Jasper is surprising her. A few caution if they are going to Atlanta, please don't go through Forsythe County.

Not wanting to cut Nora off from talking with some of the attendees, Jasper hangs back before he approaches Nora and hugs her again. He looks at her in such a loving and affectionate way until others can't help but pause and stare in their direction.

"Turn around my princess and let me have another look at you," he says. He holds her hand in his and raises their arms as Nora does a 360-degree spin.

ℰᴑᴄᴙ

Geneva walks up to the newlyweds, turns and looks back at the crowd and says, "The newlyweds will be leaving the reception in about thirty or forty minutes. The party can go on longer if you would like to stay. The musicians will be leaving shortly also, but Mr. Hempstead has brought one of those Victrolas to play some of those plastic, pancake-looking things, so we are here until your dogs start to bark," concludes Geneva.

"I ain't no way tired, yet," Octavia tells Geneva. "I'm still too excited about the wedding ceremony."

Sally Jenkins decides to take a dig at her old friend.

"You should have caught that bouquet Octavia. Mr. Willie ain't the only eligible bachelor around these parts today. You would have free ice for your ice box and free rides through all of Macon if you get hitched with him," teases Sally.

Betsy and Clara burst out laughing. Octavia throws a mean eye toward them. "Don't make me use my garbage can words with you ladies. We should not act uncouth around these straight-laced, sometimes snooty people," Octavia warns, as she smacks her lips as a symbol of having the *last* word.

"You sure you didn't hide a little jar of your special juice somewhere in the sisters' kitchen?" asks Sally. As the old folks would declare, *'Sally is still trying to get Octavia's goat.'* You know this lawn would light up if people started swiggin' on some of Mr. Willie's liquor. They'd be dancing more whether Hempstead turned on his box or not," counsels Sally.

"I told you hens before we got here, that this go be a dig-nafied event. Besides, Reverend Simpson is still close by somewhere. He is waitin' to bless Nora and Jasper as they leave to go do their love nest thang. So y'all just hold your horses," Octavia's voice is more serious now.

"Okay! Since you want to boss everybody all of a sudden," declares Betsy, with a tone of resignation.

"I 'speck we still go be friends ta-morrow laydeez. Am I callin' it right?" Octavia replies.

"Oh. Go on with all your weddin' airs, Mrs. Mother of the Groom," Sally says, with dripping sarcasm.

&0C&

Geneva delivers the exit message, as smooth as she has been all afternoon.

"Ladies and gentlemen, *and* you few youngsters in our midst, let's cheer the newlyweds on as they embark on their journey as Mr. and Mrs. Their bags are in Mr. Martin's car. They have greeted each of you to say thanks individually and now collectively. So, Reverend

Simpson, I believe, will have the last words."

"Oh! My goodness," says the reverend. "What a wonderful, almost three hours this has been. And it can still go on after the bride and groom say farewell for the evening. The food was exceptional, and we thank all the hands who helped prepare it. The beverages were so good for our thirst. The music, although scaled back with just four people, was so fitting and enjoyable. And we saw so many of you—our community here in Cloverdale—come to this wedding with joy, hope and love in your hearts for Nora and Jasper. The families of the bride and groom worked their bit of magic too. What a blessed event, all the way around.

"Let us please bow our heads," continues Reverend Simpson. "Dear Heavenly Father, thank you many, many times over for this wonderful afternoon and early evening. May you guide these two, young, newlyweds as they make their way through this often cruel and unforgiving world. Keep them in the palm of your hand. Allow them safe travels around these parts or where ever they may roam— especially Private Martin as he serves this country of ours. May they be blessed with healthy children who grow to know and love you as these two do. Keep them anchored to a good church in every nook and cranny where they may live. And above all, keep their love strong. May they always honor each other. And, finally, keep their bodies whole and healthy. Because, without your good health you are somewhat a poor man or a poor woman. These are the blessings I ask of you on their behalf. Amen!"

Geneva walks back in front of the guests and stands next to the minister. In her pleasant, but officious voice, she begins, "Even if you want to stay and enjoy the evening a little longer, please, now, go around the side yard ahead of the bride and groom. You will be given small knapsacks of rice to throw on them as they get in the DeSoto to leave.

Abigail, Cynthia, Jocelyn, and some of the younger people

were asked earlier to hand out the sacks of rice. They go ahead of the bulk of the guests. The three aunts and Octavia gather around Nora and Jasper as they take turns with good-bye hugs.

"Jasper and I can't begin to tell you how much we appreciate this lovely day you planned and toiled over with the help of so many others, just to bring us the joy and love that's still screaming in our brains, if that makes any sense," Nora says, in earnest as she dabs her tears.

Octavia jumps in, "Oh, we understand. Sho' nuff we do."

"You and Jasper deserved every bit of joy and happiness you experienced today," says Aunt Hattie.

"This was a labor of love," chimes Aunt Claudine.

"It sure was a bit hectic, but the long table covered with good food and the decorated lawn with beautiful flowers were more than many expected," adds Aunt Marilyn.

"Go now," says Hattie. "One of those tela-phones would sure come in handy tonight, just so you could call back and say you are safe. Not to tell us where you are."

"Don't none of you worry. I'm going to take such good care of *our* Nora. She will always be safe with me. That's my promise," Jasper says, with a hint of a catch in his throat. "By the way, my gift—our gift—to both houses is to get you all one of those new contraptions," Jasper announces.

With that, Jasper and Nora walk hand-in-hand around the side yard to their eager friends and neighbors waiting out front as the beautiful, early evening sun begins setting on Magnolia Street.

Chapter 24

Day One — Honeymoon

"Are you feeling tired and worn out my dear husband?" Nora asks, while smiling and staring at Jasper as he turns off the last, in-town road as they head out to Miss Lizzie's place.

"You have got to be kidding me," says Jasper, smiling back at Nora. "I could go another eight hours."

"I'm still trying to guess where we might be going for the evening—or will it be the weekend?" Nora quizzes Jasper, her voice rising.

"And do you think we will be safe once it gets dark? I mean, let's not forget what just happened to Uncle Hempstead," Nora cautions, with a drastic, but momentary mood shift.

"Didn't you believe me when I told our families I would take care of you?" asks Jasper, with a hint of disbelief in Nora's apparent unease.

"I'm so sorry. I'm about to dampen our mood and happiness. This is the last thing I want to do," Nora says, with a feigned, little girl's regret.

At the same time Nora issues her syrupy, quasi- apology, she softly places her full, opened left hand on Jasper's upper thigh and begin to rub it gently.

"Ooooh, Mrs. Martin. I don't think either one of us has work clothes to wear as we dig our car out of a ditch. That's exactly where we are going to end up, if you don't act like a good girl and let me keep my eyes on the road," Jasper warns, in an unmistakably lowered, sexy voice.

"Let's not forget, I don't have to be a good girl any longer. That was me in my *other* life. I hope this won't be a long drive, wherever you're taking us on our wedding night," coos Nora, in a slow and luring tone.

"You are a lucky lady because the drive is shorter than you can imagine, and we will arrive safely before dark," Jasper says, looking over at Nora with a sly, half-smile.

"I think I will just close my eyes for five minutes and reflect on what a wonderful day we just enjoyed," says Nora, as she yawns softly and rests the nape of her neck on the car's seat.

Jasper drives no more than another ten minutes before he stops the car at the end of the lane and right in front of the pretty little cottage where he and his bride will spend two nights and consummate their marriage.

ᔥᔐ

"Mrs. Martin, wake up. We're here," Jasper whispers softly, as he opens Nora's car door.

"Oh! I think I snuck a nap in on you. I'm so sorry, I couldn't keep my eyes open," says Nora, as she rouses herself.

"Oh, what a pretty little doll house! Where are we?" asks Nora.

"It is lovely and quaint. Isn't it?" asks Jasper "I expect we will be very comfortable here for two nights," Jasper's satisfaction is quite apparent.

Nora takes Jasper's outstretched hand and stands besides the DeSoto. Jasper leans over and embraces her, and they experience their first long, full-mouth passionate kiss as Mr. and Mrs. Jasper Martin. Both are speechless as they seem to keep sampling their new pleasure.

Jasper bends and swoops Nora off her feet as he walks on the pretty, inlaid stone path to the door of the cottage. Courtesy of Miss Lizzie, the door is unlocked.

The cottage is awash with the sweet smell of magnolias filling two earthen clay vases on the fireplace hearth.

A small circular table, with two chairs, has a clear, etched vase of long-stem white roses as its centerpiece. Close by are two heirloom-looking flutes and a bottle of champagne. A hand-written note welcoming the couple is leaning against the champagne bottle.

A settee upholstered in soft, yellow brocade fabric sits to one side of the small, parlor-like room and a second room hosts the honeymoon bed with a night stand and a kerosene lamp. A handsome, refurbished chifforobe rounds out the room.

A small, recently attached bathroom has been built on the back of the cottage with a small passageway leading to it from the bedroom. The toilet has an over-the-head chain as its disposal mechanism.

While there is no kitchen to speak of, a small sink and an ice box hug a wall near the circular table.

Miss Lizzie has appealing linens of white sheets and scalloped-edged pillow cases, a plush, white chenille bedspread, a goose-feather-filled blanket, and two chenille foot rugs on both sides of the bed. The small bathroom has white and yellow towel sets.

☙⤫☙

Jasper carries Nora to the settee and places her on it as if she is fragile porcelain. He then reaches down and slips one of Nora's shoes off and then the other shoe off the second foot. He gently starts to rub the soles of her feet before sitting and placing her feet across his lap as she has settled with her back on the settee's long arm.

"You've been in two different pair of these high shoes all day and even though you looked so gorgeous, I know you are tired," Jasper sympathizes.

"You have a right to be exhausted, too," Nora says.

Jasper listens as he rests his head on the back of the settee.

"You know, we couldn't have had a more lovely wedding if we had spent two-thousand dollars on it," Jasper says.

"We can thank both of our families—your Mother and my Aunts and Uncle Hempstead. Also, look at this pretty, but simple, pink dress he surprised me with, even after all he had already done," Nora muses.

"Yes, we are so lucky to have all of them. And now, we have each other for many, many years to come." Jasper ends his stream of consciousness, almost in a whisper.

In a whispery tone, too, Nora seems to indicate her second wind has introduced itself to her. "We've got to start on our many, many years together right now," she says, as if coming out of her stupor of fatigue.

Nora swings her feet around to the floor, sits and then leans over on Jasper's chest as if listening to his heartbeat. He immediately responds by allowing his finger tips to first explore her still-clothed breast and then pushing her up just enough to allow those same fingertips to hunt for the zipper on the back side of her dress. She then becomes an enabler and, with her eyes still shut, straightens her back as her lips search for Jasper's mouth. The newlyweds are in full-throttle kissing mode with heavy panting and hands massaging and caressing each other in ways they were never able to do inside of Jasper's car, or heaven forbid, sitting on the backyard glider at 1966 Magnolia.

"How long have I waited for a man to love and give myself to, unconditionally?" Nora asks, in a breathless whisper.

"I'm here now, my sweet queen. You don't have to wait any

longer," Jasper pants.

"Oh Jasper! I love you so much. It's so strong until it feels good and it hurts at the same time," Nora whispers.

"We've got hours, days and a lifetime for it—it—it to feel good," Jasper groans, as he picks Nora up and carries her into the small, but inviting, bedroom.

Ever the fastidious and well-trained niece and in the midst of their honeymoon passion, Nora scales a level of unconscious duty and manages to snatch the bedspread back to spare its soiling.

As Jasper struggles to get Nora out of her dress, she seems more adept at unzipping his suit pants and freeing him of his outer clothing. She then wiggles out of her dress and underwear as Jasper's excitement keeps escalating. Instead of waiting on Jasper to get rid of what seems like a fumbling third hand, Nora puts both her hands on his underwear waist band and, with all deliberate speed, frees him of that burden. With the freedom that exists with total nudity, managing the oxygen in the room becomes the secret to sustained energy and longevity or rapid flame-out. Jasper, undoubtedly, knows this delicate balance, but Nora is new to the game.

But oh! Is Nora ready for her debut!

Jasper's deep love and concern for Nora's comfort causes him to approach their first night in a slow and calculating manner. Nora's yearning is willing to forgo discomfort and caution. She wants to feel the full force and fury of Jasper's love. Before Jasper even realizes it, Nora has become the aggressor!

"Oh Jasper! Please, don't treat me like I'm going to break into little pieces! Oh—oh—please. I will be okay. Trust—trust—trust me! I—I—know my body. I can tolerate—but I can't wait. I can't wait," begs the virginal bride who feels the pressure of penetration.

"You don't have to. We can go—many—many rounds. Just let me help you feel more comfortable. Oh—oh we're on the edge of the bed," cautions Jasper. "We don't want to hit the floor," Jasper pants.

"I don't care if we end up out the front door! Just don't' stop! Don't—don't—Oh, what is happening to me?" Nora's voice is in a high pitch now.

"Oh, we, we, we are near—near—the top of the mountain again. We can keep going. We've got all night! We got the rest of our lives!" Jasper screams.

"I love you so—so—much Jasper!" Nora proclaims, as she begins to weep.

"I love you even more than I got the words to tell you!" Jasper answers, as they embrace and continue kissing and weeping together.

It is about three hours later before both of them wake up and begin to stare at each other.

"Tell me I'm not dreaming," whispers Nora. "I am Mrs. Nora Martin, at long last," she says, with certitude.

"Yes, you are! And I'm the happiest man in the world," Jasper adds, with his voice trailing. "Now, let's get about thirty minutes more of sleep."

"Why do you want to go back to sleep?" Nora asks.

"So, I can forget how hungry I am," Jasper says, without apology.

                    ഇ©രു

As Jasper falls back to sleep, Nora slips out of the bed and checks to see if the front and back doors are locked. She then goes into the bathroom to clean her face, comb her hair and to freshen up.

Jasper is coming out of his predicted thirty minute nap as Nora gets back in bed.

"We forgot to take the sandwiches out of the car," Jasper says.

"And both of our small pieces of luggage," Nora adds.

"Well, your Aunt Hattie probably put the sandwiches in a thick bag with pieces of chipped ice under them. I bet Miss Lizzie has some ice in the ice box. But don't worry. I can get breakfast from the food shack in the morning when it opens and bring the food back here to the cottage," says Jasper.

"How far are we from Miss Lizzie's Food Shack?" asks Nora.

"We are right up the lane from the restaurant. Miss Lizzie owns this cottage, too. She rents it out to people for honeymoons, for weekend stays and to pass-through travelers overnight. She has a reputation for keeping everything very clean and disinfected," Jasper says.

Still lying in bed, Nora says, in disbelief. "You mean I slept through us passing the restaurant and coming up this bumpy lane and didn't wake up until we parked out in front?"

"Yes, you figured it out at last," says Jasper, as if he got one on Nora.

ഇൽ

Jasper excuses himself and stumbles into the bathroom to do his *man-thing*.

Nora's eyes gaze with pride at Jasper's lean, well-built body with its tight buttocks. She marvels at his well-proportioned biceps and quads. She can hardly process her good fortune and the new deep well of love she is feeling for someone not of her bloodline. She mumbles a brief prayer of gratitude to her God for her wonderful GIFT!

ഇൽ

Upon Jasper's return from the bathroom, he looks at his naked bride who has wrapped the stark white sheet around her small, curvaceous body.

"Hey, do we eat, nap or play?" Jasper asks, teasingly.

"I think you know in which direction my appetite is swinging. Are you going to oblige or ignore?" asks the sassy talking Mrs. Martin.

Jasper crawls back into the lover's nest with a grin as wide as the two-lane country road that led them to this den of pleasure.

Do you want to see who has more energy—even before the sun comes up?" Nora asks in a dare.

"Oh please! No, no, no—don't scare me like that!" Jasper chuckles so hard at himself, until he goes into a strangling cough.

The newlyweds lounge, laugh and make love until it's time to pack up early Monday morning.

They welcome every sore and fatigued muscle in their well-toned bodies!

Chapter 25

Day Two — Honeymoon

"How much weight do you think we've lost since Saturday night?" Nora asks Jasper, in a teasing but triumphant tone.

"Well, on Sunday morning you started to eat the hot food I got from Miss Lizzie's. But before a fraction of the food was gone, you were attacking me again. You wouldn't eat! I couldn't eat because you kept messing with me. I didn't know you are so hot-blooded, Miss Carpenter. I would have gained five pounds or so, before this weekend, if I'd had a crystal ball," Jasper teases in response, as he stares at Nora hooking her brassiere.

"I think you are maybe changing your mind about driving back to Cloverdale this morning. Am I reading you right?" Nora coos, as she turns to meet Jasper's stare, while folding and packing her few garments.

"Oh, no sweetheart. We need to get back. My mother's house is small so you can't be so noisy when you get all heated up and excited," Jasper chuckles. "But she will, however, respect our privacy for what I pray will be a brief stay. I so want to get stateside orders and be able to have you go with me on my next assignment."

"This is my prayer, too, my sweet and gentle husband," Nora says, in a soft whisper.

She takes four steps around the bed to come face-to-face with her husband who then leans down to kiss her. He fondles with her brassiere, and Nora perks up with a broad smile.

"Don't start what you're not interested in finishing. You'll be charged with whatever law a military man gets charged with when he shirks his duty," Nora declares, in earnest.

"Oh, my goodness. The lady is serious and threatening. Let me tuck my tail, keep my hands to myself and pack my duffel bag. I'm headed toward my first scolding—or worse the guillotine," Jasper gasps, as if in fear.

"You would never make it as a funny man," Nora scoffs. "But I think you would succeed as my early morning lover," she says. "Do you want to try out for the role?"

"I see right now I'm in trouble," smiles Jasper, as he exhibits what a quick study he has become at figuring out how to unhook Nora's brassiere.

₧₨

"Congratulations, congratulations!" Miss Lizzie says in a raised voice, as Jasper and Nora enter her eatery. "I'm not surprised you're checking out a little late. Don't worry. If I know you and like you, I drop my newlyweds', late departure fee," she says, nonchalantly.

"Unh, unh unh! Y'all look like you suppose to be together. I can size up a good marriage before the last bubbles go flat in the champagne bottle," Miss Lizzie boasts, offerings her wise assessment.

"Oh, that's so kind of you to say, Miss Lizzie," Nora gushes.

"No, I mean it! I have no reason to lie about my sixth sense. I keep my mouth shut, rather than pretend and sugar coat something. You two just keep loving and respecting each other. Make sure each of you is the "other" in the Golden Rule as it states, *Do unto others as you would have them do unto you.* Yeah, y'all 'go be all right, Honey," Miss Lizzie concludes, giving Nora another once-over, visual assessment.

"You know, I thought I just about knew everything about my new bride's personality. But she had a couple of surprises for me, Miss Lizzie," Jasper says, with his dual sly and mischievous smile.

Nora clears her throat, as Miss Lizzie jumps in, "Wait…wait…

wait Mr. Jasper. Don't you go talkin' yourself into the doghouse on your—ah, ah—third day of marriage!" Miss Lizzie advises.

"You've got that right," Nora states, with an uncharacteristic roll of her eyes.

"Ha, ha, ha," chuckles Jasper. "I fooled both of you. I'm just seeing if you ladies are on your toes this Monday morning. Just a little tease to get your reaction."

"Didn't I tell you trying to be a funny man is not your best suit?" Nora reminds Jasper.

"Do you two lovebirds have time to eat a little something?" Miss Lizzie asks.

"Nora, do you want even a cup of the good chicory coffee?" asks Jasper.

"Yes, I would love that. And what about one of your hot buttermilk biscuits Miss Lizzie?" Nora adds.

"It's a deal. Now Jasper, what is your choice?" Miss Lizzie turns to face Jasper.

"The same as Nora, but with a slice of country ham with my big biscuit. You know I think I dropped a couple of pounds recently," Jasper says, in a seemingly offhanded manner.

"Yeah, newlyweds have a peculiar way of losing a little weight. And I don't need to say no 'mo." Miss Lizzie displays a broad grin, as she turns to walk back into her kitchen.

೮೦)೦೪

"We're heading back to Cloverdale a little later than I had planned," Jasper says in a detached tone, as if thinking out loud.

"Why are you rushing to get back into town?" Nora asks, with her nose crunched up.

Looking straight ahead as he drives, Jasper hesitates before he responds to Nora's question. "It's because I want to see if any mail has come to me from Uncle Sam," he answers in a stern voice.

"Oh, let's not think about any of that today. We'll go by and say hello to my aunts and pick up some of the clothes I packed to carry me through a couple of weeks. And then we'll unpack when we get to your Mother's house. I think we need to take a little nap this late afternoon before we decide on supper," Nora says, as she lays out their preconceived itinerary for the rest of the day.

Jasper seems to barely hear Nora's chirpy delivery. His entire mood has become serious and no-nonsense.

"Oh, my sweet husband. Let's not get so serious that you forget about going to heaven and back in the last—well almost two days. Our time together in that pretty little cottage was everything I had dreamed about. Let's stretch that mood and those feelings out for the next few days at least," suggests Nora.

"Nora, you know I'm still on cloud nine, but there are other issues that are crowding into my brain at the moment. Just be patient as we readjust to our return to Cloverdale," petitions Jasper, as he drives onto the paved road signaling their return to downtown Macon.

With that new jolt of reality, Jasper inexplicably turns off Main Street and drives the back route toward the colored neighborhood which leads to Hanson Park. He remains silent as he maneuvers the DeSoto around rough lumps in the quasi-patched and paved road.

Nora raises her body to survey the approaching park as if she is a first-time visitor there. She looks over to Jasper as if silently measuring his emotions. She says nothing.

Jasper steers his car onto one of the patches of grass designated for parking various modes of transport. He puts the car's parking gear in position before shifting his body toward Nora and gazing lovingly into her eyes.

"Nora, my love, I am in this place in my head where, all of a sudden, the responsibility to give you a loving, safe and comfortable life is upon me. I want very much to live up to my expectations of myself and exceed your expectations of me. I know I can do this and make *you*, and in the process, *us* happy. What I need is to maintain a level head, finish my time in Uncle Sam's Army, stay strong and healthy, find a little time to keep stroking my love for my orchestra playing, decide when I should get my college degree, when we should start our family. I'm on full throttle again in the same way I found myself contemplating our life while enduring those long and lonely nights in Basic Training. I know you will always be in my corner and by my side. I just want us to remain strong and steady. I don't ever want to lose the passion, fury and fun we discovered as our bodies and minds totally bonded this weekend. Do you understand where my heart and mind are at this moment? Going back into our family settings will make things feel different—at least at first. But I don't want us to lose anything or sacrifice any of our values to try to accommodate others. Am I making any sense?" Jasper asks, almost pleading for understanding.

"Jasper, you know we think so much alike. We want the same things out of life. There should not be a moment's worth of doubt between where we were Saturday, in front of Reverend Simpson, our families and guests, where we were as we tumbled in total ecstasy between the sheets and discovered and explored each other's body, and where we are at this moment. Every step along the way over the last two days and all the months of courtship, we were committing and recommitting ourselves to each over. Where are these fears and doubts coming from now? I don't share these emotions with you. Come on back into our nest. You are smart, confident, focused and ambitious. That's the Jasper I know. Don't you ever worry about my dedication and commitment. If I survived those smothering and possessive aunts and you survived your doting and pampering mother, we can survive and tolerate just about anything. With their innocent flaws and often frustrating ways, I think we have probably inherited, in our individual bloodlines, our families' best qualities. My sweet Jasper, we are going to be just fine. I'll go to the bank on

Uncle Ralph's money—on my prediction!" Nora begins to laugh, at her own preachy pronouncements.

As Jasper and Nora flush out their sentiments and sensitivities regarding their life ahead, Jasper begins to relax and recalibrate the positives versus the negatives. The one looming negative is the uncertainty about his current military status.

As Nora helps reign in some of Jasper's never-before-felt anxieties about his marital duties, they find themselves attempting to inch closer together in broad daylight, in their car, in the wide-open area of Hanson Park. They quickly snap back into the moment and decide the best control is to drive away and begin the process of announcing to their families their return to Cloverdale.

ℴℴℴ

Rounding the corner of Magnolia and Crescent Streets, Nora sees Aunt Marilyn puttering in one of her front yard flower beds. This is an unusual time of day—approaching noon—for Aunt Marilyn to be tending to her flowers.

Jasper pulls up to the edge of the lawn and cuts the motor on the car.

The aunt who was most resistant and wary of Nora and Jasper's budding relationship is falling all over herself with joy and excitement.

"Well hello there," Marilyn belts out. "Welcome back to Cloverdale. Of course, I'm assuming you left the community for the weekend."

Choosing to ignore her Aunt's probing comment, Nora walks to Marilyn and hugs her.

"Hi Aunt Marilyn. You couldn't make your flowers any prettier if you made a pallet here and took a nap beside them," say Nora, in a very complimentary tone. "Are Aunts Hattie and Claudine at work today?" Nora asks, keeping the conversation on point.

"Yes, they are. They were wondering if you would be returning today. Did you have a good weekend?" asks Marilyn, in a delicate tone.

"Yes, we did," injects Jasper. He offers no other information. He will let Nora tell her family about their weekend sojourn. He suspects she wants to tell all three of them at the same time.

"I got some fresh-brewed tea on the cupboard in the kitchen. It's cooled down by now. You are welcomed to get some ice out of the box and pour yourselves a glass. Hattie made sure the clothes you chose to pack are still in your luggage in the bedroom. Go on in and do what you need to do. I'll be in shortly," announces Marilyn, as she sits close to the ground on her pruning stool.

Before going through the front parlor door, Nora turns back to her aunt and says in a sincere tone, "Thanks again, Aunt Marilyn, for a beautiful wedding and reception. Your hard work certainly paid off. Jasper and I were so pleased with everything."

Jasper smiles and nods in agreement.

෨෬

"Lawdy, lawdy, lawdy," Octavia Martin shouts, as she rushes out her front screen door to the edge of her small, but tidy front yard.

"My dreams done come true for my son finding a lovely woman ta marry. How y'all doing? Did you get somethin' ta eat earlier? Bring yo' stuff in the house and settle in like we talked about last week Jasper."

"Slow down Mama and catch your breath," chuckles Jasper.

"Mrs. Martin, thank you so much for welcoming me into your home. We hope we are not going to be in your way too long. We are praying for military orders, however, that will let us be together—and not too far away from Georgia," Nora says, in a candid and sincere manner.

The smile on Octavia's face and the excitement in her eyes seem to vanish as Nora spoke her wishes for their immediate future.

Octavia does what she is expert at doing. She changes the subject and becomes the comical foil.

"When my lady friends left Sunday service with me yesterday, some neighborhood biddies—who didn't get invited to the wedding—got in our face and started tryin' to pick my tired, old brain about where was the honeymoon nest for my son an' his new bride. It ain't easy ta hold onto your Christian thoughts you hear'd a few minutes earlier when you really want to pull out your garbage can words and put them biddies back in their place. I had ta struggle to be—what's dat word—dig-na-fied. Lawdy, some of 'my people' can work my last nerves. I was not go let them make me mess up my good earned favor with the Lord. No, sirree. Not after I done struggled to not nod off during church service, " Octavia concluded.

She had accomplished her mission. Her little church tale—which had Nora and Jasper snickering at first—now had them laughing out loud.

"Mother please," begs Jasper. " It's too early in the day for you to start your comedy routines."

"I ain't making up no tall tale. I be telling the truth of what really happen on the steps of the church," declares Octavia, with a tone of finality.

&)&

Jasper tells Octavia about the pretty little cottage on Miss Lizzie's property. And how they felt it was the perfect choice. Nora sits sheepishly mum during this conversation.

"I done heard about that love nest out there in them woods. So glad you didn't have to drive far away because y'all was tired after yo' beautiful day on Saturday. Miss Nora, them fancy magazine pictures couldn't hold a candle to how pretty you look in your gown and that pink dress when y'all went off into da' sunset. What a sight!" Octavia says, as she relives the moments.

"Mrs. Martin, please call me Nora. Just Nora," Jasper's wife asks, in a low, sweet voice.

"Honey, that's my old way of respectin' all school teachers. Don't forget how important y'all are in the community. People look up ta you. Yeah they do," says Octavia.

"Thank you for that compliment. I love being a teacher," Nora smiles, as she looks directly into Octavia's eyes.

"Well, Mother, we're going to put some things on hangers in the closet of the bedroom and set ourselves up. We promise not to hog the one bathroom. Right Nora?" Jasper asks, as he cuts his eyes over to Nora, who is nodding in agreement.

"I promise you ain't go hate me when y'all leave here. I'm go be the best in-law Mother and real Mother I can be. Dat's my promise. I go' be as quiet as a church mouse. I don't know if I can say the same 'bout you newlyweds," Octavia cackles, at her own little "dig".

Jasper and Nora turn and walk down the short hallway to the small bedroom without saying a word.

છળ

"Oh Jasper. I think I need a short nap. You want to join me or go and spend some quiet time with your Mother?" Nora asks.

"I'll stretch out on the bed for a few minutes after we try to arrange our things. You promise to keep your hands to yourself, Mrs. Martin?" asks Jasper, in what's becoming his private tease about their intimate moments.

"You have no idea how sore and tender I feel right now in my private parts. Geneva and Velma warned me. I'll be okay. Maybe I'll sit in the bathtub in warm water and some Epsom salt later," Nora speculates.

"You just take your sweet time adjusting to everything. We've got a lifetime to enjoy being together," Jasper says, as he hangs some of his clothes and a few of Nora's clothes in the narrow closet.

"Leave something for me to do when I finish my nap," Nora says, as she pulls the chenille bedspread back and collapses on the soft and cushy bed.

"We're also going to have to go back over to see my aunts, in the early evening. We can visit with all three of them for a short time. We'll tell them about our choice for our wedding night, and subject ourselves to their carefully worded, but nosy questions. Oh, am I sounding like an ungrateful niece?" Nora asks, rhetorically.

"Get all of that out of your mind and try and drift off to sleep. I'll try hard not to shake the bed when I lie down next to you for a short rest. I don't plan to fall off to sleep, however. I'll go sit and chat with Mother after I get up," says Jasper. "Sweet dreams, my princess."

ଽଔଓଔ

About thirty-five minutes later Jasper tips out of the bedroom. He discovers his mother sitting in the glider, under the budding shade tree in their backyard. As he walks out toward her, he notices the seldom seen or held family Bible in her lap. He bends over and kisses her on her forehead before he sits next to her.

"A penny for your thoughts," announces Jasper.

"Oh, son. I'm glad we get 'dis time ta-gether. Look-a here, what I put in our Bible. Early morning, this here Western Union tella-gram came. The man ask fa' you by name. I told him you was not here. He ask me to tell him where you may be hidin' so he could put this in 'yo hands. I told him da truth when I say I did not know where you was. He then told me he did not think I was tellin' him da truth. I had to bite my tongue as I struggle to give him the right respeck as the authority. He done start to talk salty with me. Said he could have me put in jail for not tellin' him where you was. I told him about 'yo Saturday weddin'. He looked at me cross-wise when I say you was comin' back ta-day or ta-morrow. He say somethin' about department of whatever—and you *must* git this tella-gram in 'yo hands so you can report," Octavia finishes talking, clearly exhausted and emotional.

"Thank you for not handing this to me in front of Nora," Jasper says, as he carefully opens the yellow envelope.

He reads in silence. Octavia watches his brows tighten. She says nothing, but she stares with the kind of fixed eyes only a worried mother can display. Octavia starts to rock the glider, then she catches herself and realizes it won't allow Jasper to concentrate on what he is reading.

"Mother, I need time to absorb and think through this telegram. Please don't tell Nora I got it. I will tell you more about it later after I talk with Nora first. She is taking a nap right now. You understand once a man marries, the wife moves to the top rung of the ladder, and the Mother takes the second, but still strongest rung. I love you no less in this moment than I always have," Jasper says with a grave, wiser-by-the-minute expression.

He stands and walks to the back of the lawn—looking through the thin new leaves of the Spring season. He utters not a word.

Octavia is frozen in her spot, wringing her hands and dabbing her eyes with her ever-present rumpled, near-by hankie.

Chapter 26

Honeymoon Tell-All?

"Oh, it doesn't matter you were just about twenty miles out from Cloverdale for your wedding night—as long as you didn't have to drive through Forsythe County," pants Aunt Hattie, who has carried the narrowly-focused conversation about the weekend.

Sitting out in the backyard with Nora and Jasper, the three aunts sheepishly agreed they had tidbits of second-hand knowledge about Miss Lizzie's guest cottage—out there in the woods.

"Is it as cute as I hear tell it is?" asks Claudine. "She keeps such a tidy and well-run little kitchen, too, from what I can gather, from talk around the community."

"Yes, it's been a while since I laid eyes on Miss Lizzie here in town. She was at the post office when we spoke to each other, some six months ago," Hattie says. "If my memory serves me right, she was struggling with a heavy and awkward box of something for her business. Is she still doing okay?" asks Hattie, not particularly directing the question to either Jasper or Nora.

"I guess she's still thinking she's the best cook out there in the countryside. Huh ?" asks Marilyn, trying to sound casual in the asking.

"I didn't think you knew anything about Miss Lizzie's cooking, Aunt Marilyn," says Nora, deliberately trying to get a rise out of her aunt.

"Yes, she is a good cook and she knows it. But she is no way as good a cook as you are, Miss Marilyn," Jasper chimes in.

"Speaking of being a good cook, Aunt Marilyn has cooked us some of her delicious salmon croquettes, Jasper," Nora announces. "She told me last week this would be your surprise dinner when we returned."

"Oh, my goodness. What a surprise!" Jasper agrees, in a more youthful voice. "No wonder my mother didn't feed us before we left. She knew about this."

Jasper's mood is lifting now. He has yet to tell Nora about his telegram. And he's been struggling to act as if he is still waiting on his military assignment.

"Let's head into the kitchen, pray over the meal and start enjoying one of my favorite meals in this special home," says Jasper, in his usual comforting and familiar manner.

ဆာ

"Heyyy, you two love birds!" squeals Geneva as she opens the screen door to let Nora and Jasper into her house.

Geneva hugs Nora with an extended, silent embrace. She then turns to Jasper and puts her arm around his shoulder as they enter her front room.

"It's so good to see you. You know I heard you were back. Word got around that Jasper's car was seen earlier today coming out of Hanson Park. I had a feeling you would come by. Velma is on her way over so she can hear about where you two went this past weekend. Where did you go, if you don't mind telling? I'm sorry. I can't wait on Velma!" Geneva concludes, as she catches her breath.

"Hold your horses, Geneva," chuckles Nora. "We can visit for a little while. We just had dinner over at my house—well, my former home. My Aunt Marilyn cooked Jasper's favorite meal, her salmon croquettes."

"Yeah, they tasted better than ever," adds Jasper. "Speaking of good tasting, let me thank you again for being involved with the meal planning and everything else on Saturday. The food was outstanding—what little bit we got a chance to eat. And you and Velma were perfect bridesmaids to Nora. We couldn't have been happier with how everything turned out," Jasper concludes, with genuine gratitude.

"What more can I add to that?" asks Nora.

"Shhhh, just don't say another word. It was my honor of a lifetime. Now we can start discussing my status as future Godmother, number one," says Geneva, looking dead-on into both of their faces.

"You haven't asked us about our weekend yet," says Nora.

"Maybe I need to go out back and let you two talk for a few minutes," Jasper says, as he clears his throat.

"All I need to know is, were you tryin' to make a baby?" Geneva asks, as she starts smiling, then chuckling nervously.

Jasper and Nora look at each other and start to laugh. "You don't even know where we ended up going on Saturday night," says Nora, in a tone of incredulity.

"Well, Velma and I decided Atlanta was too far to drive, especially if you went the longer route. We then thought about where else you could go and be in a pretty setting or kind of like a nice house. After putting our heads together, we decided to go out to Miss Lizzie's cottage. Were we right?"

Nora squints her eyes, while looking back and forth into both their faces.

"I give up, Nora. Your friends are too clever and sharp, and we've got to suffer through a lifetime with them," Jasper declares, with a feigned frown on his face.

"Yep. You, Nora and all the little Martins will be in Aunt Geneva's cross-hairs," Geneva asserts, with drop-dead seriousness.

⊱⋅⋅⋅⋅⋅⊰

"Hey, I'm here!" Velma's excited voice bellows from outside Geneva's screen door.

"Come on through. I didn't latch it," says Geneva.

"How much have I missed?" asks Velma, a bit winded from her rushing.

"I know I'm outmatched now," says Jasper.

After the round of hugs between the three guests in Geneva's home are finished, Jasper says he's going to go out back to sit and meditate.

"It's not fair. I know you all started talking about the honeymoon before I got here. And did we guess right, Geneva, when we said they were out to Miss Lizzie's hidden cottage in the woods?" Velma rattles on, non-stop.

"Jasper was not interested in this juicy girls' talk so we didn't say much," says Geneva.

"And I'm not going to say too much either," announces Nora.

"Oh, come on now. You got to give us a little primer here. How will we know how to act, or what to do—when we go off into the sunset with our Mr. Right?" asks Geneva.

"Don't you remember our conversations in my bedroom while Jasper was away in Kansas? *You two* led me to believe because you were out of college, moved away from your childhood homes and on your own, you have been in a position to—how do I say this— explore a time or two with the opposite sex," Nora says, without hesitation.

"Oh, girl, you know how us women like to puff things up and act like we know more than we do," says Geneva, as Velma nods in wide-eyed agreement.

"Well, I think a woman's wedding night is sooo special, and quite private too. Is it really fair to her husband to discuss such an intimate and life altering event with her female friends?" asks Nora, as her speech pattern takes on a slower, more southern drawl.

The self-assured, speaks-her-own-mind Geneva is searching for a response.

Velma has a look on her face as she stares Geneva down.

"Oh no, I'm always the last of the two to speak."

After a deafening silence, Nora breaks the ice with, "It is beyond my vocabulary to describe! Honestly, ladies, I can't tell you what my brain lost on its way back to earth. I was on cloud nineteen—not cloud nine! All I can recall is ecstasy, pure unbridled ecstasy. You're going to have to ask Jasper if he can help me out here—and give you some details," she says, with that little girl's charm she can summon, on a dime.

With deflated appearances on their faces, Nora has to control her urge to smile.

"I—we—are so sorry to expect you to divulge the details of such a special event in your life. Don't you agree Geneva?" Velma asks, as she surprisingly, and for once, takes the speaker's *baton* from Geneva.

"Please forgive us Nora," asks Geneva, in earnest. "We have been sharing our secrets and joys since elementary school. We just thought—"

"I know, I know," says Nora. "It just hit me after I took my vows. Jasper has to be the first person whose feelings and rights I protect. As long as Jasper and I are together and have a strong and loving marriage, my family and my dear friends, like you two, have to occupy the second and third rungs of the ladder. This I feel in my gut. This does not mean I don't love you two just the same way I always have," Nora starts to choke up, as she extends her two arms for Geneva and Velma to walk into her warm embrace.

The trio becomes weepy as they embrace and hold on in silence for a minute or so.

Miss Chatter-Box breaks the spell. "Are we all close to our menstrual cycles now or are we taking on old folks ways?" asks Geneva.

"Speak for yourself, Missy. I'm enjoying this," Velma says to Geneva.

As they release their embrace, Nora initiates the new conversation. "You know, the one thing I don't look forward to is being away from my friends and family if Jasper's military orders take us maybe to the other side of the country," Nora says.

"Oh, that would give us a chance to come and visit and take a train or bus trip," suggests Velma.

"You're right. I haven't been any further than Tallahassee to the south and Birmingham going north," says Geneva.

"God forbid his next assignment takes him somewhere that I can't go with him. I don't even want to think about it. You know he is not an officer. He's a private so he doesn't have a lot of say-so over anything. Oh. well. I'll have to pray and wait. But he should be hearing something any day now," Nora lets out a weary-sounding sigh.

Not letting too much oxygen fill the cluster, Geneva jumps in with, "Can I get you all a glass of Manischewitz?" I brought a bottle back the last time I was in Atlanta, thinking I would wait for a special time to open it. This is it as far as I'm concerned."

"One glass won't hurt. Do you agree Nora?" asks Velma.

"Yes, what a good idea. As long as we only have one glass. Good thing I have some food on my stomach," says Nora.

"Oh, this is easy on you. This is not that strong stuff like Mr. Willie peddles," giggles Geneva.

Geneva leaves to pour three small glasses of the red wine. Nora and Velma chat in low tones as they sit on the parlor sofa and Nora begins to wonder if Jasper hasn't fallen off to sleep as he became more relaxed outside.

ℰℭ

"Well, I reckon y'all had a good evenin' seein' the aunts—and who else?" Octavia asks.

"Oh, we went over to Geneva's house and Velma came over soon after. The ladies visited with each other while I sat in the backyard and just relaxed," Jasper adds.

"Yes, and you needed to after eating so much of Aunt Marilyn's food. He acted like he'll never see another croquette in his life," chuckles Nora.

"'Dat was a good surprise wad'n it. Da first night back dinner?" Octavia asks.

"Sure was," Nora and Jasper almost say in unison.

"I ain't try-in ta sound like I'm tellin' you what ta do son. But you went and said the other day dat you and Nora go buy each of da two houses one of dem' tella-fone. You don't have ta go and spend y'all's money on dem thangs. Da last thang y'all need ta do is start out in a penny pinch. You know I done squirreled a little bit of money away over da years and I show can give it to y'all, if need be. 'Ya hear me now?" Octavia asks, tilting her head to follow Jasper's eyes. "I'm talkin' to you too, Miss Nora," Octavia says, as she looks over to Nora, who appears surprised.

"Mama, I have always been amazed at how resourceful you are and how you could manage to raise me on so little, but managing to build a little savings account? I had no idea you were doing that," Jasper says with amazement in his tone.

"What is mine, is sho' yours, too. It's here for the askin'. It ain't a whole lot, but it is y'all's if ya need it. And I'm finish wit' *that*. See I can say that word and some others the right way, when I stop bein' so lazy and talking too fast. I know better most of da—oops—*the* time," Octavia chuckles.

"You just continue to make me proud of you," Jasper says to Octavia, as he walks over to hug her. "I think I'm going to go and read for a short time, Nora, and turn in early. You want to join me or stay here in the kitchen with Mama for a while?" asks Jasper, as he slowly walks to the kitchen door.

"Honey, you don't have ta—*to*—stay here and be entertainin' me. Go on with yo'—oops, *your* husband," urges Octavia.

"I think I will, Mrs. Martin. I'll be in the bathroom for just a short time, then it's yours," says Nora.

"Good night, my two churins—I mean *children*, Octavia," Mrs. Martin scolds herself.

Jasper chuckles and says, "See you in the morning mother."

ഇരുട

Jasper and Nora couldn't resist staging the next passionate act of their honeymoon drama. The only difference was Nora audibly suppressing her yearnings so Mrs. Martin wouldn't be forced to be an audience of one—not seeing the action, but certainly hearing it. A week before the wedding Jasper tightened the screws on the bed's posts and oiled all wooden joints to minimize any squeaking.

The newlyweds exhausted themselves as they deliberately and uncontrollably prolonged the love-making.

Jasper was happy for the stretches of escape the passion brought to his on-again, off-again troubled mind. He knew he had to discuss the telegram's message with Nora, and later his mother. Just how would he begin the discussion with Nora and how would it end? He does not want to see the sun come up, but feels as though the darkness and dreariness of a winter's day has arrived in Macon on March 28, 1944.

ഇരുട

"Jasper, I think we need to empty the drug store shelf of Epson Salt," chuckles Nora, as she lies in Jasper arms. "What time is it anyway?" she asks.

Jasper pulls his small, army-issue, alarm clock out of the nightstand drawer and says, "It's 4:48 AM exactly."

"Why don't we take a brief nap," suggests Nora. "Then we can wake up to more fun."

"Oh, Nora, I can't sleep. I'm so full of love and worry and sadness until I can't even see straight at the moment. Let's rouse ourselves so we can have a serious talk, here."

He takes her in his arms and looks deep into her eyes. "Before

306

we got back in town late yesterday morning, my mother accepted a delivered telegram from the Army. It was my orders for my new assignment," Jasper whispers, followed by a long pause.

He gets up from the bed. She follows him and stands in front him with tears forming in her eyes.

"Oh, my goodness. If I understand what you just said, the news must not be what we want to hear. Will you have to go across country and I can't go with you?" she asks in an anxious tone.

"No, it's not even that favorable," says Jasper with a drawl.

"What is your new assignment? Can we be together? Are they trying to separate us so fast?" asks Nora, in rapid fashion and with high anxiety in her voice.

"My darling bride. I have to report to Fort Benning Army Base in Columbus, on Saturday before 2 PM. I will train for two weeks there before I am sent to Europe with a unit to join other soldiers trying to bring World War II to a victorious end. I don't know how long I will be gone. But wives certainly can't come," Jasper says very deliberately and with heavy sadness.

Nora absolutely wails on hearing the devastating news. Jasper tries to comfort her as Mrs. Martin rushes to the bedroom door—tapping it softly—and saying, "What's wrong, can I help in any way?"

Jasper raises his voice to speak above Nora's sobs, "Mother, give us a little time. I'll speak with you as soon as I can."

Chapter 27

Good-bye Too Soon

The normally confident and poised Nora is racked with emotional distress standing outside the Greyhound Bus station with Jasper. Her eyes are puffy. The whites are bloodshot. A glance of the person bent over in front of the young, uniformed soldier would suggest it is probably his aged mother or grandmother. There's even a slight tremor to the upper body.

Even though it is April 1st, this day of departure is no April Fool's joke. The last three days of the week, Nora went back to her classroom, and the children lifted her spirit out of the deep sadness of Jasper's impending departure.

"Jasper, I started to feel stronger in my classroom with the children, but now I feel like I'm having a bad dream," Nora stammers, between racking sobs. "I've been crying frequently since you got your military orders four days ago."

Nora and her husband are standing close, facing each other and holding hands. They are oblivious to others gathered outside the Greyhound station. Jasper is struggling to exhibit strength and resolve, but Nora has seen his sad eyes all week.

"The children at school will give you strength to continue when I'm away."

Through on-again, off-again heavy sobs and sniffles, Nora moans and whispers as she leans against Jasper's chest.

"This is so unfair. We've only been married a week and just

getting to know—to know each other. I don't want to be here without you. Does the Army treat other newlyweds like this?" Nora asks, nearly choking as she tries to talk.

"Sweetheart, you know this is the way the military works. They don't make decisions based on recruits' wedding dates. Uncle Sam treats the coloreds just the same as the whites about these military matters. They know nothing about my new status—that is until I give them my information about getting married while on leave. It wouldn't make a difference anyway," Jasper explains in a deliberate and calm manner.

"I want to be with you so much, Jasper. While at Miss Lizzie's cottage, I began to feel as though I want to have our first baby sooner rather than later. I thought we would be together and in about six months I would say I want to get pregnant. I know we maybe should wait, but my heart is so full of love for you. It feels like it is going to explode. Maybe having our baby would allow me to pass some of this overflowing love to our first born. Am I making any sense? You don't think—think—I'm talking out of my head, do you?" Nora stammers and cries more forcefully now, until she comes close to hyperventilating.

A few on-lookers, of mixed races, begin staring at the tortured lovebirds. Among them are couples who appear to be saying good-bye to each other, but none of them are as emotional as Nora and Jasper.

"Shh, shh. Here sweetheart, here's my handkerchief for your eyes," Jasper suggests, as he takes it from the inside pocket of his uniform jacket.

"I put two in my pocketbook this morning," Nora whispers, as she fumbles to adjust the pocketbook strap on her shoulder to open the oval-shaped purse resting on her side hip.

"Come on, let's walk further down the path so we won't be so close to the crowd," suggests Jasper. "Plus, maybe we can sneak in a sweet and long, good-bye hug."

This triggers another cascade of tears as Nora wobbles on the path, with Jasper holding her arm with one hand and toting his heavy duffel bag with the other. As they are creeping slowly away from the crowd, a young man about Jasper's age rushes over.

"Excuse me mister. Do you and your wife need any help?" he asks, with genuine concern.

"I think we're okay," Jasper says, as he looks up to face the stranger.

"I couldn't help but notice how hard your missus is taking your leaving. You don't know me, but I heard in the community that the "saxophone man"—over from the Elks Club as everybody know you—married this pretty, young school teacher. There's been lots of talk about your backyard wedding. This is how I know a little bit of 'yo business. By the way, my name is Marcus Davis," announces the man.

Nora is uncomfortable being so visible, and so emotional, around all the strangers gathered outside the station. She keeps her head down as she dabs at her eyes.

Jasper looks his peer straight in his eyes and says, "This is so nice of you to offer your help. I think I can handle this. By the way, my other name is Jasper Martin." Jasper turns a momentary stern look into an honest, disarming smile.

"I didn't mean no disrespect. Heaven knows we get enough of that from the white mens around here. I hope everything turn out all right in the Army for you. Where you headed now?" asks Marcus.

"On my way to Fort Benning Army base further south in the state, then I'll be shipped overseas to the war," Jasper states, in a matter-of-fact way.

"Good luck to you buddy," Marcus says, as he turns to walk back toward the crowd.

With this brief exchange between Jasper and Marcus Davis,

comes another torrent of tears from Nora.

"Oh, Nora, Sweetie. You are going to make yourself sick, and I'll leave here so worried. Come on, where is my little brave and strong princess? We are still in the beginning of a long and happy life together. Good-bye today doesn't mean forever. I'll probably still be able to write my award-winning-style letters to you every week. What-a-'ya think about that?" Jasper asks, lightheartedly.

Nothing seems to lighten Nora's despair. She fumbles in her pocketbook again for her second hankie. Jasper gives her an apologetic stare and again, silently engulfs her in his arms. He, too, is feeling the emotional weight of an aborted, newlywed lovers' nest. As he holds her close to his body, he feels a warm moist tear drop on one, then both of his cheeks. Nora senses what is happening because she can feel the heightened tension in his arms and torso before she feels the dampness of his tears on her face.

"Oh, Jasper, I feel like I'm about to faint. Please forgive me if I'm embarrassing you. But I've never felt so out of control of my emotions. I'm acting like a lovesick little girl. How am I going to make it over the next several months?" she asks, between sobs.

Their embraces, tears and kisses go undisturbed for a few minutes before they are jolted back to reality by a loud, surly voice that shouts out, "Are you Private Jasper Martin?" Jasper's instincts jolt him to an attention-like posture, and Nora imitates him.

"Ah! Ah, I am Private Jasper Martin, Sir," says Jasper, quickly disguising his surprise, and discreetly rubbing his face dry with his hand.

"Boy, where you been? I been calling 'yo name for damn near five minutes standin' up there outside of the station," snarls the Greyhound bus employee.

"Sir, my wife and I just moved away a short distance to—

"Just be quiet and be glad I wasn't the sergeant who's checkin' in soldiers back on the other side of the station. He wooda chewed your ass out. You would be in trouble befo' they even hauled your black bottom down to Fort Benning," the station employee scolds Jasper.

This time Nora's body, too, begins to tense up, but it's because of her uncertainty about how rude and angry the man may become.

"I know ya' been down here rubbin' on this gal and gettin' all worked up. Dats what y'all coloreds like to do. She probably already knocked up wit' a baby inside her belly," chuckles the man.

"Sir, no offense. But this is my wife, Mrs. Martin," Jasper says, in a measured and respectful way.

"Oh, y'all all claim y'all married. Probably ain't even had one of dem shotgun weddings. She probably be huggin' up with some other low-life man before the bus can even go twenty miles down the road," the station employee concludes, with a hint of self-satisfaction.

As Nora feels Jasper's body stiffen even more and hears what she thinks is him grinding his teeth, her body begins to tremble, uncontrollably.

"My wife is a bit nervous sir, with all the excitement of me leaving this afternoon. If you'll excuse us, we'll head back toward the station so I can process in," says Jasper, in a cautious manner. He holds Nora's hand tighter as they tip around the man's burly frame.

"You betta' hope you ain't in trouble," says the arrogant and hostile man, managing to have the last words.

Nora starts sniffling again. Jasper looks down at her and squeezes her hand tighter. "We are not going to let that fool upset us and mock our love for each other. We know we are an officially married couple. It was done in front of our God and our family. We have played by all *their* laws and rules," Jasper reassures her.

Chapter 28

The Melting Pot

Jasper's forehead is pressed, childlike, against the window of the bus. His eyes capture none of the countryside scenery, however. He stares in silence and is oblivious to the voices and movement around him.

Annoyed by the bumpy ride on Georgia State Route 22, Jasper relives over and over his last minutes with his beloved Nora. So quickly, he feels alternately angry and haunted because of the ugly encounter with the Greyhound worker. He debates in his mind if he was enough of a man in defending his wife's honor. He wonders why didn't he dispute the stereotypical thinking that colored women are loose in their moral behavior. And their loyalty is transactional. And they are breeders of any convenient and pleasurable man's babies.

Between his simmering anger and painful sadness, Jasper nods off fitfully. His neck muscles are overworked as he is constantly jerking his head back into position.

After twenty minutes on the road the bus driver tells his passengers Fort Benning—near the Georgia/Alabama state line—is about 110 miles away. The bus is occupied by Army recruits only and pulled out of the terminal in Macon around 3:10 PM. Jasper knows his misery and fatigue will not end quickly.

He and Nora had not slept very much in recent nights. They cuddled, talked and made love until the wee hours of the morning. He so appreciated Octavia spending long, early evenings out of the house visiting with her lady friends. She made every effort to afford them the privacy and intimacy she knew would go a long way during their separation.

"Hey, Private Martin. You look like a man who is already drifting alone out there on a raft in the ocean," says the stranger, bending down to read Jasper's name plate on the left-chest position of his uniform.

Jasper comes out of his trance and offers a silent, quizzical stare into the young, colored man's face. "Yeah, my mind is off into some place other than this bus," Jasper says.

"I'm Benjamin Gaston. Like you, I'm a Private," says the man, as he offers his hand for a shake.

Raising up in his seat, Jasper introduces himself. "I'm Jasper Martin from Macon. Where are you from?" asks Jasper

"I'm from Fort Valley. I boarded the bus in Atlanta, however. I was up there a few days carousing with the pretty ladies. You may have noticed a few of us were already on when the bus got to Macon," Benjamin says. " I assume you've done basic, right? Most people on this bus are, after a few days at Fort Benning, being shipped over to the war zone in Europe."

"I don't even want to think of going that far," Jasper says, in a drawl.

"Well, you'd better get ready. The handwriting is on the wall for us enlisted folks. Of course, they are sending a lot of officers over there too, even some of the colored Tuskegee Airmen pilots are needed to help wrap this war up," Benjamin spews, in a knowing voice.

"You have to excuse me. I need to take a short cat nap so I will be in a better mood to talk. No offense, man," says Jasper, as he releases a long yawn.

"Yeah, I'll catch you later," says Benjamin, as he turns and walks toward the back of the bus.

THE DEBT

ುೂ಄

Jasper rouses himself about forty minutes later. He suddenly realizes he is engulfed in a brief period of dissociation. He has to remind himself where he is, and that he and Nora are not in the same space. They are no longer together.

As he sits silently staring out the window again, the sadness reemerges as he thinks Nora is probably still struggling and trying to adjust to their new circumstances. He tries to minimize the issue by reminding himself of how intelligent and strong Nora is. How she weathered the weeks he was away in Basic Training in Kansas. He hopes she will be happier in getting back to her normal routine. Jasper's mind becomes flooded to the point that he detects a rare headache brewing. He closes his eyes only to see Nora smiling up at him almost exactly one-week to the hour they were married.

A knot lodges in his chest. He fears he is on the edge of exposing some never-before-known weakness or vulnerability. Was he about to lose control? Embarrass himself in front of these men? Jasper realizes his sweaty palms have a death grip on the seat's rickety arm rests. He quickly jerks his head around to see who is observing his uncharacteristic behavior. But these men don't know him. They may be acting weird, too. They may feel bereft like he does. These feeling are so new and alien to Jasper.

He suddenly channels his mother's wisdom about being afraid.

"Nine times out of ten, Jasper, the other boys around you are more afraid than you are. They're pretending, too. They're trying not to let anyone else 'peep their hold card.' Perhaps you're scared, too," Octavia's voice tells young Jasper, *"People could only pretend so long. Either walk away from the situation or reveal your true feelings. You help yourself and relieve other people around you of their stress."*

Jasper quickly concludes this may not apply to many military situations. He shifts in his seat which is next to a small, pull-down utility bench. This design allows him to be free of a seat mate. He has stuffed his duffel bag into the space. This time, he turns his back towards the aisle as he positions his entire frame on its left side to look out of the now-dusty window. His body posture and anti-social manner are screaming to others that he does not care to be bothered. In this instance, misery does not love company.

॥౭౭౩॥

Jasper finds the training and drills at Fort Benning's Embarkment Camp to be brutal and demanding. This is where soldiers are housed and readied, or quick-trained for embarkation overseas.

On day five of Embarkation Camp—word starts to filter down among the enlisted ranks that a major and deadly battle will take place in France in a place called Normandy. The entire base is buzzing about what's going to happen. To Jasper and his fellow comrades there is a renewed urgency assigned to all manner of base activity and training.

॥౭౭౩॥

Every break in Jasper's training routines allows his brain, wittingly or unwittingly, to focus right back on how much he aches for Nora's touch. He misses the feel of her soft, dewy skin and her petite but curvy frame, intentionally brushing up against him in the tight spots around their small bedroom. He grins as he recalls accusing her of altering his penchant for being punctual about everything— even getting out of the house on time for mundane errands. Nora could cause him to stop dead in his tracks and disrobe to climb back in bed with her. His heartbeat quickens every time he allows himself to wallow in those wonderful, recent memories.

॥౭౭౩॥

Fourteen days later Jasper finds himself in a Seaboard Air Line Railroad car on his way to Charleston, South Carolina. The heat is suffocating inside the car in spite of the open windows. The clacking and knocking of the train's joints, bolts and other hardware as well as the train's unrelenting jerks, makes it next to impossible to cat nap or even read. And the icing on this distasteful cake is all the billowing smoke coming through the windows from the train's coal-burning engine room.

A couple of the soldiers attempt to talk to each other as well as Jasper. He has a good excuse for not being bothered. He points to one of his ears signaling he can't hear what the other person is saying. This suits him just fine. He is still in a lonely and dark head space, and no attempts at socializing interest him in the least bit.

∞

Jasper has been to Charleston once before to perform with an orchestra. He remembers how beautiful the stately homes are and how soothing the coastal shoreline can be. He was allowed in this section of Charleston only in the convoy of traveling musicians being driven to an elaborate wedding reception at one of Charleston's estates right on the waterfront. He amuses himself for a moment when he thinks of how impressed Nora would be to see this lovely city. But now, Charleston had a different and less lustrous appeal. This would be his last touch stone on American soil once he climbed the gang plank to the ship taking the anxious soldiers over to Europe. He prayed silently and earnestly for a smooth sail to Europe. He knows his whole life rests on going over and returning safely to Nora's loving arms.

∞

Jasper has studied the pecking order of the enlisted ranks well enough to know, the man standing at the entrance to the gang plank is a Master Sargent. He has a large Army-issue bull horn in his hand and he shows his pride and arrogance in bellowing, "Okay, you half-stepping recruits, haul ass on up the gang plank and act like you're proud to go fight for your freedom."

317

THE DEBT

The slouching and robot-like troops seem to self-correct their posture as they move ahead carrying heavy and awkward gear. Jasper knows he is in for an unknown and out-of-his-control situation. All he can wish for is a leader who will have a modicum of respect for commanding colored troops in a difficult and challenging environment. Oh, how he longs to see Nora and his mother. His private thoughts embarrass him. He is thinking like a child and not like a grown, twenty-three year old, proud colored Private in Uncle Sam's Army.

∞)(∞

After processing in and having their names checked against the ship's manifest, the colored enlisted men head to the berthing compartments. There are dozens of men squeezing around each other looking for their bunk. Each has been given a bunk or rack number. The bedroom he and Nora had in his mother's house seems spacious by comparison to the racks. Everything is crammed together. There is not an inch of personal privacy space once you lift your behind out of your rack. Jasper finds his rack and throws his duffel bag on it before sitting to catch his breath.

Jasper immediately tries to assess his surroundings. He sees few smiles or expressions of contentment. He assumes the half-dozen people talking in pairs probably met on the loading dock. Jasper reverently opens his duffel bag, unzips an interior compartment and pulls out some carefully wrapped black and white photographs. He smiles as he looks at Nora's last year's school picture she has given him. There are pictures of Nora sitting at a piano, Nora as a toddler, Octavia in her back yard smiling and a professional glossy picture of the Ellis Walker Orchestra with Jasper sitting on the front saxophone line. As soon as he can get a mailing address to Nora, she will send him some of their wedding pictures Henry Turner will have processed by then.

∞)(∞

After sitting in the Port of Charleston all night, the ship takes off for England early in the morning. The commotion from the troops

318

trying to settle themselves in such confining quarters, raised a level of noise that never subsided. No one got much sleep on the first night aboard the ship. And the projected four-and-a-half-day sail across the Atlantic portends another level of discomfort Jasper is dreading. He really doesn't know what to expect.

Jasper realizes on his first night aboard ship he cannot afford to remain so detached from his comrades. He knows he needs to become acquainted with and act friendly toward a few of them. And especially those sleeping in the near-by racks, two of whom are already experiencing seasickness.

"Hey, buddy. You 'go be okay over there?" Jasper asks the one closest to him by raising his head and looking a couple of bunk beds down the line.

The young guy sheepishly flags his hand in a go-away gesture, as he holds a round metal can to his mouth with his other hand. At the moment, there appears to be no space where he can isolate himself from the others.

Jasper is probably feeling lucky that his stomach is settled. He wishes his mind would settle down, however, and cease worrying about Nora and wondering how she is feeling. They briefly talked about her going back to live in her home with her aunts. Nora knows they would be wounded if she made any other decision while Jasper is away. Jasper helped her take some of her clothing back, but she tearfully told her aunts she would spend a couple of days longer with Mrs. Martin. They understood.

&)(&

The morning reveille, on day two, is a most unwelcome sound. Again, Jasper did not rest well in his rack, and the military breakfast is a third-tier meal if Jasper thinks of Miss Lizzie's or Aunt Marilyn's cooking. On this second morning on board, the waves are choppy. There is a misty rain at sea and the colored troops are ready for their on-board chores.

The work orders are assigned by arrangement or numbers on the bunks. Jasper's bunk section is assigned the duties of mopping the decks several times a day. Some other sections will have duties such as clean the latrines several times a day, or clean the cooking utensils and wipe up the mess halls after each meal, polish the railings and any brass-ware aboard the two-deck vessel. These were the cleaning orders for the colored enlisted. The white enlisted soldiers were given less strenuous duties, if given any duties at all. The butler-type duties designed to help the senior enlisted white soldiers and the white officers aboard, were always delegated to higher-ranking colored enlistees.

The young dude who tried to engage Jasper on the bus leaving Macon, is the leader of the mopping crew. His rack is four bunks removed from Jasper's rack.

"Hey. Does the cat still have your tongue this morning, Private Martin?" Benjamin asks Jasper, in a sarcastic tone.

Jasper turns to discover who has that heavy, yet familiar voice.

"You have to excuse my not-so-friendly attitude on the ride from Macon to Fort Benning a couple of weeks or so ago. I was about as downcast as I have ever been in my adult life," responds Jasper.

"Come on let's get started here before those old peckers start raising their voices and barking the same orders we heard right after breakfast," Benjamin warns, in a near whisper.

"Whatever you say," answers a disinterested Jasper.

Benjamin turns and raises his voice to about fifteen guys in Army work fatigues.

"Okay, this is how we are going to tackle these deck mopping duties. And going forward, just call me Ben. Yeah, Ben from Fort Valley, Georgia," he says, with an air of confidence.

"Now how many times a day do we have to clean the decks behind these slouches?" asks a recruit, standing at the back of the cluster.

"Why don't each one of you say your name the first time you talk today. This way we will know how you pronounce it. I know you have your name on your short sleeve field shirt, but it helps us to say your name the way you want us to. You may be called out of your name or anything unpleasant by *them*, if you know what I mean," says Ben, in a protective tone.

"Well, my name is Jessie," says the soldier, who had just asked the question.

"As often as it looks dirty, I suspect. But certainly after breakfast and all the meals, which is why we had better get started. We don't need nobody in our asses first thing this morning. The mops are over there in the corner, with the pine cleaner. I was told the first buckets of clean water are in the supply room on both levels. After that, there are pulley-type contraptions where we lower the buckets into the ocean and raise the clean ocean water back onto the two decks," Ben concludes his instructions.

"I'm Augustus," shouts another soldier. "Who don' been assigned to which deck. And who put you in charge, Mr. Ben?"

"Here's my duty sheet. I'll help clean on the top deck where the whites are assigned. Seven of you will come with me to clean up there. The other seven will clean this deck which is our area. I've been told the Master Sergeant will check both decks to see if the cleaning meets the right standards. Put your best effort forward soldiers," Ben says in a stern, but respectful tone.

"Private Ben, you still didn't tell me who made you the head nigger?" asks Augustus, in an insistent tone.

"Well, when I was in the holding area in Atlanta before boarding the Greyhound bus to Macon to pick up most of you all heading to Fort Benning, one of the white Sergeants told me I would be in charge of the deck cleaning men. It is as simple as that. And by the way Private Augustus—ah, what's your last name?" asks Ben, trying to sound casual.

"My last name is Wilson, Private Ben," announces the more youthful looking soldier. "And what is your last name, since you 'go be our boss, of sorts?"

"Please Private Augustus Wilson, none of us should call each other nigger. They refer to us enough using that word. We should not be in the business of insulting our own—if you understand what I'm saying. And, by the way, my surname is Gaston. And I am no one's boss. We are all of the same colored man's standing on this sail over to France. Let's all remember who should be the friends here, and who should bear our watching. Let us not be easily confused," Ben states, in an effort to disguise his irritation.

"Hey, I'm Gilbert Sims from a little town called Anniston, Alabama. Let's start out on the good foot here. We don't need to be hainty and all that with each other," Gilbert says, looking around trying to make eye contact with some of the other guys. "Don't y'all agree?" he asks.

"I'm Paul Sparks from Tallahassee, Florida, and I know we don't need to be trying to get nobody's dandruff up," Paul says, in a how-dare-you tone.

"Okay. Come on over and look at my sheet here so you will know which deck you'll be mopping until we drop anchor," says Ben, acting very much the person who has re-asserted his low-level leadership.

It doesn't take Jasper long to realize he is among a mixed group of mature acting, early twenty year olds and a few teenagers who are greener than green and a little hot-headed to boot. He wonders how he will remain calm in this group and keep his head down so he can daydream about his sweet Nora.

To Be Continued...

ACKNOWLEDGMENTS

Over my lifespan, many people of varying personalities have played a role—before my eyes—within my dreams—and in my light-of-day imagination—in this, my first novel, *THE DEBT.* Any resemblance or likeness of any known person or persons is purely coincidental.

Valerie Connelly, my editor for the past two years, has not entertained my penchant for being a serial "wannabe novelist" who shelves her manuscript and does disappearing acts. She is the consummate editor, visual artist, publishing company owner and all-around creative magician.

My first creative writing workshop mentor was Hildie Block. I refuse to recall how long ago she encouraged my first cerebral spark of my novel's protagonist, Nora Carpenter. Jane Tarrant, my neighbor and friend, introduced me to Hilde and encouraged me to write.

My fairly-new friend and Links, Inc. sister, Jeanette Conrad-Ellis, JD., referred me to Valerie who was her editor and publisher for her six-volume "tween" series.

My tech guru, Franklin Mills, who rescued me on too many occasions to recall, was my Mr. Fix-it. He not only served as my Dell and MacBook tutor, but he maintained and repaired lapsed "technical memory."

My son-in-law, Tony Martin, was my back-up tech person. Also, he rescued my stalled writing after my eye surgery by setting up my new and much larger Apple Display Monitor. Of course, I needed a tutorial session or two.

A few friends and family members have been encouraging through my on-again, off-again writing odyssey. A few years ago, Brenda Welburn identified and added writing programs on my device. The author of three published books, she is a model of writing discipline and perseverance. I should be so focused.

My cousin, Cornelia Wills, Ed.D, a published author, encouraged me to keep my head down and write. My other Wills cousin and Wills family Matriarch, Clarice Wills-Reid, MD, always makes us feel everything is possible. My sister-in-law, Jeannine Otis, a creative force in her own right, has always been so positive. Lifelong friend

Otto Stallworth, MD, a recently published memoirist, is inspiring.

Yvette Moss Hunt, Brenda Stallworth Devrouax, Felicia Watkins and Joseph Ramsey, Lt. Col, USAF, Ret., Angela Parham, and Shemariah Williams have recently become aware that my manuscript had been taken from the shelf, dusted off and readied to swim or sink. My early-on-informed friends Billy Hall, Flavia Walton, Ph.D., Patricia Knight Gary, Harriet Ecton, Hazel Bristow, Patrice Frazier, Sheila Dunheimer, Nell Braxton Gibson, Jennifer Dargan, and Hala Jabbour are nevertheless surprised.

So many people travel our roads with us, and my heart-felt gratitude goes out to each and every one of these wonderful people who grace this stage of the journey on my life's road.

ABOUT THE AUTHOR

Brenda Wills Otis

Brenda Otis, a former high school English teacher, also enjoyed an eighteen-year career in the medium of television—first as an on-air public affairs moderator, then an award-winning news producer, a co-creator and debut producer of the Ace Award-nominated BET News, and a programming executive in the PBS system. This first-time novelist is a grandmother, a community activist and a philanthropist. She lives with her husband, Amos, in northern Virginia.

www.ingramcontent.com/pod-product-compliance
Lightning Source LLC
Chambersburg PA
CBHW041750010726
47507CB00009B/346